I0654761

Adjutant General's Office

Roster of Ohio Volunteers

in the service of the United States - War with Spain

.

Adjutant General's Office

Roster of Ohio Volunteers
in the service of the United States - War with Spain

ISBN/EAN: 9783337234645

Printed in Europe, USA, Canada, Australia, Japan

Cover: Foto ©Andreas Hilbeck / pixelio.de

More available books at **www.hansebooks.com**

ROSTER

OF

OHIO VOLUNTEERS

IN THE

SERVICE OF THE UNITED STATES,

WAR WITH SPAIN.

Prepared under direction of
HERBERT B. KINGSLEY,
Adjutant General of Ohio.

COLUMBUS, OHIO:
J. L. Trauger, State Printer.
1898.

PREFACE.

✿

THIS roster was prepared for use of charitable organizations. It is a complete roster of Ohio Volunteers who were mustered into the United States service with original muster. The recruits mustered since the original muster of organization, not having, up to the time of the publication of this roster been reported to this office, are not contained herein.

HERBERT B. KINGSLEY,

Adjutant General of Ohio.

Commissioned Officers, Field and Staff.

First Regiment Ohio Volunteer Infantry.

COLONEL.
Charles B. Hunt.

LIEUTENANT COLONEL.
[1]Paul M. Millikin.

MAJORS.
Thomas W. Thomas. [2]John Proctor.
Samuel W. Kennedy.

REGIMENTAL ADJUTANT.
Russell P. Reeder.

SURGEON.
Frank W. Hendley.

ASSISTANT SURGEONS.
Gilbert I. Cullen. Herbert E. Twitchell.

QUARTERMASTER.
George I. Hopf.

BATTALION ADJUTANTS.
[3]Harry S. Bryan. Adolph R. Diehl.
[4]William H. Latham. William M. Olhaber.
Harry Terrell.

CHAPLAIN.
Howard Henderson.

[1]Promoted from Capt. Co. 1 1st O. V.
I., May 14, 1898.
[2]Promoted from Capt. Co. C 1st O. V.
I., May 14, 1898.

[3]Promoted to 1st Lieut. Co. F 1st O.
V. I., May 14, 1898.
[4]Promoted to 1st Lieut. Co. H 1st O.
V. I., May 14, 1898.

Line Officers.

First Regiment Ohio Volunteer Infantry.

CAPTAINS.

Co.	
B.	Earnest P. Diets.
H.	Percy H. Hawkins.
I.	¹Paul M. Millikin.
A.	Charles Becht.
C.	²John Proctor.
D.	William Hayes.
E.	August W. Margedant.

Co.	
G.	Charles W. Pieper.
K.	Fred. L. Davidson.
L.	William M. Sullivan.
C.	³Harry Havlin.
F.	⁴Herman O. Moeller.
I.	⁵Charles F. Hake, Jr.
M.	Cassilly C. Cook.

¹Promoted to Lieut. Col. 1st O. V. 1., May 14, 1898.
²Promoted to Maj. 1st O. V. I., May 14, 1898.
³Vice John Proctor promoted.

⁴Promoted from 1st Lieut. Co. H 1st O. V. I.
⁵Promoted from 1st Lieut. Co. I 1st O. V. I. Vice Millikin promoted.

FIRST LIEUTENANTS.

Co.	
B.	Robert L Davis.
H.	¹Herman O. Moeller.
I.	²Charles F. Hake, Jr.
A.	William Schuster.
C.	³Harry Havlin.
E.	⁴George Ayers.
G.	Alexander Frank.
K.	Henry J. Pfiester.

Co.	
L.	Joseph L. McCarter.
C.	⁵Robert L. Dunning.
D.	⁶Charles P. Clark.
F.	⁷Harry S. Bryan.
I.	⁸Anton Folger.
H.	⁹William H. Latham.
M.	William R Collins.
E.	¹⁰Oliver P. Branch.

¹Promoted to Capt. Co. F 1st O. V. I., May 14, 1898.
²Promoted to Capt. Co. I 1st O. V. I., May 14, 1898.
³Promoted to Capt. Co. C 1st O. V. I., May 14, 1898.
⁴Resigned and hon. dis. July 18,1898.
⁵Promoted from 2nd Lieut. 1st O. V. I. Vice Havlin promoted.

⁶Promoted from 2nd Lieut. Co. D 1st O. V. I.
⁷Promoted from Batt. Adj. 1st O. V. I.
⁸Vice Charles F. Hake, Jr., promoted.
⁹Promoted from Batt. Adjt. 1st O. V. I. Vice Herman O. Moeller promoted.
¹⁰Promoted from 2nd Lieut. Co. E 1st O. V. I., July 21, 1898.

SECOND LIEUTENANTS.

Co.	
B.	Marcus H. Folger.
H.	Desire L. Sence.
A.	George A. Fisher.
C.	¹Robert L. Dunning.
D.	²Charles P. Clark.
E.	³Oliver P. Branch.
G.	William McMiller.
K.	Thomas Henry Pfeiffer.

Co.	
L.	Charles Benton Hoover.
C.	⁴Charles F. Laur.
D.	⁵Frederick Raine, Jr.
F.	Harry C. Williams.
I.	Eugene M. Shinkle.
M.	Joseph E. Boylan.
E.	⁶Charles A. Cox.

¹Promoted to 1st Lieut. Co. C 1st O. V. I., May 14, 1898.
²Promoted to 1st Lieut. Co. D 1st O. V. I., May 14, 1898.
³Promoted to 1st Lieut. Co. E 1st O.

V. I., July 21, 1898. Vice George Ayers resigned.
⁴Vice Robert L. Dunning promoted.
⁵Vice Charles P. Clark promoted.
⁶Vice Oliver P. Branch promoted.

Commissioned Officers, Field and Staff.

Second Regiment Ohio Volunteer Infantry.

COLONEL.
Julius A. Kuert.

LIEUTENANT COLONEL.
Edward S. Bryant.

MAJORS.
Worthington Kautzman.   John D. Leitner.
Perle A. Campbell.

REGIMENTAL ADJUTANT.
Adolph B. Collier.

SURGEON.
Frank D. Bain.

ASSISTANT SURGEONS.
C. L. Mueller.   L. J. Stueber.

QUARTERMASTERS.
¹N. H. Colwell.   ²Milroy Pool.

BATTALION ADJUTANTS.
Edward K. Campbell.   Cliffe Deming.
O. L. Albright.

CHAPLAIN.
C. B. Crawford.

¹Resigned and hon. dis. June 25, 1898.   ²Vice N. H. Colwell resigned.

Line Officers.

Second Regiment Ohio Volunteer Infantry.

CAPTAINS:

Co.
A.   Tilman L. Lafferty.
B.   James W. Marston.
C.   Frank M. Bell.
D.   Edward S. Matthias.
F.   Lucius C. Bennett.
G.   J. Guy Deming.
H.   Archie M. Fassig.

Co.
I.   [1]Henry J. May.
K.   W. J. White.
L.   John G. Hoegner.
E.   Lorenzo D. Gasser.
M.   Samuel W. Ennis.
I.   [2]Albert S. Clucker.

[1]Resigned and hon. dis July 11, 1898.

[2]Promoted from 1st Lieut. Co. I 2nd O. V. I., July 20, 1898.

FIRST LIEUTENANTS.

Co.
A.   Ralph E. Barnd.
B.   Joseph Gloeser.
C.   M. D. Reichelderfer.
D.   Robert Webster.
E.   Joseph B. Sohn.
F.   R. E. Graham.
G.   Pearl Humphreys.

Co.
H.   John P. Beam.
I.   [1]Albert S. Clucker.
K.   William S. Wilson.
L.   Charles O. Brokaw.
M.   Alfred N. Wilcox.
I.   [2]Rezin D. Smith.

[1]Promoted to Capt. Co. I 2nd O. V. I., July 20, 1898. Vice Henry J. May resigned.

[2]Vice Albert S. Clucker promoted.

SECOND LIEUTENANTS.

Co.
B.   Frank Moody.
C.   John M. Bingham.
D.   Elias W. Martz.
E.   Frank J. Dildine.
F.   W. E. Green.
G.   James A. Pool.
H.   James W. Smith.

Co.
I.   [1]Ralph V. Couts.
K.   Frank C Hatch.
L.   Roy E. Layton.
A.   Frank M. Biggs.
M.   John P. Miller.
I.   [2]Carl C. Rutledge.

[1]Resigned and hon. dis. July 10, 1898.

[2]Vice Ralph V. Couts resigned.

Commissioned Officers, Field and Staff.

Third Regiment Ohio Volunteer Infantry.

COLONEL.
Charles Anthony.

LIEUTENANT COLONEL.
William J. White.

MAJORS.
Robert E. Campbell.   Patrick J. Curren.
William H. Gross.

REGIMENTAL ADJUTANT.
Charles F. Startzman.

SURGEON.
James E. Shellenberger.

ASSISTANT SURGEONS.
Fred C. Weaver.   David King Gotwald.

QUARTERMASTER.
Clarence S. Ramsey.

BATTALION ADJUTANTS.
[1]Benjamin M. Marshall.   Mahara D. Barnes.
Edwin S. Dollinger.   [2]Charles A. Fay.

CHAPLAIN.
Clarence E. Gardner.

[1]**Resigned** and hon. dis. June 24, 1808 [2]Vice. Benj. M. Marshall, resigned

Line Officers.

Third Regiment Ohio Volunteer Infantry.

CAPTAINS.

Co.
B. William H. Bradbury.
C. Robert E. Horner.
F. Thomas Q. Bowles.
H. George G. Bambach.
I. Benjamin F. Boyer.
L. William T. Amos.

Co.
M. Harry R. Allen.
D. George W. Leonard.
A. ¹Henry O. Weaver.
G. ²William W. White.
E. John F. Locke.
K. McPherson Brown.

¹Promoted from 2nd Lieut. Co. A 3rd
O. V. I.

²Promoted from 1st Lieut. Co. G 3rd
O. V. I.

FIRST LIEUTENANTS.

Co.
A. Henry E. Finfrock.
B. Fred L. Bernard.
C. Jacob E. Yount.
F. Arthur G. Jenkins.
G. ¹William W. White.
H. Rush P. Tyler.
I. Wesley W. K. Hamilton.

Co.
L. Henry M. Theurer.
M. William E. Adair.
D. Walter C. Gifford.
G. ²Arthur E. West.
E. Peyton R. Emery.
K. James F. Hubbard.

¹Promoted to Capt. Co. G 3rd O. V. I.,
May 16, 1898.

²Promoted from 2nd Lieut. Co. G 3rd
O. V. I., May 16, 1898.

SECOND LIEUTENANTS.

Co.
A. ¹Henry O. Weaver.
B. Michael J. Bahin.
C. Ray M. Gilbert.
D. George A. Burkett.
G. ²Arthur E. West.
H. Eugene R. Young.
I. Guy E. Manning.

Co.
L. Emerson V. Moore.
M. James M. Runyan.
A ³Ziba L. Ramsey.
F. John P. Gorman.
G. ⁴George H. Wood.
E. E. Arnett Smith.
K. Harry D. Mitchell.

¹Promoted to Capt. Co. A 3rd O. V. I.,
May 16, 1898.
²Promoted to 1st Lieut. Co. G 3rd O.

V. I. May 16, 1898. Vice William W.
White promoted.
³Vice Henry O. Weaver promoted.
⁴Vice Arthur E. West promoted.

Commissioned Officers, Field and Staff.

Fourth Regiment Ohio Volunteer Infantry.

COLONEL.
Alonzo B. Coit.

LIEUTENANT COLONEL.
Cyrus B. Adams.

MAJORS.
John C. Speaks.   Charles V. Baker.
John L. Sellers.

REGIMENTAL ADJUTANT.
Mac Lee Wilson.

SURGEON.
Edward M. Semans.

ASSISTANT SURGEONS.
Thompson B. Wright.   Henry M. Taylor.

QUARTERMASTER.
George B. Donavin.

BATTALION ADJUTANTS.
Thomas P. Williams.   Harry W. Krumm.
Edward M. Fullington.

CHAPLAIN.
James C. Schindel.

Line Officers.

Fourth Regiment Ohio Volunteer Infantry.

CAPTAINS.

Co.		Co.	
A.	Joseph J. Walsh.	H.	¹Stanley R. Pritchard.
B.	Will S. White.	I.	Lewis H. Palmer.
C.	Thomas R. Biddle.	K.	Burt H. Greiner.
D.	Charles F. Sellers.	L.	Fred M. French.
E.	William L. Vincent.	M.	Burr J. Bostwick.
F.	Joseph D. Potter.	H.	²James W. Smith.
G.	Fred W. Peters.		

¹Discharged July 26, 1898.

²Promoted from 1st Lieut. Co. H 4th O. V. I., August 1, 1898.

FIRST LIEUTENANTS.

Co.		Co.	
A.	Harry Graham.	H.	¹Frank B. Pratt.
B.	Frank L. Oyler.	I.	Fred S. Whiley.
C.	Arthur W. Reynolds.	K.	William B. McCloud.
D.	Jay R. Turner.	L.	Charles E. Bigler.
E.	Charles O. Updyke.	M.	Charles G. Duffy.
F.	Clyde R. Modie.	H.	²James W. Smith.
G.	Fred S. Titus.	H.	³Kinney Funk.

¹Resigned and hon. dis. June 27, 1898.
²Promoted from 2nd Lieut. Co. H, July 6, 1898. Promoted to Capt. Co. H 4th

O. V. I., August 1 1898. Vice Stanley R. Pritchard discharged.
³Promoted from 2nd Lieut. Co. H 4th O. V. I., August 1, 1898.

SECOND LIEUTENANTS.

Co.		Co.	
A.	Cyrus W. Grandstaff.	I.	W. H. Hause.
B.	William B. Hamill.	L.	Sherman E. Ward.
C.	Frank A. Alexander.	M.	George Florence.
D.	¹Frank Otte.	K.	Oscar O. Koeppel.
E.	J. M. Fugate.	H.	³Kinney Funk.
F.	Nathan A. McCoy.	D.	⁴Abe Newlove.
G.	Thomas E. Andrews.	H.	⁵Forrest C. Briggs.
H.	²James W. Smith.		

¹Resigned and hon. dis. July 12, 1898.
²Promoted to 1st Lieut. Co. H 4th O. V. I., July 6, 1898. Vice Frank B Pratt resigned.
³Vice James W Smith promoted. Pro-

moted to 1st Lieut. Co. H 4th O. V. I., August 1, 1898, Vice James W. Smith promoted.
⁴Vice Frank Otte resigned.
⁵Vice Kinney Funk promoted.

Commissioned Officers, Field and Staff.

Fifth Regiment Ohio Volunteer Infantry.

COLONEL.
Cortland L. Kennan.

LIEUTENANT COLONEL.
Daniel C. Stearns.

MAJORS.
Charles F. Cramer.   James P. Woodworth.
Arthur K. A. Liebich.

REGIMENTAL ADJUTANT.
Frederick B. Dodge.

SURGEON.
William P. Love.

ASSISTANT SURGEONS.
John S. Windisch.   Charles Dexter Noble.

QUARTERMASTER.
Bennoni F. Du Perow.

BATTALION ADJUTANTS.
Edward W. Dissette.   William M. Barrett.
William F. Herringshaw.

CHAPLAIN.
Samuel J. McConnell.

Line Officers.

Fifth Regiment Ohio Volunteer Infantry.

CAPTAINS.

Co.		Co.	
A.	Wilbur S. Pole.	H.	James A. Freed.
C.	Daniel H. Pond.	K.	Edward A. Noll.
D.	Edward W. Kennedy.	M.	Jerome S. Burrows.
E.	Herman B. Williams.	L.	Walter S. Bauder.
F.	Charles X. Zimmerman.	B.	Joseph C. Beardsly.
G.	Albert W. Davis.	I.	Edwin G. Lane.

FIRST LIEUTENANTS.

Co.		Co.	
A.	William E. Gilmore.	L.	Claude E. Monck.
B.	Corbett E. Southam.	H.	Harry W. Ulrich.
E.	Charles C. Maltbie.	C.	Burton O. Squier.
F.	Hiland B. Wright.	K.	William J. De Witt.
G.	Frederick H. De Witt.	B.	Harry L. Andrus.
M.	Harry P. Bosworth.	I.	Edward W. Briggs.

SECOND LIEUTENANTS.

Co.		Co.	
C.	James E. Wertman.	A.	Harry D. Savage.
D.	Mose Barry.	E.	James W. Maltbie.
F.	Daniel Fovargue.	H.	Fred C. Porter.
G.	Edgar G. Martin.	L.	Montague W. Mountcastle.
K.	Ralph A. Tingle.	B.	William J. Lawson.
M.	Charles R. Tuttle.	I.	William J. Graham.

Commissioned Officers, Field and Staff.

Sixth Regiment Ohio Volunteer Infantry.

COLONEL.
William V. McMaken.

LIEUTENANT COLONEL.
William O. Bulger.

MAJORS.

Sanford B. Stanbery.   [1]William E. Gillett.
George P. Parker.

REGIMENTAL ADJUTANT.
William H. Porter.

SURGEONS.

[2]Arthur L. Osborn.   [3]Park L. Myers.

ASSISTANT SURGEONS.

[4]Park L. Myers.   [5]Fred L. Albritton.
John D. Howe.

QUARTERMASTERS.

[6]Edward W. Rydman.   [7]Eugene E. Newman.

BATTALION ADJUTANTS.

Herbert D. Draper.   Frederick M. Baumgardner.
J. E. Melville Milne.

CHAPLAIN.
Thomas J. Harbaugh.

[1]Promoted from Capt. Co. I 6th O. V.
I., May 16, 1898.
[2]Resigned and hon. dis. July 7, 1898.
[3]Promoted from Asst. Surg. 6th O. V.
I., July 12, 1898.
[4]Promoted to Surg. 6th O. V. I., July

12, 1898. Vice Arthur L. Osborn resigned.
[5]Vice Park L. Myers promoted.
[6]Appointed Capt. Co. I 6th O. V. I. and
transferred to the line as such May 16,
1898, to rank from May 12, 1898.
[7]Vice Edward W. Rydman, transferred.

Line Officers.

Sixth Regiment Ohio Volunteer Infantry.

CAPTAINS.

Co.		Co.	
A.	Jacob M. Weier.	H.	Lloyd W. Howard.
B.	Charles E. Stroud.	I.	¹William E. Gillett.
C.	John A. Gekle.	K.	Louis E. Fouke.
D.	Franklin P. Culp.	L.	Frank I. Howells.
E.	Charles L. Langel.	I.	²Edward W. Rydman.
F.	Joseph A. Musser.	M.	James F. Crandall.
G.	John A. Weier.		

¹Promoted to Maj. 6th O. V. I., May
16, 1898, to fill an original vacancy.

²Transferred from Q. M. May 16, 1898.
Vice William E. Gillett promoted.

FIRST LIEUTENANTS.

Co.		Co.	
A.	Fred H. Zurfluh.	G.	Frank Outcalt.
B.	Rolla D. Chase.	H.	Charles A. Morrison.
C.	Edward R. Smiley.	I.	Jesse A. Douglas.
D.	Howard F. Noble.	K.	Myron C. Cox.
E.	Samuel Diehl.	L.	Oliver B. Waters.
F.	Charles W. Jackson.	M.	Harry B. Lewis.

SECOND LIEUTENANTS.

Co.		Co.	
A.	Edwin M. Barnum.	H.	Frank L. Matthews.
B.	Frank A. Vincent.	I.	Ed. Welsh.
C.	William T. Teitz.	K.	Clarence E. Myers.
D.	George W. Cunningham.	L.	Harry C. Bussell.
F.	James W. Frankfather.	E.	Sebring C. Fisk.
G.	Melvin W. McConkey.	M.	Wesley E. King.

Commissioned Officers, Field and Staff.

Seventh Regiment Ohio Volunteer Infantry.

COLONEL.
Arthur L. Hamilton.

LIEUTENANT COLONEL.
Hamlin D. Burch.

MAJORS.
Judson H. Hovey.   'Edward U. Wiedler.
Walter A. Irvine.

REGIMENTAL ADJUTANT.
Tiffin Gilmore.

SURGEON.
David A. Rannells.

ASSISTANT SURGEONS.
Reuben M. Bonar.   Edward F. Waddle.

QUARTERMASTER.
Jacob Houk.

BATTALION ADJUTANTS.
William T. Watkins.   James N. Purdum.
James M. Woltz.

CHAPLAIN.
John M. Life.

'Died July 15, 1898, Chillicothe, O.

Line Officers.

Seventh Regiment Ohio Volunteer Infantry.

CAPTAINS.

Co.
A. Thomas D. Binckley.
B. Frank S. Lowry.
D. William L. West.
E. Baxter D. McClain.
F. Elmer E. Blizzard.
G. George W. Brandle.

Co.
H. Carmi A. Thompson.
I. Jonathan T. Millhouse.
K. Louis N. Gerber.
L. William A. Castle.
M. Fred C. Wooster.
C. Verne M. Bovie.

FIRST LIEUTENANTS.

Co.
A. Dell W. Stinchcomb.
B. Albert O. Sloane.
D. James H. Rhodes.
E. ¹Edward M. Gross.
F. Charles A. McClure.
G. Carlos B. Allen.
H. Luther B. Hurst.

Co.
I. Charles B. McQuigg.
K. Edward L. Jones.
L. Fred S. Russell.
M. John E. Burke.
C. Joseph W. Good.
E. ²Louis S. Hanshumaker.

¹Resigned and hon. dis. July 25, 1898.

²Promoted from 2nd Lieut. Co. E 7th O. V. I., August 9, 1898.

SECOND LIEUTENANTS.

Co.
B. Herbert W. Brooks.
D. Otis A. True.
E. ¹Frank O. Brooks.
F. Charles B. Compton.
G. George C. Crawford.
H. Robert S. Franklin.
I. Edward E. Corn.

Co.
L. Raymond H. Bell.
M. John S. Burton.
K. Stamper W. Andrews.
A. Arthur J. Teal.
C. Charles W. H. Needham.
E. ²Louis S. Hanshumaker.
E. ³Charles W. Hare.

¹Resigned and hon. dis. May 30, 1898.
²Vice Frank O. Brooks resigned. Promoted to 1st Lieut. Co. E 7th O. V. I.
Vice Edward M. Gross resigned.
³Vice Louis S. Hanshumaker promoted.

Commissioned Officers, Field and Staff.

Eighth Regiment Ohio Volunteer Infantry.

COLONEL.
Curtis V. Hard.

LIEUTENANT COLONEL.
Charles W. F. Dick.

MAJORS.
Edward Vollrath.   Charles C. Weybrecht.
Frederick C. Bryan.

REGIMENTAL ADJUTANT.
Alexander W. Maynes.

SURGEON.
Emmer C. Farquhar.

ASSISTANT SURGEONS.
George H. Wuchter.   Allen V. Smith.

QUARTERMASTER.
Herman L. Kuhns.

BATTALION ADJUTANTS.
Charles F. Schaber.   Andrew T. Weybrecht.
George M. Wright.

CHAPLAINS.
[1]Isaiah N. Kieffer.   [2]James O. Campbell.

[1]Died June 23, 1898.   [2]Vice Isaiah N. Kieffer, died.

Line Officers.

Eighth Regiment Ohio Volunteer Infantry.

CAPTAINS.

Co.
A. Marquis A. Charlton.
B. Herman O. Feederle.
C. Tully O. Deibler.
D. Frank C. Gerlach.
E. William M. Hill.
F. John A. Leininger.

Co.
G. Frank C. Lee.
H. Ammon B. Critchfield.
I. Henry L. Willis.
K. Elliott L. Gyger.
L. Marcus A. Fisher.
M. Fred S. Marquis.

FIRST LIEUTENANTS.

Co.
A. John W. Birk.
B. Harry J. Blackburn.
C. Kaiser W. Taylor.
D. William E. Barnard.
E. George O. Anderson.
F. August Weidman.
G. ¹Fred C. Hile.

Co.
H. Sanford M. Swarts.
I. Philip Yost.
K. Edgar E. Brosius.
L. William M. Burson.
M. Charles H. Hughes.
G. ²Herbert E. Bolick.

¹Resigned and hon. dis. June 21, 1898. ²Promoted from 2nd Lieut. Co. G 8th O. V. I., July 6, 1898.

SECOND LIEUTENANTS.

Co.
A. Guy D. Swingley.
B. William O. Rutherford.
C. Orlando R. Edwards.
D. Gustave W. Unger.
E. Robert T. Hall.
F. Herbert S. Spidel.
H. Marion S. Robison.

Co.
K. George Heer.
L. Herbert C. Smart.
M. Walter S. Bradford.
G. ¹Herbert E. Bolick.
I. Dudley J. Hard.
G. ²Charles S. Hoover.

¹Promoted to 1st Lieut. Co. G 8th O. V. I., July 6, 1898. Vice Fred C Hile resigned. ²Vice Herbert E. Bolick promoted.

Commissioned Officers, Field and Staff.

Ninth Battalion Ohio Volunteer Infantry.

MAJOR.
Charles Young.

ASSISTANT SURGEONS.

[1]John H. Dickerson.   [2]William Guy Wren.

[1]Resigned and hon. dis. August 8, 1898.   [2]Vice John H. Dickerson resigned.

QUARTERMASTER.
Walter S. Thomas.

BATTALION ADJUTANTS.

[1]Emanuel D. Bass.   [2]Wilson Ballard.

[1]Promoted to 1st Lieut. Co. D 9th Batt.   [2]Promoted from 2nd Lieut. Co. B 9th
O. V. I., August 11, 1898. Vice Wm. H.   Batt. O. V. I.
Brooks resigned.

Line Officers.

Ninth Battalion Ohio Volunteer Infantry.

CAPTAINS.

Co.
A. Robert R. Rudd.
B. ¹James H. Hopkins.
C. Harry H. Robinson.

Co.
D. John C. Fulton.
B. ²Deaton J. Brooks.

¹Resigned and hon. dis. July 31, 1898.

²Promoted from 2nd Lieut. Co. B 9th Batt. O. V. I., July 27, 1898.

FIRST LIEUTENANTS.

Co.
A. John R. Rudd.
B. Charles C. Caldwell.
C. James W. Smith.

Co
D. ¹William H. Brooks.
D. ²Emanuel D. Bass.
D. William H. Brooks.

¹Resigned and hon. dis. August 8, 1898

²Promoted from Batt. Adjt. 9th Batt. O. V. I.

SECOND LIEUTENANTS.

Co.
A. William F. Ellicott.
B. ¹Deaton J. Brooks.
C. James W. Braselton.

Co.
D. Alfred A. Moore.
B. ²Wilson Ballard.
B. ³Woodson P. Welsh.

¹Promoted to Capt. Co. B 9th Batt. O. V. I., July 27, 1898. Vice James H. Hopkins resigned.

²Vice Deaton J. Brooks promoted. Promoted to Batt. Adjt. 9th Batt. O. V. I. Vice Emanuel D. Bass promoted.
³Vice Wilson Ballard promoted.

Commissioned Officers, Field and Staff.

Tenth Regiment Ohio Volunteer Infantry.

COLONEL.
Henry A. Axline.

LIEUTENANT COLONEL.
Edward O. Dana.

MAJORS.
Arlington U. Betts.   Otto M. Schade.

REGIMENTAL ADJUTANT.
William G. Welbon.

SURGEON.
William A. Westervelt.

ASSISTANT SURGEONS.
James J. Erwin.   Charles W. Newton.

QUARTERMASTER.
Abner H. Bedell.

CHAPLAIN.
Carlos H. Hanks.

Line Officers.

Tenth Regiment Ohio Volunteer Infantry.

CAPTAINS.

Co.		Co.	
A.	John R. McQuigg.	G.	Myer Geleerd.
B.	Edward N. Ogram.	H.	Arthur W. S. Irvine.
C.	Henry Frazee.	I.	Clifford W. Fuller.
D.	Hazen B. Norton.	K.	Edward D. Shurmer.
E.	Horace E. Smith.	L.	Charles A. Reynolds.
F.	Herman Werner.	M.	Lowe K. Emerson.

FIRST LIEUTENANTS.

Co.		Co.	
A.	Harry P. Shupe.	G.	Charles A. Yost.
B.	John H. Caunter.	H.	Burnett F. Bliss.
C.	Frederick M. Fanning.	I.	George H. Gibson.
D.	Sanford H. Howland.	K.	Ralph T. Hatch.
E.	Grant S. Taylor.	L.	Walter V. Black.
F.	John M. Straub.	M.	Verner H. Guthrie.

SECOND LIEUTENANTS.

Co.		Co.	
A.	Harry W. Morgenthaler.	G.	Reuben C. Lemmon.
B.	David A. Keister.	H.	Frank L. Schelling.
C.	Perry E. Hathaway.	I.	Morris J. Shupe.
D.	William E. McBain.	L.	Wilbur H. Phillips.
E.	Rodney W. Bell.	M.	Samuel J. McGrew.
F.	John Percy Colwell.	K.	William G. Meade.

Commissioned Officers, Field and Staff.

First Regiment Ohio Volunteer Light Artillery.

MAJOR.
Charles T. Atwell.

SURGEON.
Henry M. W. Moore.

QUARTERMASTER.
James H. Perley.

BATTALION ADJUTANT.
Howard O. Fulkerson.

Line Officers.

First Regiment Ohio Volunteer Light Artillery.

CAPTAINS.

Bat.
A. George T. McConnell.
C. Charles W. Corbin.

Bat.
G. William C. Miller.
H. Frank T. Stewart.

FIRST LIEUTENANTS.

Bat.
A. Julius A. Blasis.
C. Charles V. Paul.

Bat.
G. Charles F. Sowersby.
H. Charles A. Field.

SECOND LIEUTENANTS.

Bat.
A. Walter E. Eddy.
C. Philip J. Sprague.
G. Francis E. Symons.
H. Harold M. Bush.

Bat.
A. Arthur L. Schwartz.
C. William E. Stockdale.
G. Charles W. Kellenberger.
H. Levi White Hunt.

Commissioned Officers, Field and Staff.

First Regiment Ohio Volunteer Cavalry.

LIEUTENANT COLONEL.
Matthias W. Day.

MAJORS.
Webb C. Hayes.   James E. Runcie.

REGIMENTAL ADJUTANT.
Arthur C. Rogers.

SURGEON.
Frank E. Bunts.

ASSISTANT SURGEON.
Charles H. Castle.

QUARTERMASTER.
[1]Thomas S. Grasselli.   [2]Ralph B. Day.

[1]Resigned and hon. dis. July 27, 1898.   [2]Vice Thomas S. Grasselli resigned

SQUADRON ADJUTANTS.
Paul Howland.   George A. J. Gampher.

Line Officers.

First Regiment Ohio Volunteer Cavalry.

CAPTAINS.

Troop.		Troop.	
A.	Russell E. Burdick.	E.	Henry De H. Waite.
B.	Henry W. Corning.	F.	Frederick W. Beekman.
C.	William M. Scofield.	H.	Fred J. Herman.
D.	Byron L. Bargar.	G.	George L. Converse.

FIRST LIEUTENANTS.

Troop.		Troop.	
A.	Carlyle L. Burridge.	F.	Walter D. Cline.
B.	Frank W. Wood.	H.	C. Edward Patton.
C.	James M. Shallenberger.	G.	Max C. Fleischmann.
D.	William D. Forsyth.	E.	²Norton S. Monsarrat.
E.	¹David B. Burgert.		

¹Resigned and hon. dis. July 11, 1898.   ²Promoted from 2nd Lieut. Troop D 1st O. V. C., July 15, 1898.

SECOND LIEUTENANTS.

Troop.		Troop.	
A.	Henry E. Doty.	F.	Robert G. Wuichet.
B.	Sheldon Cary.	H.	Joseph L. Hagemeyer.
C.	George W. Van Camp.	C.	²William C. Bailey.
D.	¹Norton S. Monsarrat.	D.	³Paul Loving.
E.	Donn C. Mitchell.	G.	⁴John T. Huntington.

¹Promoted to 1st Lieut. Troop E 1st O. V. C., July 15, 1898. Vice David B. Burgert resigned.

²Resigned and hon. dis. August 10, 1898.
³Vice Norton S. Monsarrat promoted.
⁴Vice William C. Bailey resigned.

ROSTER

OF

OHIO VOLUNTEERS.

ADA

Borden, Roy A., Pr. Co. B 5th O. V. I.
Christopher, Arthur, Pr. Co. G 2nd O.
V. I.
Davis, Elmer F., Pr. Co. B 5th O. V. I.
Dobbins, Ray R., Pr. Co. G 2nd O.V.I.
Doling, Ralph O., Pr. Co. B 2nd O.V.I.
Morrow, John H., Pr. Tr. D 1st O.
V. C.

Routson, Albert A., Pr. Co. G 2nd O.
V. I.
Stokes, Clarence E., Pr. Co. G 2nd O.
V. I.
Worrell, Harry L., Pr. Co. I 2nd O.V.I.
Young, Frank L., Pr. Co. G 2nd O.V.I.

ADAM'S MILLS

Collins, Bert, Pr. Co. F 7th O. V. I.

Guild, Thomas A., Pr. Co. F 7th O.
V. I.

ADAMSVILLE

Bagent, George F., Pr. Co. G 7th O.V. I.

ADRIAN, MICH.

Jordan, Charles A., 1st Sergt. Tr. E 1st O. V. C.

ÆTNA

Wilkins, Clarence D., Pr. Co. K 7th O. V. I.

AKRON

Abrahams, David, Pr. Co. F 10th O.
V. I.
Allison, George D., Pr. Co. B 8th O.
V. I.
Barber, Edward P., Pr. Co. B 8th O.
V. I.
Bender, Elwood C., Pr. Co. B 8th O.
V. I.
Bordner, William H., Pr. Co. B 8th O.
V. I.
Bowman, Robert H., Pr. Co. B 8th O.
V. I.
Brennan, Patrick, Pr. Co. F 10th O.V.I.
Brigger, Albert, Pr. Co. F 10th O.V.I.
Brigger, Arthur, Pr. Co. F 10th O.V.I.
Brown, David W., Sergt. Maj. 8th O.
V. I.
Brown, Frank H., Pr. Co. I 10th O.V.I.

Brown, Gerald H., Pr. Co. B 8th O.
V. I.
Bruner, William T., Pr. Co. I 10th O.
V. I.
Burla, Frank T., Pr. Co. B 8th O. V. I.
Cameron, Wilford E., Pr. Co. B 8th O.
V. I.
Campbell, Harry E., Pr. Co. B 8th O.
V. I.
Cass, Claud A., Corp. Co. B 8th O.V.I.
Chaffee, Dan., Pr. Co. F 10th O. V. I.
Chandler, William G., Pr. Co. F 10th
O. V. I.
Chapin, Robert H., Pr. Co. B 8th O.
V. I.
Christensen, Charles F., Pr. Co. B 8th
O. V. I.
Clark, Claud B., Pr. Co. B 8th O. V. I.

Cooper, Heber, Musician Co, C 8th
O. V. I.
Coyle, John W., Musician Co, G 8th
O. V. I.
Craighton, Ossian C., Pr. Co, B 8th O.
V. I.
Cranz, Clarence A., Sergt. Co, B 8th O.
V. I.
Cranz, Earl, Sergt. Co, B 8th O. V. I.
Crook, Alfred, Pr. Co, F 10th O. V. I.
Crumrine, Charles C., Corp. Co, B 8th
O. V. I.
Decker, Monroe, Pr. Co, F 10th O.V.I.
Deckert, Richard, Pr. Co, F 10th O.
V. I.
Deeds, Wilbur C., Corp. Co, F 10th
O. V. I.
Dice, Jesse P., Pr. Co, F 10th O. V. I.
Dice, William M., Pr. Co, F 10th O.
V. I.
Didion, William, Artificer Co B 8th
O. V. I.
Diehl, Fred H., Pr. Co, B 8th O. V. I.
Dorrance, John M., Pr. Co, B 8th O.
V. I.
Eakens, Burt H., Pr. Co, B 8th O. V. I.
Eckel, Gustave, Pr. Co, F 10th O. V. I.
Eckler, Adam, Jr., Pr. Co, F 10th O.
V. I.
Edgar, Edward E., Pr. Co, F 10th O.
V. I.

Fink, Joseph R., Pr. Co, F 10th O.V.I.
Fuchs, Clemons, Pr. Co, F 10th O.V.I.
Gahwolf, Mike, Corp. Co, F 10th O.V.I.
Gaillard, Armand, Pr. Co, F 10th O.
V. I.
Gale, Clarence W., Pr. Co, F 10th O.
V. I.
Gallagher, Thomas, Pr. Co, F 10th O.
V. I.
Geis, Clarence J., Pr. Co, F 10th O.V.I.
Goddard, Frank C., Pr. Co, B 8th O.
V. I.
Goodall, Albert, Pr. Co, F 10th O. V. I.
Grether, Lewis J., Pr. Co, B 8th O.V.I.
Groesel, Ernest, Pr. Co, B 8th O. V. I.
Hackett, William T., Pr. Co, F 10th
O. V. I.
Hall, Harry E., Q. M. Sergt. Co, D 9th
Bat. O. V. I.
Hanscom, Austin B., Pr. Co, B 8th O.
V. I.
Harden, Frank, Pr. Co, F 10th O. V. I.
Harris, Earl M., Pr. Co, F 10th O.V.I.
*Harriss, Walter H., Musician Co, H
8th O. V. I.
Haushalter, Fred G., Pr. Co, B 8th O.
V. I.
Hawn, Acton F., Pr. Co, F 10th O.V.I.
Heldding, Charles T., Pr. Co, B 8th O.
V. I.
Heller, Meck, Pr. Co, B 8th O. V. I.
Herwick, Adam C., Pr. Co, F 10th O.
V. I.

Herwick, Frank P., Pr. Co, F 10th
O. V. I.
Hill, Clarence M., Sergt. Co, F 10th
O. V. I.
Hinkle, Oliver C., Pr. Co, F 8th O.V.I.
Hollinger, John H., Sergt. Co, F 10th
O. V. I.
Holloway, Albert C., Pr. Co, B 8th O.
V. I.
Honodle, Edward H., Pr. Co, B 8th O.
V. I.
Hoover, Charles R., Pr. Co, F 10th
O. V. I.
Hough, D. Leslie, Pr. Co, F 10th O.
V. I.
Houghland, Harry D., Pr. Co, B 8th
O. V. I.
Howe, Henry J., Pr. Co, F 10th O.V.I.
Hutton, Willis, Pr. Co, F 10th O. V. I.
Ish, Watson W., Pr. Co, F 10th O.V.I.
Johnson, Arthur C., Pr. Co, B 8th O.
V. I.
Jones, William, Pr. Co, B 8th O. V. I.
Kapp, Martin D., Pr. Co, F 10th O.V.I.
Keck, Harry E., Pr. Co, B 8th O. V. I.
Keck, Ira, Artificer Co, F 10th O. V. I.
Keller, Harry E., Pr. Co, F 10th O.V.I.
Kelso, Wallace A., Pr. Co, F 10th O.
V. I.
Kiefer, George, Corp. Co, F 10th O.V.I.
Klingenhagen, Carl, Corp. Co, F 10th
O. V. I.
Klingler, George W., Pr. Co, F 10th
O.V. I.
Koons, George, Pr. Co, F 10th O. V. I.
Kramer, Gottlieb F., Pr. Co, F 10th
O. V. I.
Kraver, Charles W., Wagoner Co, B
8th O. V. I.
Lappin, Emery W., Corp. Co, F 10th
O. V. I.
Le Doux, Henry, Pr. Co, F 10th O.V.I.
Le Fevre, Milton, Pr. Co, F 10th O.
V. I.
Lewis, Sam, Pr. Co, F 10th O. V. I.
Lillich, Daniel F., Pr. Co, B 8th O.V.I.
Limbert, James, Corp. Co, F 10th O.
V. I.
Longacre, Ellsworth H., Pr. Co, B 8th
O. V. I.
Love, William H., Pr. Co, B 8th O.V.I.
Mahoney, Denis J., Pr. Co, F 10th O.
V. I.
McCann, John, Pr. Co, F 10th O. V. I.
McDonald, Angus, Pr. Co, F 10th O.
V. I.
McTammany, John, Musician Co, E 8th
O. V. I.
Meier, Julius C., Q. M. Sergt. Co, F
10th O. V. I.
Mellor, E. Carroll, Corp. Co, F 10th
O. V. I.
Metzler, Frank M., Pr. Co, F 10th O.
V. I.
Miller, William, Pr. Co, F 10th O.V.I.

Discharged.

Moll, George J., Corp. Co. F 10 O.V.I.
Morrison, Joseph C., Corp. Co. B 8th O. V. I.
Morthland, David, Pr. Co. F 10th O. V. I.
Myers, Joseph, Corp. Co. F 10th O.V.I.
Nelson, Paul E., Pr. Co. F 10th O.V.I.
Nigh, William D., Pr. Co. F 10th O. V. I.
Noland, William E., Pr. Co. F 10th O. V. I.
Palmer, William R., Ch. Mus. 8th O. V. I.
Parker, Harry W., Pr. Co. F 10th O. V. I.
Pittinger, Joseph, Pr. Co. F 10th O.V.I.
Prange, Harry B., Pr. Co. F 10th O. V. I.
Prier, Otis E., Sergt. Co. B 8th O.V.I.
Quine, Harry S., Pr. Co. B 8th O.V.I.
Rabe, Henry J., Pr. Co. F 10th O.V.I.
Radaff, Abraham, Musician Co. F 10th O. V. I.
Reinecke, Charles, Pr. Co. F 10th O. V. I.
Reinhard, James, Pr. Co. F 10th O.V.I.
Robinson, Edson M., Pr. Co. B 8th O. V. I.
Rogers, George W., Pr. Co. B 8th O. V. I.
Roussert, Albert, Musician Co. B. 8th O. V. I.
Roussert, Leo, Pr. Co. F 10th O. V. I.
Ruedy, Henry, Pr. Co. F 10th O. V. I.
Russell, Walter C., 1st Sergt. Co. F 10th O. V. I.
Ruttman, Daniel W., Musician Co. B 8th O. V. I.
Rynn, John A., Pr. Co. F 10th O. V. I.
Schoenduve, Carl, Sergt. Co. F 10th O. V. I.
Seybold, Carl, Wagoner Co. F 10th O. V. I.
Shaffer, Harvey G., Corp. Co. F 10th O. V. I.
Shaffer, Lyman E., Pr. Co. B 8th O. V. I.
Sharp, Frank B., Pr. Co. F 10th O.V.I.
Slater, William, Pr. Co. F 10th O.V.I.
Slattery, M. T., Pr. Co. F 10th O. V. I.
Smith, Edward J., Pr. Co. F 10th O. V. I.
Snyder, Milo D., Musician Co. G 8th O. V. I.
Spafford, Augustius W., Musician Co. F 10th O. V. I.

Speck, Earnest H., Pr. Co. F 10th O. V. I.
Spencer, William A., Pr. Co. B 8th O. V. I.
Spofford, Willis B., Pr. Co. B 8th O. V. I.
Sprague, Arthur E., Pr. Co. B 8th O. V. I.
Staub, Otis G., Pr. Co. F 10th O. V. I.
Steigner, Harry, Pr. Co. F 10th O.V.I.
Sues, Frank, Pr. Co. F 10th O. V. I.
Tannyhill, Franklin, Corp. Co. B 8th O. V. I.
Thomas, David R., Pr. Co. B 8th O. V. I.
Thomas, James R., Sergt. Co. B 8th O. V. I.
Trauger, Charles C., Pr. Co. F 10th O. V. I.
Treap, Harry F., Sergt. Co. B 8th O. V. I.
Treen, Harry, Pr. Co. F 10th O. V. I.
Vermillion, Richard S., Pr. Co. F 10th O. V. I.
Walker, James A. G., Pr. Co. L 8th O. V. I.
Walkup, Royal A., Corp. Co. B 8th O. V. I.
Walkup, William E., 1st Sergt. Co. B 8th O. V. I.
Warner, Charles H., Pr. Co. F 10th O. V. I.
Whalon, George, Corp. Co. F 10th O. V. I.
Wheeler, Walter R., Pr. Co. B 8th O. V. I.
Whitestone, David, Pr. Co. B 8th O. V. I.
Williams, Idris C., Pr. Co. B 8th O. V. I.
Wilson, Bertie E., Pr. Co. F 10th O. V. I.
Wise Ora F., Sergt. Co. F 10th O. V. I.
Woehler, Henry C., Pr. Co. A 8th O. V. I.
Woods, Frank F., Pr. Co. B 8th O.V.I.
Woods, James, Pr. Co. F 10th O. V. I.
Worthington, William W., Musician Co. C 8th O. V. I.
Wright, George W., Pr. Co. F 10th O. V. I.
Yohey, George E., Pr. Co. B 8th O. V. I.
Young, Joseph, W., Sergt. Maj. 8th O. V. I.
Yontz, William, Corp. Co. F 10th O. V. I.

ALBION

Baylor, Lorenzo, Pr. Co. C 8th O.V.I.
Edwards, Orla P., Pr. Co. C 8th O.V.I.

Snoddy, Allen C., Pr. Co. C 8th O.V.I.

ALGER

Stimmel, Pary D., Pr. Co. I 2nd O.V.I.

ALLEGHENY, PA.

Hogan, William P., Pr. Bat. C 1st O. V. A.

Payne, William H., Pr. Co. D 9th Bat. O. V. I.

ALLIANCE

Baker, Fred. Pr. Co. K 8th O. V. I.
Ballard, Whitcomb A., Corp. Co. K 8th O. V. I.
Bankerd, William W., Pr. Co. K 8th O. V. I.
Bardo, Oby, Pr. Co. K 8th O. V. I.
Bartley, Charles E., Pr. Co. K 8th O. V. I.
Bourguard, Edward E., Pr. Co. K 8th O. V. I.
Bowman, Curtis J., Pr. Co. K 8th O.V.I.
Brosius, Harry E., 1st Sergt. Co. K 8th O. V. I.
Buel, Henry V., Pr. Co. K 8th O. V. I.
Cannon, Benjamin, Pr. Co. K 8th O. V. I.
Cooper, Charles F., Sergt. Co. K 8th O. V. I.
Clapsaddle, John H., Corp. Co. K 8th O. V. I.
*Crowl, Calvin D., Artificer Co. K 8th O. V. I.
Crowl, Isaac W., Pr. Co. K 8th O. V. I.
Crubaugh, Clyde B., Sergt. Co. K 8th O. V. I.
Davis, Herbert C., Pr. Co. K 8th O.V.I.
Davis, Louis J., Pr. Co. K 8th O. V. I.
Dobson, Harry M., Sergt. Co. K 8th O. V. I.
Douglas, Neal. Pr. Co. K 8th O. V. I.
Eckert, Calvin, Pr. Co. K 8th O. V. I.
Eells, Milton R., Pr. Co. K 8th O. V. I.
Gilbert, Robert S., Pr. Co. K 8th O. V. I.
Gilhuly, Joseph A., Pr. Co. K 8th O. V. I.
Grubb, Loyal, Pr. Co. K 8th O. V. I.
Hoover, Charles S., Sergt. Maj. 8th O. V. I.
Hopps, Lucius, Pr. Co. K 8th O. V. I.
Jarrett, William S., Corp. Co. K 8th O. V. I.
Kirkwood, Daniel E., Pr. Co. K 8th O. V. I.

Knowles, William R., Corp. Co. K 8th O. V. I.
Kreigbaum, Frank, Pr. Co. K 8th O. V. I.
Leu, Harry W., Pr. Co. K 8th O. V. I.
Marchand, Aubrey W., Pr. Co. I 8th O. V. I.
Maus, Walter B., Pr. Co. K 8th O. V. I.
McCowen, Charles H., Pr. Co. K 8th O. V. I.
Miller, Orva, Pr. Co. K 8th O. V. I.
Miller, Wallace, Pr. Co. K 8th O. V. I.
Moyer, Lloyd F., Sergt. Co. K 8th O. V. I.
Newcomer, Jesse, Pr. Co. K 8th O.V.I.
Osborn, Bert R., Pr. Co. K 8th O. V. I.
Patterson, John O., Pr. Co. K 8th O. V. I.
Reynolds, Aldun, Musician Co. K 8th O. V. I.
Richards, Joseph E., Pr. Co. K 8th O. V. I.
Richards, Martin A., Pr. Co. K 8th O. V. I.
Robertson, Alexander, Pr. Co. K 8th O. V. I.
Scott, John M., Pr. Co. K 8th O. V. I.
Seacrist, Edd, Pr. Co. K 8th O. V. I.
Shaffer, Ira J., Pr. Co. K 8th O. V. I.
Silver, Edwin B., Sergt. Co. K 8th O. V. I.
Silver, James A., Pr. Co. K 8th O. V. I.
Sourbeck, Alva L., Pr. Co. K 8th O.V.I.
Sullivan, Michael, Pr. Co. K 8th O.V.I.
Teeters, Carl D., Pr. Co. E 8th O.V.I.
Urig, Edmond J., Pr. Co. K 8th O.V.I.
Walser, Richard, Pr. Co. K 8th O. V. I.
White, Charles L., Corp. Co. K 8th O. V. I.
Zang, Fred. J., Pr. Co. K 8th O. V. I.
Zuber, Charles H., Pr. Co. K 8th O.V.I.
Zuber, George A., Musician Co. K 8th O. V. I.

ALTOONA, PA.

Ishler, James A., Pr. Co. K 7th O. V. I.

AMANDA

Kernes, Doid, Pr. Co. I 4th O. V. I.
Lape, Theodore I., Pr. Co. I, 4th O.V.I.

Terry, Nelson E., Pr. Co. I 4th O. V. I.

AMSTERDAM, N. Y.

Hurley, John, Pr. Co. M 5th O. V. I.

° Discharged.

ANDERSONVILLE

Hixson, Benj. F., Pr. Co. H 7th O.V.I.
McCollister, Chauncey, Pr. Co. H 7th O. V. I.
McCollister, James C., Pr. Co. H 7th O. V. I.

Overley, Kell, Pr. Co. H 7th O. V, I.
Rhoads, William H., Pr. Co. H 7th O. V. I.
Throckmorton, Geo. L., Pr. Co. H 7th O. V. I.

ANDOVER

Griffis, Albert L., Pr. Tr. B, 1st O. V. C.   Tossell, William J., Pr. Co. E 5th O.V.I.

ANGOLA

Broyles, Ezra E., Corp. Co. C 7th O.V.I.
Broyles, John W., Pr. Co. C 7th O.V.I.

Markin, Charles C., Pr. Co. B 2d U. S. V. E.
Whittaker, Aaron, Pr. Co. C 7th O.V.I.

ANNA

Dill, Omer R., Corp. Co. L 3rd O. V. I.

ANNAPOLIS

Charlton, Wilber J., Pr. Co. A 8th O.V. I.

ANSONIA

Spielman, Morrison E., Pr. Co. C 3rd O. V. I.

ANTWERP

Bernardin, Frank L., Pr. Co. M 2nd O. V. I.
Boylan, Samuel, Pr. Co. M 2nd O. V. I.
Cline, Edwin, Pr. Co. M 2nd O. V. I.
Curtis, John W., Corp. Co. M 2nd O. V. I.
Cussen, James F., Corp. Co. M 2nd O. V. I.
Cussen, Thomas, Pr. Co. M 2nd O.V.I.
Dreibelbiss, Oscar M., Pr. Co. M 2nd O. V. I.
Jaderstrom, Lewis W., Pr. Co. M 2nd O. V. I.
Kauffman, Bert J., Pr. Co. M 2nd O.V.I.
Kerns, Edward, Pr. Co. M 2nd O. V. I.
Kline, Adam H., Wagoner Co. M 2nd O. V. I.

McCalla, John H., Sergt. Co. M 2nd O. V. I.
McCreary, Lionel D., Pr. Co. M 2nd O. V. I.
Mooney, John H., Pr. Co. M 2nd O.V.I.
Munson, Charles E., Pr. Co. M 2nd O. V. I.
Traxler, Ernest D., Pr. Co. M 2nd O. V. I.
Van Horn, Harmon, Pr. Co. M 2nd O. V. I.
Wilson, James E., Pr. Co. M 2nd O.V.I.
Woodcox, Wallace, Pr. Co. M 2nd O. V. I.
Zeigler, Bert A., Pr. Co. M 2nd O. V. I.

ANTIOCH

Pryor, Isaac M., Pr. Co. D 7th O. V. I.

ARCANUM

Cline, George D., Pr. Co. C 3rd O. V. I.   Hoffman, Victor W., Corp. Co. C 3rd O. V. I.

ARENO

Carter, James M., Pr. Co. M 2nd O.V.I.   Shepherd, John R., Pr. Co. M 2nd O. V. I.

ARTHUR

Morris, Elijah C., Pr. Co. M 6th O.V.I.   Wade, Dan, Pr. Co. M 6th O. V. I.

3—R. O. V.

ASHLAND

Abrams, Edwin T., Pr. Co. C 8th O.V.I.
Bott, La Roy F., Pr. Co. C 8th O. V. I.
Buchter, Stanley D., Pr. Co. C 8th O. V. I.
Clark, Jess M., Sergt. Co. C 8th O. V. I.
Closson, John D., Pr. Co. C 8th O.V.I.
Downs, Robert F., Pr. Co. C 8th O.V.I.
Ewing, Tom C., Pr. Co. C 8th O. V. I.
Frey, Alvin C., Pr. Co. C 8th O. V. I.
Gardner, Alfred G., Pr. Co. C 8th O.V.I.
Gilletly, Fred H., Pr. Co. C 8th O. V. I.
Hayes, Frederick C., Pr. Co. C 8th O. V. I.
Hetzel, Peter, Corp. Co. C 8th O. V. I.
Hockensmith, Charles A., Pr. Co. C 8th O. V. I.
Lersch, Arthur, Pr. Co. C 8th O. V. I.

Long, C. LeRoy, Pr. Co. C 8th O. V. I.
McCray, Benjamin W., Pr. Co. C 8th O. V. I.
Miller, Charles F., Pr. Co. C 8th O.V.I.
Patterson, Jay H., Pr. Co. C 8th O.V.I.
Plank, Joshua M., Pr. Co. C 8th O.V.I.
Redding, Frank, Pr. Co. C 8th O. V. I.
Renn, John Z., Pr. Co. C 8th O. V. I.
Ridgley, Roy E., Pr. Co. C 8th O. V. I.
Rittenhouse, Emmet C., Pr. Co. C 8th O. V. I.
Robinson, Louis J., Pr. Co. C 8th O. V. I.
Schoff, Willie F., Pr. Co. C 8th O.V.I.
Tallon, Bernard, Pr. Co. C 8th O. V. I.
Way, Charley, Pr. Co. C 8th O. V. I.
Woods, William, Pr. Co. C 8th O. V. I.

ASHLAND, KY.

Callahan, Madison J., Musician Co. I 7th O. V. I.

ASHTABULA

Clark, William K., Pr. Co. E 5th O.V.I.
Collar, Dwight O., Sergt. Co. E 5th O. V. I.
Dietz, Robert C., Pr. U. R. 3rd O. V. I.

Good, Charles A., Wagoner Co. E 5th O. V. I.
Hillman, Bert E., Pr. Co. E 5th O. V. I.

ATHENS

Baker, Edward J., Pr. Co. B 7th O.V.I.
Bartlett, Harry G., Musician Co. B 7th O. V. I.
Bean, William H., Pr. Co. B 7th O.V.I.
Blakeley, Jesse N., Pr. Co. B 7th O.V.I.
Bordee, Benjamin H., Sergt. Co. B 7th O. V. I.
Brown, Guy H., Pr. Co. B 7th O. V. I.
Brown, Harry W., Pr. Co. B 7th O.V.I.
Brown, Justus, Pr. Co. B 7th O. V. I.
Brown, William A., Pr. Co. B 7th O V. I.
Cage, Daniel W., Pr. Co. B 7th O. V. I.
Carpenter, Eber, Pr. Co. K 7th O. V. I.
Charter, Howard, Corp. Co. B 7th O V. I.
Cochran, Malcolm S., Pr. Co. B 7th O. V. I.
Cullums, Edward N., Pr. Co. B 7th O. V. I.
Dalton, Frank Hadley, 1st Sergt. Co. B 7th O. V. I.
Dalton, Ralph A., Corp. Co. B 7th O V. I.
Davis, Lee, Pr. Co. B 7th O. V. I.
Davis, Thomas E., Pr. Co. B 7th O.V.I.
Edmundson, Clyde, Corp. Co. B 7th O. V. I.
Faires, William C., Sergt. Co. B 7th O. V. I.
Gabriel, Earl, Pr. Co. B 7th O. V. I.
Gabriel, William R., Pr. Co. B 7th O. V. I.

Gates, George W., Pr. Co. B 7th O.V.I.
Gibson, Ned C., Pr. Co. B 7th O. V. I.
Gist, John D., Corp. Co. B 7th O. V. I.
Graf, Albert, Pr. Co. B 7th O. V. I.
Hawk, Hadley C., Pr. Co. B 7th O.V.I.
Headley, Sanford A., Corp. Co. B 7th O. V. I.
Kaler, Joseph W., Pr. Co. B 7th O.V.I.
Kinkade, Charles R., Pr. Co. B 7th O. V. I.
Kinkade, Millard F., Pr. Co. B 7th O. V. I.
Kirkendall, Emmett R., Pr. Co. B 7th O. V. I.
Laughlin, Charley H., Pr. Co. B 7th O. V. I.
Mariner, Charles, Pr. Co. K 7th O. V. I.
McKinstry, Koss T., Pr. Co. B 7th O. V. I.
Milligan, Albert, Pr. Co. B 7th O. V. I.
Morrison, Harry D., Pr. Co. B 7th O. V. I.
North, Eli T., Sergt. Co. B 7th O. V. I.
Peters, John H., Pr. Co. B 7th O. V. I.
Pickering, Charles O., Pr. Co. B 7th O. V. I.
Poston, Charles H., Pr. Co. B 7th O. V. I.
Rabe, Frank A., Pr. Co. B 7th O. V. I.
Rasmusson, Hugh P., Pr. Co. B 7th O. V. I.
Richmond, Earl, Pr. Co. B 7th O.V.I.
Rose, Frank C., Pr. Co. B 7th O. V. I.

Root, Chas., Q. M. Sergt. Co. B 7th O. V. I.
Sackett, Guy A., Pr. Co. B 7th O. V. I.
Salters, Elza, Pr. Co. B 7th O. V. I.
Sickels, Lester E., Pr. Co. B 7th O.V.I.
Six. Pater P., Pr. Co. B 7th O. V. I.
Skinner, William D., Sergt. Co. B 7th O. V. I.
Slaughter, David C., Pr. Co. B 7th O. V. I.
Staflinger, Fitch H., Artificer Co. B 7th O. V. I.
Stearns, Clifford H., Corp. Co. B 7th O. V. I.
Sutton, Herbert E., Pr. Co. B 7th O.V.I.
Thompson, Bernard H., Musician Co. B, 7th O. V. I.
Thompson, Hart, Pr. Co. B 7th O. V. I.
Woodworth, Erwin C., Pr. Co. B 7th O. V. I.

AUBURN

Husted, Don B., Pr. Co. C 10th O. V. I.

BARBERTON

Durant, George L., Pr. Co. B 8th O.V.I.
King, Jesse W., Corp. Co. B 8th O.V.I.
Melbourn, Edmond W., Pr. Co. B 8th O. V. I.

BARLOW

Lawton, Leonard C., Pr. Co. B 2nd U. S. V. E.

BARNESVILLE.

Ellis, Ross, Pr. Co. D 3rd O. V. I.

BASCOM

Corner, Charles N., Pr. Co. E 2nd O. V. I.
Leitner, Charles A., Pr. Co. E 2nd O. V. I.
Taylor, Charles W. G., Pr. Co. A 10th O. V. I.

BATAVIA

Glancy, Homer B., Sergt. Co. M 1st O. V. C.
Parrott, Edmund K., Corp. Co. M 1st O. V. C.
Parrott, Dale K., Pr. Co. M 1st O.V.C.
Stirling, William A., Pr. Co. I 10th O. V. I.
Zenike, John C., Pr. Co. M 1st O. V. C.

BEATTY

Stewart, Perry Mc., Pr. Co. B 3rd O. V. I.

BEAVER, PA.

Leslie, Darraugh, Pr. Co. L 8th O.V.I.

BELLE CENTRE

Mitchell, Walter E., Pr. Co. F 2nd O. V. I.
Smith, James R., Pr. Co. I 2nd O. V. I.

BELLEFONTAINE

Allmon, Frank J., Sergt. Co. F 2nd O. V. I.
Arnold, Howard Glen, Pr. Co. F 2nd O. V. I.
Bassett, James H., Pr. Co. F 2nd O. V. I.
Bell, Elbert M., Pr. Co. F 2nd O. V. I.
Bennett, Charles E., Bat. Sergt. Maj. 2nd O. V. I.
Bickham, John R., Pr. Co. F 2nd O. V. I.
Bishop, Curtis L., Pr. Co. F 2nd O.V.I.
Black, Will W., Pr. Co. F 2nd O. V. I.
Braden, Robert C., Pr. Co. F 2nd O. V. I.
Brown, Harry E., Pr. Co. F 2nd O.V.I.
Bryan, John N., Pr. Co. F 2nd O. V. I.

Campbell, Harold F., Pr. Co. F 2nd O. V. I.
Davidson, E. W., Pr. Co. F 2nd O.V.I.
Detrick, Earl F., Sergt. Co. F 2nd O. V. I.
Detrick, Emmett G., Corp. Co. F 2nd O. V. I.
Dowell, Perry C., Pr. Co. F 2nd O.V.I.
Downing, Art. E., Pr. Co. F 2nd O.V.I.
Driggs, Charles P., Pr. Co. F 2nd O. V. I.
Ewing, Jasper, Pr. Co. F 2nd O. V. I.
Fulton, Albert M., Pr. Co. F 2nd O. V. I.
Fultz, Samuel S., Artificer Co. F 2nd O. V. I.
Ginn, Robert, Pr. Co. F 2nd. O. V. I.
Hawker, Edward S., Sergt. Co. F 2nd O. V. I.
Hulsiger, William T., Corp. Co. F 2nd O. V. I.
Jackson, Walter H., Pr. Co. F 2nd O. V. I.
Kemper, Roy, Pr. Co. F 2nd O. V. I.
Kitchen, William B., Pr. Co. F 2nd O. V. I.
Knox, Ira B., Pr. Co. F 2nd O. V. I.
Lane, Cory Levi, Pr. Co. B 4th O.V.I.
Law, Albert, Pr. Co. F 2nd O. V. I.
Liggett, David A., Corp. Co. F 2nd O. V. I.
Lloyd, Robert J., Pr. Co. F 2nd O.V.I.
Lowe, Herman G., Pr. Co. F 2nd O. V. I.

Maxwell, Sidney R., Pr. Co. F 2nd O. V. I.
Miller, Huber M., Pr. Co. F 2nd O.V.I.
Millner, Jesse M., Wagoner Co. F 2nd O. V. I.
Moore, Chas. H., Pr. Co. F 2nd O.V.I.
Pash, Harry W., Pr. Co. F 2nd O.V.I.
Patterson, John M., Pr. Co. F 2nd O. V. I.
Pheneger, Edwin B., Corp. Co. F 2nd O. V. I.
Riegler, Marion P., Corp. Co. F 2nd. O. V. I.
Riley, Ned, Pr. Co. F 2nd O. V. I.
Robinaugh, Harley J., Corp. Co. F 2nd O. V. I.
Rutter, Frank E., Sergt. Co. F 2nd O. V. I.
Stelzig, John E., Pr. Co. F 2nd O.V.I.
Stevenson, Gail, Pr. Co. F 2nd O. V. I.
Stilwell, Harry W., Sergt. Co. F 2nd O. V. I.
Straight, Ora R., Pr. Co. F 2nd O.V.I.
Thompson, Edward, Pr. Co. F 2nd O. V. I.
Thompson, Ernest, Pr. Co. F 2nd O. V. I.
Wall, James T., Pr. Co. F 2nd O. V. I.
Wallace, Will G., Pr. Co. F 2nd O.V.I.
West, Samuel H., Pr. U. R. 2nd O.V.I.
Whitlock, William G., Pr. Co. F 2nd O. V. I.

BELLEVUE, KY.

Dresselhaus, George H., Pr. Co. B 2nd U. S. V. E.

BELLEVUE, O.

Miller, LeRoy E., Pr. Tr. B 1st O.V.C.

Shattuc, Edwin S., Pr. Co. C 10th O. V. I.

BELLVILLE

Green, Jesse B., Pr. Co. B 5th O. V. I.

BEREA

Alber, Robert J., Pr. Co. D 5th O.V.I.
Baisch, Frank G., Pr. Co. D 5th O.V.I.
Baker, Andrew A., Pr. Co. D 5th O. V. I.
Barendt, Frank E., Pr. Co. D 5th O. V. I.
Barendt, Fred A., Pr. Co. D 5th O.V.I.
Bennett, William H., Pr. Co. D 5th O. V. I.
Belter, Edward F., Pr. Co. D 5th O. V. I.
Bohn, Frank A., Pr. Co. D 5th O.V.I.
Buhrer, John G., Pr. Co. D 5th O.V.I.
Burnham, Victor G., Pr. Co. D 5th O. V. I.

Chevalier, Lyle L., Pr. Co. D 5th O. V. I.
Colvin, Benjamin W., Pr. Co. D 5th. O. V. I.
Cooper, Charles W., Pr. Co. D 5th O. V. I.
Corrigan, Thomas G., Pr. Co. D 5th O. V. I.
Crawford, David C., Pr. Co. D 5th O. V. I.
Crawford, Walter J., Pr. Co. D 5th O. V. I.
Dodd, Herbert L., Pr. Co. D 5th O. V. I.
Eckert, Carl J., 1st Sergt. Co. D 5th O. V. I.

Ferguson, Chauncey E., Pr. Co. D 5th O. V. I.
Fessler, Jacob, Pr. Co. D 5th O. V. I.
Finley, Carl F., Pr. Co. D 5th O. V. I.
Fuller, Albert J., Sergt. Co. D 5th O. V. I.
Geiger, Frank J., Pr. Co. D 5th O.V.I.
Goehner, Fred H., Pr. Co. D 5th O. V. I.
Hartman, Martin C., Pr. Co. D 5th O. V. I.
Hauck, Charles F., Pr. Co. D 5th O. V. I.
Headley, Clyde W., Pr. Co. D 5th O. V. I.
Heckelman, Christian A., Pr. Co. D 5th O. V. I.
Herscheider, Joseph E. J., Pr. Co. D 5th O. V. I.
Hubbard, George A., Jr., Pr. Co. D 5th O. V. I.
Hyman, William, Pr. Co. D 5th O.V.I.
Johnson, James R., Pr. Co. D 5th O. V. I.
Jordan, Edward L., Pr. Co. D 5th O. V. I.
King, Henry D., Pr. Co. D 5th O. V. I.
Kobie, William B., Pr. Co. D 5th O. V. I.
Kraft, Fred F., Pr. Co. D 5th O. V. I.
Krafton, Edward C., Pr. Co. D 5th O. V. I.
Le Duke, Francis A., 2nd Sergt. Co. D 5th O. V. I.
Lewis, Seth A., Pr. Co. D 5th O. V. I.
Marks, Thomas, Corp. Co. D 5th O. V. I.
Martin, Albert H., Pr. Co. D 5th O. V. I.
Mehl, George W., Pr. Co. D 5th O.V.I.
Nelson, John H., Pr. Co. D 5th O.V.I.

Neubauer, Ernest H., Pr. Co. D 5th O. V. I.
Newcomb, Adrian G., Corp. Co. D 5th O. V. I.
Nickels, Frank G., Pr. Co. D 5th O. V. I.
O'Hare, Edward, Pr. Co. D 5th O.V.I.
Peter, George A., Pr. Co. D 5th O.V.I.
Poots, Charles F., Pr. Co. D 5th O.V.I.
Pope, John H., Pr. Co. D 5th O. V. I.
Pszenitzki, Frank J., Pr. Co. D 5th O. V. I.
Pszenitzki, Paul J., Pr. Co. D 5th O. V. I.
Schaal, William G., Pr. Co. D 5th O. V. I.
Schaibly, John G., Corp. Co. D 5th O. V. I.
Scheurenbrand, Fred C., Pr. Co. D 5th O. V. I.
Schmidt, George J., Corp. Co. D 5th O. V. I.
Schneider, George, Pr. Co. D 5th O. V. I.
Shoop, Ora J., Sergt. Co. D 5th O. V. I.
Shute, Arthur J., Pr. Co. D 5th O.V.I.
Stephenson, Frank S., Corp. Co. D 5th O. V. I.
Taylor, Frank M., Pr. Co. D 5th O.V.I.
Wadel, Max L., Pr. Co. D 5th O. V. I.
Walker, Barton J., Pr. Co. D 5th O. V. I.
Webber, Joseph, Pr. Co. D 5th O.V.I.
Whitney, Alfred C., Pr. Co. D 5th O. V. I.
Wieseke, George R., Musician Co. D 5th O. V. I.
Winsor, Leroy E., Pr. Co. D 5th O. V. I.
Winsor, Ona J., Pr. Co. D 5th O. V. I.
Woodcock, Sam., Sergt. Co. D 5th O. V. I.

BERLINVILLE

Grose, Peter L., Pr. Co. G 5th O. V. I.

BEVERLY

Worstell, John C., Pr. Co. D 7th O.V.I.

BIG PLAIN

Grubb, William D., Pr. Co. E 3rd O. V. I.

Holloway, Newton J., Pr. Co. E 3rd O. V. I.
Meagher, Frank, Pr. Co. I 1st O. V. I.

BIG PRAIRIE

Derry, Lawrence, Pr. Co. H 8th O.V.I.

Merkel, Eugene D., Pr. Co. H 8th O. V. I.

BIRMINGHAM

Latteman, Carl, Pr. Co. I 5th O. V. I.

BLADEN

Halley, John R., Pr. Co. C 7th O. V. I.
Halley, Samuel T., Pr. Co. C 7th O.V.I.
Harrington, Perne, Pr. Co. C 7th O.
V. I.

Jeffers, Thomas, Pr. Co. C 7th O. V. I.
Warden, Richard W., Pr. Co. C 7th O.
V. I.

BLISSFIELD, MICH.

Howard, Victor D., Pr. Tr. E 1st O. V. C.

BLOOMDALE

Brandeberry, Irvy E., Pr. Co. H 2nd
O. V. I.
Callan, Edward M., Pr. Co. H 2nd O.
V. I.
Campbell, Boyd E., Pr. Co. H 2nd O.
V. I.
Campbell, Robert P., Pr. Co. H 2nd
O. V. I.
Colbert, Daniel G., Pr. Co. H 2nd O.
V. I.
Coldwell, Wilbert, Pr. Co. H 2nd O.
V. I.
Conley, Abe B., Pr. Co. B 2nd O. V. I.
Corey, George E., Pr. Co. H 2nd O.V.I.
Cramer, Samuel M., Sergt. Co. H 2nd
O. V. I.
Crum, Chance C., Corp. Co. H 2nd O.
V. I.
Deihl, Thomas E., Pr. Co. H 2nd O.
V. I.
Dicken, Guy, Corp. Co. H 2nd O. V. I.
Douglas, Archibald, Pr. Co. H 2nd O.
V. I.
Douglas, Wallace B., Bat. Sergt. Maj.
2nd O. V. I.
Drake, Charles, Pr. Co. H 2nd O. V. I.
Drake, David F., Pr. Co. H 2nd O.V.I.
England, Ray, Pr. Co. H 2nd O. V. I.
Enos, John J., Corp. Co. H 2nd O. V. I.
Fasig, Walter S., Sergt. Co. H 2nd O.
V. I.
Frankfather, Earl, Pr. Co. H 2nd O.V.I.
Frankfather, Guy, Pr. Co. H 2nd O.V.I.
Fry, Delos, Pr. Co. H 2nd O. V. I.
Gale, Stanley, Pr. Co. II 2nd O. V. I.
Griffith, Harold, E., Pr. Co. H 2nd
O. V. I.
Hamblin, Franklin A., Pr. Co. H 2nd
O. V. I.
Hamblin, John W., Pr. Co. H 2nd O.
V. I.
Harn, Milton, Pr. Co. H 2nd O. V. I.
Hoofman, John M., Pr. Co. H 2nd
O. V. I.
Hoover, Irwin B., Pr. Co. H 2nd O.V.I.
Krieger, Henry M., Pr. Co. H 2nd O.
V. I.
Kripliver, Louis M., Pr. Co. H 2nd
O. V. I.
Loman, Allen, Pr. Co. H 2nd O. V. I.
Long, Elmer J., Pr. Co. H 2nd O. V. I.
Mapes, James B., Pr. Co. H 2nd O.V.I.
McLaughlin, John D., Pr. Co. H 2nd
O. V. I.

Miller, David L., Corp. Co. H 2nd O.
V. I.
Miller, Jesse, Pr. Co. H 2nd O. V. I.
Monroe, Redmond B., Pr. Co. H 2nd
O. V. I.
Olmstead, Walter T., Pr. Co. H 2nd
O. V. I.
Ordway, James H., Pr. Co. H 2nd O.
V. I.
Parmenter, Earl L., Pr. Co. H 2nd O.
V. I.
Pelton, William H., Pr. Co. H 2nd O.
V. I.
Pepple, Charles A., Pr. Co. H 2nd O.
V. I.
Pepple, Dodie W., Pr. Co. H 2nd O.
V. I.
Porter, Sylvester D., Pr. Co. H 2nd O.
V. I.
Richard, Clarence, Pr. Co. H 2nd O.
V. I.
Richard, Florentine, Pr. Co. H 2nd O.
V. I.
Richard, William H., Corp. Co. H 2nd
O. V. I.
Robbins, Lander V., Q. M. Sergt. Co.
H, 2nd O. V. I.
Ropp, John A., Pr. Co. H 2nd O. V. I.
Rosebrook, Jesse, Pr. Co. H 2nd O.V.I.
Rosendale, Scott E., Pr. Co. H 2nd O.
V. I.
Sautimire, George S., Sergt. Co. H 2nd
O. V. I.
Shaw, Harry W., Pr. Co. H 2nd O.V.I.
Shelt, Harry E., Sergt. Co. H 2nd O.
V. I.
Simon, Frank, Pr. Co. H 2nd O. V. I.
Simon, Willis E., 1st Sergt. Co. H 2nd
O. V. I.
Skinner, Charles B., Pr. Co. H 2nd O.
V. I.
Slotterbeck, Clyde, Pr. Co. H 2nd O.
V. I.
Snyder, Guy M., Corp. Co. H 2nd O.
V. I.
Snyder, Milton H., Pr. Co. H 2nd O.
V. I.
Speck, Edward, Pr. Co. H 2nd O. V. I.
Stecker, John M., Pr. Co. H 2nd O.V.I.
Stockman, Henry R., Pr. Co. H 2nd
O. V. I.
Sweetland, Daniel L., Pr. Co. H 2nd
O. V. I.

Underwood, Chauncey, Pr. Co. H 2nd
O. V. I.
Wakefield, Clyde W., Pr. Co. H 2nd
O. V. I.

Whitcomb, Thomas J., Pr. Co. H 2nd
O. V. I.
Yates, John, Pr. Co. H 2nd O. V. I.
Yonker, Arthur H., Pr. Co. H 2nd O.
V. I.

BLOOMINGBURG

Creath, Owen W., Pr. Co. D 8th O.V.I.

BLOOMINGTON

Aldrige, John A., Pr., Co. M 3rd O.V.I.

BLOOMVILLE

Carew, Charles W., Pr. Co. E 2nd O. V I.

BLUFFTON

Owens, Otto J., Pr. Co. B 2nd O. V. I.

BOGGS

McKean, John W., Pr. Co. C 7th O.V.I.

BOLIVAR

App, Floyd T., Pr. Co. C 10th O. V. I.

BOND'S FERRY

Haas, Charles, Pr. Co. C 2nd U.S.V.E.

BOURNEVILLE

Miller, Wesley Ray, Pr. Co. H 7th O. V. I.

BOWLING GREEN

Bowen, Edward E., Pr. Co. H 10th
O. V. I.
Bates, James G., Pr. Co. K 2nd O. V. I.
Carr, Wilber O., Pr. Co. K 2nd O.V.I.
Dawson, John C., Pr. Co. K 2nd O.V.I.
Glover, Ralph N., Pr. Co. H 10th O.V.I.
Hall, Walter L., Pr. Co. C 10th O. V. I.
Harmon, Henry, Pr. Co. K 2nd O. V. I.
Jolley, George A., Pr. Co. H 10th O.V.I.

Jolley, Jesse D., Pr. Co. H 10th O. V. I.
Myers, Leon L., Corp. Co. K 2nd O.
V. I.
Reese, Edward T., Pr. Co. H 10th O.
V. I.
Sears, Foster, Pr. Co. C 10th O. V. I.
Shimer, Harvey, Pr. Co. K 2nd O. V. I.
Ward, Ervie, Pr. Co. K 2nd O. V. I.

BOWMAN

Woring, Doctor L., Pr. Co. B 7th O. V. I.

BOYD

Carey, Charlie, Pr. Co. C 3rd O. V. I

BRADFORD

Conaway, Harry, Pr. Co. K 3rd O. V. I.
Crane, Urlin S., Pr. Co. C 3rd O. V. I.
Dickey, Vernard, Pr. Co. C 3rd O. V. I
Eller, Hayes B., Pr. Co. C 3rd O. V. I.
Eller, Orlan T., Pr. Co. C 3rd O. V. I.
Feaster, William, Pr. Co. K 3rd O. V. I.

Galligan, Thomas, Corp. Co. K 3rd O.
V. I.
Maurer, Fred W., Pr. Co. C 3rd O.V.I.
Miller, William Orton, Pr. Co. C 3rd
O. V. I.

Purdy, William, Pr. Co. C 3rd O. V. I.
Roop, William, Pr. Co. K, 3rd O. V. I.
Stone, Fernan F., Pr. Co. C 3rd O. V. I.

Vore, Harry B., Pr. Co. C 3rd O. V. I.
Wade, David E., Pr. Co. C 3rd O. V. I.
Waitman, Earl C., Pr. Co. C 3rd O.V.I.

BRANDON

Channell, Charles H., Pr. Co. L 4th O. V. I.

Lockwood, Charles, Pr. Co. L 4th O. V. I.

BRICETON

Bruner, William I., Pr. Co. M 2nd O. V. C.
Mulcahy, Michael J., Pr. Co. M 2nd O. V. C.

Sprague, Jacob F., Pr. Co. M 2nd O. V. C.
Sutter, John H A., Corp Co. M 2nd O. V. C.

BRECKSVILLE

Dillow, Frank H., Pr. Co. L 5th O.V.I.

BRIGGS

Prewett, George M., Pr. Co. D 7th O. V. I.

BRIGGSDALE

Briggs, J. Merton, Hospital Steward, 10th O. V. I.

BRITTAIN

Spade, Charles A., Pr. Co. B 8th O.V.I.

BROOKLYN

Becker, John P., Sergt. Co. F 5th O.V.I.
Blickert, Edward A., Pr. Co. B 10th O. V. I.
Butera, Mike B., Pr. Co. I 10th O.V.I.

Schlund, Frank J., Jr., Pr. Co. B 10th O. V. I.
Steffen, Gustav, Pr. Co. I 10th O. V. I.

BROUGHTON

Harrow, Steele, Pr. Co. M 2nd O. V. I.
Miller, George E., Pr. Co. M 2nd O. V. I.

Robinson, Herman C., Pr. Co. M 2nd O. V. I.
Robinson, Joseph L., Pr. Co. M 2nd O. V. I.

BRUNO

Miller, Murry A., Pr. Co. K 7th O.V.I.

BRYAN

Amsbaugh, Charles R., Corp. Co. E 6th O. V. I.
Bolins, Richard F., Pr. Co. E 6th O. V. I.
Boucher, Charles F., Corp. Co. E 6th O. V. I.
Brown, Frank W., Pr. Co. E 6th O. V. I.
Bucklew, Andrew J., Pr. Co. E 6th O. V. I.
Burgoyne, Boyd W., Pr. Co. E 6th O. V. I.

Carroll, Earl C., Pr. Co. E 6th O. V. I.
Connin, Wilson, Musician Co. E 6th O. V. I.
Davis, William H., Sergt. Co. E 6th O. V. I.
Doolittle, Orrin J., Pr. Co. E 6th O. V. I.
Elder, Clark F., Pr. Co. E 6th O. V. I.
Engle, John E., Pr. Co. E 6th O. V. I.
Ensign, Loren E., Pr. Co. E 6th O.V.I.
Farber, Adolph D., Pr. Co. E 6th O. V. I.

Fay, Irwin D., Pr. Co. E 6th O. V. I.
Fether, Louis C., 1st Sergt. Co. E 6th
O. V. I.
Fisher, John P., Musician Co. E 6th
O. V. I.
Frehse, Fred E., Pr. Co. E 6th O.V.I.
Gabriel, Charles R., Pr. Co. E 6th O.
V. I.
Gabriel, Henry, Corp. Co. E 6th O.V.I.
Hummel, William S., Sergt. Co. E 6th
O. V. I.
Kelley, William A., Pr. Co. E 6th O.
V. I.
Kosier, William T., Corp. Co. E 6th
O. V. I.
Kurtz, Herman J., Pr. Co. E 6th O.V.I.
La Bounty, Stanford M., Pr. Co. E 6th
O. V. I.
Laeiss, Fred W., Pr. Co. E 6th O.V.I
Lambert, Charles T., Pr. Co. E 6th
O. V. I.
Leidigh, Mark, Wagoner Co. E 6th O.
V. I.
Mason, John C., Pr. Co. E 6th O.V.I.
Mavis, Charles P., Corp. Co. E 6th O.
V. I.
Moore, Edward M., Pr. Co. E 6th O.
V. I.
Newman, Charles P., Pr. Co. E 6th
O. V. I.

Newman, James S., Pr. Co. E 6th O.
V. I.
Reynolds, William, Artificer, Co. E 6th
O. V. I.
Robinson, Robert T., Pr. Co. E 6th
O. V. I.
Rodigkict, Theodore A., Pr. Co. E 6th
O. V. I.
Saddoris, James I., Pr. Co. E 6th O.
V. I.
Saddoris, John E., Pr. Co. E 6th O.V.I.
Schmidt, John, Pr. Co. E 6th O. V. I.
Shoemaker, Charles J., Pr. Co. E 6th
O. V. I.
Spangler, Arthur G., Pr. Co. E 6th
O. V. I.
Spangler, Omar L., Pr. Co. E 6th O.
V. I.
Storer, Frank, Pr. Co. E 6th O. V. I.
Thomas, Floyd S., Pr. Co. E 6th O.
V. I.
Warner, Daniel E., Sergt. Co. E 6th
O. V. I.
Warren, Garfield O., Pr. Co. E 6th
O. V. I.
Wetmore, Francis M., Sergt. Co. E 6th
O. V. I.
Whitney, Charles, Pr. Co. E 6th O.V.I.
Yates, Elmer E., Pr. Co. E 6th O.V.I.

BUCKLAND

Bowsher, Walter F., Pr. Co. L 2nd O.
V. I.
Gahret, Wilbur C., Pr. Co. L 2nd O.
V. I.

McAdams, Otto Marion, Pr. Co. L 2nd
O. V. I.

BUCHTEL.

Wetzel, Louis, Pr. Co. I 10th O. V. I.

BUCYRUS

Bacon, Fred W., Pr. Co. A 8th O.V.I.
Bechman, Harry T., Pr. Co. A 8th O.
V. I.
Beer, Frederick T., Corp. Co. A 8th
O. V. I.
Beer, William C., Pr. Co. A 8th O.V.I.
Belzner, Charles F., Pr. Co. A 8th O.
V. I.
Bittikofer, Charles L., Pr. Co. A 8th
O. V. I.
Bland, Ebbie N., Pr. Co. A 8th O.V.I.
Breymaier, William J., Pr. Co. A 8th
O. V. I.
Brown, John B., Pr. Co. A 8th O.V.I.
Bryant, Charles F., Pr. Co. A 8th O.
V. I.
Burroughs, Edgar A., Artificer Co. A
8th O. V. I.
Burwell, William M., Pr. Co. A 8th
O. V. I.
Christie, Robert L., Pr. Co. A 8th O.
V. I.

Coulter, Edward J., Pr. Co. A 8th O.
V. I.
Cramer, John C., Sergt. Co. A 8th O.
V. I.
Crim, John B., Pr. Co. A 8th O. V. I.
Deardorff, Charles W., Musician Co. A
8th O. V. I.
Dinkel, Christopher, Pr. Co. A 8th O.
V. I.
Ferrell, Charles F., Pr. U. R. 8th O.
V. I.
Fisher, Cyrus, Pr. Co. A 8th O. V. I.
Foreman, Charles W., Pr. Co. A 8th
O. V. I.
Foreman, Homer A., Pr. Co. A 8th
O. V. I.
Fulton, James E., Musician 8th O.
V. I.
Hill, James P., Pr. Co. A ... O. V. I.
Hillis, Emmer G., Pr. Co. A 8th O.V.I.
Hillis, William D., Pr. Co. A 8th O.
V. I.

Holland, Harry H., Pr. Co. A 8th O. V. I.

Hubbell, Walter M., Pr. Co. A 8th O. V. I.

Humiston, Alva S., Sergt. Co. A 8th O. V. I.

Jones, Charles V., Pr. U. R. 8th O.V.I.

Keplinger, Charles C., Pr. Co. A 8th O. V. I.

Kerr, Robert W., Corp. Co. A 8th O. V. I.

Kinninger, George E., Corp. Co. A 8th O. V. I.

Leitz, Harry W., Pr. Co. A 8th O.V.I.

McCracken, Jay C., Pr. Co. A 8th O. V. I.

Minick, Jesse H., Pr. Co. A 8th O.V.I.

Monnette, Ephriam G., Pr. Co. A 8th O. V. I.

Moore, John James, Pr. Co. A 8th O. V. I.

Morrow, Harry W., Pr. Co. A 8th O. V. I.

Nedele, Lewis S., Sergt. Co. A 8th O. V. I.

Nelson, Samuel H., Pr. Co. A 8th O. V. I.

Orr, Benjamin L., Pr. Co. A 8th O.V.I.

Raub, Charles W., Musician Co. A 8th O. V. I.

Raymond, Samuel, Wagoner Co. A 8th O. V. I.

Reber, William F., Corp. Co. A 8th O. V. I.

Reid, Edward G., Sergt. Maj. 8th O. V. I.

Rettig, Edward, Pr. Co. A 8th O. V. I.

Rice, Orlando C., Pr. Co. A 8th O.V.I.

Rodey, Edward, 1st Sergt. Co. A 8th O. V. I.

Shanks, Charley E., Pr. Co. A 8th O. V. I.

Stahl, Frederick, Pr. Co. A 8th O.V.I.

Stailey, Milton W., Sergt. Co. A 8th O. V. I.

Taylor, Roscoe F., Pr. Co. A 8th O. V. I.

Thoman, Charles F., Sergt. Co. A 8th O. V. I.

Volk, Henry E., Corp. Co. A 8th O. V. I.

West, Joseph E., Corp. Co. A 8th O. V. I.

Winner, Harry R., Pr. Co. A 8th O. V. I.

Wise, Edward M., Pr. Co. A 8th O.V.I.

Woolweber, Otto, Prin. Musician 8th O. V. I.

BUDGEVILLE.

Paxton, George S., Pr. Co. L 10th O. V. I.

BULLITT PARK

Sams, David R., Pr. Co. F 4th O. V. I.

BURTON

Randa, Isaac, Pr. Co. M 5th O. V. I.

CABLE

Beck, Marsh, Pr. Co. D 3rd O. V. I.   Jones, Lee R., Pr. Co. D 3rd O. V. I.

CADMUS

Drummond, Charles E., Pr. Co. C 7th O. V. I.

CALDWELL

Wheeler, Clement, Pr. Bat. C 1st O. V. A.

CAMBRIDGE

Scott, Charles W., Pr. Co. K 8th O.V.I   Zimmerman, Frank B., Pr. Co. A 10th O. V. I.

CAMDEN

Ayliffe, Ora C., Pr. Co. I 5th O. V. I.

CAMPBELL P. O.

Stamper, James A., Pr. Co. B 2nd U. S. V. Eng.

CANAL WINCHESTER

Boyd, Eber Lee, Pr. Co. B 4th O. V. I.

Bennett, Charles C., Pr. Co. B 4th O. V. I.

CANTON

Aderholt, Robert K., Pr. Co. I 8th O. V. I.
Anthony, Louis H., Pr. Co. F 8th O. V. I.
Aughinbaugh, William, Pr. Co. L 8th O. V. I.
Bahler, Charles, Sergt. Co. L 8th O.V.I.
Bailey, Rezin M., Q. M. Sergt. 8th O. V. I.
Baird, Henry, Pr. Co. F 8th O. V. I.
Balizet, John E., Pr. Co. L 8th O.V.I.
Berlin, Henry L., Pr. Co. L 8th O.V.I.
Bessi, Joe, Pr. Co. F 8th O. V. I.
Biery, Philip, Corp. Co. F 8th O. V. I.
Black, John P., Pr. Co. L 8th O. V. I.
Blinn, Albert H., Pr. Co. L 8th O.V.I.
Bloomfield, Clement O., 1st Sergt. Co. F 8th O. V. I.
Bock, Charles G., Pr. Co. I 8th O.V.I.
Bolander, Walter, Pr. Co. F 8th O.V.I.
Bowman, Albert T., Pr. Co. I 8th O. V. I.
Bressler, Roscoe L., Pr. Co. L 8th O. V. I.
Broiske, Henry, Pr. Co. F 8th O. V. I.
Browning, John H., Pr. Co. L 8th O. V. I.
Buch, Victor, Sergt. Co. F 8th O. V. I.
Buckwalter, Samuel W., Pr. Co. I 8th O. V. I.
Burwell, James B., Pr. Co. I 8th O.V.I.
Cantleberry, Joseph N., Pr. Co. F 8th O. V. I.
Carr, Don M., Pr. Co. I 8th O. V. I.
Chaddock, Ollie, Pr. Co. F 8th O. V. I.
Cheveraux, Paul S., Musician Co. I 8th O. V. I.
Clay, Uriah E., Pr. Co. L 8th O. V. I.
Clark, William W., Jr., Pr. Co. I 8th O. V. I.
Clewell, Charles Walter, Sergt. Co. F 8th O. V. I.
Coleman, J. W., Pr. Co. F 8th O. V. I.
Conrad, Harry E., Pr. Co. L 8th O.V.I.
Converse, Norris M., Sergt. Co. I 8th O. V. I.
Copthorne, Harold S., Pr. Co. I 8th O. V. I.
Corey, James A., Pr. Co. I 8th O. V. I.
Cowley, George A., Pr. Co. L 8th O.V.I.
Crumm, Thomas M., Wagoner Co. I 8th O. V. I.
Daniels, John Walker, Pr. Co. L 8th O. V. I.
Dannemiller, Augustus F., Pr. Co. I 8th O. V. I.

Danber, John G., Pr. Co. I 8th O. V. I.
Davis, James F., Pr. Co. F 8th O. V. I.
De Muth, Benjamin A., Corp. Co. I 8th O. V. I.
Donze, Albert, Pr. Co. F 8th O. V. I.
Donze, Julius E., Pr. Co. I 8th O. V. I.
Draime, Frank J., Pr. Co. L 8th O.V.I.
Eckstine, Frank, Pr. Co. F 8th O. V. I.
Erdman, Walter L., Pr. Co. I 8th O. V. I.
Eschliman, David, Sergt. Co. F 8th O. V. I.
Essner, Joseph E., Pr. Co. I 8th O.V.I.
Febay, Warren W., Pr. Co. I 8th O.V.I.
Ferguson, Clark, Sergt. Co. F 8th O. V. I.
Filliez, George E., Pr. Co. F 8th O.V.I.
Flanagan, Barney, Pr. Co. F 8th O.V.I.
Flory, Charles W., Pr. Co. L 8th O.V.I.
Freed, Preston C., Pr. Co. I 8th O.V.I.
Freeman, Thomas, Pr. Co. F 8th O.V.I.
Genkes, William D., Pr. Co. L 8th O. V. I.
Gibson, Ralph S., Pr. Co. I 8th O. V. I.
Gloss, William, Pr. Co. F 8th O. V. I.
Goodyear, Ira C., Pr. Co. F 8th O.V.I.
Gotshall, Charles E., 1st Sergt. Co. L 8th O. V. I.
Grable, Albert C., Pr. Co. I 8th O. V. I.
Graham, Charles R., Pr. Co. L 8th O. V. I.
Graham, William B., Sergt. Co. L 8th O. V. I.
Greenwald, Howard M., Corp. Co. L 8th O. V. I.
Grossklaus, William, Pr. Co. F 8th O. V. I.
Gween, Herman H., Pr. Co. F 8th O. V. I.
Hadley, Glen W., Pr. Co. I 8th O.V.I.
Hadley, William L., Pr. Co. I 8th O. V. I.
Hagy, William E., Pr. Co. I 8th O.V.I.
Harbert, Charles, Pr. Co. F 8th O. V. I.
Harding, Charles S., Pr. Co. L 8th O. V. I.
Harding, Elmer F., Pr. Co. I 8th O.V.I.
Harding, Howard A., Pr. Co. I 8th O. V. I.
Harrington, Ralph E., Pr. Co. I 8th O. V. I.
Haus, John R., Sergt. Co. L 8th O.V.I.
Heisler, Jacob W., Pr. Co. I 8th O.V.I.
Herdlicka, Jared, Pr. Co. L 8th O. V. I.
Herdlicka, Joseph, Corp. Co. L 8th O. V. I.

Hill, John M., Pr. Co. F 8th O. V. I.

Holman, John W., Corp. Co. L 8th O. V. I.

Houser, Charles J., Corp. Co. I 8th O. V. I.

Hudson, James Arthur, Sergt. Co. L 8th O. V. I.

Hurford, Perkins, Corp. Co. F 8th O. V. I.

Jahant, George A., Pr. Co. L 8th O.V.I

Jones, Benjamin D., Pr. U. R. 8th O. V. I.

Kaiser, Harmon, Pr. Co. L 8th O. V. I.

Knorzer, Ludwig, Pr. Co. F 8th O.V.I.

Lantz, Charles W., Musician Co. F 8th O. V. I.

Lape, John H., Jr., Pr. Co. L 8th O.V.I.

Lape, Melvin B., Pr. Co. L 8th O. V. I.

Leahy, William P., Corp. Co. F 8th O. V. I.

Leslie, Levi, Pr. Co. L 8th O. V. I.

Linn, Wilson F., Pr. Co. I 8th O. V. I.

Longley, George, Pr. Co. L 8th O.V.I.

Lorimer, Robert A., Pr. Co. I 8th O.V.I.

Lothamer, Philip I., Pr. Co. I 8th O. V. I.

Meister, George, Pr. Co. F 8th O. V. I

Metz, Fred T., Pr. Co. L 8th O. V. I.

Metzger, A. H., Pr. Co. F 8th O. V. I.

Miday, Eugene J., Pr. Co. L 8th O. V. I.

Miller, Harry C., Pr. Co. I 8th O. V. I

Miller, Roscoe C., Pr. Co. L 8th O.V.I.

Miller, William H., Artificer Co. F 8th O. V. I.

Misch, Eugene, Pr. Co. F 8th O. V. I.

Moreland, Harvey C., Corp. Co. L 8th O. V. I.

Mosgrove, Oliver P., Pr. Co. L 8th O. V. I.

Munaw, Welker A., Pr. Co. I 8th O. V. I.

Myers, Walter W., Pr. Co. F 8th O.V.I.

Olinger, Edward, Pr. U. R. 8th O. V. I.

Oppenheimer, Otto J., Hospital Steward 8th O. V. I.

Orth, Otis, Pr. Co. F 8th O. V. I.

Penfield, Earnest, Pr. Co. F 8th O. V. I.

Pennock, Frederick R., Pr. Co. L 8th O. V. I.

Pfirman, Franklin, Pr. U. R. 8th O.V.I.

Piero, Oliver J., Pr. Co. I 8th O. V. I.

Prendeville, James P., Pr. Co. F 8th O. V. I.

Provines, James, Pr. Co. I 8th O. V. I.

Pruden, Charles E., Wagoner Co. L 8th O. V. I.

Pumphrey, Ernest M., Pr. Co. L 8th O. V. I.

Quaill, Theodore L., Pr. Co. I 8th O. V. I.

Raber, Ernst, Corp. Co. F 8th O. V. I.

Ralston, Robert J., Pr. Co. L 8th O.V.I.

Rea, Charles T., Corp. Co. I 8th O. V. I

Rea, George, Sergt. Co. I 8th O. V. I.

Reimensnyder, Charles C., Pr. Co. L 8th O. V. I.

Renner, Edward C., Corp. Co. I 8th O. V. I.

Rich, Elmer, Pr. Co. L 8th O. V. I.

Ringle, Homer G., Corp. Co. I 8th O. V. I.

Robinson, John E., Pr. Co. F 8th O. V. I.

Rohrer, John S., Jr., Pr. Co. K 8th O. V. I.

Rubin, Christian, Pr. Co. F 8th O. V. I.

Russell, Albert M., Musician Co. I 8th O. V. I.

Saeger, Roy S., Corp. Co. I 8th O.V.I.

Schauweker, James T., Pr. Co. I 8th O. V. I

Schicker, Frank, Pr. Co. F 8th O. V. I.

Schroyer, John W., Pr. Co. F 8th O. V. I.

Seeger, Lucius E. D., Pr. Co. I 8th O. V. I.

Seikel, Frank A., Pr. Co. L 8th O. V. I.

Seese, Dorsey, Pr. Co. L 8th O. V. I.

Sheaffer, Robert H., Pr. Co. F 8th O. V. I.

Sheldon, George T., Pr. Co. I 8th O. V. I.

Sherry, Clifford E., Pr. Co. L 8th O.V.I.

Simpson, Charles H., Pr. Co. L 8th O. V. I.

Sliker, Harry W., Pr. Co. I 8th O. V. I.

Smith, John H., Corp. Co. F 8th O.V.I.

Snyder, Joseph C, Pr. Co. L 8th O.V.I.

Spangler, Charles, Pr. Co. I 8th O.V.I.

Spangler, John A., Pr. Co. I 8th O.V.I.

Spotts, Hugh J., Pr. Co. I 8th O. V. I.

Spotts, Ralph L., 1st Sergt. Co. I, O. V. I.

Steadman, Harry K., Musician Co. F 8th O. V. I.

Stokey, Fred E., Pr. Co. K 8th O. V. I.

Streby, Ed., Pr. Co. F 8th O. V. I.

Stump, John A., Sergt. Co. L 8th O.V.I.

Tarner, Charles E., Pr. Co. L 8th O.V.I.

Terrett, Edward P., Sergt. Co. I 8th O. V. I.

Tucker, William D., Pr. Co. F 8th O. V. I.

Uebelhart, William J., Pr. Co. K 8th O. V. I.

Ungashick, Frank A., Pr. Co. I 8th O. V. I.

Vogelgesang, Alfred L., Artificer Co. I 8th O. V. I.

Voglesang, Elmer J., Pr. Co. L 8th O. V. I.

Wagner, Edwin, Pr. Co. F 8th O. V. I.

Wagner, Frank L., Pr. Co. I 8th O.V.I.

Walcutt, Burt, Pr. Co. F 8th O. V. I.

Warner, John H., Corp. Co. L 8th O. V. I.

Weidman, George, Sergt. Co. F 8th O. V. I.

Whipple, John L., Sergt. Co. I 8th O. V. I.

White, Homer, Wagoner Co. F 8th O. V. I.

Wilkinson, Paul, Pr. Co. F 8th O. V. I.
Wingerter, Edward J., Pr. Co. I 8th . O. V. I.
Winters, George E., Pr. Co. L 8th O. V. I.
Wise, Homer A., Sergt. Co. I 8th O. V. I.

Wise, Warren S. C., Musician Co. L 8th O. V. I.
Witter, Charles A., Pr. Co. I 8th O.V.I.
Young, John J., Pr. Co. F 8th O. V. I.
Young, Joseph S., Pr. Co. L 8th O.V.I.

CARLTON

Butericks, Joseph N., Pr. Co. L 7th O. V. I.

Webb, R. L., Pr. Co. L 7th O. V. I.

CARLWICK

Paxton, James B., Pr. Co. L 10th O.V.I.

CARROLL

Wagner, Herman L., Pr. Co. I 1th O. V. I.

CARROLLTON

Handley, Winfield H., Pr. Co. I 5th O. V. I.
Hardesty, Marion, Pr. Co. I 5th O. V. I.

Maple, Charles, Pr. Co. I 5th O. V. I.
Taylor, Robert N., Pr. Co. E 8th O.V.I.

CATAWBA

Laymond, Clinton C., Pr. Co. C 3rd O. V. I.

CATTLETTSBURG, KY.

Prymale, Miles E., Pr. Co. B 2nd U. S. V. E.
Ratcliffe, Guy H., Pr. Co. B 2nd U. S. V. E.

Smith, Frederick J., Pr. Co. B 2nd U. S. V. E.

CECIL

Rudolph, Charles, Pr. Co. M 2nd O.V.I.

White, Fred. A., Pr. Co. M 2nd O. V. I.

CELINA

Carter, Daniel V., Pr. Co. D 2nd O.V.I.

CENTERBURG

Dally, Vincent L., Pr. Co. B 4th O.V.I.

Herrod, Louis M., Musician Co. L 4th O. V. I.

CHAGRIN FALLS

Hulbert, George W., Jr., Pr. Co. A 10th O. V. I.
Judd, Clarence E., Pr. Co. A 10th O. V. I.

Le Roy, Bernard R., Sergt. Co. A 2nd U. S. V. E.
Sheffield, Guy L., Musician Co. L 5th O. V. I.

CHAMBERSBURG

Brown, Herschell V., Pr. Co. L 10th O. V. I.

Chambers, William F., Pr. Co. C 7th O. V. I.

CHANDLERSVILLE

Waxler, Howard E., Pr. Co. L 10th O. V. I.

CHARDON

Johnson, Sherman, Pr. Co. M. 5th O. V. I.

CHARLOE

Martin, Gary W., Pr. Co. M 2nd O.V.I.
Garman, John H., Pr. Co. M 2nd O.V.I.
Shaffer, Ora L., Pr. Co. M 2nd O. V. I.
Young, Clyde, Pr. Co. M 2nd O. V. I.

CHATHAM

McMullen, Calvin C., Pr. Co. G 7th O. V. I.

CHESHIRE

Call, Emory, Pr. Co. C 7th O. V. I.
Plants, Jerome, Pr. Co. C 7th O. V. I.
Reynolds, Pearl, Pr. Co. C 7th O. V. I.
Swisher, Benjamin W., Pr. Co. L 7th O. V. I.

CHICAGO, ILL.

Callahan, Martin, Pr. Co. C 10th O.V.I.

CHILLICOTHE

Alberts, James W., Pr. Co. G 7th O.V.I.
Ankrom, Harry, Pr. Co. H 7th O. V. I.
Barnes, Arthur F., Pr. Co. H 7th O.V.I.
Barrett, Walter S., Pr. Co. F 7th O.V.I.
Bohnen, Gustave S., Pr. Co. H 7th O. V. I.
Briggs, Major Lee, Pr. Co. H 7th O. V. I.
Brown, William E., Sergt. Maj. 7th O. V. I.
Cleveland, Charles P., Pr. Co. H 7th O. V. I.
Cutright, William A., Pr. Co. H 7th O. V. I.
Duncan, Charles H., Pr. Co. G 7th O. V. I.
England, Asa, Pr. Co. H 7th O. V. I.
England, Chas. H., Corp. Co. H 7th O. V. I.
Gettle, Fred W., Pr. Co. K 7th O.V.I.
Gilsdorf, Charles, Pr. Co. K 7th O.V.I.
Gudgen, Harry C., Pr. Co. H 7th O. V. I.
Hall, Frank D., Pr. Co. H 7th O. V. I.
Hall, Robert J., Pr. Co. H 7th O. V. I.
Hammel, Edson B., Pr. Co. L 7th O. V. I.
Hand, Harry E., Corp. Co. H 7th O. V. I.
Harring, Delona, Pr. Co. B 2nd U. S. V. E.
Hayes, Orson J., Pr. Co. G 7th O. V. I.
Houser, Louis S., Pr. Co. K 7th O.V.I.
Hedrick, William E., Q. M. Sergt. Co. H. 7th O. V. I.
Howson, John Harold, Pr. Co. H 7th O. V. I.
Hugill, Homer, Artificer Co. H 7th O. V. I.
Isbani, William L., Pr. Co. A 7th O.V.I.
Jeff, James D., Pr. Co. K 7th O. V. I.
Jones, Charley, Pr. Co. H 7th O. V. I.
Johnson, Jacob, Pr. Co. K 7th O. V. I.
Johnson, John, Pr. Co. H 7th O. V. I.
Kelley, James Wm., Jr., Pr. Co. H 7th O. V. I.

Kelly, Clarence, Pr. Co. H 7th O. V. I.
King, Thomas, Pr. Co. K 7th O. V. I.
Kirsch, Fred, Jr., Pr. Co. H 7th O.V.I.
Korst, Albert, Pr. Co. K 7th O. V. I.
Korst, Louis E., Pr. Co. H 7th O.V.I.
Krick, Frank, Pr. Co. H 7th O. V. I.
Markham, Ernest, Wagoner Co. H 7th O. V. I.
Mason, Geo. E., Pr. Co. H 7th O.V.I.
McCoy, Arthur Lee, 1st Sergt. Co. H 7th O. V. I.
McDonald, Lawrence E., Pr. Co. H 7th O. V. I.
McFarrin, Albert W., Pr. Co. H 7th O. V. I.
Miller, Charles, Pr. Co. H 7th O. V. I.
Miller, George E., Pr. Co. H 7th O. V. I.
Miller, Jacob, Jr., Pr. Co. H 7th O. V. I.
Miller, John F., Pr. Co. H 7th O. V. I.
Minshall, Wm. E., Pr. Co. H 7th O.V.I.
Nation, Carey, Pr. Co. H 7th O. V. I.
Overly, Noah, Pr. Co. K 7th O. V. I.
Pross, Wm. L., Pr. Co. H 7th O. V. I.
Quick, Harvey S., Pr. Co. H 7th O.V.I.
Raper, Ernest W., Pr. Co. H 7th O.V.I.
Reed, Parker C., Pr. Co. H 7th O.V.I.
Reed, William H., Pr. Co. I 7th O.V.I.
Renick, George S., Pr. Co. I 7th O.V.I.
Renick, Joseph D., Pr. Co. H 7th O. V. I.
Rice, Edgar D., Pr. Co. F 7th O. V. I.
Scheer, Edward W., Batt. Sergt. Maj. 7th O. V. I.
Schneff, August, Pr. Co. H 7th O. V. I.
Sears, Walter J., Pr. Co. H 7th O.V.I.
Socin, Frank E., Hospital Steward 7th O. V. I.
Somers, Clark, Sergt. Co. H 7th O.V.I.
Stewart, Thomas C., Pr. Co. F 7th O. V. I.
Stewart, William H., Sergt. Co. H 7th O. V. I.
Stitt, John G., Pr. Co. H 7th O. V. I.
Story, Samuel C., Pr. Co. H 7th O.V.I.

Swatman, Titus A., Pr. Co. H 7th O. V. I.
Taylor, Horace S., Pr. Co. A 7th O.V.I.
Thorne, Jesse, Pr. Co. H 7th O. V. I.
Vance, Walter A., Pr. Co. I 7th O.V.I.
Voorhes, Ralph L., Musician Co. H 7th O. V. I.
Whetstone, William, Pr. Co. H 7th O. V. I.

Wolcott, Wm. A., Sergt. Co. H 7th O. V. I.
Wolfe, Arthur, Pr. Co. F 7th O. V. I.
Wood, Joseph D., Q. M. Sergt. 7th O. V. I.
Woods, Charles H., Pr. Co. I 7th O. V. I.

CHIPPEWA LAKE

Nelson, Henry W., Pr. Co. B 5th O. V. I.

CHRISTIANSBURG

Brelsford, Harley H., Corp. Tr. D 1st O. V. C.

CINCINNATI

Adams, John C., Pr. Co. M 10th O.V.I.
Adamson, Harry, Pr. Co. K 1st O.V.I.
Adkins, Charles O., Pr. Co. K 1st O. V. I.
Aichele, Harry, Sergt. Co. D 1st O.V.I.
Albertz, Joseph F., Pr. Co. A 1st O.V.I.
Albiez, Edward, Pr. Co. C 2nd U. S. V. E.
Albietz, Albert, Pr. Co. M 10tn O. V. I.
Allen, John E., Pr. Co. K 1st O. V. I.
Ames, Frank D., Q. M. Sergt. Co. M 1st O. V. I.
Ammann, Joseph, Musician Co. C 1st O. V. I.
Anderson, Robert C., Jr., Pr. Co. G 1st O. V. I.
Anderson, Thomas D., Sergt. Co. B 2nd U. S. V. E.
Andrews, Edward, Pr. Tr. H 1st O.V.C.
Andrews, Thorton L., Pr. Co. M 1st O. V. I.
Anezanne, Frank, Hospital Steward 1st O. V. I.
Ange, Harry L., Pr. Co. B 1st O. V. I.
Apple, Milton D., Musician Co. B 1st O. V. I.
Arata, Joseph A., Sergt. Co. F 1st O. V. I.
Armstrong, John, Pr. Co. K 1st O.V.I. 1st O. V. I.
Assel, Frederick, Pr. Co. M 10th O.V.I.
Atkins, Albert, Pr. Co. B 1st O. V. I.
Atkins, William D., Pr. Co. F 1st O. V. I.
Bachman, Fred H., Pr. Co. F 1st O. V. I.
Bachtrup, William, Pr. Co. K 1st O. V. I.
Badhorn, Albert, Pr. Co. K 1st O.V.I.
Baker, Frederick B., Pr. Co. M 10th O. V. I.
Baldwin, William E., Pr. Co. M 10th O. V. I.
Ballhaus, Emil, Pr. Co. A 1st O. V. I.
Balzhiser, Maurice J., Pr. Co. B 1st O. V. I.

Barenscheer, Fred W. J., Pr. Co. F 1st O. V. I.
Barnes, George M., Pr. Co. M 10th O. V. I.
Barnett, Michael, Pr. Co. D 1st O.V.I.
Barr, George W., Pr. Co. D 1st O. V. I.
Barrett, Harry S., Pr. Co. M 1st O.V.I.
Barrett, William, Pr. Co. I 1st O. V. I.
Barry, Morris M., Pr. Co. H 1st O.V.I.
Batter, George, Pr. Co. M 1st O. V. I.
Battist, Gustav, Pr. Co. M 10th O.V.I.
Bauersfeld, Edward J., Pr. Co. D 1st O. V. I.
Baumgartner, William J., 11th Corp. Co. M 10th O. V. I.
Bazell, Earl M., Pr. Co. F 1st O. V. I.
Beach, Charles H. C., Pr. Co. F 1st O. V. I.
Beatty, John A., Pr. Co. B 2nd U.S.V.E.
Bebb, William T., Jr., Pr. Co. K 1st O. V. I.
Beck, Joseph E., Pr. Co. B 1st O. V. I.
Beck, Tilden J., Pr. Co. C 1st O. V. I.
Becker, Albert J., Sergt. Co. C 1st O. V. I.
Beckett, William P., Pr. Co, A 1st O. V. I.
Beckman, Harry J., Pr. Co. B 2nd U. S. V. E.
Beebe, Albert, Q. M. Sergt. Co. I 1st O. V. I.
Beel, Joseph, Pr. Co. B 1st O. V. I.
Beil, Charles, Pr. Co. I 1st O. V. I.
Belt, Arthur, Pr. Co. M 1st O. V. I.
Bender, Edward, Pr. Co. G. 1st O.V.I.
Beneker, Fred H., Pr. Tr. G 1st O.V.C.
Bennett, Eugene C., Pr. Co. H 1st O. V. I.
Bercaw, William H., Pr. Co. M 10th O. V. I.
Bergen, Walter H., Musician Co. B 1st O. V. I.
Bergmark, Alf., Pr. Co. B 2nd U. S. V. E.
Bernstein, Hugo, Pr. Co. K 1st O.V.I.

Bertling, Ernst Frederick, Pr. Co. K 1st O. V. 1.

Bethke, Fred, 3rd Corp. Co. A 1st O. V. I.

Bickett, Earl H., Pr. Tr. G 1st O. V. C.

Biersmith, William F., Pr. Co. G 1st O. V. I.

Billhorn, William, Pr. Co. B 1st O.V.I.

Birmingham, Arthur H., 3rd Sergt. Co. M 16th O. V. I.

Birt, William H., Artificer Co. K 1st O. V. I.

Birt, William H., Pr. Co. M 1st O.V.I.

Bishop, Loren, Pr. Co. H 1st O. V. I.

Bisping, Louis H., Pr. Co. D 1st O. V. I.

Black, Charles, Sergt. Co. G 1st O.V.I.

Black, Charles R., 1st Sergt. Co. F 1st Blackman, Max, Corp. Co. K 1st O. V. I.

Bland, James W., Pr. Co. C 2nd U. S. V. E.

Blevin, Alfred, Pr. Co. I 1st O. V. I.

Blumberg, Frank, 1st Corp. Co. A 1st O. V. I.

Boehmer, Harry W, Pr. Co. D 1st O. V. I.

Boellinger, Frank, Pr. Co. H 1st O.V.I.

Bogen, William, Pr. Co. M 10th O.V.I.

Bold, William, Pr. Co. I 1st O. V. I.

Bolton, Robert M., Pr. Co. D 1st O. V. I.

Booth, William A., Pr. Co. C 2nd U. S. V. E.

Bower, Alexander McG., Pr. Co. K 1st O. V. I.

Bowman, Robert Rogers, Sergt. Co. K 1st O. V. I.

Bowman, Theodore, Pr. Co. I 1st O. V. I.

Boyer, Charles K., Pr. Co. H 1st O.V.I.

Brachman, Fred. E., Pr. Tr. H 1st O. V. C.

Brand, Fred W., Pr. Co. I 1st O. V. I.

Brauer, Emil, Pr. Co. C 1st O. V. I.

Braun, Frederick, Pr. Co. M 10th O. V. I.

Breen, John, Pr. Co. A 2nd U.S.V.E. S. V. E.

Breitenbach, John G., Corp. Co. F 1st O. V. I.

Brenner, Philip C., Q. M. Sergt. Co. A 1st O. V. I.

Brestel, Edward J., 4th Sergt. Co. A 1st O. V. I.

Briggs, William H., Pr. Co. C 1st O. V. I.

Brinke, William C. Aufdem, Pr. Co. K 1st O. V. I.

Brockman, William, Pr. Co. B 2nd U. S. V. E.

Broermann, Henry L., Pr. Co. B 2nd U. S. V. E.

Brooker, William, Pr. Co. M 1st O.V.I.

Brooks, Albert, Corp. Tr. H 1st O.V.C.

Brooks, Taylor L., Corp. Co. I 1st O. V. I.

Brucker, Joseph, Pr. Co. C 1st O. V. I.

Brueck, William, Pr. Co. F 1st O. V. I.

Bruening, William, Pr. Co. G 1st O. V. I.

Buckenberger, Louis, Pr. Co. M 1st O. V. I.

Buckley, James J., Pr. Co. C 2nd U. S. V. E.

Buren, Otto, Pr. Co. L 3rd O. V. I.

Burke, Martin T., Pr. Co. H 1st O.V.I.

Bullard, Edward I., Pr. Co. K 1st O. V. I.

Burch, Owen S., Wagoner Co. C 1st O. V. I.

Burnes, William, 1st Sergt. Co. A 1st O. V. I.

Burns, Henry F., Pr. Co. K 1st O.V.I.

Burns, Patrick, Pr. Co. B 2nd U. S. V. E.

Burroughs, Albert, Pr. Co. A 1st O.V.I.

Butler, George W., Pr. Co. G 1st O. V. I.

Buttleworth, Harry L., Pr. Co. D 1st O. V. I.

Byrnes, Stephen, Artificer Co. M 10th O. V. I.

Cadwallader, Warren W., Pr. Co. G 1st O. V. I.

Cagney, James, Pr. Co. 2nd U.S.V.E.

Caine, Albert H., Pr. Co. I 1st O. V. I.

Caldwell, Horace, Pr. Co. M 10th O. V. I.

Carr, Charles P. J. P., Pr. Co. C 1st O. V. I.

Carr, James, Pr. Co. H 1st O. V. I.

Carroll, Edwin J., Musician Co. H 1st O. V. I.

Carroll, John D., Pr. Co. I 1st O. V. I.

Carroll, William B., Pr. Co. M 10th O. V. I.

Carroll, William H., Corp. Co. H 1st O. V. I.

Carson, Harry C., Corp. Co. M 1st O. V. I.

Casazza, Joseph, Pr. Co. F 1st O. V. I.

Casteller, Joseph, Pr. Co. B 2nd U. S. V. E.

Cella, Joseph, Pr. Co. I 1st O. V. I.

Chamberlain, Louis W., Pr. Co. C 1st O. V. I.

Chard, Daniel, Sergt. Tr. H 1st O.V.C.

Chard, Thomas J., Corp. Tr. H 1st O. V. C.

Chatten, Harry B., Pr. Co. B 2nd U. S. V. E.

Cherry, Jesse B., Pr. Co. H 1st O.V.I.

Chisman, Thomas F., Pr. Co. D 1st O. V. I.

Christopher, Leroy, Pr. Co. B 1st O. V. I.

Chumley, Bert, Sergt. Co. H 1st O.V.I.

Clawson, Charles P., Pr. Co. B 1st O. V. I.

Clayton, Charles L., Corp. Tr. H 1st O. V. C.

Clinch, Joseph A., Corp. Co. H 1st O. V. I.
Clift, Ernest S., Pr. Co. M 10th O.V.I.
Clott, Charles G., Pr. Co. M 10th O. V. I.
Clover, Thomas H., Pr. Co. M 1st O. V. I.
Clyde, Charles A., Pr. Co. B 1st O.V.I. V. I.
Coburn, John Fletcher, Pr. Co. B 2nd U. S. V. E.
Cochran, Edward W., Pr. Co. K 1st O. V. I.
Coger, Julius E., Pr. Co. B 1st O. V. I.
Cook, Albert G., Pr. Co. D 1st O. V. I.
Cook, Levi, Sergt. Co. G 1st O. V. I.
Cokell, Richard B., Pr. Co. I 1st O.V.I.
Collins, Edward W., Pr. Co. C 1st O. V. I.
Collins, John L., Hos. Co. H 1st O.V.I.
Colborn, Wade H., Pr. Co. M 1st O. V. I.
Connelly, Harry B., Pr. Tr. H 1st O. V. C.
Connor, George A., Pr. Co. I 1st O. V. I.
Conzett, John J., Hos. Co. H 1st O.V.I.
Cooper, Cassius, Pr. Co. G 1st O. V. I.
Corin, Volney W., Corp. Co. H 1st O. V. I.
Corry, Anthony, Pr. Co. B 2nd U.S.V.E.
Conrady, Fred W., Pr. Co. M 1st O. V. I.
Courson, Samuel, Pr. Co. I 1st O. V. I.
Cowie, Patrick, Pr. Co. M 1st O. V. I.
Craft, Louis T., Pr. Co. C 1st O. V. I.
Crambert, Frank, Pr. Co. M 10th O. V. I.
Crandell, Samuel B., 1st Sergt. Co. I 1st O. V. I.
Craver, Alfred B., Pr. Co. M 1st O.V.I.
Cresap, Albert W., Musician Co. B 2nd U. S. V. E.
Cribbins, John P., Pr. Co. M 10th O. V. I.
Crigler, Wallace P., Pr. Co. G 1st O. V. I.
Crofton, William, Pr. Co. H 1st O.V.I.
Cromwell, Robert, Pr. Co. M 1st O. V. I.
Crynes, Joseph M., Pr. Co. M 10th O. V. I.
Cuban, William, Pr. Co. M 1st O. V. I.
Curnayn, William L., Pr. Co. C 1st O. V. I.
Cunningham, J. H., Pr. Tr. H 1st O. V. C.
Curry, William M., Corp. Tr. H 1st O. V. C.
Curtin, Patrick, Pr. Co. B 2nd U. S. V. E.
Curwood, Edward, Q. M. Sergt. Co. D 1st O. V. I.
Cutter, Alpheus, Jr., Pr. Co. I 1st O. V. I.
Daly, Garrett W., Sergt. Co. H 1st O. V. I.

4—R. O. V.

Dassell, Ed. T., Pr. Co. L 3rd O. V. I.
Davison, Thomas, Pr. Co. F 1st O.V.I.
Day, Edgar J., Pr. Co. K 1st O. V. I.
Decker, Louis, Pr. Co. G 1st O. V. I.
Degnan, Joseph F., Sergt. Co. M 1st O. V. I.
Deitsch, Answell E., 9th Corp. Co. M 10th O. V. I.
Deitz, George W., Pr. Co. A 1st O.V.I.
Deitz, Henry, Pr. Co. A 1st O. V. I.
Delaney, John A., Pr. Co. C 2nd U. S. V. E.
Delaney, William, Pr. Co. K 1st O.V.I.
Delano, Frank W., 7th Corp. Co. M 10th O. V. I.
De Laurier, Benjamin, Pr. Co. M 10th O. V. I.
DeLong, A. Daniel, Sergt. Tr. H 1st O. V. C.
De Lotal, John A., Sergt. Co. G 1st O. V. I.
De Neck, Henri, Pr. Co. G 1st O. V. I.
Denecke, Ferdinand M., Pr. Co. A 1st O. V. I.
Denkamp, William, Pr. Co. M 1st O. V. I.
Dennig, William E., Corp. Co. C 2nd U. S. V. E.
Dennis, Joseph, Musician Co. C 1st O. V. I.
Demmons, George N., Pr. Co. M 1st O. V. I.
Denterlein, George T., Pr. Co. C 1st O. V. I.
Determan, Andrew, Pr. Co. D 1st O. V. I.
Deutschman, John J., Pr. Co. D 1st O. V. I.
Deuterlein, Lawrence, Corp. Co. C 1st O. V. I.
Devlin, John C., Pr. Co. G 1st O. V. I.
Deye, J. John, Pr. Tr. H 1st O. V. C.
Dieckmann, Ernest, Pr. Co. M 1st O.
Dieckmann, Gustav, Pr. Co. F 1st O. V. I.
Dieckman, Louis H., Pr. Co. M 10th O. V. I.
Dieckmann, William, Pr. Co. H 1st O. V. I.
Diegmueller, Charles, Pr. Co. D 1st O. V. I.
Diehl, George J., Pr. Co. D 1st O. V. I.
Diehl, Adolph R., Batt. Sergt. Maj. 1st O. V. I.
Dietrich, Rud. H., Pr. Tr. H 1st O.V.C.
Dietz, John, Pr. Tr. H 1st O. V. C.
Dix, John N., Corp. Tr. H 1st O.V.C.
Doan, Clifford H., Corp. Co. G 1st O. V. I.
Dorhagen, Harry, Pr. Co. C 1st O.V.I.
Donnelly, Joseph M., Pr. Co. I 1st O. V. I.
Donnersberg, Henry A., Pr. Co. I 1st O. V. I.
Dombaugh, Val. E., Hospital Steward 1st O. V. I.
Doran, James, Pr. Co. M 1st O. V. I.

Doughman, Edgar M., Pr. Co. M 10th O. V. I.

Dudley, Edward G., Pr. Co. F 1st O. V. I.

Dunton, Philo Alfred, Pr. Co. K 1st O. V. I.

Drake, Roy N., Farrier Tr. H 1st O. V. C.

Draut, William, Pr. Co. G 1st O. V. I.

Durham, Clyde, Pr. Tr. H 1st O. V. C.

Earl, Colfax E., Pr. Co. I 1st O. V. I.

Ebbrecht, Albert, Pr. Co. D 1st O. V. I.

Eckert, Allen R., Farrier Tr. H 1st O. V. C.

Eckert, Charles A., Corp. Co. I 1st O. V. I.

Eckert, Peter J., Pr. Co. M 1st O. V. I.

Egbers, George, Pr. Co. M 10th O.V.I.

Egleston, Arthur H., Corp. Co. M 1st O. V. I.

Egleston, James A., Pr. Co. M 1st O. V. I.

Ehlers, Willard E., Pr. Co. I 1st O.V.I.

Ellenrieder, Charles, Pr. Co. H 1st O. V. I.

Elliott, Francis A., Pr. Co. B 2nd U. S. V. E.

Elliott, Thomas J., Pr. Co. C 2nd U. S. V. E.

Elwert, William, Pr. Co. M 10th O.V.I.

Elwood, William, Pr. Tr. H 1st O.V.C.

Engle, John A., Pr. Co. M 10th O.V.I.

Ensfelder, George J., Pr. Co. B 2nd U. S. V. E.

Enoch, Harry R., Pr. Co. I 1st O. V. I.

Emerson, Dean, Corp. Co. M 1st O. V. I.

Ernst, John C., Pr. Co. C 2nd U. S. V. E.

Enlass, William B., Pr. Co. A 1st O.V.I.

Evans, Benjamin F., Pr. Co. H 1st O. V. I.

Fagin, Homer A., Pr. Co. M 1st O.V.I.

Falk, Edward W., Pr. Co. F 1st O.V.I.

Fallis, Harry T., Pr. Co. I 1st O. V. I.

Farrell, Thomas P., Pr. Co. M 10th O. V. I.

Faust, Otto, Pr. Co. H 1st O. V. I.

Fay, Ernest S., Pr. Co. K 1st O. V. I.

Fay, James M., Pr. Co. B 1st O. V. I.

Fee, Darlington E., Pr. Co. I 1st O. V. I.

Felbel, Jacob, Pr. Co. M 1st O. V. I.

Feldman, William, Pr. Co. B 2nd U. S. V. E.

Fennessy, David V., Pr. Co. A 1st O.V.I.

Field, Joseph F., Pr. Co. G 1st O. V. I.

Fink, Karl, Pr. Co. M 1st O. V. I.

Fink, William, Pr. Co. M 1st O. V. I.

Finkler, William F., Pr. Co. M 10th O. V. I.

Finn, John J., Pr. Co. F 1st O. V. I.

Fishbach, John, Pr. Co. C 1st O. V. I.

Fisher, Charles, Corp. Co. H 1st O.V.I.

Fisher, Charles T., Pr. Co. A 1st O.V.I.

Fisher, Eben F., Pr. Co. A 1st O. V. I.

Fleisch, Robert, Pr. Co. M 10th O.V.I.

Flinker, Joseph, Pr. Co. B 2nd U. S. V. E.

Floerken, John, Corp. Co. B 1st O.V.I.

Flower, Otto E., Corp. Co. H 1st O. V. I.

Flowers, Christ W. T., Pr. Co. F 1st O. V. I.

Flynn, John P., Pr. Co. H 1st O. V. I.

Foellger, Christian, 4th Corp. Co. A 1st O. V. I.

Fogarty, Thomas F., Pr. Co. D 1st O. V. I.

Folger, William H., Q. M. Sergt. Co. B 1st O. V. I.

Folk, Harry, Pr. Co. M 1st O. V. I.

Foster, William E., Pr. Co. G 1st O. V. I.

Fox, Frank J., Pr. Co. I 1st O. V. I.

Fox, Thomas J., Pr. Co. I 1st O. V. I.

Fraid, Charles, Pr. Co. B 1st O. V. I.

Franman, Walter W., Sergt. Co. C 1st O. V. I.

Frech, Harry, Pr. Co. I 1st O. V. I.

Frech, Henry G., Pr. Co. D 1st O. V. I.

Freyn, William, Pr. Co. G 1st O. V. I.

Frick, Harry R., Pr. Tr. H 1st O. V. C.

Friend, Charles W., Pr. Co. H 1st O. V. I.

Frickhofen, Fred, Corp. Co. B 1st O. V. I.

Friel, Anthony, Pr. Co. M 1st O. V. I.

Frietsch, Sigmund, Jr., Hospital Steward 1st O. V. I.

Frintz, John T., Pr. Co. F 1st O. V. I.

Frohman, George, Pr. Co. D 1st O. V. I.

Frueh, John, Pr. Co. K 1st O. V. I.

Fruehe, George William, Pr. Tr. H 1st O. V. C.

Fiihn, Martin, Pr. Co. B 2nd U.S.V.E.

Fuchs, George P., Pr. Co. M 1st O.V.I.

Fuchs, Louis H., Pr. Co. H 1st O. V. I.

Fulweiler, Robert M., Pr. Co. B 2nd U. S. V. E.

Funk, George B., Sergt. Co. M 1st O. V. I.

Gabriel, Charles E., Pr. Co. M 10th O. V. I.

Galbraith, Leslie P., Pr. Co. K 1st O. V. I.

Gampfer, Chas., Pr. Tr. H 1st O. V. C.

Gampfer, Fernand H., Pr. Co. F 1st O. V. I.

Gampfer, Louis J., 1st Sergt. Tr. H 1st O. V. C.

Garber, William C., Pr. Co. C 1st O. V. I.

Garrison, Wallace Bruce, Pr. Co. G 1st O. V. I.

Gastl, John, Pr. Co. B 2nd U. S. V. E.

Gatch, John H., Pr. Co. C 2nd U. S. V. E.

Gates, Robert Dudley, Q. M. Sergt. Co. K 1st O. V. I.

Gauder, Fredrich, Pr. Co. B 2nd U. S. V. E.

Geiz, Charles C., Pr. Co. G 1st O. V. I.

Geldrick, Albert, Pr. Co. A 1st O. V. I.
Gellenbeck, Fred, Corp. Co. D 1st O.
V. I.
Geng, George, Pr. Co. M 10th O. V. I.
Gerland, George, Pr. Co. I 1st O. V. I.
Geyer, Henry, Pr. Co. B 1st O. V. I.
Gibbins, Thomas, Pr. Co. B 1st O. V. I.
Gibson, William H., Pr. Co. C 2nd
U. S. V. E.
Gilligan, William F., Pr. Co. M 1st O.
V. I.
Gilmore, William, Sergt. Co. H 1st O.
V. I.
Glascock, Reginald P., Pr. Co. F 1st
O. V. I.
Gleason, Thomas, Pr. Co. D 1st O.V.I.
Goeller, Peter, Pr. Co. C 2nd U.S.V.E.
Gollenstin, John, Pr. Co. H 1st O. V. I.
Gordon, Bertram, Pr. Co. H 1st O.V.I.
Gormley, Thomas P., Pr. Co. M 10th
O. V. I.
Gosling, Jerome C., Pr. Tr. H 1st O.
V. C.
Gourjon, John E., 1st Sergt. Co. B 1st
O. V. I.
Gove, Herbert, Pr. Co. B 1st O. V. I.
Graf, Andrew, Pr. Tr. H 1st O. V. C.
Grafious, Walter J., Pr. Co. A 1st O.V.I.
Graham, Ernest A., Corp. Co. G 1st
O. V. I.
Granger, George R., Pr. Tr. H 1st O.
V. C.
Gregory, David E., Pr. Co. F 1st O.
V. I.
Grell, Joseph, Wagoner Co. A 1st O.V.I.
Green, Ben, Pr. Co. K 1st O. V. I.
Green, George G., Pr. Co. I 1st O.V.I.
Gribbelle, Harry, Corp. Co. B 1st O.
V. I.
Griesser, William J., Pr. Tr. B 1st O.
V. C.
Grimsley, William, Pr. Co. B 1st O.V.I.
Grennan, Lawrence E., Jr., Pr. Co. K
1st O. V. I.
Greuber, Grant, Pr. Co. F 1st O. V. I.
Guertler, George, Pr. Co. D 1st O. V. I.
Gulick, Robert H., Corp. Co. B 1st O.
V. I.
Gullerman, Peter, Pr. Co. G 1st O.V.I.
Gustetter, Alfred L., Pr. Co. I 1st O.
V. I.
Gutman, Chas. W., Pr. Tr. H 1st O.
V. C.
Haake, Gustav F., Pr. Co. M 10th O.
V. I.
Haigh, Sim C., Pr. Co. D 1st O. V. I.
Hake, Harry H., Pr. Co. C 1st O. V. I.
Haley, Charles A., Pr. Co. H 1st O.V.I.
Hall, Benjamin F., Pr. Co. A 1st O.V.I.
Halpin, William, Jr., Pr. Co. C 1st O.
V. I.
Haney, Edgar E., Pr. Co. M 1st O.V.I.
Haney, William E., Pr. Co. F 1st O.
V. I.
Hamilton, Albert A., Pr. Co. I 1st O.
V. I.

Hamilton, John A., Pr. Co. M 1st O.
V. I.
Hamilton, James C., Artificer Co. D
1st O. V. I.
Hamel, Harry, Pr. Tr. H 1st O. V. C.
Hammel, Osmar F., Pr. Co. M 10th
O. V. I.
Hannaford, Paul H., Pr. Co. C 1st O.
V. I.
Hanning, John Harmon, Corp. Co. B
2nd U. S. V. E.
Hansfeld, Benzara, Pr. Co. M 10th O.
V. I.
Harden, Alva J., Corp. Tr. H 1st O.V.C.
Hardy, John D., Pr. Co. H 1st O.V.I.
Harris, James, Pr. Co. B 1st O. V. I.
Hartford, Frank, Pr. Co. D 1st O. V. I.
Hartlieb, Louis, Pr. Co. A 1st O. V. I.
Hartman, Edward A., Pr. Co. C 1st O.
V. I
Haungs, Dennis B., Pr. Co. I 1st O.
V. I.
Hatt, William, Pr. Co. K 1st O. V. I.
Havlin, Joseph, Pr. Co. H 1st O. V. I.
Hayner, Fred C., Pr. Co. A 1st O. V. I.
Hayward, Philip, Pr. Co. B 1st O. V. I.
Healey, Francis R., Pr. Co. K 1st O.
V. I.
Heatley, William C., Pr. Co. A 1st O.
V. I.
Heaton, Daniel, 2nd Sergt. Co. M 10th
O. V. I.
Heger, Charles, Pr. Co. M 10th O.V.I.
Heidebrink, George H., Pr. Co. D 1st
O. V. I.
Heinz, Charles J., Pr. Co. B 1st O. V. I.
Hehemann, Anthony, Pr. Co. B 1st O.
Helfenrider, Emil, Pr. Co. C 2nd U.
S. V. E.
Helman, Clifford A., Sergt. Tr. H 1st
O. V. C.
Helmholz, Henry W., Pr. Co. B 2nd
U. S. V. E.
Hemmer, Bernard A., Pr. Co. G 1st
O. V. I.
Henn, Charles, Pr. Co. M 1st O. V. I.
Hennessy, Edward A., Pr. Co. C 1st
O. V. I.
Hennessy, Edward J., Pr. Co. C 2nd
U. S. V. E.
Henling, Joseph J., Wagoner Co. G 1st
O. V. I.
Henslee, Charles C., Pr. Co. B 1st O.
V. I.
Herbert, Henry E., Sergt. Co. K 1st
O. V. I.
Herbrich, Emil, Pr. Co. C 1st O. V. I.
Herrier, John, Pr. Co. G 1st O. V. I.
Herron, Howard J., Pr. Co. L 3rd O.
V. I.
Hertenstein, William J., Musician Co.
M 10th O. V. I.
Hertzberger, John, Pr. Co. D 1st O.V.I.
Hertzler, Ira A., Pr. Co. H 1st O. V. I.
Hessling, John, Pr. Co. D 1st O. V. I.
Hewitt, William C., Jr., Pr. Co. B 2nd
U. S. V. E.

Hicks, Robert A., Pr. Co. H 1st O.V.I.
Higdon, Albert, Pr. Co. M 10th O.V.I.
Higgins, Thomas R., Wagoner Co. M 10th O. V. I.
Hilgeman, Joseph G., Pr. Co. B 2nd U. S. V. E.
Hillengass, Fred, Pr. Co. M 3rd O.V.I.
Hines, Thomas J., Pr. Co. G 1st O.V.I.
Hinman, William A., Pr. Co. A 1st O. V. I.
Hirnikel, George, Pr. Co. A 1st O.V.I.
Hirsch, Bertram F., Pr. Co. I 1st O. V. I.
Hoard, James, Pr. Co. C 2nd U.S.V.E.
Hoare, Harry M., Pr. Co. C 1st O. V. I.
Hoer, Harry, Pr. Co. M 1st O. V. I.
Hoff, John A., Pr. Co. C 1st O. V. I.
Hoffert, Frederick, Pr. Co. B 2nd U. S. V. E.
Holderer, Charles, Pr. Co. B 1st O.V.I.
Holmes, James Edward, Pr. Co. B 2nd U. S. V. E.
Holtmeier, Joseph, Pr. Co. D 1st O.V.I.
Holtz, Louis J., Pr. Co. H 1st O. V. I.
Hommedien, Herbert S. S., Corp. Co. M 1st O. V. I.
Hoorman, Charles F., Corp. Co. K 1st O. V. I.
Hopkins, James M., Pr. Co. F 1st O. V. I.
Hornbrook, Ike E., Pr. Co. B 2nd U. S. V. E.
Horstman, William, Pr. Co. G 1st O. V. I.
Howe, Benjamin F., Pr. Co. B 2nd U. S. V. E.
Hubbarth, Frank, Pr. Co. K 1st O.V.I.
Huber, George, Jr., Pr. Co. M 1st O. V. I.
Huber, George M., 12th Corp. Co. M 10th O. V. I.
Huber, John L., Pr. Co. M 1st O. V. I.
Hull, Alfred B., Sergt. Co. F 1stO.V.I.
Humphreys, Thomas A., Pr. Co. M 10th O. V. I.
Hypp, Albert G., Sergt. Co. B 2nd U. S. V. E.
Husted, Vernon C., Pr. Co. F 1st O. V. I.
Huston, Frederick L., Pr. Co. C 2nd U. S. V. E.
Hyland, George W., Pr. Co. I 1st O. V. I.
Hyman, Aaron, Corp. Co. D 1st O.V.I.
Irvine, Robert W., Pr. Tr. H 1st O.V.C.
Isham, Frank S., Pr. Co. G 1st O.V.I.
Ives, Bernard F., Pr. Co. B 1st O. V. T.
Jackson, Robert D., Pr. Co. D 1st O. V. I.
Jaeger, John, Pr. Co. M 10th O. V. I.
Jaegle, Henry A., Pr. Co. M 10th O. V. I.
James, Frank, Pr. Co. A 1st O. V. I.
Janson, Joseph A., Pr. Co. M 10th O. V. I.
Jauch, Jacob, Pr. Co. K 1st O. V. I.
Jeffries, Edward, Pr. Co. A 1st O. V. I.

Jenny, Walter F., Pr. Co. C 1st O.V.I.
Jenny, William L., Sergt. Co. C 1st O. V. I.
Jergens, Charles, Wagoner Co. M 1st O. V. I.
Jester, Eugene E., Pr. Co. G 1st O.V.I.
Jochem, Matheas, Pr. Co. H 1st O.V.I.
Johns, Charles R., Sergt. Co. B 1st O. V. I.
Johnson, Don L., Pr. Co. F 1st O.V.I.
Johnson, Charles E., Pr. Co. K 1st O. V. I.
Johnson, James J., Sergt. Co. G 1st O. V. I.
Jones, William, Pr. Co. M 10th O.V.I.
Jordan, Charles, Pr. Co. H 3rd O.V.I.
Jordan, Charles R., Pr. Co. C 2nd U. S. V. E.
Joslyn, Albert R., Artificer Co. C 1st O. V. I.
Kadow, William H., 2nd Sergt. Co. A 1st O. V. I.
Kaplan, Frank H., Pr. Co. K 1st O. V. I.
Kappauf, Charles H., Jr., 8th Corp. Co. M 10th O. V. I.
Karl, Charley H., Pr. Co. F 1st O.V.I.
Kaufman, Christian, Pr. Co. B 1st O. V. I.
Kaulfersch, William C., Pr. Tr. H 1st O. V. C.
Keller, Jacob W., Pr. Co. H 1st O.V.I.
Keller, Turner A., Pr. Co. H 1st O.V.I.
Kelly, Charles A., Pr. Co. H 1st O.V.I.
Kemp, Walter S., Pr. Co. G 1st O.V.I.
Kennedy, William W., Pr. Co. C 2nd U. S. V. E.
Kempf, Dominick, Corp. Co. M 1st O. V. I.
Kempster, James W. H., Pr. Tr. H 1st O. V. C.
Kestner, John P., Pr. Tr. H 1st O.V.C.
Keyes, Herman M., Pr. Co. M 1st O. V. I.
Kiechler, Charles, Pr. Co. B 1st O.V.I.
Kiehl, Alexander, Pr. Co. G 1st O.V.I.
Kiessling, William, Pr. Co. C 1st O.V.I.
Kilb, Louis H., Pr. Co. D 1st O. V. I.
Kildow, Josiah, Pr. Co. M 1st O. V. I.
Kilgour, Henry C., Pr. Co. K 1st O. V. I.
King, John W., Musician Tr. H 1st O. V. C.
Kirkpatrick, William D., Pr. Co. C 2nd U. S. V. E.
Kissane, Thomas, Pr. Co. C 1st O. V. I.
Klineman, Charles H., Corp. Co. C 1st O. V. I.
Klipfel, Alois, Pr. Co. G 1st O. V. I.
Knabe, Harvey, Pr. Co. C 2nd U. S. V. E.
Knapp, Joseph J., Pr. Co. M 1st O.V.I.
Koehler, William, Pr. Co. F 1st O.V.I.
Koenig, August, Pr. Co. F 1st O. V. I.
Korbett, George, Pr. Co. F 10th O.V.I.
Kountz, Theodore J., Pr. Co. G 1st O. V. I.

Kramer, Charles, Pr. Co. C 2nd U. S. V. E.
Kramer, Frank A., Corp. Co. F 1st O. V. I.
Kramer, William C., Pr. Co. A 1st O. V. I.
Kramig, Fred, Pr. Co. M 10th O. V. I.
Krause, Julius A., Pr. Co. G 1st O.V.I.
Kreiger, Benj. H., Pr. Tr. H 1st O.V.C.
Kresling, Albert H., Pr. Co. K 1st O. V. I.
Krohne, William L., Pr. Co. D 1st O. V. I.
Krueger, William F., Musician Co. K 1st O. V. I.
Krug, Henry J., Pr. Co. M 10th O.V.I.
Krumm, George, Pr. Co. I 1st O. V. I.
Krumpelbeck, Jerome, 6th Corp. Co. A 1st O. V. I.
Kuehling, Theodore J., Pr. Co. D 1st O. V. I.
Kuhn, Phillip, Pr. Co. C 2nd U.S.V.E.
Kumpf, Edward, Corp. Co. B 1st O.V.I.
Kunzler, John O., Pr. Co. F 1st O.V.I.
Lammers, Albert, Pr. Co. M 10th O.
Lamy, Charles, Pr. Co. M 1st O. V. I.
Landers, James, Pr. Co. D 1st O. V. I.
Landherr, Edward G., Pr. Co. B 2nd U. S. V. E.
Lanksweirt, Oscar J., Pr. Co. A 1st O. V. I.
Larkin, Thomas, Pr. Co. M 10th O.V.I.
Larrus, Frank, Pr. Co. M 1st O. V. I.
Laudenbach, Frank, Pr. Co. D 1st O. V. I.
Laurie, Archibald, Jr., Sergt. Co. B 1st O. V. I.
Laurie, John A., Corp. Co. B 1st O.V.I.
Lavin, Edward P., Pr. Co. M 10th O. V. I.
Lawrence, George W., Wagoner Co. I 1st O. V. I.
Learned, Harry M., Pr. Co. M 1st O. V. I.
Leighner, Albert, 1st Corp. Co. M 10th O. V. I.
Lennon, William H., Pr. Co. H 1st O. V. I.
Less, Joseph, Pr. Co. C 1st O. V. I.
Lewis, William E., Pr. Co. F 1st O.V.I.
L'Hommedieu, Richard, Pr. Co. M 1st O. V. I.
Lichtenfeld, James E., Pr. Co. H 1st O. V. I.
Lieberwood, William P., Pr. Co. I 1st O. V. I.
Liermann, Frederick A., Pr. Co. C 1st O. V. I.
Light, Alvin L., Pr. Co. F 1st O. V. I.
Lingenfelter, James, Pr. Co. D 1st O. V. I.
Linger, Louis C., Pr. Co. M 1st O.V.I.
Lipps, Nickolas, Pr. Tr. H 1st O. V. C.
Lipps, Frederick, Pr. Co. B 2nd U. S. V. E.
Locke, Edward, Pr. Co. C 1st O. V. I.

Loewenstine, Jacob H., Pr. Co. K 1st O. V. I.
Loftus, John L., Pr. Co. M 10th O.V.I.
Logue, John, Pr. Co. M 10th O. V. I.
Long, John T., Pr. Co. M 1st O. V. I.
Long, Robert L., Pr. Co. M 1st O.V.I.
Lohmyer, Meinolf, Corp. Co. K 1st O. V. I.
Lorenz, William H., Pr. Co. C 1st O. V. I.
Lotz, Alvin J. E., Pr. Co. B 1st O. V. I.
Luckey, Louis L., Pr. Co. H 1st O.V.I.
Lukens, Benjamin P., Pr. Co. A 1st O. V. I.
Lutz, Joseph, Pr. Co. H 1st O. V. I.
Lutz, William J., Pr. Co. M 1st O. V. I.
Lynch, John, Pr. Co. C 1st O. V. I.
Lyon, David, Pr. Co. B 5th O. V. I.
Mackey, Joseph V., Pr. Co. B 1st O. V. I.
Mackey, Thomas, Pr. Co. B 1st O.V.I.
Macready, John H., Pr. Co. B 1st O. V. I.
Maddox, Clifton, Pr. Co. I 1st O. V. I.
Madigan, John, Pr. Co. C 2nd U. S. V. E.
Magill, Wesley W., Pr. Co. K 1st O. V. I.
Maithrie, Emil, Pr. Co. D 1st O. V. I.
Malloy, John J., Pr. Co. M 1st O. V. I.
Malone, Bartly, Pr. Co. C 2nd U. S. V. E.
Maltby, John, Pr. Co. G 1st O. V. I.
Manning, John A., Pr. Co. M 10th O. V. I.
Manning, William J., Pr. Co. B 2nd U. S. V. E.
March, Wesley S., Sergt. Co. M 1st O. V. I.
Marsh, Charles H., 3rd Sergt. Co. A 1st O. V. I.
Martin, Charles P., Pr. Co. A 1st O.V.I.
Martin, Harry, Pr. Co. G 1st O. V. I.
Martin, Harry C., Jr., Pr. Co. K 1st O. V. I.
Martin, John D., Pr. Co. K 1st O.V.I.
Marzinzeck, Charles B., Pr. Co. G 1st O. V. I.
Maschnot, Adam J., Pr. Co. C 1st O. V. I.
Mason, James, Sergt. Co. D 1st O.V.I.
Masteo, John G., Pr. Co. I 1st O. V. I.
Mathes, Charles, Pr. Co. D 1st O. V. I.
Mathie, Robert A., Pr. Co. K 1st O. V. I.
May, John, Pr. Co. A 1st O. V. I.
McCabe, Joseph, Sergt. Co. D 1st O. V. I.
McCabe, Victor, 1st Sergt. Co. D 1st O. V. I.
McCarthy, John, Pr. Co. M 1st O.V.I.
McCarthy, Peter F., Pr. Co. G 1st O. V. I.
McCormack, William, Pr. Co. F 1st O. V. I.
McCrosky, Fred. B., Sergt. Co. C 2nd U. S. V. E.

McDermott, Thomas F., Pr. Co. I 1st O. V. I.
McDonald, James, Pr. Co. K 1st O.V.I.
McFadden, Charley J., Pr. Co. M 10th O. V. I.
McGechin, Milton R., 4th Corp. Co. M 10th O. V. I.
McGee, Ray, Pr. Co. M 10th O. V. I.
McGrann, James J., Pr. Co. F 1st O. V. I.
McGrann, John J., Pr. Co. I 1st O.V.I.
McKinney, Daniel L., Pr. Co. G 1st O. V. I.
McKnight, Louis C., Pr. Co. I 1st O. V. I.
McLeisch, Charles, Pr. Tr. H 1st O. V. C.
Medecke, John E., Pr. Co. F 1st O.V.I.
Meehan, William F., Corp. Co. C 2nd U. S. V. E.
Meinhardt, Frank, Pr. Co. B 2nd U. S. V. E.
Meinze, Frederick, Pr. Co. B 1st O.V.I.
Meissner, George, Musician Co. H 1st O. V. I.
Meyer, Frank J., Pr. Co. D 1st O. V. I.
Meyer, Frederick, Pr. Co. B 2nd U. S. V. E.
Meyer, George, Pr. Tr. H 1st O. V. C.
Meyer, Henry, Pr. Co. B 2nd U.S.V.E.
Meyer, Philip, Jr., 5th Corp. Co. M 10th O. V. I.
Meyers, Edward F., Pr. Co. H 1st O. V. I.
Meyers, Henry F., Pr. Co. F 1st O.V.I.
Meyers, Mitchell P., Pr. Co. B 2nd U. S. V. E.
Middendorf, George H., Q. M. Sergt. Co. M 10th O. V. I.
Miller, Charles E., Sergt. Co. C 2nd U. S. V. E.
Miller, Frederick W., Corp. Co. G 1st O. V. I.
Miller, Jacob, Pr. Co. M 1st O. V. I.
Miller, William E., Pr. Co. A 1st O.V.I.
Milligan, Alfred W., Pr. Tr. H 1st O. V. C.
Millward, Charles, Pr. Co. A 1st O.V.I.
Millward, Henry H., Pr. Co. F 1st O. V. I.
Minning, William, Pr. Co. D 1st O.V.I.
Mitchell, Gregor, Q. M. Sergt. Co. F 1st O. V. I.
Mitchell, James, Sergt. Co. C 2nd U. S. V. E.
Mitchell, John, Pr. Co. M 1st O. V. I.
Mitchell, William, Artificer Co. H 1st O. V. I.
Moeller, Clifford, Pr. Co. A 1st O.V.I.
Moeller, Clemens, Pr. Co. D 1st O. V. I.
Moeller, Edward H., Sergt. Tr. H 1st O. V. C.
Moeller, George A., Pr. Co. C 1st O. V. I.
Moeser, Hermann F. H., Pr. Co. C 1st O. V. I.

Mohrmann, William, Pr. Co. C 2nd U. S. V. E.
Molony, Isaac W., Pr. Tr. H 1st O.V.C.
Molson, Thomas, Pr. Co. I 1st O. V. I.
Monahan, William F., Pr. Co. B 2nd U. S. V. E.
Moore, Thomas H., Pr. Co. B 2nd U. S. V. E.
Moore, William J., Pr. Co. I 1st O.V.I.
Morel, Henry, Pr. Co. D 1st O. V. I.
Morris, Frank D., Pr. Co. A 1st O.V.I.
Moser, Louis L., Pr. Co. I 1st O. V. I.
Moylan, Maurice, Pr. Co. I 1st O. V. I.
Mueller, William E., Q. M. Sergt. Co. C 1st O. V. I.
Muench, Charles F., Pr. Co. A 1st O. V. I.
Mulaney, Mathew J., Pr. Co. M 10th O. V. I.
Mulcahy, John, Pr. Co. B 1st O. V. I.
Muller, George, Pr. Co. M 10th O.V.I.
Muller, William C., Pr. Co. C 1st O. V. I.
Munk, Sigmund, Pr. Tr. G 1st O.V.C.
Murnahan, Edward J., Wagoner Co. D 1st O. V. I.
Murphy, Andrew J., 5th Sergt. Co. A 1st O. V. I.
Murphy, Jerome, Pr. Co. H 1st O.V.I.
Murphy, Luke, Pr. Co. C 2nd U. S. V. E.
Murphy, Michael, Pr. Co. M 10th O. V. I.
Murphy, Richard, Corp. Co. D 1st O. V. I.
Murray, George, Pr. Co. A 1st O. V. I.
Murray, James Edward, Pr. Co. B 2nd U. S. V. E.
Murray, Walter T., Pr. Co. B 1st O.V.I.
Nacher, Otto, Pr. Co. B 1st O. V. I.
Nagel, Charles A., Pr. Co. F 1st O.V.I.
Neff, Victor F., Pr. Co. F 1st O. V. I.
Neil, Oscar C., Sergt. Tr. H 1st O.V.C.
Neuhaus, Charles J., Pr. Co. K 1st O. V. I.
Nevin, Thomas A., Pr. Co. B 2nd U. S. V. E.
Newell, John P., Pr. Co. H 1st O.V.I.
Nichols, Alfred, Sergt. Co. I 1st O.V.I.
Nickols, Andrew J., Pr. Co. B 2nd U. S. V. E.
Noll, Fred., Q. M. Sergt. Tr. H 1st O. V. C.
Noll, Henry, Pr. Co. D 1st O. V. I.
Nolan, Dennis J., Pr. Co. D 1st O. V. I.
Nolte, John F., Wagoner Co. H 1st O. V. I.
Nortman, Joseph, Pr. Co. C 2nd U. S. V. E.
Oberhelman, Henry E., Pr. Co. A 1st O. V. I.
O'Day, John E., Pr. Co. F 1st O. V. I.
Oettinger, Walter, Pr. Co. M 10th O. V. I.
O'Keefe, Edward J., Wagoner Co. K 1st O. V. I.

O'Keefe, Thomas A., Pr. Co. M 10th O. V. I.
Olhaber, William M., Regt. Sergt. Maj. 1st O. V. I.
Oligee, Richard, Pr. Co. F 1st O. V. I.
Oliver, Frank J., Pr. Co. H 1st O.V.I.
O'Neal, Michael, Pr. Co. D 1st O. V. I.
Orr, Benton, Pr. Co. G 1st O. V. I.
Ortman, Charles, Corp. Co. D 1st O. V. I.
Oyler, Isaac A., Pr. Co. F 1st. O. V. I.
Owen, Charles J., Corp. Co. G 1st O. V. I.
Padgett, John E., Pr. Co. F 1st O.V.I.
Paine, Wilmot K., Corp. Tr. H 1st O. V. C.
Parker, James, Pr. Co. G 1st O. V. I.
Parkison, William H., Corp. Co. C 2nd U. S. V. E.
Parry, Richard W., Sergt. Co. C 1st O. V. I.
Paschen, Frank, Corp. Co. D 1st O.V.I.
Patton, Richard, Pr. Co. K 1st O.V.I.
Payne, Frank A., Musician Co. I 1st O. V. I.
Pence, William L., Pr. Co. K 1st O.V.I.
Penn, Harry, Pr. Co. M 10th O. V. I.
Perchment, John W., Pr. Co. C 2nd U. S. V. E.
Perk, Harry J., Sergt. Co. F 1st O.V.I.
Perrotss, Raphael, Pr. Co. C 2nd U. S. V. E.
Peterson, Louis E., 1st Sergt. Co. H 1st O. V. I.
Pfeffer, Charles S., Pr. Co. C 2nd U. S. V. E.
Pfeiffer, Joseph, Pr. Co. C 1st O. V. I.
Pfetzing, John A., Corp. Co. C 1st O. V. I.
Phares, George C., Signal Co. H 1st O. V. I.
Phares, Walter L., Pr. Co. G 1st O.V.I.
Phelan, Peter H., Jr., Pr. Tr. H 1st O. V. C.
Pieper, Joe H., Pr. Co. H 1st O. V. I.
Pinkerton, Eugene, Pr. Co. H 1st O. V. I.
Pinkerton, William D., Pr. Co. H 1st O. V. I.
Pinney, Martin J., 4th Sergt. Co. M 10th O. V. I.
Pipes, Armour Scott, Pr. Co. B 2nd U. S. V. E.
Pirman, William H., Pr. Tr. H 1st O. V. C.
Platt, James, Corp. Co. I 1st O. V. I.
Platts, George E., Pr. Co. G 1st O.V.I.
Poast, Peter P., Jr., Pr. Co. F. 1st O. V. I.
Polen, Washington D., Pr. Co. H 1st O. V. I.
Preis, John, Pr. Co. C 2nd U. S. V. E.
Price, James, Pr. Co. M 10th O. V. I.
Prindsack, Joseph B., Pr. Co. B 2nd U. S. V. E.
Proctor, Thomas A., Pr. Co. M 10th O. V. I.

Quirk, Patrick J., Pr. Co. H 1st O.V.I.
Radcliffe, Harry B., Pr. Co. H 1st O. V. I.
Radford, George E., Pr. Co. C 2nd U. S. V. E.
Rahm, August G., Sergt. Co. B 1st O. V. I.
Raine, Fred, Jr., Batt. Sergt. Maj. 1st O. V. I.
Ranes, Frank L., Artificer Co. I 1st O. V. I.
Ramsdell, Risher W., Musician Co. M 1st O. V. I.
Ramsey, Stanley M., Pr. Tr. H 1st O. V. C.
Rappold, Louis, Pr. Tr. H 1st O. V. C.
Rathbone, St. George I., Pr. Co. C 2nd S. V. E.
Reas, John F., Pr. Co. F 1st O. V. I.
Rectanus, Louis R., Pr. Co. H 1st O. V. I.
Redfield, Charles J., Batt. Sergt. Maj. 1st O. V. I.
Reed, George A. S., Pr. Co. I 1st O. V. I.
Reese, Charles, Pr. Co. G 1st O. V. I.
Regan, Charles, Pr. Co. C 2nd U. S. V. E.
Rehner, Charles, Artificer Co. M 1st O. V. I.
Reinhardt, Charles, Pr. Co. A 1st O.V.I.
Reinhold, Louis G., Pr. Co. B 2nd U. S. V. E.
Reinken, Henry C., Jr., Pr. Co. D 1st O. V. I.
Reinstadtler, Harry W., Pr. Co. B 2nd U. S. V. E.
Reisser, John, Pr. Co. M 1st O. V. I.
Renneberg, Reinhart G., Corp. Co. K 1st O. V. I.
Reynolds, Arthur R., Pr. Co. I 1st O. V. I.
Reynolds, William L., Pr. Co. F 1st O. V. I.
Rexford, Clarence E., Pr. Co. B 1st O. V. I.
Rhodes, Albert, Pr. Co. G 1st O. V. I.
Rhodes, Robert, Pr. Co. C 2nd U. S. V. E.
Rice, Charles, Pr. Co. C 1st O. V. I.
Rice, Charles, Jr., Pr. Co. D 1st O. V. I.
Rice, William, Pr. Co. G 1st O. V. I.
Richardson, Herman E., Pr. Co. C 2nd U. S. V. E.
Ricke, Henry B., Pr. Co. M 10th O.V.I.
Riedemann, Henry L., Pr. Co. B 1st O. V. I.
Riggs, Edward N., Pr. Co. M 10th O. V. I.
Ringel, Conrad, Pr. Tr. H 1st O. V. C.
Ringel, George L., Pr. Tr. H 1st O. V. C.
Roberts, Gerald, Pr. Tr. H 1st O.V.C.
Robinson, David W., Pr. Co. M 1st O. V. I.

Robinson. John W., Pr. Co. C 1st O. V. I.
Rodecker, George W., Pr. Co. M 10th O. V. I.
Roegge. Harry, Corp. Co. F 1st O.V.I.
Roemmich, Frederick, Pr. Co. B 1st O. V. I.
Rooney. John J., Pr. Co. A 1st O. V. I.
Ropp, John, Sergt. Co. M 1st O. V. I.
Roseboom, Jesse G., Pr. Co. C 2nd U. S. V. E.
Ross, Harry H., Pr. Co. A 1st O. V. I.
Rost, George H., Pr. Co. M 1st O.V.I.
Rousch, Thomas, Pr. Co. B 1st O.V.I.
Roy, William P., 6th Corp. Co. M 10th O. V. I.
Rudd, William L., Musician Co. F 1st O. V. I.
Rump, Clemens G., Pr. Co. A. 1st O. V. I.
Runte. John S., Pr. Co. I 1st O. V. I.
Ruppert, Anthony, Pr. Co. M 10th O. V. I.
Rusk, Clifford E., Corp. Tr. H 1st O V. C.
Russell, William J., Jr., Pr. Tr. H 1st O. V. C.
Ryan, John J., Pr. Co. F 1st O. V. I.
Ryan, Robert J., Pr. Co. C 1st O. V. I.
Sachs, William A., Artificer Co. A 1st O. V. I.
Sagars, George W., Pr. Co. K 1st O. V. I.
Sanders, Francis W., Pr. Co. B 1st O. V. I.
Sauer, John, Pr. Co. D 1st O. V. I.
Saunders, William, Pr. Co. M 1st O. V. I.
Scanlan, James J., Pr. Co. B 2nd U. S. V. E.
Schachleiter, Harry, Pr. Co. C 1st O. V. I.
Schaefer, Charles B., Pr. Co. B 2nd U. S. V. E.
Schafer, Henry, Pr. Co. M 1st O. V. I.
Schaller, Louis, Pr. Co. M 1st O. V. I.
Schanenberg, Henry A., Pr. Co. F 1st O. V. I.
Scharf, John, Pr. Co. D 1st O. V. I.
Schath, Edwin, Pr. Co. I 1st. O. V. I.
Schatzman, Edward, Pr. Co. D 1st O. V. I.
Schayer, Isadore, Pr. Co. B 1st O. V. I.
Scheidt, Anthony, Corp. Co. F 1st O. V. I.
Scheidt, Jacob, Pr. Co. M 1st O. V. I.
Schindler, Charles O., Pr. Co. G 1st O. V. I.
Schimmel, John, Pr. Co. M 10th O.V.I.
Schlenck, Robert, Pr. Co. K 1st O.V.I.
Schmidt, George, 5th Sergt. Co. M 10th O. V. I.
Schmidt, George, Pr. Co. B 2nd U. S. V. E.
Schmidt, Joseph J., Pr. Co. G 1st O. V. I.

Schmidt, Robert, Pr. Co. D 1st O. V. I.
Schmehling, Martin, Pr. Co. M 1st O. V. I.
Schmitker, Benjamin, Pr. Co. A 1st O. V. I.
Schmuck, Frank E., Pr. Co. M 1st O. V. I.
Schneider, Anthony E., Pr. Co. G 1st O. V. I.
Schneider, Charles B., Sergt. Co. F 1st O. V. I.
Schoenfeld, Ferdinand W., Musician Co. A 1st O. V. I.
Schoone, Charles A., Pr. Co. F 1st O. V. I.
Schoone, 'Louis E., Pr. Co. D 1st O. V. I.
Schroder, Bernard, Pr. Co. B 1st O. V. I.
Schroeder, Frederick A., Saddler Sergt. 1st O. V. C.
Schulte, George H., Pr. Co. I 1st O. V. I.
Schulte, Henry, Pr. Co. I 1st O. V. I.
Schuetz, Jacob, 1st Sergt. Co. M 10th O. V. I.
Schwall, August S., Pr. Co. A 1st O.V.I.
Schwall, Walter, Pr. Co. A 1st O.V.I.
Schwarz, Theodore, Pr. Co. D 1st O. V. I.
Schweickart, Louis F., Musician Co. M 1st O. V. I.
Schwesinger, William H., Pr. Co. G 1st O. V. I.
Search, Edwin H., Pr. Co. C 1st O.V.I.
Searcy, Edward C., Pr. Co. A 1st O.V.I.
Seib, Howard, Pr. Co. B 1st O. V. I.
Seifert, John, Pr. Co. M 1st O. V. I.
Seiler, Emil, Pr. Co. B 2nd U. S. V. E.
Seiver, Frederick J., Pr. Co. I 1st O. V. I.
Sess, Fred, Pr. Co. M 1st O. V. I.
Seyler, Louis, Pr. Tr. H 1st O. V. C.
Shafer, Albert O., Corp. Co. I 1st O. V. I.
Shafer, Frank G., Pr. Co. I 1st O. V. I.
Shafer, George H., Corp. Co. I 1st O. V. I.
Shambaugh, George H., Pr. Co. B 1st O. V. I.
Shanahan, Daniel F., Pr. Co. C 1st O V. I.
Shank, Rienzi R., Pr. Co. C 1st O.V.I.
Sharts, Joseph W., Corp. Co. C 1st O. V. I.
Shier, Frank, Pr. Co. C 1st O. V. I.
Sholes, Clarence L., Pr. Co. C 1st O. V. I.
Shumate, Frank, Pr. Co. C 2nd U. S. V. E.
Shull, George, Pr. Co. C 1st O. V. J
Simcoe, Harry W., Pr. Co. C 2nd U. S. V. E.
Siminger, Harry, Pr. Co. M 1st O.V.I.
Simpkinson, Harry B., Pr. Co. B 1st O. V. I.

Simon, William G., Pr. Co. M 10th O. V. I.
Simms, Harry O., Pr. Co. G 1st O.V.I.
Sincoe, John W., 10th Corp. Co. M 10th O. V. I.
Smith, Benjamin, Pr. Co. M 10th O. V. I.
Smith, Charles H., Pr. Co. M 10th O. V. I.
Smith, Charles J., Pr. Co. M 10th O. V. I.
Smith, Edward F., Pr. Co. F 1st O.V.I.
Smith, Edward W., Pr. Co. A 1st O.V.I.
Smith, George C., Band Leader 1st O. V. I.
Smith, George, Sr., Pr. Co. B 1st O.V.I.
Smith, Harry, Pr. Co. F 1st O. V. I.
Smith, Harry, Pr. Co. H 1st O. V. I.
Smith, Henry, Pr. Co. B 2nd U.S.V.E.
Smith, Jacob, Pr. Co. B 2nd U. S. V. E.
Smith, James H., Pr. Co. M 1st O.V.I.
Smith, John H., Pr. Co. M 10th O.V.I.
Smith, Michael, Pr. Co. M 1st O. V. I.
Smith, Peter D., Pr. Co. B 2nd U. S. V. E.
Smith, Robert B., Pr. Co. B 2nd U. S. V. E.
Smith, Thomas, Pr. Co. C 1st O. V. I.
Smith, William J., Pr. Co. C 2nd U. S. V. E.
Snyder, Andrew C., Pr. Co. C 2nd U. S. V. E.
Snyder, David A., Musician Co. I 1st O. V. I.
Solomon, Thomas E., Wagoner Tr. H 1st O. V. C.
Speers, Charles H., Pr. Co. M 1st O. V. I.
Sperry, George, Pr. Co. M 10th O.V.I.
Splatt, Frank S., Pr. Co. K 1st O. V. I.
Splatt, Ralph A., Pr. Co. K 1st O. V. I.
Spring, Edward, Jr., Pr. Tr. H 1st O. V. C.
Springmeier, William H., Pr. Co. C 1st O. V. I.
Stadlmann, Michael, Pr. Co. B 1st O. V. I.
Stanfer, William C., Pr. Co. A 2nd U. S. E.
Stanley, Charles, Pr. Co. M 10th O.V.I.
Staples, Edward F., Pr. Co. C 2nd U. S. V. E.
Starry, Edward K., Pr. Co. C 2nd U. S. V. E.
Statzenger, Frederick, Pr. Co. C 2nd U. S. V. E.
Steele, Thomas P., Pr. Co. M 1st O. V. I.
Stein, Lee, Pr. Co. F 1st O. V. I.
Steinman, James G., Pr. Co. I 1st O. V. I.
Stephens, Elijah, Pr. Co. C 2nd U. S. V. E.
Stephenson, William S., Pr. Tr. H 1st O. V. C.
Stone, Richard A., Pr. Tr. H 1st O.V.C.
Stolz, Edward, Pr. Co. B 1st O. V. I.

Strickland, William T., Pr. Co. K 1st O. V. I.
Strobridge, Nelson W., Pr. Tr. H 1st O. V. C.
Stith, Horace W., Pr. Co. I 1st O. V. I.
Stuart, Joseph L., 5th Corp. Co. A 1st O. V. I.
Stix, Walter H., Pr. Co. B 1st O. V. I.
Street, Frank W., Pr. Co. K 1st O.V.I.
Stuber, Frederick M., Pr. Co. I 1st O. V. I.
Suleman, Charles A., Pr. Co. H 1st O. V. I.
Sullivan, Daniel H., 1st Sergt. Co. G 1st O. V. I.
Sullivan, Michael D., Pr. Co. K 1st O. V. I.
Sutten, John M., Sergt. Co. B 2nd U. S. V. E.
Sutter, Fred J., Pr. Tr. G 1st O. V. C.
Sweeney, Joseph B., Pr. Co. H 1st O. V. I.
Sweeney, Martin, Pr. Co. M 1st O.V.I.
Sylvester, Frank, Pr. Co. F 1st O. V. I.
Sylvester, Henry, Pr. Co. M 10th O. V. I.
Tacy, Charles K., Corp. Co. H 1st O. V. I.
Taecklenborg, Charles, Pr. Co. D 1st O. V. I.
Tamme, Louis J., Pr. Co. M 10th O. V. I.
Taylor, Robert P., Pr. Co. G 1st O.V.I.
Teaney, George B., Pr. Co. M 1st O. V. I.
Tenney, Charles E., Pr. Co. B 1st O. V. I.
Tenney, Wilson R., Pr. Co. B 1st O.V.I.
Thieben, Herman, Pr. Co. H 1st O.V.I.
Thiele, Albert C., Pr. Co. K 1st O.V.I.
Theis, Nicholas, Pr. Co. A 1st O. V. I.
Theiss, Charles, Jr., Pr. Co. G 1st O. V. I.
Thomann, Henry, Pr. Co. A 1st O. V. I.
Thomas, Edward A., Pr. Co. A 1st O. V. I.
Thomas, Harry I., Pr. Co. C 1st O.V.I.
Thompson, Frank P., Corp. Co. M 1st O. V. I.
Thompson, Elmer E., Pr. Co. H 1st O. V. I.
Tieman, Louis, Pr. Co. I 1st O. V. I.
Tillotson, Harry A., Pr. Co. I 1st O. V. I.
Tittmann, Henry, Pr. Co. D 1st O. V. I.
Toben, Thomas A., Pr. Co. C 2nd U. S. V. E.
Todd, James H., Pr. Co. I 1st O. V. I.
Toebben, Harry I., Musician Co. M 10th O. V. I.
Tompkins, Harry L., Pr. Co. C 2nd U. S. V. E.
Trageser, Peter, 2nd Corp. Co. A 1st O. V. I.
Tranor, Harry H., Pr. Co. B 1st O.V.I.
Traut, Burke D., Pr. Co. K 1st O.V.I.
Tressler, John T., Pr. Co. H 1st O.V.I.

Troutine, Charles, Pr. Co. M 1st O.V.I.
Ture, Frank, Pr. Co. B 1st O. V. C.
Turrell, John H., Pr. Co. C 2nd U. S. V. E.
Underhill, Whittington T., Pr. Co. B, 1st O. V. I.
Ury, Felix A., Pr. Co. M 10th O. V. I.
Vadersen, Otto, 2nd Corp. Co. M 10th O. V. I.
Valentine, Arthur B., Pr. Co. G 1st O. V. I.
Vance, Henry L., Pr. Co. H 1st O.V.I.
Van Arnum, John, Pr. Co. B 1st O.V.I.
Van Dyke, Ben., Musician Tr. II 1st O. V. C.
Van Duzen, John J., Q. M. Sergt. Co. II. 1st O. V. I.
Van Pelt, Eddie, Pr. Co. M 10th O.V.I.
Van Pelt, Edward R., Pr. Co. F 1st O. V. I.
Van Pelt, Stanley Farren, Pr. Co. K 1st O. V. I.
Varner, William Henry, Pr. Co. B 2nd U. S. V. E.
Venable, Russell Vernon, Musician Co. B 2nd U. S. V. E.
Viet, Henry L., Pr. Co. B 1st O. V. I.
Voegeli, Charles, Pr. Co. M 1st O.V.I.
Voegeli, William O., Pr. Tr. II 1st O. V. C.
Volker, August J., Corp. Co. B 2nd U. S. V. E.
Volz, Frank J., Musician Co. G 1st O. V. I.
Volz, Philip J., Pr. Co. G 1st O. V. I.
Von Felde, Frederick, Pr. Co. M 10th O. V. I.
Voss, Henry, Pr. Co. C 1st O. V. I.
Wachtendorf, Fred. G., Sergt. Co. B 2nd U. S. V. E.
Wade, Thomas, Pr. Co. H 1st O. V. I.
Wagner, Elmer C., Pr. Co. I 1st O.V.I.
Wagner, Henry, Pr. Co. C 1st O. V. I.
Wagner, Henry, Pr. Co. C 2nd U. S. V. E.
Wagner, Jacob, Pr. Co. G 1st O. V. I.
Wagner, John, Pr. Co. K 1st O. V. I.
Wahl, Joseph, Pr. Co. M 1st O. V. I.
Wait, Frank K., Pr. Co. B 1st O. V. I.
Walk, Joseph, Pr. Co. M 1st O. V. I.
Walker, Everett R., Musician Co. F 1st O. V. I.
Wall, George F., Corp. Co. C 1st O.V.I.
Wallace, Joseph N., Pr. Co. B 1st O. V. I.
Wallace, Walter, Sergt. Co. B 1st O. V. I.
Walsh, Edward, Pr. Co. C 1st O. V. I.
Walsh, Edward A., Corp. Co. G 1st O. V. I.
Walsh, William J., Pr. Co. C 2nd U. S. V. E.
Ward, Guy, Pr. Co. F 1st O. V. I.
Weaver, James D., Pr. Co. C 1st O.V.I.
Webb, J. Frank, Pr. Tr. H 1st O. V. C.
Webb, William H. C., Corp. Co. F 1st O. V. I.

Weber, Charles J., Sergt. Co. D 1st O. V. I.
Weber, John, Pr. Co. G 2nd O. V. I.
Wedig, Henry W., Jr., Corp. Co. K 1st O. V. I.
Wehmhoff, Fred, Pr. Co. D 1st O. V. I.
Weibel, Raymond O., Pr. Co. G 1st O. V. I.
Weibel, Samuel, Corp. Co. G 1st O.V.I.
Weich, J. Arthur, Pr. Co. K 1st O.V.I.
Weich, Elmer J., Musician Co. C 2nd U. S. V. E.
Weidman, Joseph C., Pr. Co. A 1st O. V. I.
Weisner, Joseph, Pr. Co. M 1st O.V.I. O. V. I.
Weiss, Louis J., Corp. Co. M 1st O.V.I.
Welch, Austin J., Pr. Co. B 2nd U. S. V. E.
Welge, Harry, Pr. Co. C 1st O. V. I.
Wenng, John, Corp. Co. M 1st O.V.I.
Wenning, Emil C., Pr. Co. M 10th O. V. I.
Werden, Derward B., Sergt. Co. H. 1st O. V. I.
West, James A., Sergt. Tr. H 1st O.V.C.
Wessling, George W., Pr. Tr. II 1st O. V. C.
Westmeier, Henry C., Pr. Co. M 10th O. V. I.
Wewer, Leonard J., Pr. Co. M 10th O V. I.
Weyler, Frank, Corp. Co. I 1st O. V. I.
Whaley, William J., Pr. Tr. H 1st O. V. C.
Wherle, Jacob, Pr. Co. G 1st O. V. I.
White, Ambrose, Jr., Corp. Co. K 1st O. V. I.
White, Elliott P., 1st Sergt. Co. K 1st O. V. I.
White, Fred A., Jr., Pr. Co. F 1st O. V. I.
Whiteford, Robert C., Pr. Co. C 2nd U. S. V. E.
Whitemann, Jacob, Pr. Co. D 1st O. V. I.
Whitteker, Elliott, Corp. Co. M 1st O. V. I.
Wibbelsmann, Bernhard, Pr. Co. D 1st O. V. I.
Widmeyer, Charles W., Pr. Co. A 1st O. V. I.
Widner, William, Jr., Corp. Co. C 2nd U. S. V. E.
Wilkin, Nicholas, Jr., Pr. Co. F 1st O. V. I.
Williams, David J., Pr. Co. H 1st O. V. I.
Williams, Grant H., Pr. Co. H 1st O. V. I.
Williams, Louis, Pr. Co. H 1st O. V. I.
Williams, Scott, Corp. Co. M 1st O.V.I.
Williams, Willie H., Pr. Co. F 1st O. V. I.
Williamson, Howard E., Pr. Co. K 1st O. V. I.

Williamson, Richard, Pr. Co. K 1st O. V. I.
Willett, George S., Pr. Co. D 1st O. V. I.
Willet, John, Pr. Co. M 1st O. V. I.
Wilson, Albert L., Pr. Tr. H 1st O. V. C.
Wilson, Edward F., Pr. Co. A 1st O. V. I.
Wilson, Henry B., Pr. Co. C 2nd U. S. V. E.
Wimmer, John J., Pr. Co. F 1st O.V.I.
Wimmer, Louis, Corp. Co. F 1st O.V.I.
Wimmer, William, Pr. Tr. H 1st O. V. C.
Winkelman, William, Pr. Co. G 1st O. v. I.
Winter, Frank J., Trumpeter Co. A 1st O. V. I.
Wirthwine, Harry H., Pr. Co. C 1st O. V. I.
Wittels, Jacob, Pr. Co. M 10th O. V. I.
Woest, Herman, Jr., Musician Co. H 1st O. V. I.
Woeste, Daniel W., Pr. Co. A 1st O. V. I.
Wolsefer, Charles F., Pr. Co. G 1st O. V. I.
Wood, Horace M., Sergt. Co. B 2nd U. S. V. E.
Worst, Oliver G. E., Pr. Co. I 1st O. V. I.
Worthington, John S., Pr. Co. H 1st O. V. I.
Woycke, Eugene P., Pr. Co. B 2nd U. S. V. E.
Wright, Benjamin A., Pr. Tr. H 1st O. V. C.
Wright, Chester, Pr. Co. I 1st O. V. I.
Wright, Ray S., 3rd Corp. Co. M 10th O. V. I.

Wright, Walter C., Pr. Co. H 1st O. V. I.
Wright, William N., Corp. Co. M 1st O. V. I.
Wuest, Charles, Pr. Co. C 2nd U. S. V. E.
Wuest, George J., Pr. Tr. H 1st O. V. C.
Wulfeck, Wallace E., Wagoner Co. B 1st O. V. I.
Wulfekamp, William Henry, Corp. Co. B 2nd U. S. V. E.
Wunderlich, Willie, Pr. Co. H 1st O. V. I.
Wunderlich, William J., Musician Co. K 1st O. V. I.
Wurz, Charles J., Pr. Co. M 10th O. V. I.
Wyle, Edward W., Pr. Co. M 1st O. V. I.
Yahrans, William E., Pr. Co. C 1st O. V. I.
Yanch, John, Q. M. Sergt. Co. G 1st O. V. I.
Yates, Fred, Pr. Co. H 1st O. V. I.
Yither, Philip H., Pr. Co. M 10th O. V. I.
Young, Charles E., Pr. Co. H 1st O. V. I.
Young, Frank, Corp. Co. D 1st O. V. I.
Young, William, Pr. Co. I 1st O. V. I.
Yuille, George M., Pr. Co. K 1st O. V. I.
Zahn, Armin, Pr. Co. M 10th O. V. I.
Zapf, Andrew, Pr. Co. M 10th O. V. I.
Zench, William, Pr. Co. A 1st O. V. I.
Zins, Edward S., Pr. Co. A 1st O. V. I.
Zint, John G., Pr. Co. M 1st O. V. I.
Zimmer, Alex., Pr. Co. B 1st O. V. I.
Zimpelman, Jacob F., Pr. Co. K 1st O. V. I.

CIRCLEVILLE

Ambrose, William R., Pr. Co. M 4th O. V. I.
Anderson, Hartley J., Pr. Co. M 4th O. V. I.
Baer, Henry C., Pr. Co. M 4th O. V. I.
Bailey, John S., Pr. Co. M 4th O. V. I.
Baker, John L., Pr. Co. M 4th O. V. I.
Bales, Blenn R., Pr. Co. M 4th O. V. I.
Barker, William J., Pr. Co. M 4th O. V. I.
Baughman, James, Wagoner Co. M 4th O. V. I.
Baughman, Joseph, Pr. Co. M 4th O. V. I.
Bostwick, Charles A., Sergt. Co. M 4th O. V. I.
Brady, George, Pr. Co. M 4th O. V. I.
Brannan, Charles, Pr. Co. M 4th O.V.I.
Brown, Edward M., Pr. Co. M 4th O. V. I.
Brown, Mason J., Pr. Co. M 4th O.V.I.

Bussert, Wayne, Pr. Co. M 4th O. V. I.
Caldwell, Job D., Pr. Co. M 4th O. V. I.
Crayne, John Mouser, Corp. Co. M 4th O. V. I.
Crissinger, Frank, Pr. Co. M 4th O. V. I.
Crites, Clifford W., Pr. Co. M 4th O. V. I.
Crum, Charles K., 1st Sergt. Co. M 4th O. V. I.
Darby, William, Pr. Tr. D 1st O. V. C.
Donnelly, Fred. L., Pr. Co. M 4th O. V. I.
Doyle, John, Pr. Co. M 4th O. V. I.
Edgington, George C., Pr. Co. M 4th O. V. I.
Evans, David J., Pr. Co. M 4th O. V. I.
Fisher, William C., Pr. Co. M 4th O. V. I.
Flemming, Robert, Pr. Co. M 4th O.V.I.
Fletcher, Bradley, Pr. Co. M 4th O.V.I.

Forsythe, Bert N., Pr. Co. M 4th O.V.I.
Friley, Charles R., Pr. Co. M 4th O.V.I.
Haines, George L., Pr. Co. M 4th O.
  V. I.
Hammell, Lewis C., Pr. Tr. D 1st O.
  V. C.
Hane, William A., Pr. Co. M 4th O.V.I.
Henry, Stephen J., Sergt. Co. M 4th
  O. V. I.
Hernstein, Philip G., Pr. Co. M 4th O.
  V. I.
Hughes, Harry L., Sergt. Co. M 4th
  O. V. I.
Irwin, George G., Pr. Co. M 4th O.V.I.
Jackson, Albert, Pr. Co. M 4th O. V. I
Kashner, John H., Corp. Co. M 4th
  O. V. I.
Kinney, Daniel, Pr. Co. M 4th O. V. I.
Lape, William, Pr. Co. M 4th O. V. I.
Lewis, Leotus E., Pr. Co. M 4th O.V.I.
Lilley, Frank P., Pr. Co. M 4th O. V. I.
Lowe, Charles F., Sergt. Co. M 4th O.
  V. I.
Lower, William, Pr. Co. M 4th O. V. I.
McHale, Thomas, Pr. Co. M 4th O.V.I.
McKenzie, David, Pr. Co. M 4th O.V.I.
Miller, Frank M., Pr. Co. M 4th O.V.I.
Miller, Jacob W., Pr. Co. M 4th O.V.I.
Mowery, Arlow F., Corp. Co. M 4th
  O. V. I.

Moyer, Harvey E., Pr. Co. M 4th O.
  V. I.
Murray, Marshall E., Corp. Co. M 4th
  O. V. I.
Palm, Joseph, Pr. Co. M 4th O. V. I.
Radcliffe, Frank C., Sergt. Maj. 4th
  O. V. I.
Redman, George H., Pr. Co. M 4th O.
  V. I.
Reeder, William B., Corp. Co. M 4th
  O. V. I.
Roof, Charles E., Pr. Co. M 4th O.V.I.
Shaffer, Samuel, Pr. Co. M 4th O. V. I.
Spangler, Samuel, Pr. Co. M 4th O.V.I.
Spires, James E., Pr. Co. M 4th O.V.I.
Strawser, Harry, Pr. Co. M 4th O. V. I.
Tatman, Ed., Pr. Co. M 4th O. V. I.
Taylor, Ed., Pr. Co. M 4th O. V. I.
Thompson, Leroy M., Corp. Co. M 4th
  O. V. I.
Thorn, Fred, H., Pr. Co. M 4th O. V. I.
Titus, Charles M., Artificer Co. M 4th
  O. V. I.
Walker, Edward, Pr. Co. M 4th O.V.I.
Warner, B. Frank, Sergt. Co. M 4th
  O. V. I.
Warner, William A., Pr. Co. M 4th O.
  V. I.
Wright, Homer A., Pr. Co. M 4th O.
  V. I.
Yowell, Harry, Pr. Co. M 4th O. V. I.

CLARK CO.

Baker, Ira, Pr. Co. B 3rd O. V. I.   Dean, Henry K., Pr. Co. B 3rd O.V.I.

CLARKE

Ports, Delbert H., Pr. Co. H 8th O. V. I.

CLEARPORT

Raynolds, George E., Pr. Co. I 4th O. V. I.

CLEVELAND

Adams, David, Corp. Co. B 10th O.V.I.
Addis, William J., Corp. Co. K 5th
  O. V. I.
Adolph, Henry M., Pr. Co. C 10th O.
  V. I.
Aichler, Bert, Pr. Tr. B 1st O. V. C.
Ake, Jay F., Corp. Co. C 10th O. V. I.
Alden, Henry C., Pr. Co. B 10th O.V.I.
Alexander, Chas A., Q. M. Sergt. Co.
  C 10th O. V. I.
Allen, George I., Pr. Tr. A 1st O.V.C.
Allen, Karl C., Pr. Tr. A 1st O. V. C.
Ammon, Jay R., 8th Sergt. Tr. C 1st
  O. V. C.
Anderson, Clarence W., Pr. Bat. A 1st
  O. V. A.
Anderson, George H., Pr. Co. K 10th
  O. V. I.

Anderson, Henry, Pr. Co. K 10th O.
  V. I.
Andrews, William W., Pr. Tr. B 1st
  O. V. C.
Ankert, Louis, Corp. Co. K 5th O. V. I.
Anspeck, Frank W., Pr. Bat. A 1st O.
  V. A.
Apfil, Oscar C., Pr. Tr. C 1st O. V. C.
Apple, Ward B., Pr. Co. K 5th O. V. I.
Aring, Ernest H., Pr. Co. B 10th O.V.I.
Arndt, Fred W., Pr. Co. C 5th O.V.I.
Arrivee, Joseph H., Corp. Co. B 5th
  O. V. I.
Arthur, George G., Sergt. Co. B 10th
  O. V. I.
Astrup, Charles E., Pr. Co. K 5th O.
  V. I.
August, Albert, Pr. Co. I 5th O. V. I.

Aulenbacher, Louis, Corp. Co. C 10th O. V. I.
Auxer, Fred P., Q. M. Sergt. Co. K 5th O. V. I.
Bailer, Louis A., Pr. Tr. B 1st O.V.C.
Bailey, Arthur R., Pr. Co. I 10th O.V.I.
Baker, Andrew G., Pr. Tr. G 1st O. V. C.
Baker, Harry C., Pr. Co. K 5th O.V.I.
Baker, William, Pr. Co. I 5th O. V. I.
Barber, Dwight L., Pr. Bat. A 1st O. V. A.
Barnstein, Carl, Pr. Co. F 5th O. V. I.
Bartholomew, William I., Pr. Co. C 5th O. V. I.
Bartlett, Edwin L., Pr. Co. L 5th O. V. I.
Bassett, Ira S., Sergt. Co. B 10th O. V. I.
Bastian, Charles, Pr. Co. A 10th O.V.I.
Bastie, Frank F., Pr. Co. C 10th O.V.I.
Bates, Elihu M., Pr. Co. B 10th O.V.I.
Batten, Harry H., 5th Sergt. Tr. A 1st O. V. C.
Battenfeld, Ferdinand, Corp. Co. B 10th O. V. I.
Baxa, Thomas P., Pr. Co. C 10th O.V.I.
Baxter, James F., Pr. Co. A 10th O.V.I.
Beck, Albert W., Pr. Co. K 10th O.V.I.
Beckman, Adolph A., Pr. Bat. A 1st O. V. A.
Beebe, Arthur L., Pr. Tr. A 1st O.V.C.
Beiler, Joseph B., Pr. Tr. B 1st O.V.C.
Belcher, John, Pr. Co. A 10th O. V. I.
Bell, Franklyn M., Pr. Tr. A 1st O. V. C.
Bell, George, Pr. Co. I 5th O. V. I.
Bellemore, Peter, Pr. Co. A 10th O.V.I.
Below, George W., Pr. Co. B 10th O. V. I.
Benarfa, Augustus J., Musician Co. F 5th O. V. I.
Bencke, Carl F., Corp. Co. K 5th O.V.I.
Bender, George C., Pr. Tr. C 1st O. V. C.
Bennett, Harry E., Pr. Tr. C 1st O.V.C.
Bently, Harry M., Pr. Tr. B 1st O.V.C.
Berg, George A., Pr. Co. L 5th O.V.I.
Bernard, Paul H., Pr. Bat. A 1st O. V. A.
Rezena, Louis L., Pr. Bat. A 1st O. V. A.
Bienhoff, Max, Pr. Co. I 5th O. V. I.
Biercer, Ernest C., Pr. Tr. A 1st O. V. C.
Bigus, John A., Pr. Co. B 10th O. V. I.
Binyon, Edward A., Pr. Tr. A 1st O. V. C.
Bishop, Neil H., Pr. Tr. A 1st O.V.C.
Bishop, Roy N., Pr. Tr. A 1st O.V.C.
Black, Lewis A., Pr. Tr. G 1st O. V. C.
Blackstock, James G., Pr. Co. I 10th O. V. I.
Blake, William J., Pr. Co. C 10th O.V.I.
Blickensderfer, Michael R., Pr. Tr. C 1st O. V. C.
Bliss, William F., Pr. Co. B 10th O.V.I.

Boam, Andrew D., Pr. Co. K 5th O.V.I.
Boardman, James T., Corp. Co. C 10th O. V. I.
Boettishes, William J., Jr., Corp. Co. B 10th O. V. I.
Bole, Benjamin P., Sergt. Maj 1st O. V. C.
Bolton, Will M., Pr. Tr. A 1st O.V.C.
Bond, George M., Pr. Tr. A 1st O.V.C.
Bonesteel, Ralph L., Pr. Co. C 5th O. V. I.
Booth, Frank W., Q. M. Sergt. Co. I 5th O. V. I.
Born, Carl P., Jr., Pr. Tr. A 1st O.V.C.
Bould, William, Pr. Co. B 5th O. V. I.
Bourne, Benjamin R., Pr. Co. A 3rd O. V. I.
Bourne, John K., Pr. Tr. A 1st O.V.C.
Bowles, Chauncey, Pr. Co. D 9th Batt. O. V. I.
Boyd, John D., Pr. Co. L 5th O. V. I.
Bradley, Frank L., Pr. Tr. C 1st O. V. C.
Bradley, Linnius M., Pr. Tr. B 1st O. V. C.
Brady, Clinton J., Q. M. Sergt. Co. B 5th O. V. I.
Bram, Edward W., Pr. Bat. A 1st O. V. A.
Bram, Samuel G., Corp. Bat. A 1st O. V. A.
Breit, Louis, Pr. Co. A 10th O. V. I.
Breman, John C., Pr. Co. C 10th O.V.I.
Bretschneider, Max B., Pr. Co. B 5th O. V. I.
Brewster, John H., Corp. Co. C 10th O. V. I.
Brewster, William, Pr. Co. K 5th O.V.I.
Briggs, Charles W., Pr. Co. F 5th O. V. I.
Britton, Schuyler P., 6th Sergt. Tr. A 1st O. V. C.
Brock, Charles, Pr. Co. I 5th O. V. I.
Brock, Collins J., Pr. Co. K 5th O.V.I.
Brockway, Clarence M., Pr. Tr. A 1st O. V. C.
Brooks, Albert L., Q. M. Sergt. Co. C 5th O. V. I.
Brown, James, Pr. Co. D 9th Batt. O. V. I.
Brown, Royal L. L., Pr. Tr. C 1st O. V. C.
Brown, William, Pr. Co. F 5th O. V. I.
Brunnell, Ebon N., Corp. Co. A 10th O. V. I.
Brunner, Conrad, Pr. Co. A 10th O. V. I.
Brush, William H., Q. M. Sergt. Co. B 10th O. V. I.
Bryant, Charles L., Pr. Bat. A 1st O. V. A.
Bubak, Lada C., Pr. Co. C 10th O.V.I.
Buesser, William H., Pr. Co. L 5th O. V. I.
Bulkley, Henry G., Pr. Tr. A 1st O. V. C.
Bundy, Archie P, Pr. Co. C 5th O V.I.

Bundy, Charles C., 1st Sergt. Co. I 10th O. V. I.

Burhenn, Louie E., Pr. Co. I 10th O. V. I.

Burke, George, Pr. Co. B 10th O. V. I.

Burke, James, Pr. Co. B 10th O. V. I.

Burke, John J., Pr. Co. I 5th O. V. I.

Burkheiser, Martin N., Pr. Tr. A 1st O. V. C.

Burns, Daniel J., Corp. Co. B 5th O. V. I.

Burton, Harry E., Corp. Co. L 5th O. V. I.

Burton, William H., Pr. Co. K 5th O. V. I.

Buss, William, Pr. Co. K 5th O. V. I.

Byrnes, William J., Pr. Co. I 10th O. V. I.

Callaghan, Charles, Pr. Tr. B 1st O. V. C.

Calleher, Eugene, Pr. Co. F 5th O.V.I.

Camp, William N., Pr. Co. B 10th O. V. I.

Campbell, Charles C., Pr. Tr. B 1st O. V. C.

Campbell, Franklin S., Pr. Tr. B 1st O. V. C.

Canfield, Birtley K., 5th Sergt. Tr. C 1st O. V. C.

Canfield, Ulyssus S. G., Pr. Co. B 10th O. V. I.

Carle, Charles W., Pr. Co. K 5th O.V.I.

Carlton, Frank R., Pr. Tr. C 1st O.V.C.

Carman, Oliver G., Pr. Co. C 10th O. V. I.

Carroll, John, Pr. Tr. B 1st O. V. C.

Carson, Thomas J., Pr. Co. I 10th O. V. I.

Cartner, Alexander L., Pr. Co. C 5th O. V. I.

Cass, John E., Pr. Co. C 10th O. V. I.

Casterline, Frank H., Sergt. Co. K 5th O. V. I.

Castigon, Edward W., Pr. Co. C 10th O. V. I.

Caulkins, Albert, 8th Corp. Co. I 10th O. V. I.

Cauthard, Harry F., Pr. Co. I 10th O. V. I.

Cawthra, Frank, Pr. Co. L 5th O. V. I.

Cawthra, Winfield, Pr. Co. L 5th O.V.I. V. I.

Cenes, John, Pr. Bat. A 1st O. V. A.

Chaloner, Henry, Pr. Tr. C 1st O.V.C.

Chandler, Zachariah M., Pr. Tr. A 1st O. V. C.

Chapp, Charles C., Pr. Tr. A 1st O. V. C.

Chester, Robert C., Pr. Tr. A 1st O. V. C.

Chrisford, James W., Pr. Bat. A 1st O. V. A.

Christman, Edwin D., Pr. Co. K 5th O. V. I.

Christy, Patrick, Pr. Co. B 5th O. V. I.

Cills, Albert G., Pr. Bat. A 1st O.V.A.

Claffey, Edward, Corp. Co. A 10th O. V. I.

Clark, George H., Pr. Co. A 10th O. V. I.

Clark, Gleeland E., Corp. Co. F 5th O. V. I.

Clark, Herbert R., Pr. Co. I 10th O. V. I.

Clark, John J., Pr. Co. K 10th O. V. I.

Clark, Junius B., Pr. Co. A 10th O.V.I.

Clark, Rupert, Pr. Co. L 5th O. V. I.

Clark, William P., Pr. Co. C 3rd O.V.I.

Clarke, Daniel, Pr. Co. I 5th O. V. I.

Clarke, William G., Pr. Bat. A 1st O. V. A.

Class, William A., Pr. Co. F 5th O.V.I.

Cleary, John J., Pr. Co. B 10th O. V. I.

Cleland, James H., 4th Sergt. Co. I 10th O. V. I.

Clements, George F., Pr. Co. B 10th O. V. I.

Clemes, Arthur W., Pr. Tr. B 1st O. V. C.

Clough, Joseph B., 4th Corp. Co. I 10th O. V. I.

Clure, Albert H., Pr. Tr. A 1st O.V.C.

Cobbledick, William, Pr. Co. A 2nd U. S. V. E.

Cody, Arthur P., Pr. Tr. A 1st O. V. C.

Coffey, Fred W., Pr. Tr. B 1st O.V.C.

Cohen, Isaac, Pr. Co. C 10th O. V. I.

Cole, Frank H., Pr. Co. L 5th O. V. I.

Coleman, Arthur F., Pr. Co. F 10th O. V. I.

Coleman, Fred, Pr. Co. I 5th O. V. I.

Coleman, Maxwell J., Pr. Co. I 5th O. V. I.

Collins, Francis A., Pr. Tr. A 1st O. V. C.

Collings, Frederick, Pr. Bat. A 1st O. V. A.

Collins, George P., Pr. Co. L 5th O.V.I.

Comstock, John M., Reg. Sergt. Maj. 5th O. V. I.

Conkey, Thomas A., Pr. Bat. A 1st O. V. A.

Connelly, Thomas, Pr. Co. H 10th O. V. I.

Connor, Friend D., Pr. Tr. A 1st O. V. C.

Connor, Michael M., Pr. Co. B 10th O. V. I.

Cook, Francis P., Pr. Tr. G 1st O.V.C.

Cook, Frederick L., Pr. Co. C 5th O. V. I.

Cook, Howard E., Corp. Co. I 5th O. V. I.

Cooke, Milton W., Pr. Co. I 10th O. V. I.

Copeland, Harvey L., Corp. Co. B 5th O. V. I.

Copeland, Mark A., Pr. Co. K 10th O. V. I.

Corrigan, James R., Pr. Co. C 5th O. V. I.

Cormier, Frederick, Sergt. Co. B 5th O. V. I.

Farr, Asa A., Pr. Tr. C 1st O. V. C.
Farr, Edwin W., Pr. Co. I 10th O.V.I.
Farr, William E., 3rd Corp. Co. I 10th O. V. I.
Farrell, Alfred, Pr. Co. I 5th O. V. I.
Faust, Robert R., Pr. Co. C 5th O.V.I.
Fawcett, Frank E., Corp. Co. K 10th O. V. I.
Fawcett, William H., Pr. Co. I 5th O. V. I.
Feaney, Thomas, Pr. Co. B 10th O. V.I.
Fegan, Edward J., Pr. Co. C 10th O.V.I.
Feinkohl, Fred, Pr. Co. B 10th O. V. I.
Felhaber, Frank C., Corp. Bat. A 1st O. V. A.
Ferbert, Otto H., Pr. Tr. B 1st O.V.C.
Fernandez, Robert J., Pr. Co. B 10th O. V. I.
Ferrell, Harry D., Pr. Co. L 5th O.V.I.
Ferris, Raymond A., Pr. Co. K 10th O. V. I.
Ferris, Robert B., Pr. Co. I 10th O.V.I.
Ficken, Harry, Artificer Co. K 5th O. V. I.
Fiedler, George R., Pr. Co. K 10th O. V. I.
Filkins, Frank L., Corp. Co. B 5th O. V. I.
Finger, Chas. W., Pr. Co. B 10th O. V. I.
Fink, Josef, Musician Co. I 10th O.V.I.
Fisher, Alexander, Pr. Co. B 5th O.V.I.
Fisher, Arthur J., Corp. Co. A 10th O. V. I.
Fisher, Charles A., Pr. Bat. A 1st O. V. A.
Fisher, William H., Pr. Co. L 5th O. V. I.
Fisk, Charles W., Pr. Co. C 5th O.V.I.
Fitzpatrick, Clarkson, Pr. Co. A 10th O. V. I.
Flinn, Harold L., Pr. Tr. B 1st O.V.C.
Flower, Andrew G., Hospital Steward 5th O. V. I.
Foehl, Gustave A., Pr. Co. F 5th O. V. I.
Fogarty, William, Pr. Co. A 10th O. V. I.
Follansbee, Edwin C., Pr. Co. K 10th O. V. I.
Ford, James O., Sergt. Co. B 2nd U. S. V. E.
Fortune, Albert V., Pr. Co. K 5th O. V. I.
Forwick, Benjamin, Pr. Co. I 10th O. V. I.
Foster, Frank G., Pr. Co. M 5th O.V.I.
Fowler, Leroy, Corp. Co. D 9th Batt. O. V. I.
Fowler, Walter G., Pr. Tr. A 1st O. V. C.
Fox, John N., Musician Tr. C 1st O. V. C.
Frances, Jesse A., Pr. Co. B 5th O.V.I.
Frank, Fred, Pr. Co. C 10th O. V. I.
Frank, Max, Pr. Co. B 10th O. V. I.
Frankel, David, Pr. Co. B 5th O. V. I.

Franklin, Albert, Wagoner Co. D 9th Batt. O. V. I.
Franklin, Thomas W., Pr. Co. B 10th O. V. I.
Frazior, William B., Pr. Co. I 10th O. V. I.
Freeman, Edson T., Pr. Co. K 5th O. V. I.
Freeman, George H., Corp. Co. B 10th O. V. I.
Freeman, William H., Pr. Tr. C 1st O. V. C.
Freedman, Morris H., Pr. Co. L 5th O. V. I.
Freiberger, Jacob, Pr. Co. A 10th O. V. I.
French, Charles L., Pr. Co. L 5th O. V. I.
Freund, Edward H., Corp. Tr. A 1st O. V. C.
Friesman, William H., Hospital Steward 5th O. V. I.
Friestad, Ole M., Bat. Sergt. Maj. 5th O. V. I.
Frost, Huron J., 1st Sergt. Co. K 5th O. V. I.
Fuller, Lafayette, Pr. Co. K 10th O. V. I.
Funk, Charles B., Pr. Co. B 5th O.V.I.
Futz, Robt. O., Pr. Tr. C 1st O. V. C.
Gadban, Edmund, Musician Co. B 5th O. V. I.
Gales, Benjamin, Pr. Co. D 9th Batt. O. V. I.
Gallagher, Joseph P., Pr. Co. L 5th O. V. I.
Gallagher, Michael, Pr. Co. A 10th O. V. I.
Gamble, William F., Pr. Tr. C 1st O. V. C.
Garber, Charlie H., Pr. Co. A 10th O. V. I.
Garvey, Michael E., Pr. Co. B 10th O. V. I.
Gavan, Frank W., Pr. Co. I 10th O.V.I.
Geckler, Charles F., 1st Sergt. Co. C 10th O. V. I.
Gedecke, Herman C., Pr. Co. K 5th O. V. I.
Gehres, Harry C., Pr. Co. B 5th O.V.I.
Geiger, John M., Corp. Co. C 5th O. V. I.
Geiger, Otto J., Pr. Co. B 5th O. V. I.
Gellner, Emil, Pr. Co. A 10th O. V. I.
Gensemer, Dubbs K., Pr. Bat. A 1st O. V. A.
Gibbons, Harry J., Musician Bat A 1st O. V. A.
Gibson, Albert M., Pr. Bat. A 1st O. V. A.
Gibson, Robert C., Pr. Tr. B 1st O. V. C.
Gibson, Samuel W., Sergt. Bat. A 1st O. V. A.
Gibson, William A., Pr. Bat. A 1st O. V. A.

Gibson, William A., Pr. Co. F 5th O. V. I.
Gilchrist, Joseph A., Sergt. Tr. B 1st O. V. C.
Gilbert, William, Wagoner Co. C 10th O. V. I.
Gilmore, Burdette G., Pr. Co. F 5th O. V. I.
Gilmore, Michael C., Pr. Co. K 10th O. V. I.
Gill, William C., 4th Sergt. Co. C 5th O. V. I.
Gillis, Carl B., Pr. Tr. A 1st O. V. C.
Gilson, Adam, Pr. Co. L 5th O. V. I.
Gleason, Charles A., Corp. Co. C 5th O. V. I.
Gleason, Edward J., Pr. Bat. A 1st O. V. A.
Gleeson, Frank T., Pr. Co. I 10th O. V. I.
Glenn, Jack, Corp. Co. D 9th Batt. O. V. I.
Glueck, John G., Sergt. Co. C 10th O. V. I.
Gohr, Carl, Pr. Co. I 5th O. V. I.
Goodale, Herman C., Pr. Co. K 5th O. V. I.
Goode, James W., Pr. Co. B 10th O.V.I.
Goodhue, Allan E., 1st Sergt. Co. K 10th O. V. I.
Goodsell, Clare, Pr. Co. F 5th O. V. I.
Gordon, Robert, Pr. Co. I 5th O. V. I.
Gosnick, Otto, Pr. Co. C 10th O. V. I.
Goucher, Paul B., Corp. Co. C 5th O. V. I.
Gray, Harry P., Pr. Co. L 5th O. V. I.
Graham, Albert L., Pr. Co. M 5th O. V. I.
Grant, Thomas D., Pr. Tr. G 1st O. V. C.
Grasgreen, Saul, Pr. Co. A 10th O. V. I.
Greber, George W., Pr. Co. B 10th O. V. I.
Green, Thomas W., Corp. Co. F 5th O. V. I.
Greenberg, Jesse, Corp. Co. F 5th O. V. I.
Greeves, J. Gardner, Pr. Tr. B 1st O. V. C.
Grenlock, Fred. W., Pr. Co. I 5th O. V. I.
Gresham, Walter H., Pr. Co. F 5th O. V. I.
Gresmuck, Frank W., Pr. Bat. A 1st O. V. A.
Griesser, Frank, Pr. Co. C 10th O.V.I.
Griesser, Fred, Pr. Co. C 10th O. V. I.
Grigsby, William A., Pr. Co. K 5th O. V. I.
Groff, George E., Pr. Co. I 5th O.V.I.
Gronow, Benjamin, Pr. Co. B 10th O. V. I.
Gronow, Harry, Pr. Co. B 10th O. V. I.
Groot, George, Pr. Tr. A 1st O. V. C.
Groot, William S., Pr. Tr. A 1st O.V.C.
Gruettner, William F., 1st Sergt. Co. F 5th O. V. I.

Grugel, Gustav, Pr. Co. I 10th O.V.I.
Guentzler, Harry W., Pr. Tr. C 1st O. V. C.
Gunday, Henry S., Pr. Tr. A 1st O.V.C.
Gundel, John, Pr. Co. A 10th O. V. I.
Gundermann, Harry J., Pr. Co. I 10th O. V. I.
Gunnarsen, Christian B., Pr. Co. B 5th O. V. I.
Gunton, Walter C., Pr. Co. B 5th O. V. I.
Gustawes, John G., Pr. Co. K 5th O.V.I.
Gustawes, Herman G., Pr. Co. A 10th O. V. I.
Guthmann, Fred, Pr. Co. I 10th O.V.I.
Gutman, August W., Pr. Tr. C 1st O. V. C.
Haffner, Fred, Pr. Co. I 10th O. V. I.
Hageman, William, Pr. Co. B 5th O. V. I.
Hagen, William F., Q. M. Sergt. Co. F 5th O. V. I.
Hagerty, James, Pr. Co. I 5th O. V. I.
Haker, George C., Sergt. Co. I 5th O. V. I.
Haldy, William O., Sergt. Bat. A 1st O. V. A.
Halford, William D., Pr. Co. K 5th O. V. I.
Hamilton, Harry K., Pr. Tr. G 1st O. V. C.
Hamilton, John F. J., Pr. Co. F 5th O. V. I.
Hamley, John, Pr. Co. A 10th O. V. I.
Hammer, Ben, Pr. Co. B 5th O. V. I.
Hammer, Max, Pr. Co. I 5th O. V. I.
Hanna, Edward Raymond, Pr. Bat. A 1st O. V. A.
Hank, Bert J., Pr. Co. A 10th O. V. I.
Hannay, Allan K., Pr. Co. L 5th O. V. I.
Hanschild, Arthur J., Pr. Co. B 5th O. V. I.
Hannschild, Frank G., Pr. Bat. A 1st O. V. I.
Hardesty, Eugene, Pr. Tr. C 1st O. V. C.
Harper, Lewis B., Pr. Co. K 5th O.V.I.
Harriman, Alfred L., Pr. Co. F 5th O. V. I.
Harrington, William H., Pr. Co. C 10th O. V. I.
Harris, Cyrus M., Pr. Tr. A 1st O.V.C.
Harris, John, Pr. Co. D 9th Batt. O. V. I.
Hart, Benjamin F., Pr. Co. K 10th O. V. I.
Hart, John, Pr. Tr. C 1st O. V. C.
Hartz, Dave E., Pr. Co. I 10th O. V. I.
Harvey, Ernest R., Pr. Tr. G 1st O. V. C.
Harvey, Finis D., Pr. Co. K 10th O. V. I.
Harvey, Harry A., Pr. Co. C 5th O.V.I.
Harvey, William A., Pr. Co. K 10th O. V. I.

Hasbrouck, Niles B., Corp. Tr. A 1st O. V. C.
Haskell, John M., Pr. Tr. A 1st O.V.C.
Haskins, James E., Pr. Co. I 5th O.V.I.
Hawkens, William E., Pr. Co. A 2nd U. S. V. E.
Hays, William J., Pr. Tr. A 1st O.V.C.
Hayes, Ernest W., Pr. Bat. A 1st O. V. A.
Hayman, William R., Musician Co. K 5th O. V. I.
Heffron, Dominic, Pr. Co. I 5th O.V.I.
Heid, Otto A., Pr. Co. I 5th O. V. I.
Heidecker, Joseph, Pr. Co. L 5th O.V.I.
Heinzman, Joseph, Corp. Co. C 10th O. V. I.
Helm, Joseph C., Pr. Co. C 10th O. V. I.
Helman, William, Pr. Co. K 10th O. V. I.
Henderson, Walter L., Pr. Co. B 5th O. V. I.
Henderson, William P., Pr. Co. L 5th O. V. I.
Hennessy, Edward J., Musician Co. B 10th O. V. I.
Henry, James, Pr. Co. A 2nd U. S. V. E.
Herbert, Charles H., Pr. Co. F 5th O. V. I.
Herman, Eugene, Pr. Co. I 5th O. V. I.
Herrmann, Max K., Pr. Co. K 5th O. V. I.
Hesche, Charles, Pr. Bat. A 1st O. V. A.
Hess, George, Musician Tr. C 1st O. V. C.
Hewitt, Clarence W., Pr. Co. A 10th O. V. I.
Hewitt, Ernest E., Pr. Co. B 5th O.V.I.
Hickman, John, Pr. Co. K 3rd O. V. I.
Hill, Boyden C., Pr. Co. L 5th O. V. I.
Hill, Louis E., 3rd Sergt. Tr. A 1st O. V. C.
Hilliard, Newton H., Pr. Co. K 5th O. V. I.
Hirschling, Frederick O., Sergt. Co. B 10th O. V. I.
Hirstius, August J., Pr. Bat. A 1st O. V. A.
Hlavacek, John J., Pr. Co. B 5th O. V. I.
Hoag, Benjamin W., Pr. Co. K 10th O. V. I.
Hoard, William J., Pr. Co. A 10th O. V. I.
Hodapp, Paul, Pr. Co. C 5th O. V. I.
Hodge, Frank D., Pr. Co. C 5th O.V.I.
Hoeltz, Louis J., Pr. Co. I 10th O.V.I.
Hoettinger, John G., Sergt. Co. C 10th O. V. I.
Hoffman, Andrew J., Musician Co. I 5th O. V. I.
Hoffman, John P., Pr. Co. K 5th O.V.I.
Hoffman, Robert, Pr. Co. I 10th O.V.I.
Hogan, Frank J., Pr. Co. I 10th O.V.I.
Holden, Rollin T., Jr., Pr. Tr. A 1st O. V. C.

Hollander, Karl, Pr. Co. B 5th O.V.I.
Hollenbach, Frank B., Pr. Co. C 5th O. V. I.
Hollis, Albert B., Pr. Co. C 5th O.V.I.
Hollister, Cornelius T., Pr. Tr. A 1st O. V. C.
Holter, Irwin B., Pr. Co. A 10th O.V.I.
Holton, Edward C., 7th Sergt. Tr. C 1st O. V. C.
Honey, Charles F., Corp. Co. A 10th O. V. I.
Hopkins, Emery V. K., Pr. Tr. B 1st O. V. C.
Hopkins, William J., Pr. Co. B 10th O. V. I.
Hoppensack, Justus F., Pr. Bat. A 1st O. V. A.
Hook, Frank A., Pr. Co. F 5th O.V.I.
Hoover, Charles M., Pr. Co. L 5th O. V. I.
Hoppe, Fred, Musician Co. G 5th O. V. I.
Horne, William, Pr. Co. D 9th Batt. O. V. I.
Horton, Erward V., Pr. Co. I 5th O. V. I.
Hosman, Joseph A., Pr. Co. C 5th O. V. I.
Houghton, Henry S., Pr. Tr. A 1st O. V. C.
Houghton, Tom, Pr. Co. F 5th O.V.I.
Howells, William L., Pr. Co. B 10th O. V. I.
Howey, William F., Pr. Co. A 10th O. V. I.
Howk, Harry M., Pr. Co. F 5th O.V.I.
Hudson, Alanson, Corp. Co. A 10th O. V. I.
Huettich, Rudolph C., Pr. Tr. B 1st O. V. C.
Huge, Charles, Pr. Co. K 5th O. V. I.
Hughes, George S., Pr. Tr. C 1st O. V. C.
Hughes, George W., Pr. Co. C 5th O. V. I.
Hughes, Glen T., Pr. Co. K 10th O.V.I.
Hughes, John E., Musician Co. I 5th O. V. I.
Hull, Robert C., Corp. Co. K 10th O. V. I.
Humelbaugh, Frank E., Pr. Co. A 10th O. V. I.
Humphrey, Wellington D., Pr. Co. K 5th O. V. I.
Hunt, William J., Sergt. Co. F 5th O. V. I.
Huntsman, John M., Pr. Co. B 10th O. V. I.
Hurley, James, Pr. Co. K 10th O. V. I.
Husbands, William A., Bat. Sergt. Maj. 5th O. V. I.
Hutchinson, Clarence H., Corp. Co. A 10th O. V. I.
Huxtable, Arthur J., Pr. Co. A 10th O. V. I.
Iago, Ralph A., Pr. Co. K 10th O.V.I.
Irwin, William, Pr. Co. A 10th O. V. I.

Isham, William, Corp. Co. C 5th O. V. I.
Jackson, Daniel, Pr. Co. D 9th Batt. O. V. I.
Jacobi, Edward W., Pr. Bat. A 1st O. V. A.
Jacobi, William R., Pr. Bat. A 1st O. V. A.
Jacobson, Albert W., Pr. Tr. C 1st O. V. C.
Jacobson, Gustav, Pr. Co. I 5th O.V.I.
James, Frank E., Pr. Co. C 5th O.V.I.
James, Guy M., Pr. Co. M 5th O. V. I.
James, Thomas, Pr. Tr. B 1st O. V. C.
Jamison, James K., Pr. Co. I 10th O. V. I.
Jasperson, Rudolph, Farrier Tr. C 1st O. V. C.
Jefferson, Henry, Sergt. Co. D 9th Batt. O. V. I.
Jenkins, Thomas A., Pr. Co. C 5th O. V. I.
Jennings, Patrick, Pr. Co. I 5th O.V.I.
Johns, Thomas W., Pr. Bat. A 1st O. V. A.
Johnson, Albert, Pr Co. C 5th O. V. I.
Johnson, Charles, Pr. Bat. A 1st O. V. A.
Johnson, Charles W., Pr. Tr. A 1st O. V. C.
Johnson, James E., Pr. Co. M 5th O. V. I.
Jones, Benjamin D., 12th Corp. Co. I 10th O. V. I.
Jones, Evan J., Pr. Co. K 10th O.V.I.
Joslyn, Alfred B., Pr. Co. F 5th O.V.I.
Joslyn, Louis B., Pr. Co. M 5th O.V.I.
Judd, Myron E., Pr. Co. B 5th O. V. I.
Kaltenmayer, Frank J., Corp. Co. I 5th O. V. I.
Kamm, Harry C., Pr. Co. B 10th O.V.I.
Kane, Gustav, Pr. Tr. C 1st O. V. C.
Kappenmacher, Gustav, Pr. Co. C 10th O. V. I.
Karnatz, Rudolph C., Pr. Co. I 10th O. V. I.
Kavanaugh, John W., Musician Co. B 10th O. V. I.
Keating, David T., Pr. Tr. A 1st O. V. C.
Keating, Maurice R., Pr. Co. C 10th O. V. I.
Keenan, John II., Corp. Co. I 5th O. V. I.
Keeshan, Michael, Corp. Co. I 5th O. V. I.
Keim, Harry W., 1st Sergt. Co. I 5th O. V. I.
Kelch, Samuel M., Pr. Co. I 5th O.V.I.
Kellar, Oscar, Pr. Co. C 5th O. V. I.
Kelley, Edward, Pr. Tr. C 1st O. V. C.
Kelley, Walter S., Corp. Co. I 5th O. V. I.
Kellogg, William R., Pr. Tr. A 1st O. V. C.
Kendis, Abie, Pr. Co. B 5th O. V. I.

Kennedy, Martin J., Pr. Co. B 5th O. V. C.
Kenney, Charles B., Pr. Co. F 5th O. V. I.
Kenney, Clarke E., Pr. Tr. C 1st O. V. I.
Kensinger, John I., Pr. Co. I 5th O.V.I.
Kepler, Harry L., Pr. Co. M 5th O.V.I.
Killinger, Charles G., Pr. Co. I 5th O. V. I.
King, Dewick, Pr. Co. I 10th O. V. I.
King, Tom, Pr. Tr. B 1st O. V. C.
Kingzett, William E., Pr. Bat. A 1st O. V. A.
Kintzler, Robert L., Pr. Co. K 10th O. V. I.
Kirk, Willie, Pr. Co. I 5th O. V. I.
Klein, Edward, Pr. Co. B 5th O. V. I.
Klein, George, Pr. Co. B 5th O. V. I.
Klein, Herman, Pr. Co. I 5th O. V. I.
Klockert, Henry, Pr. Bat. A 1st O.V.A.
Klopfstein, Samuel, Pr. Co. B 10th O. V. I.
Kluth, Robert, Pr. Co. F 5th O. V. I.
Knapp, Albert S., Pr. Co. F 5th O.V.I.
Kober, Joseph, Sergt. Co. A 10th O.V.I.
Koch, Jacob C., Pr. Co. B 10th O. V. I.
Kohler, Ferdinand, Pr. Co. I 5th O.V.I.
Kolsom, John, Pr. Co. I 5th O. V. I.
Kortonick, Louie, Pr. Co. C 10th O. V. I.
Kortonick, Tony, Pr. Co. C 10th O.V.I.
Kortz, John, Pr. Co. B 10th O. V. I.
Kosel, Charles J., Pr. Tr. G 1st O.V.C.
Kovach, Geza, Pr. Co. B 10th O. V. I.
Kranz, George R., Pr. Tr. B 1st O.V.C.
Krause, Henry C., Pr. Co. F 5th O.V.I.
Kreiger, Otto, Artificer Co. C 10th O. V. I.
Kremil, Frank, Pr. Tr. A 1st O. V. C.
Kuchenbecker, Fred H., Pr. Co. L 5th O. V. I.
Kuehn, Charles F., Pr. Co. C 10th O. V. I.
Kuehn, Louis, Pr. Co. K 5th O. V. I.
Kulish, Quido A., Pr. Bat. A 1st O. V. A.
Kusta, John, Jr., Musician Co. B 5th O. V. I.
Lacey, William C., Sergt. Co. L 5th O. V. I.
Lackmann, Frederick W., Pr. Co. A 10th O. V. I.
Lanckton, Edward G., Pr. Co. B 5th O. V. I.
Land, Nelson A., Pr. Co. K 10th O.V.I.
Langford, John, Pr. Co. B 5th O. V. I.
Langdon, Horace G., Corp. Co. B 5th O. V. I.
Lamb, Eugene H., Pr. Co. I 10th O. V. I.
Larimer, John M., Pr. Co. K 10th O. V. I.
Larimer, Melvin G., Artificer Co. K 10th O. V. I.
Latimer, Howard J., 1st Sergt. Co. C 5th O. V. I.

Laughlin, Charles L., Pr. Tr. G 1st O.
V. C.
Lawrence, Cloyd, Pr. Co. I 5th O. V. I.
Lawrence, James, Pr. Co. K 10th O.
V. I.
Lawrence, Walter H., Pr. Co. B 5th O.
V. I.
Lawyer, William J., Corp. Bat. A 1st
O. V. A.
Leland, Frederick K., Pr. Bat. A 1st
O. V. A.
Lenthall, John C., Pr. Co. I 10th O.
V. I.
Lenthall, William J., Pr. Co. K 10th
O. V. I.
Leopold, Otto F., Pr. Tr. A 1st O.V.C.
Letterle, Frank, Pr. Co. F 5th O. V. I.
Lever, Clarence C., Pr. Co. M 5th O.
V. I.
Levington, Robert H., Pr. Co. I 5th O.
V. I.
Lewis, Charles, Pr. Co. I 10th O. V. I.
Lewis, Charles H., Pr. Co. B 5th O.
V. I.
Lewis, Clarence A., Pr. Co. A 2nd U.
S. V. E.
Lewis, Daniel A., Pr. Co. A 3rd O.V.I.
Lewin, Frank, Pr. Co. B 5th O. V. I.
Lewis, Harry E., Pr. Co. D 9th Batt.
O. V. I.
Lewis, James P., Pr. Co. C 5th O. V. I.
Lewis, John L., Pr. Co. F 10th O. V. I.
Lewis, Theophilus, Pr. Tr. B 1st O.
V. C.
Leyland, George E., Pr. Co. K 5th O.
V. I.
Lichtenberg, Charles, Corp. Co. C 10th
O. V. I.
Lindow, Gustav, Pr. Co. C 10th O. V. I.
Lineham, James L., Pr. Tr. G 1st O.
V. C.
Linton, William B., Pr. Co. A 2nd U.
S. V. E.
Little, William, Pr. Tr. B 1st O. V. C.
Litwack, Morris, Pr. Co. F 5th O. V. I.
Lloyd, Howard, Pr. Tr. C 1st O. V. C.
Lloyd, Sanford L., Pr. Co. C 5th O.V.I.
Lockard, Oliver P., Pr. Co. C 10th O.
V. I.
Loewe, Fred E., Pr. Co. I 10th O.V.I.
Long, Charles F., Pr. Co. I 5th O.V.I.
Longtin, Hubert, Pr. Co. A 10th O.V.I.
Lothrop, Louis J., Pr. Co. B 10th O.V.I.
Loucks, Fred, Pr. Tr. C 1st O. V. C.
Loucks, Harry, Pr. Tr. C 1st O. V. C.
Louder, William E., Pr. Co. E 5th O.
V. I.
Love, Harry O., 5th Corp. Co. I 10th
O. V. I.
Lowe, John C., Pr. Co. L 5th O. V. I.
Lyman, Harry E., Pr. Co. I 5th O.V.I.
Lyon, Earnest, Pr. Co. B 5th O. V. I.
Machlener, Henry, Pr. Co. I 10th O.
V. I.
Mackay, William A., Pr. Co. C 5th O.
V. I.

Mackley, Harry S., Corp. Co. L 5th
O. V. I.
MacNeil, Howard E., Pr. Co. L 5th
O. V. I.
Macpherson, John, Wagoner Co. B 5th
O. V. I.
Madison, Clarence C., Pr. Bat. A 1st
O. V. A.
Maedje, Charles A., Corp. Co. L 5th O.
V. I.
Maher, Charles, Pr. Co. C 10th O. V. I.
Mahon, James, Pr. Co. C 10th O. V. I.
Mahrdt, John, Pr. Co. I 10th O. V. I.
Majors, Carl L., Pr. Co. I 10th O.V.I.
Maloney, Andrew, Pr. Co. B 10th O.
V. I.
Mann, Frank, Pr. Co. D 9th Batt. O.
V. I.
Mansfield, Harvey, 1st Sergt. Tr. A 1st
O. V. C.
Marion, Walter G., Pr. Co. D 9th Batt.
O. V. I.
Markow, Paul M., Pr. Co. K 10th O.
V. I.
Marks, Franklin H., Corp. Co. K 10th
O.V.I.
Marlett, Charley C., Corp. Co. K 10th
O. V. I.
Marsh, Aura C., Pr. Co. M 5th O. V. I.
Martin, Glenn W., Pr. Co. K 10th O.
V. I.
Martin, Paul, Pr. Co. C 10th O. V. I.
Martin, William G., Pr. Co. C 5th O.
V. I.
Martins, Bodd, Pr. Tr. B 1st O. V. C.
Mashek, Charles H., Musician Co. E
5th O. V. I.
Mashek, Otto, Musician Co. K 5th O.
V. I.
Mason, Thomas, Wagoner Co. I 10th
O. V. I.
Masten, Irvin J., Chief Musician 5th
O. V. I.
May, John, Pr. Co. B 5th O. V. I.
McAllister, Collin, Pr. Tr. A 1st O.V.C.
McArthur, Archibald, Pr. Co. B 5th O.
V. I.
McCarthy, George C., Artificer Co. A
10th O. V. I.
McCarthy, Thomas J., Pr. Co. C 10th
O. V. I.
McClain, Clement L. V., Pr. Co. A
10th O. V. I.
McCloskey, James, Pr. Co. I 5th O.V.I.
McClusky, John J., Pr. Co. L 5th O.V.I.
McCool, Patrick E., Pr. Co. B 5th O.
V. I.
McCormack, Frank W., Pr. Co. I 10th
O. V. I.
McCormick, John T., Pr. Co. L 5th O.
V. I.
McCormick, William, Pr. Co. K 5th O.
V. I.
McCormick, William T., Pr. Co. B 10th
O. V. I.
McConnell, Walter R., Pr. Tr. A 1st
O. V. C.

McCracken, Oliver P., Pr. Bat. A 1st O. V. A.

McCullough, William A., Pr. Co. K 5th O. V. I.

McCullough, William J., Pr. Co. I 5th O. V. I.

McDonald, James, Pr. Co. I 5th O.V.I.

McDonald, John T., Pr. Co. B 10th O. V. I.

McFerran, Joseph W., Pr. Co. L 5th O. V. I.

McGeen, Joseph, Pr. Tr. B 1st O. V. C.

McGovern, James, Pr. Co. C 10th O. V. I.

McGowan, John, Musician Co. A 10th O. V. I.

McGregor, John Corp. Tr. B 1st O. V. C.

McGuire, Newton L., Corp. Co. C 10th O. V. I.

McIsaac, Daniel, Pr. Co. K 10th O.V.I.

McKay, Robert F., Pr. Tr. G 1st O. V. C.

McKearney, Stephen R., Pr. Bat. A 1st O. V. A.

McKeown, Thomas P., Pr. Co. C 10th O. V. I.

McKoy, James, Pr. Tr. C 1st O. V. C.

McNamara, Thomas, Pr. Co. B 10th O. V. I.

McMahon, Harry R., Pr. Tr. A 1st O. V. C.

McMillen, Henry E., Jr., Q. M. Sergt. Co. K 10th O. V. I.

McNulty, Joseph, Pr. Co. I 5th O. V. I.

McPheeters, John, Corp. Co. D 9th Batt. O. V. I.

McPherson, William D., Pr. Co. K 5th O. V. I.

McQuinn, Oscar A., Pr. Co. F 5th O. V. I.

McSweeney, Edward, Pr. Bat. A 1st O. V. A.

Mead, Charles N., Pr. Tr. A 1st O.V.C.

Meade, William G., 3rd Sergt. Co. I 10th O. V. I.

Meech, William J., Pr. Co. L 5th O. V. I.

Meinke, William H., Pr. Tr. C 1st O. V. C.

Melick, John, Pr. Tr. G 1st O. V. C.

Mellen, Harry J., Pr. Co. L 5th O. V. I.

Merkel, Arthur E., Pr. Tr. A 1st O. V. C.

Messmer, Charles, Pr. Co. L 5th O.V.I.

Metcalf, Arthur C., Pr. Co. A 10th O. V. I.

Metzger, Jacob J., Sergt. Co. K 5th O. V. I.

Meyers, Albert J., Pr. Co. B 5th O.V.I.

Meyer, Charlie N., Pr. Co. B 5th O.V.I.

Meyer, Frank, Pr. Co. I 5th O. V. I.

Meyer, Joseph, Pr. Co. A 10th O.V.I.

Meyer, Otto G., 7th Corp. Co. I 10th O. V. I.

Michael, Levi, Pr. Tr. G 1st O. V. C.

Mill, Edward, Pr. Tr. B 1st . O. V. C.

Millar, Joseph H., 2nd Sergt. Tr. A 1st O. V. C.

Millard, H. Alfred, Pr. Tr. B 1st O. V. C.

Miles, Alfred G., Sergt. Tr. B 1st O. V. C.

Miller, Calvin J., Wagoner Co. A 10th O. V. I.

Miller, Frank E., Corp. Co. K 5th O. V. I.

Miller, Harry, Pr. Co. I 10th O. V. I.

Miller, Herman C., Pr. Tr. B 1st O. V. C.

Miller, Leonard, Pr. Co. K 5th O. V. I.

Miller, Miles R., Pr. Co. C 5th O. V. I.

Miller, Otto H., 2nd Sergt. Tr. C 1st O. V. C.

Miller, William J., Sergt. Co. A 10th O. V. I.

Milton, Charles H., Pr. Co. M 5th O. V. I.

Minnemeyer, Edward G., Jr., Pr. Co. I 10th O. V. J.

Minshall, Harry, Artificer Co. I 10th O. V. I.

Mills, Edward J., Pr. Co. K 5th O. V. I.

Mills, William L., Musician Co. C 10th O. V. I.

Mitermiler, Anton R., Musician Co. K 10th O. V. I.

Mitro, Andrew, Pr. Tr. B 1st O. V. C.

Mobley, Grier P., Pr. Co. B 5th O.V.I.

Molyneaux, Robert T., 2nd Sergt. Co. I 10th O. V. I.

Moore, Frank, Musician Co. D 9th Batt. O. V. I.

Monosmith, Edward H., Sergt. Co. K 10th O. V. I.

Monroe, Morris G., Pr. Co. C 5th O. V. I.

Monroe, Walter J., Sergt. Co. B 10th O. V. I.

Moravec, Frank, Pr. Co. B 10th O.V.I.

Morgan, George E., Corp. Co. C 5th O. V. I.

Morgan, Perry L., Pr. Co. I 10th O. V. I.

Morley, John E., Sergt. Tr. B 1st O. V. C.

Morris, Arthur B., Musician Co. D 9th Batt. O. V. I.

Morse, Charles B., Pr. Tr. A 1st O. V. C.

Morse, Herbert M., Pr. Co. F 5th O. V. I.

Morton, William E., Corp. Bat. A 1st O. V. A.

Motter, Wallace, Pr. Co. A 2nd U. S. V. E.

Mouson, George T., Pr. Co. I 5th O. V. I.

Moxon, John R., Sergt. Bat. A 1st O. V. A.

Mudge, Frederick T., Sergt. Bat. A 1st O. V. A.

Muir, Thomas J., Pr. Co. A 10th O.V.I.

Mulloy, John W., Pr. Co. K 10th O. V. I.

Munn, Frank J., Sergt. Co. B 5th O. V. I.

Munn, William G., Sergt. Co. C 10th O. V. I.

Murphy, Martin W., Pr. Co. C 5th O. V. I.

Murphy, Michael J., Sergt. Co. I. 5th O. V. I.

Murphy, Robert E., Pr. Co. A 10th O. V. I.

Murphy, Robert E., Pr. Tr. C 1st O. V. C.

Myers, Patrick, Pr. Co. D 9th Batt. O. V. I.

Myers, Robert H., Pr. Co. I 10th O. V. I.

Mylechraine, James A., Pr. Co. K 5th O. V. I.

Naab, Henry, Corp. Tr. A 1st O. V. C.

Najy, Illes, Pr. Co. L 5th O. V. I.

Nash, William F., 1st Sergt. Tr. C 1st O. V. C.

Neal, Daniel L., Pr. Tr. C 1st O. V. C.

Nejedly, Albert E., Corp. Co. L 5th O. V. I.

Nelson, Raymond C., Pr. Tr. C 1st O. V. C.

Nelson, William, Pr. Co. D 9th Batt. O. V. I.

Nicholson, Vincent E., Q. M. Sergt. Co. A 10th O. V. I.

Nickel, Charles, Pr. Co. F 5th O. V. I.

Nightingale, Robert J., Pr. Co. L 5th O. V. I.

Nilson, Ed., Pr. Co. I 5th O. V. I.

Newhouse, Clement L., Sergt. Co. A 10th O. V. I.

Newton, Harley L., Pr. Co. K 5th O. V. I.

Niver, Clarence B., Artificer Co. C 5th O. V. I.

Noble, Richard, Pr. Tr. B 1st O. V. C.

Nolan, William, Pr. Tr. C 1st O. V. C.

Nonzak, James, Pr. Co. B 5th O. V. I.

Noville, Carl F., Pr. Bat. A 1st O.V.A.

Nunrar, Adolph G., Sergt. Co. I 5th O. V. I.

Nye, Ralph, Pr. Tr. B 1st O. V. C.

O'Brien, Joseph W., Pr. Co. L 5th O. V. I.

O'Brien, William J., Pr. Bat. A 1st O. V. A.

O'Connor, John Z., Pr. Co. A 10th O. V. I.

O'Dell, Burton A., Corp. Co. A 10th O. V. I.

O'Donnell, Harry J., Pr. Co. F 5th O. V. I.

O'Donnell, Michael, Pr. Co. I 5th O. V. I.

O'Neill, Edward, Pr. Tr. C 1st O.V.C.

O'Neill, John Richard, Pr. Co. A 10th O. V. I.

O'Malley, John W., Pr. Tr. B 1st O. V. C.

O'Rourke, John, Pr. Co. K 10th O.V.I.

O'Rourke, Richard D., Pr. Bat. A 1st O. V. A.

O'Sullivan, Charles J., Pr. Tr. B 1st O. V. C.

Ollom, Charles R., Corp. Co. I 5th O. V. I.

Olson, John, Saddler Bat. A 1st O.V.A.

Opre, Harry E., Pr. Co. L 5th O. V. I.

Osborne, Ralph A., Pr. Co. F 5th O. V. I.

Oswald, Benjamin J., Corp. Co. L 5th O. V. I.

Ott, Charles J., Pr. Co. B 10th O. V. I.

Owens, James F., Pr. Co. A 10th O. V. I.

Owens, Lewis, Pr. Co. C 10th O. V. I.

Page, Clarence W., Pr. Co. L 5th O.V.I.

Palda, Leo J., Pr. Co. A 10th O. V. I.

Palmer, Augustus W., Pr. Co. B 5th O. V. I.

Palmer, Charles J., Musician Co. K 10th O. V. I.

Palmer, Dan J., Pr. Co. A 10th O. V. I.

Palmer, Granville E., 3rd Sergt. Tr. C 1st O. V. C.

Parisen, George B., Corp. Co. K 5th O. V. I.

Parks, Merton M., Pr. Co. B 5th O. V. I.

Parsons, George A., Pr. Co. C 5th O. V. I.

Patterson, Walter K., Musician Bat. A 1st O. V. A.

Paulitzky, Matthias, Pr. Co. I 5th O.V.I.

Pejano, Archie F., Pr. Tr. C 1st O.V.C.

Pellettier, John, Pr. Co. I 5th O. V. I.

Pender, John J., Jr., Pr. Co. M 5th O. V. I.

Perkins, Douglas, Jr., Corp. Tr. C 1st O. V. C.

Perkins, George A., Pr. Bat. A 1st O. V. A.

Peters, Oscar J., Pr. Co. I. 5th O. V. I.

Peters, Theodore C., Q. M. Sergt. Co. L 5th O. V. I.

Peters, Will F., Pr. Co. L 5th O. V. I.

Peterson, Axtell E., Corp. Co. F 5th O. V. I.

Peterson, Charles, Pr. Co. I 5th O.V.I.

Peterson, Herman, Pr. Co. B 5th O. V. I.

Petterson, Karl J., Pr. Tr. C 1st O.V.C.

Pfaff, Charles, Pr. Co. L 5th O. V. I.

Pfaffmann, Frederick W., Pr. Tr. C 1st O. V. C.

Phillips, Herbert A., Pr. Bat. A 1st O. V. A.

Phillips, William, Pr. Co. B 10th O. V. I.

Pickert, Richard, Pr. Co. I 5th O. V. I.

Pierce, Eugene J., Pr. Co. A 10th O. V. I.

Pim, Henry, Corp. Co. D 9th Batt. O. V. I.

Pinney, Warren L., Pr. Co. E 5th O. V. I.

Platt, John, Corp. Co. I 5th O. V. I.
Plotz, Frederick, Pr. Co. B 5th O.V.I.
Plumb, George E., Pr. Co. L 5th O.V.I.
Pohlman, William H., Corp. Co. B 5th O. V. I.
Poley, Charles H., Pr. Co. K 5th O.V.I.
Porter, Charles W., Pr. Co. B 10th O. V. I.
Potter, George, Musician Co. I 10th O. V. I.
Powell, Austin C., Pr. Bat. A 1st O. V. A.
Power, Homer, Pr. Co. A 10th O. V. I.
Prange, Emil F., Pr. Bat. A 1st O.V.A.
Pratt, Clyde E., Pr. Co. B 10th O. V. I.
Price, Joseph H., Pr. Co. C 10th O.V.I.
Price, Will E., Sergt. Co. C 10th O.V.I.
Purdy, William W., Pr. Bat. A 1st O. V. A.
Putsky, William F., Pr. Co. A 10th O. V. I.
Quay, Cephas W., Pr. Tr. B 1st O.V.C.
Quinlan, Frank, Pr. Co. I 10th O.V.I.
Quinn, Charles, Pr. Co. A 2nd U. S. V. E.
Radder, Fred, Corp. Co. B 10th O.V.I.
Radke, Anton, Pr. Co. B 5th O. V. I.
Rafter, Edward C., Pr. Co. B 10th O. V. I.
Rainey, Frank M., Pr. Tr. A 1st O.V.C.
Ralya, Harry B., Pr. Co. F 5th O.V.I.
Randall, Walter W., Pr. Co. C 10th O. V. I.
Ranke, Fred A., Pr. Co. M 5th O. V. I.
Ransom, Charles G., 1st Sergt. Co. B 10th O. V. I.
Rash, William Arthur, Pr. Co. C 10th O. V. I.
Raymond, Robert E., Pr. Co. B 10th O. V. I.
Read, George J., Pr. Co. C 5th O.V.I.
Record, Quince, Musician Co. L 5th O. V. I.
Reed, Burt J., Pr. Co. M 5th O. V. I.
Reed, Charles E., Pr. Co. I 10th O.V.I.
Reed, Charles P., Pr. Co. F 5th O.V.I.
Reeder, Schrole, Pr. Co. K 5th O. V. I.
Reese, William R., Pr. Tr. C 1st O.V.C.
Regan, Joseph, Pr. Co. I 10th O. V. I.
Rehark, Charles A., Corp. Co. F 5th O. V. I.
Reid, William H., Sergt. Co. K 10th O. V. I.
Reilly, William J., Pr. Co. B 10th O. V. I.
Reisdorf, Edward J., Artificer Co. L 5th O. V. I.
Reisdorph, William, Pr. Co. B 5th O. V. I.
Reuss, Fred G., Pr. Co. I 10th O.V.I.
Revere, Paul A., Q. M. Sergt. Co. I 10th O. V. I.
Reynolds, Thomas, Pr. Co. B 5th O. V. I.
Rezner, John S., Pr. Co. A 10th O.V.I.
Rhoads, John A., Pr. Co. L 5th O. V. I.
Rice, Clyde V., Pr. Tr. B 1st O. V. C.

Richards, Gomer D., Pr. Co. H 10th O. V. I.
Rickards, Raymond L., Pr. Co. B 5th O. V. I.
Richardson, Samuel H., Pr. Bat. A 1st O. V. A.
Riggs, Wesley, Pr. Co. I 5th O. V. I.
Rix, Ira B., Corp. Co. K 10th O. V. I.
Robejsek, James, Pr. Co. I 5th O.V.I.
Robb, Reginald H., Corp. Co. I 5th O. V. I.
Robbins, Clarence C., Corp. Co. A 10th O. V. I.
Roberts, Alvord V., Sergt. Bat. A 1st O. V. A.
Roberts, Edward, Pr. Co. D 9th Batt. O. V. I.
Roberts, James T., Musician Co. C 10th O. V. I.
Robinson, Abe, Pr. Co. B 10th O. V. I.
Robinson, John, Pr. Co. D 9th Batt. O. V. I.
Rock, Edward H., Pr. Co. C 10th O. V. I.
Rodermond, Charles B., 1st Sergt. Co. A 10th O. V. I.
Rodocker, Charles P., Pr. Co. I 5th O. V. I.
Rodsensky, Otto F., Pr. Co. B 5th O. V. I.
Roemer, Harry A., Corp. Co. C 5th O. V. I.
Roemer, Harvey H., Musician Co. C 5th O. V. I.
Rogers, Frank, Musician Co. F 5th O. V. I.
Rolfe, Guy M., Pr. Co. K 5th O. V. I.
Roney, Lorenza J., Corp. Co. A 10th O. V. I.
Roth, Emil A., Pr. Co. A 10th O. V. I.
Root, Henry O., Corp. Co. B 5th O. V. I.
Rowley, Walter D., Pr. Co. K 5th O. V. I.
Ruff, Joseph, Pr. Co. A 10th O. V. I.
Russell, Alexander, Pr. Co. C 5th O. V. I.
Russell, Charles C., Pr. Co. B 5th O. V. I.
Russell, George G., Pr. Co. A 10th O. V. I.
Russon, Henry R., Pr. Bat A 1st O. V. A.
Ruthven, Neil, Pr. Co. C 5th O. V. I.
Ryan, John L., Pr. Co. B 5th O. V. I.
Ryder, Clarence A., Pr. Co. C 10th O. V. I.
Ryder, John R., Pr. Co. C 10th O. V. I.
Sabine, Fred R., Pr. Co. F 5th O.V.I.
Sackwitz William, Pr. Bat. A 1st O. V. A.
Sage, David A., Guidon Bat. A 1st O. V. A.
Salewski, Samuel, Pr. Co. K 5th O.V.I.
Sanderson, Charles W., Pr. Co. B 5th O. V. I.

Sanderson, William, Pr. Tr. A 1st O. V. C.

Sapp, Hayden C., Sergt. Co. L 5th O. V. I.

Sattler, Joseph A., Pr. Co. K 10th O. V. I.

Sauenskey, Charles H., Pr. Co. L 5th O. V. I.

Sawyer, Harry B., Pr. Tr. A 1st O.V.C.

Schaar, Vincent D., Pr. Co. C 10th O. V. I.

Schaffer, Charles C., Pr. Bat. A 1st O. V. A.

Schaffer, Frank F., Pr. Tr. G 1st O. V. C.

Scheuring, Oscar, Pr. Co. C 10th O.V.I.

Sclawr, William, Pr. Co. I 5th O. V. I.

Schliess, Frank C., Pr. Co. M 3rd O. V. I.

Schmenk, Frank B., Pr. Co. K 10th O. V. I.

Schmenk, Henry B., Pr. Co. K 10th O. V. I.

Schmidt, Gustaf, Artificer Co. B 5th V. I.

Schmitt, John C., Pr. Tr. B 1st O.V.C.

Schmitz, Ludwig, Wagoner Co. I 5th O. V. I.

Schmunk, Walter G., Pr. Bat. A 1st O. V. A.

Schneider, Carl F., Pr. Co. F 5th O. V. I.

Schneider, Fank F., Pr. Co. B 5th O. V. I.

Schneider, Frederick, Pr. Bat. A 1st O. V. A.

Schneider, Herbert L., Corp. Bat. A 1st O. V. A.

Schneider, Michael J., Sergt. Co. B 5th O. V. I.

Schofield, Sherman W., Pr. Tr. A 1st O. V. C.

Schorn, Fred F., Pr. Co. C 5th O.V.I.

Schott, Otto, Jr., Pr. Co. I 10th O.V.I.

Schubert, Carl W., Corp. Co. B 10th O. V. I.

Schuler, Clarence C., Pr. Co. C 5th O. V. I.

Schultz, Louie F., Pr. Co. A 10th O. V. I.

Schroeder, John M., Pr. Co. B 5th O. V. I.

Schurdell, Edward H., Pr. Co. I 10th O. V. I.

Schwab, Clyde, Pr. Co. B 5th O. V. I.

Schwab, Daniel P., Pr. Tr. C 1st O. V. C.

Schwab, Frank W., Pr. Tr. C 1st O. V. C.

Schwahn, William H., Pr. Co. I 10th O. V. I.

Schwarz, Peter W., Pr. Co. F 5th O. V. I.

Schwentner, Frank F., Pr. Bat. A 1st O. V. A.

Scofield, Donald C., Corp. Co. B 10th O. V. I.

Scott, Edwin C., Pr. Co. K 5th O. V. I.

Scott, Sydney B., Sergt. Co. F 5th O. V. I.

Sealand, Frank N., Pr. Tr. A 1st O. V. C.

Seckel, Albert, Pr. Co. K 5th O. V. I.

Seidman, Adolph, Pr. Co. I 5th O.V.I.

Seifert, Albin, Pr. Co. A 10th O. V. I.

Seith, Daniel P., Sergt. Co. K 5th O. V. I.

Seith, Henry A., Pr. Co. K 5th O. V. I.

Seith, Louis F., Pr. Co. I 5th O. V. I.

Sellers, Samuel L., 10th Corp. Co. I 10th O. V. I.

Selmin, Edward E., Pr. Co. M 5th O. V. I.

Semon, Frank R., Sergt. Co. K 10th O. V. I.

Semon, John C., Pr. Co. C 5th O. V. I.

Senne, Adam, Pr. Co. I 10th O. V. I.

Seward, J Carl, Pr. Tr. B 1st O. V. C.

Shanks, Charles B., 2nd Sergt. Tr. A 1st O. V. C.

Sharp, Charles, Corp. Co. D 9th Batt. O. V. I.

Shaw, Vernon R., Pr. Tr. C 1st O.V.C.

Shaw, William A., Pr. Co. L 5th O.V.I.

Shaw, William, Pr. Tr. B 1st O. V. C.

Sheffield, Leander V., Pr. Co. A 10th O. V. I.

Sheffield, Ray, Pr. Co. A 2nd U. S. V. E.

Shelsinger, Albert W., Pr. Tr. C 1st O. V. C.

Sherbarth, Albert, Pr. Co. I 5th O. V. I.

Sheridan, Henry H. K., 4th Sergt. Tr. C 1st O. V. C.

Sherwood, Charles F., 1st Sergt. Tr. B 1st O. V. C.

Shikowsky, Emil, Pr. Co. C 10th O.V.I.

Shilling, John M., Pr. Co. B 10th O. V. I.

Shorb, Orren E., Pr. Tr. C 1st O.V.C.

Shupe, John P., Corp. Co. A 10th O. V. I.

Shute, Arthur S., Pr. Co. F 5th O.V.I.

Sicha, Antone E., Pr. Co. I 5th O.V.I.

Sill, James B., Sergt. Co. F 5th O.V.I.

Simmonds, Harry, Pr. Co. C 5th O.V.I.

Simmons, George S., Jr., Pr. Co. F 5th O. V. I.

Sindelar, Joseph, Musician Co. C 5th O. V. I.

Singletary, Howard A., Corp. Bat. A 1st O. V. A.

Sitzenstock, Carl A., Pr. Co. A 10th O. V. I.

Skeel, Louis A., Pr. Bat. A 1st O.V.A.

Skinner, Finlay C., Pr. Tr. G 1st O. V. C.

Sladden, Edwin C., Pr. Co. K 10th O. V. I.

Slater, Adolph, Pr. Co. C 10th O. V. I.

Slemmons, William C., Pr. Tr. C 1st O. V. C.

Slousky, Henry A., Pr. Co. A 10th O. V. I.

Slosson, Howard B., Pr. Co. A 10th O. V. I.

Smick, John F., Pr. Bat. A 1st O.V.A.

Smies, George H., Pr. Bat. A 1st O. V. A.

Smith, Albert E., Pr. Tr. A 1st O.V.C.

Smith, Augustus E., Pr. Co. F 5th O. V. I.

Smith, Cassius J., Pr. Tr. B 1st O.V.C.

Smith, Cortez B., Pr. Tr. C 1st O. V. C.

Smith, Frank B., Pr. Co. F 5th O.V.I.

Smith, John, Pr. Co. B 5th O. V. I.

Smith, Norton T., Pr. Tr. A 1st O.V.C.

Smith, Pard H., Sergt. Tr. B 1st O. V. C.

Smith, Wellington J., Pr. Co. C 5th O. V. I.

Smith William F., Pr. Co. F 5th O.V.I.

Smith, William H., Pr. Bat. A 1st O. V. A.

Snuth, Herbert A., Pr. Bat. A 1st O. V. A.

Snyder, Hurbert M., Pr. Co. B 10th O. V. I.

Soeder, Henry, Pr. Co. I 10th O. V. I.

Sommers, James, Pr. Co. D 9th Batt. O. V. I.

Spear, Leon S., Pr. Co. K 10th O.V.I.

Spears, James, Musician Co. M 5th O. V. I.

Spitz, Coleman, Pr. Co. I 5th O. V. I.

Spitz, Jack, Pr. Co. L 5th O. V. I.

Sprengle, David S., Pr. Co. F 5th O. V. I.

Stafford, Benjamin F., Jr., Corp. Co. K 10th O. V. I.

Stair, John, Pr. Co. D 9th Batt. O.V.I.

Stanton, Arthur H., Pr. Tr. B 1st O. V. C.

Starkweather, William J., Jr., 6th Sergt. Tr. C 1st O. V. C.

Starrett, Arthur J., Corp. Co. K 10th O. V. I.

Stedrousky, Stephen A., Pr. Co. C 10th O. V. I.

Steen, Andrew S., Pr. Co. I 10th O.V.I.

Stein, George, Pr. Co. I 5th O. V. I.

Stevens, Allan W., Pr. Co. G 5th O.V.I.

Stevens, George, Pr. Tr. A 1st O.V.C.

Stevens, William L., 6th Corp. Co. I 10th O. V. I.

Stewart, Floyd A., Sergt. Co. D 9th Batt. O. V. I.

Stewart, Julius, Pr. Co. L 5th O. V. I.

Stewart, Samuel C., Pr. Co. C 5th O. V. I.

Stewart, Samuel T., 1st Corp. Co. I 10th O. V. I.

Stewart, Seth, Pr. Co. D 9th Batt. O. V. I.

Stone, Charles E., Pr. Tr. B 1st O. V. C.

Stotter, Joe, Corp. Co. C 10th O. V. I.

Straka, Joseph F., Pr. Co. C 10th O.V.I.

Strauss, Louis, Pr. Co. K 6th O. V. I.

Strauss, Solomon, Pr. Co. I 5th O.V.I.

Strickland, William, Pr. Co. G 5th O. V. I.

Stroeiner, Adolf, Pr. Co. A 10th O. V. I.

Struck, Emil, Pr. Tr. C 1st O. V. C.

Studer, Thomas, Pr. Co. A 10th O.V.I.

Sturge, Thomas, Pr. Co. F 5th O. V. I.

Suck, John C., Pr. Co. K 5th O. V. I.

Suitil, John F., Pr. Co. B 10th O. V. I.

Sullivan, Daniel, Pr. Co. B 5th O.V.I.

Sunderland, Ralph, Pr. Tr. B 1st O. V. C.

Sutter, Berton D., Pr. Bat. A 1st O. V. A.

Sutton, Hal., Pr. Co. I 10th O. V. I.

Swaffield, Harry, Pr. Co. C 10th O.V.I.

Swartwood, Josiah B., Pr. Co. A 10th O. V. I.

Talkes, Stephen H., Pr. Tr. B 1st O. V. C.

Tate, Eugene, Pr. Co. D 9th Batt. O. V. I.

Tavernie, Peter, Pr. Tr. C 1st O. V. C.

Taylor, Clarence E., Pr. Bat. A 1st O. V. A.

Taylor, Frederick C., Chief Trumpeter 1st O. V. C.

Taylor, Percy S., Pr. Co. B 5th O.V.I.

Taylor, Reginald E., Pr. Tr. G 1st O. V. C.

Taylor, William E., Pr. Co. K 5th O. V. I.

Teahan, Daniel M., Pr. Co. B 5th O. V. I.

Te Linde, William, Pr. Bat. A 1st O. V. A.

Terrett, Thomas C., Pr. Bat. A 1st O. V. A.

Tharp, Charles W., Pr. Co. A 2nd U. S. V. E.

Thiessen, Frederick, Pr. Bat. A 1st O. V. A.

Thoemmes, William T., Pr. Co. C 10th O. V. I.

Thomas, Edward A., Pr. Co. K 5th O. V. I.

Thomas, Edward P., Pr. Co. 5th O. V. I.

Thompson, Clarence E., Pr. Bat. A 1st O. V. A.

Thompson, Harry A., 2nd Sergt. Co. C 5th O. V. I.

Thompson, Tod T., Pr. Co. B 10th O. V. I.

Throup, Alfred, Pr. Co. B 5th O. V. I.

Toland, Daniel, Pr. Co. L 5th O. V. I.

Tompkins, Edmund B., 5th Sergt. Co. I 10th O. V. I.

Toomey, John M., Pr. Co. K 5th O.V.I.

Tovell, Fred H., 9th Corp. Co. I 10th O. V. I.

Tracy, Jerry A., Pr. Bat. A 1st O.V.A.

Traxler, Edwin A., Pr. Co. B 5th O. V. I.

Tuck, Thomas B., Pr. Co. B 5th O.V.I.

Turner, Frank G., Sergt. Co. K 5th O. V. I.

Tuttle, Horace B., Corp. Tr. A 1st O. V. C.

Twitchell, George F., Pr. Co. I 10th O. V. I.

Twitchell, Lee D., Pr. Tr. A 1st O.V.C.

Tyler, Ralph H., Pr. Co. C 10th O.V.I.

Tyler, Roy D., Pr. Co. C 5th O. V. I.

Ubessax, Frank C., Pr. Co. K 5th O. V. I.

Udell, Merton A., Pr. Tr. C 1st O.V.C.

Uhlir, Frank J., Pr. Co. C 5th O. V. I.

Updegrove, Doane J., Pr. Co. C 5th O. V. I.

Urack, Max H., Pr. Co. K 10th O.V.I.

Vacha, Edward J., Pr. Co. B 5th O.V.I.

Vanderwerf, Martin E., Corp. Co. B 5th O. V. I.

Vaughan, George J., Pr. Co. C. 5th O. V. I.

Vaupel, Albert H. C., 2nd Corp. Co. I 10th O. V. I.

Venning, Ralph J., 4th Sergt. Tr. A 1st O. V. C.

Villard, Allen J., Pr. Co. L 5th O. V. I.

Vincent, Richard R., 1st Sergt. Co. L 5th O. V. I.

Vining, William W., Blacksmith Bat. A 1st O. V. A.

Vinton, Charles A., Pr. Bat. A 1st O. V. A.

Volk, Frederick G., Pr. Bat. A 1st O. V. A.

Vormelker, Herman A., Pr. Co. I 5th O. V. I.

Voukorm, Fred, Principal Musician 5th O. V. I.

Wabel, Francis E., Corp. Bat. A 1st O. V. I.

Wachs, Adam R., Wagoner Co. K 5th O. V. I.

Wadkins, Lem., Pr. Co. D 9th Batt. O. V. A.

Wagner, Charles W., Pr. Tr. C 1st O. V. C.

Wagner, Fred, Pr. Co. I 10th O. V. I.

Wald, Frederick W., Pr. Co. K 10th O. V. I.

Waldo, Harold P., Pr. Co. B 10th O. V. I.

Walker, Charles S., Pr. Co. K 5th O. V. I.

Walsh, James L., Pr. Co. I 10th O.V.I.

Walter, Eugene, Pr. Tr. A 1st O. V. C.

Walter, Louis P., Pr. Co. K 10th O.V.I.

Walters, Edward L., Q. M. Sergt. F. and S. 5th O. V. I.

Walworth, Louis M., Pr. Co. K 5th O. V. I.

Wamser, Charles, Pr. Co. I 5th O. V. I.

Warfel, George W., Corp. Co. A 10th O. V. I.

Warington, James, Pr. Co. I 5th O. V. I.

Warner, Carl F., Pr. Co. C 5th O.V.I.

Warnke, George A., Corp. Co. I 5th O. V. I.

Waters, George F., Pr. Co. L 5th O.V.I.

Waterbury, Roy W., Pr. Co. B 5th O. V. I.

Watson, Frank, Pr. Co. C 10th O. V. I.

Watters, Harry, Pr. Tr. C 1st O. V. C.

Weaser, Joseph F., Pr. Co. M 5th O. V. I.

Weaver, Franklin C., Pr. Co. B 10th O. V. I.

Weaver, Orlando L., Pr. Bat. A 1st O. V. A.

Weber, Harry F., Corp. Co. L 5th O. V. I.

Weber, William, Pr. Co. I 10th O.V.I.

Weber, William S., Pr. Co. C 10th O. V. I.

Wehagen, John H., Pr. Bat. A 1st O. V. A.

Wehle, Oscar C., Pr. Co. L 5th O. V. I.

Wehr, Adam, Pr. Tr. C 1st O. V. C.

Weik, Louis D., Pr. Co. K 5th O. V. I.

Weiss, Morris, Pr. Co. B 10th O. V. I.

Wells, George J., Pr. Co. I 10th O.V.I.

Wells, William, Pr. Co. I 5th O. V. I.

Welsch, Bernhard, Pr. Co. I 5th O.V.I.

Welsh, John, Pr. Co. C 10th O. V. I.

Welsh, William, Pr. Tr. C 1st O. V. C.

Wenzel, Edward H., Pr. Tr. C 1st O. V. C.

Werner, Fred., Pr. Co. I 5th O. V. I.

West, Edward, Pr. Co. A 10th O. V. I.

Weston, Frank J., Pr. Tr. B 1st O.V.C.

Wheeler, Frank W., Corp. Co. K 10th O. V. I.

White, Arthur H., Pr. Co. C 10th O.V.I.

White, Henry C., Sergt. Tr. B 1st O. V. C.

White, Howard C., Pr. Co. C 5th O. V. I.

White, Robert H., Corp. Co. A 10th O. V. I.

Whitney, Stanley A., Pr. Co. K 10th O. V. I.

Wiegert, Harry, Pr. Co. I 5th O. V. I.

Wileman, Abram N., Pr. Co. I 10th O. V. I.

Wiley, Craig, Pr. Co. D 9th Batt. O. V. I.

Wilhelm, Ray C., Pr. Co. A 10th O.V.I.

Winter, Frank F., Pr. Tr. C 1st O.V.C.

Williams, Albert I., Corp. Co. D 9th Batt. O. V. I.

Williams, Chester S., Pr. Co. I 10th O. V. I.

Williams, David C., Pr. Co. K 10th O. V. I.

Williams, Edward M., Pr. Co. I 10th O. V. I.

Williams, James, Pr. Co. I 5th O. V. I.

Williams, Samuel M., Pr. Co. L 5th O. V. I.

Williams, William, Pr. Co. C 10th O. V. I.

Williams, William H., Corp. Co. K 10th O. V. I.

Williams, William P., Sergt. Bat. A 1st O. V. A.

Witte, Edward H., Pr. Co. I 10th O. V. I.

Witte, George A., Pr. Co. I 10th O.V.I.

Wolfram, Alfonzo J., Pr. Co. A 10th O. V. I.

Wood, Roy A., Pr. Co. B 5th O. V. I.

Wood, William, Pr. Co. D 9th Batt. O. V. I.

Woodman, Fred A., Pr. Co. F 5th O. V. I.

Woodruff, William, Pr. Co. H 5th O. V. I.

Woods, Joseph J., Pr. Tr. A 1st O.V.C.

Wright, Roscoe L., Pr. Tr. B 1st O. V. C.

Wrobbel, Edward, Pr. Co. A 10th O. V. I.

Wyman, Burt E., Pr. Co. F 5th O.V.I.

Yates, George L., Pr. Co. D 9th Batt. O. V. I.

Yoos, Fred W., Pr. Tr. C 1st O. V. C.

Young, John M., Pr. Tr. C 1st O.V.C.

Young, Robert E., Sergt. Co. L 5th O. V. I.

Zadrow, Paul J., Pr. Bat. A 1st O.V.A.

Zeitner, August W. F., Pr. Tr. C 1st O. V. C.

Zimmer, Henry, Pr. Co. K 10th O.V.I.

Zimmer, William, Pr. Co. K 10th O. V. I.

Zimmerman, William C., Pr. Co. B 5th O. V. I.

Zoller, Edward, Pr. Co. B 10th O. V. I.

CLIPPER MILLS

Thivener, Thomas, Pr. Co. C 7th O. V. I.

CLYDE

Aldrich, Clare D., Pr. Co. I 6th O.V.I.

Aldrich, Eugene M., Pr. Co. I 6th O. V. I.

Anderson, Sherwood B., Pr. Co. I 6th O. V. I.

Becker, Lewis, Corp. Co. I 6th O. V. I.

Berrigan, Frank, Artificer Co. I 6th O. V. I.

Bennett, Warner, Pr. Co. I 6th O. V. I.

Bishop, Fred, Pr. Co. I 6th O. V. I.

Brown, Eugene E., Pr. Co. I 6th O.V.I.

Buzzell, Arthur R., Pr. Co. I 6th O. V. I.

Cooper, Howard J., Pr. Co. I 6th O. V. I.

Covill, William H., Pr. Co. I 6th O.V.I.

Crockett, Elijah B., Pr. Co. I 6th O. V. I.

Dennis, Charles L., Pr. Co. I 6th O.V.I.

Dennis, Mack A., Corp. Co. I 6th O. V. I.

Eisenhard, John W., Pr. Co. I 6th O. V. I.

Elliott, Joel B., Wagoner Co. I 6th O. V. I.

Engler, William B., Pr. Co. I 6th O. V. I.

Ford, Caddie E., Corp. Co. I 6th O.V.I.

Gallagher, Ernest J., Pr. Co. I 6th O. V. I.

Geiger, Edward J., Pr. Co. I 6th O.V.I.

Gettius, George F., Sergt. Co. I 6th O. V. I.

Gray, George N., Pr. Co. I 6th O. V. I.

Haff, Merrit C., Pr. Co. I 6th O. V. I.

Harris, Ura G., Corp. Co. I 6th O.V.I.

Hawk, Chancey, Pr. Co. I 6th O. V. I.

Hess, Reuben W., Jr., Pr. Co. I 6th O. V. I.

Holtz, William A., Pr. Co. I 6th O.V.I.

Houser, Ora L., Pr. Co. I 6th O. V. I.

Jessop, Walter F., Pr. Co. I 6th O. V. I.

Lee, Albert F., Pr. Co. I 6th O. V. I.

Lemmon, Charles N., Pr. Co. I 6th O. V. I.

Lemmon, George W., Pr. Co. I 6th O. V. I.

Lemmon, Leroy, Sergt. Co. I 6th O. V. I.

Lemmon, Mack, Pr. Co. I 6th O. V. I.

May, James H., Corp. Co. I 6th O.V.I.

Mann, Edward, Pr. Co. I 6th O. V. I.

Mann, Robert, Pr. Co. I 6th O. V. I.

McCleary, Charles M., Pr. Co. I 6th O. V. I.

Miller, Harkness, Corp. Co. I 6th O. V. I.

Moffat, Dana C., Pr. Co. C 6th O. V. I.

Needham, William H., Pr. Co. I 6th O. V. I.

Parkhurst, David J., Pr. Bat. C 1st O. V. A.

Raymond, Charles, Sergt. Co. I 6th O. V. I.

Rife, Charles H., Pr. Co. I 6th O. V. I.

Robinson, Alvin I., 1st Sergt. Co. I 6th O. V. I.

Robinson, Howard H., Pr. Co. I 6th O. V. I.

Robinson, Mack, Corp. Co. I 6th O. V. I.

Sargeant, Harry D., Pr. Co. I 6th O. V. I.

Sargeant, William A., Pr. Co. I 6th O. V. I.

Scanlan, Jerrie N., Pr. Co. I 6th O.V.I.

Scott, Ernest W., Pr. Co. I 6th O. V. I.

Scott, William E., Pr. Co. I 6th O.V.I.

Sellinger, William, Sergt. Co. I 6th O. V. I.

Selvey, Manley C., Pr. Co. I 6th O.V.I.

Smith, Robert S., Pr. Co. I 6th O.V.I.

Sowell, Norris W., Pr. Co. I 6th O.V.I.

Sowell, Scott L., Corp. Co. I 6th O. V. I.

Stark, Horace, Pr. Co. I 6th O. V. I.

Stieff, Cloyd A., Pr. Co. I 6th O. V. I.
Stieff, George G., Pr. Co. I 6th O.V.I.
Strong, Frederick G., Pr. Co. I 6th O.
V. I.
Trump, Scott W., Pr. Co. I 6th O.V.I.
Trump, William C., Pr. Bat. C 1st O.
V. A.
Vickery, Bert, Pr. Co. I 6th O. V. I.

Weeks, Fred E., Sergt. Co. I 6th O.
V. I.
Westbrook, Frank J., Pr. Co. I 6th
O. V. I.
Wickersham, Adam M., Pr. Co. I 6th
O. V. I.
Wilson, Burton J., Pr. Co. I 6th O.V.I.

COALGROVE

Kelly, Frank, Pr. Co. I 7th O. V. I.
Kelly, James M., Pr. Co. I 7th O. V. I.
Moseman, William M., Pr. Co. I 7th
O. V. I.

Palmer, Emory W., Pr. Co. I 7th O.
V. I.
Zimmerman, Oscar J., Pr. Co. I 7th O.
V. I.

COAL RUN

Weiss, Jacob T., Pr. Co. D 7th O. V. I.

COLLAMER

Robinson, Harry L., Pr. Co. I 5th O. V. J.

COLLEGE HILL

Harris, Clinton B., Corp. Co. C 2nd
U. S. V. E.

Wild, Walter R., Pr. Co. I 1st O. V. I.

COLLINS

Perkins, Jay W., Pr. Co. G 5th O. V. I.

Shaw, Floyd L., Pr. Co. G 5th O. V. I.

COLLINWOOD

Burroughs, Charles D., 3rd Sergt. Co.
C 5th O. V. I.
Cosford, Ernest G. B., Pr. Co. F 5th
O. V. I.
Cushman, Fred L., Pr. Co. M 5th O.
V. I.
Dady, Edwin C., Pr. Co. I 5th O. V. I.
Dady, Roy M., Pr. Co. I 5th O. V. I.

Farmer, Willard A., Artificer Co. E 5th
O. V. I.
Glaser, Charles, Pr. Co. I 5th O. V. I.
Hoffman, Elic. A., Pr. Co. B 5th O.V.I.
Sobey, Percy W., Pr. Co. I 5th O. V. I.
Williams, Frederick G., Wagoner Co.
L 5th O. V. I.

COLTON

Jackson, Chester D., Musician Co. C 6th O. V. I.

COLUMBUS

Abraham, Thomas, Pr. Co. D 9th Batt.
O. V. I.
Acker, John S., 5th Sergt. Co. A 4th
O. V. I.
Affleck, Edward T., Jr., Corp. Bat. H
1st O. V. A.
Allen, Ethan H., Pr. Co. A 2nd U. S.
V. E.
Allen, Robert S., Pr. U. R. 9th Batt.
O. V. I.
Alexander, Ernest, Pr. Co. D 9th Batt.
O. V. I.
Algeo, Thomas B., Pr. Bat. H 1st O.
V. A.

Anderson, Harry T., Pr. Bat. H 1st O.
V. A.
Anderson, Lewis, Musician Co. F 4th
O. V. I.
Anderson, William, Pr. Co. D 9th
Batt. O. V. I.
Andrews, Lucius B., Q. M. Sergt. Co.
A 4th O. V. I.
Anthony, Carl H., Sergt. Bat. H 1st
O. V. A.
Amrine, William F., Pr. U. R. 4th O.
V. I.
Arlidge, Charles A., Pr. Co. F 6th O.
V. I.

Armadale, Elwood A., Pr. Co. D 9th
Batt. O. V. I.
Armstrong. Paul, Sergt. Co. C 4th O.
V. I.
Arthur. Joseph, Pr. Co. B 4th O. V. I.
Ashley, Arthur, Pr. Tr. D 1st O. V. C.
Auld, James Albert, 4th Sergt. Co. A
4th O. V. I.
Baehr, George S., Pr. Co. C 4th O.V.I.
Baker, Zachary T., Pr. Bat. H 1st O.
V. A.
Balsley. Lloyd W., Pr. Co. C 4th O.V.I.
Balz, Christian F.! Pr. Bat. H 1st O.
V. A.
Bame, Frank H., Pr. Co. A 2nd U. S.
V. E.
Barber, William, Jr., Pr. Co. D 9th
Batt. O. V. I.
Bargar, Frederick C., Sergt. Tr. D 1st
O. V. C.
Barker, Harry L., Sergt. Co. C 4th O.
V. I.
Barlow. Moses H., Pr. Co. F 4th O.V.I.
Barnes. Perry M., Pr. Co. A 4th O.V.I.
Barnett, William M., Corp. Co. B 9th
Batt. O. V. I.
Barnhart. Cyrus, Pr. U. R. 4th O. V. I.
Bauer, Charles F., Pr. Co. C 4th O.V.I.
Bauman, Ora A., Pr. Co. A 3rd O.V.I.
Beals, Harry, Pr. Bat. H 1st O. V. A.
Beatty, John W., Pr. Co. D 9th Batt.
O. V. I.
Belcher, Walter C., Pr. Co. B 9th Batt.
O. V. I.
Benjamin, Charles H., Pr. Tr. D 1st
O. V. C.
Benkert, Louis, Pr. U. R. 4th O. V. I.
Bennett, William C., Pr. Bat. H 1st O.
V. A.
Bergwitz, William B., Pr. Co. A 4th
O. V. I.
Bethel, Ellsworth, Pr. Co. D 9th Batt.
O. V. I.
Biddle, Edward M., 1st Sergt. Co. C 4th
O. V. I.
Biddle, Frank C., Corp. Co. C 4th O.
V. I.
Bigelow, Madison, Pr. Co. E 3rd O.V.I.
Billett. Arthur J., Pr. Co. A 3rd O.V.I.
Blake, Monroe H., Pr. Tr. G 1st O.
V. C.
Blakley. Worley S., Pr. Co. F 4th O.
V. I.
Bliss, Amos L., Pr. Bat. H 1st O.V.A.
Bliss, Marvel W., Pr. Co. C 4th O.V.I.
Bodkins. George W., Pr. Co. A 2nd
U. S. V. E.
Boehm. John, Pr. Co. I 5th O. V. I.
Bolden, Samuel, Pr. Co. B 9th Batt.
O. V. I.
Bolin, Charles E., Corp. Co. B 4th O.
V. I.
Bonn, Oliver H., Corp. Co. A 4th O.
V. I.
Bopp. Edwin C., Pr. Bat. H 1st O.V.A.
Bourne, Benjamin R., Pr. Co. A 3rd
O. V. I.

Bowen, Charles T., Pr. Co. F 4th O.
V. I.
Boyer, Charles H., Pr. Co. A 10th O.
V. I.
Bradfield. Albert D., Pr. Co. E 10th O.
V. I.
Braim, John W., Sergt. Co. A 2nd U.
S. V. E.
Branson, John S., Pr. Tr. D 1st O.V.C.
Braunschweig, John, Pr. Co. A 2nd U.
S. V. E.
Brewer, Claude L., Pr. Co. C 10th O.
V. I.
Brodbeck, Edward, Pr. Tr. D 1st O.
V. C.
Bromley, Noel L., Sergt. Co. D 9th
Batt. O. V. I.
Brooks, James, Pr. Go. D 9th Batt. O.
V. I.
Brown, Charles Frank, Pr. Co. B 4th
O. V. I.
Brown, James W., Pr. Co. B 4th O.V.I.
Brown, John E., Sergt. Co. B 9th Batt.
O. V. I
Brown, Joshua K., Jr., Pr. Bat. H 1st
O. V. A.
Brown, Oliver T., Pr. Co. B 4th O.V.I.
Brown, Roy H., Pr. Co. K 3rd O. V. I.
Brown, Wallace S., Pr. Co. A 4th O.
V. I.
Bright, Walter S., Pr. Co. A 4th O.V.I.
Brixner, Ollie L., Pr. Co. A 4th O.V.I.
Bruce, Horace J., Pr. Bat. H 1st O.V.A.
Buchenberg, Alvin E., Sergt. Co. A 2nd
U. S. V. E.
Buckingham, Fred, Pr. Co. B 4th O.
V. I.
Buehler, John W., Pr. Co. C 4th O.V.I.
Bulger, John. Pr. U. R. 4th O. V. I.
Bun. Frank H., Hospital Steward 4th
O. V. I.
Burke, Edward J., Pr. Co. A 2nd U.
S. V. E.
Burkett, Dora V., Pr. Tr. D 1st O.V.C.
Burkett, John M., Pr. Co. B 2nd U. S.
V. E.
Buroker, James A., Pr. Co. E 10th O.
V. I.
Burett, Emil, Pr. Co. E 10th O. V. I.
Burton, Horatio C., Pr. Co. A 3rd O.
V. I.
Buskirk, Thomas, Pr. Co. A 4th O.V.I.
Butcher, Alfred, Corp. Co. D 9th Batt.
O. V. I.
Butcher, Fred E., Pr. Bat. H 1st O.V.A.
Butler, Arza E., Pr. Co. C 4th O. V. I.
Butler, Mike J., Pr. Bat. H 1st O.V.A.
Butler, William, Pr. Co. B 4th O. V. I.
Butterworth, Robert B., Pr. Bat. H 1st
O. V. A.
Butterworth, William H., Pr. Bat. H 1st
O. V. A.
Calkins, Arda H., Pr. Bat. H 1st O.
V. A.
Calkins, William B., Pr. Bat. H 1st O.
V. A.

Campbell, James C., Pr. Tr. D 1st O.
V. C.
Capell, Samuel P., Corp. Co. B 4th O.
V. I.
Carroll, Frank, Pr. Co. A 4th O. V. I.
Carroll, John, Pr. Co. F 4th O. V. I.
Carson, Samuel K., Pr. Co. A 4th O.
V. I.
Carter, Lewis M., Artificer Co. C 4th
O. V. I.
Chamberlain, Ben. W., Pr. Co. A 4th
V. I.
Chandler, Howard B., Corp. Bat. H
1st O. V. A.
Chandler, Lawrence B., Pr. Bat. H 1st
O. V. A.
Chapman, John W., Pr. Tr. D 1st O.
V. C.
Charles, William S., Pr. Co. C 4th O.
V. I.
Clemens, Joseph B., Pr. Co. B 4th O.
V. I.
Clemens, Samuel B., Pr. Co. C 10th O.
V. I.
Cloud, Charles M., Pr. Co. E 10th O.
V. I.
Clover, Thomas, Pr. Co. M 1st O. V. C.
Coble, Andrew, Pr. Co. B 9th Batt. O.
V. I.
Cockins, Hayes R., Pr. Co. A 4th O.
V. I.
Coe, Dean B., Pr. Tr. G 1st O. V. C.
Coleman, Charles Pr. Co. D 9th Batt.
O. V. I.
Collins, Lorenzo D., Pr. Co. A 2nd U.
S. V. E.
Conner, Harry O., Pr. Co. A 2nd U.
S. V. E.
Conti, John M., Corp. Co. B 4th O.V.I.
Conway, Eugene J., Pr. U. R. 4th O.
V. I.
Cook, Harry L., Pr. Co. C 4th O. V. I.
Cook, John W., Pr. U. R. 4th O. V. I.
Cook, Otto F., Pr. Co. C 4th O. V. I.
Cooper, Cliney, Pr. Co. B 9th Batt.
O. V. I.
Cooper, Leroy, Pr. Co. D 9th Batt. O.
V. I.
Cordner, John O., Pr. Co. C 4th O.V.I.
Corson, William, Pr. Co. F 4th O.V.I.
Coughlin, Daniel, Pr. Co. C 10th O.
V. I.
Craig, Owen, Pr. Co. C 10th O. V. I.
Crawford, John J., Pr. Co. C 4th O.V.I.
Creager, Charles E., Bat. Sergt. Maj.
4th O. V. I.
Creamer, Michael S., Pr. U. R. 4th O.
V. I.
Crooks, Howard M., Pr. Tr. D 1st O.
V. C.
Cruzen, Jacob W., Pr. Tr. D 1st O.V.C.
Cummins, Henry R., Pr. Co. B 4th O.
V. I.
Cunningham, Elmer T., Pr. Co. A 4th
O. V. I.
Danel, Joseph R., Pr. Co. B 4th O. V. I.
Daugherty, Jerome, Pr. Co. D 4th O.
V. I.

Davie, John B., Pr. Co. A 4th O. V. I.
Davis, David S., Pr. Co. C 4th O. V. I.
Davis, Dean D., Pr. Bat. G 1st O.V.A.
Davis, Harry A., Pr. Co. C 4th O. V. I.
Davis, Joseph W., Corp. Co. B 4th O.
V. I.
Davis, Leo, Pr. Co. A 10th O. V. I.
Davis, Shell P., Pr. U. R. 4th O. V. I.
Davis, Thomas D., Pr. Tr. G 1st O.
V. C.
Davis, William, Pr. Co. B 9th Batt.
O. V. I.
Davis, William R., Pr. U. R. 4th O.V.I.
Day, Moses, Pr. Co. B 9th Batt. O.
V. I.
Dearth, Earnest, Pr. Co. C 4th O. V. I.
Dempesey, Marion, Pr. Co. E 10th O.
V. I.
Dent, Homer A., Pr. Bat. H 1st O.V.A.
Dent, Joseph W., Pr. Co. C 4th O. V. I.
Devan, Charles, Pr. Co. E 10th O. V. I.
Devine, William P., Pr. Co. A 2nd U.
S. V. E.
Dickson, James F., Jr., Pr. Co. L 4th
O. V. I.
Diers, Henry, Pr. Co. K 3rd O. V. I.
Dixon, Herbert B., Pr. Co. F 4th O.V.I.
Dixon, Lovett F., Pr. Co. C 4th O.V.I.
Drake, George, Trumpeter Tr. D 1st
O. V. C.
Drake, George, Pr. Co. K 3rd O. V. I.
Drake, Ross, Pr. Co. K 3rd O. V. I.
Dodd, Homer C., Pr. Bat. H 1st O.V.A.
Dougherty, Leonard L., Pr. Bat. H 1st
O. V. A.
Douse, Frank, Pr. Co. F 10th O. V. I.
Dubois, Edward L., Pr. Co. C 4th O.
V. I.
Dunlap, Roland, Sergt. Co. F 4th O.
V. I.
Drury, Robert B., Pr. Bat. H 1st O.
V. A.
Dyar, Harry S., Pr. Bat. H 1st O.V.A.
Eastburn, Franklin, Pr. Tr. D 1st O.
V. C.
Easton, Fred L., Pr. Co. C 4th O. V. I.
Eaton, Walter M., Pr. Bat. H 1st O.
V. A.
Ebner, Jacob, Pr. Co. G 4th O. V. I.
Edington, William J., Pr. Co. A 4th
O. V. I.
Edmonson, Harry A., Pr. Bat. H 1st
O. V. A.
Eichorn, Harry E., Corp. Co. C 4th
O. V. I.
Eldridge, Wilbur T., Corp. Tr. D 1st
O. V. C.
Elliott, Reuben J., Pr. Co. E 10th O.
V. I.
Essex, John P., Jr., Pr. Co. I 10th O.
V. I.
Ethell, Frank T., Sergt. Co. B 4th O.
V. I.
Evans, Walter G., Pr. Tr. D 1st O. V. C.
Farahay, William I., Pr. Co. B 4th O.
V. I.
Feeney, Joseph, Musician Co. C 4th O.
V. I.

Fitzgerald, Edwin P., Pr. Co. F 4th O. V. I.
Fleck, James S., Pr. Co. A 4th O. V. I.
Fleck, Harry M., Pr. Co. A 4th O. V. I.
Fogle, Joshua K., Pr. Co. A 3rd O.V.I.
Ford, Samuel, Wagoner Co. C 4th O. V. I.
Fowler, William, Pr. Co. B 9th Batt. O. V. I.
Francklyn, Alan C., Pr. Tr. D 1st O. V. C.
Freeman, George D., Jr., Corp. Co. F 4th O. V. I.
Freeman, Harry C., Pr. Bat. H 1st O. V. A.
Freeman, Stanton S., Q. M. Sergt. Tr. D 1st O. V. C.
French, Samuel W., Pr. Co. A 4th O. V. I.
Frizzell, Edward, Pr. Co. B 5th O. V. I.
Fuller, Reuben H., Pr. Tr. G 1st O. V. C.
Fuller, William, Pr. Co. E 10th O.V.I.
Fullerton, Rutherford, Pr. Tr. D 1st O. V. C.
Gard, Wardsworth, Sergt. Bat. H 1st O. V. A.
Garrisan, John L., Pr. Co. E 10th O. V. I.
Gee, Eugene C., Pr. Co. A 4th O. V. I.
Gepler, Otho E., Trumpeter Tr. D 1st O. V. C.
Geren, Carl B., Pr. Co. A 10th O.V.I.
Getren, George, Pr. Co. F 10th O.V.I.
Gilbert, Howard, Pr. Co. B 9th Batt. O. V. I.
Gilmore, George W., 1st Sergt. Bat. H 1st O. V. A.
Goodrich, David, Pr. Co. A 10th O.V.I.
Gorley, Clarence, Pr. Co. A 4th O.V.I.
Graham, Frank, Pr. Co. A 4th O. V. I.
Graham, John, Corp. Co. I 5th O. V. I.
Graham, Jos. A., Pr. Co. A 4th O.V.I.
Graham, William Earl, Pr. Co. B 4th O. V. I.
Grandstaff, Morley P., Wagoner Co. A 4th O. V. I.
Grate, Frank A., Pr. Co. F 4th O. V. I.
Graves, James W., Pr. Co. D 9th Batt. O. V. I.
Gray, William F., Pr. U. R. 4th O.V.I.
Green, Armitage, Pr. Co. F 6th O.V.I.
Green, Charles W., Pr. U. R. 9th Batt. O. V. I.
Green, Elmer E., Pr. Co. B 4th O. V. I.
Green, Herbert W., Pr. Co. I 10th O. V. I.
Green, Wilfred, Corp. Co. B 9th Batt. O. V. I.
Greenlee, Earl C., Pr. Co. F 4th O.V.I.
Griffon, John C., Pr. Co. A 10th O.V.I.
Grimes, William, Pr. Co. D 9th Batt. O. V. I.
Grimm, Arthur A., 1st Sergt. Co. F 4th O. V. I.
Groce, Charles O., Pr. Co. F 4th O.V.I.
Guitner, Albert, Pr. Co. F 4th O. V. I.

Guthier, John M., Pr. Co. F 6th O.V.I.
Haggard, James S., Pr. U. R. 9th Batt. O. V. I.
Hale, Moses, Pr. Co. B 9th Batt. O. V. I.
Hall, John R., Pr. Co. D 9th Batt. O. V. I.
Haly, William S., Sergt. Co. F 4th O. V. I.
Hamilton, Charles O., Pr. Co. M 1st O. V. C.
Hamilton, Edwin Forrest, Pr. Co. H 7th O. V. I.
Hamilton, Ernest O., Saddler Tr. D 1st O. V. C.
Hampton, William E., Pr. Co. B 5th O. V. I.
Hance, William, Pr. U. R. 4th O. V. I.
Handley, Scott J., Pr. Co. F 4th O. V. I.
Hankee, Fred, Pr. Co. B 4th O. V. I.
Hanway, Albert L., Pr. Co. A 4th O. V. I.
Hardesty, Thomas M., Corp. Tr. D 1st O. V. C.
Hardman, Thomas E., Pr. Bat. H 1st O. V. A.
Harley, Matthew J., Pr. Co. B 9th Batt. O. V. I.
Harper, Martin A., Pr. Co. B 4th O.V.I.
Harris, Earnest H., Pr. Co. B 9th Batt. O. V. I.
Harris, Edward, Pr. Co. D 9th Batt. O. V. I.
Harris, Starling, Pr. Co. B 9th Batt. O. V. I.
Harrod, S. Riley, Sergt. Co. C 4th O. V. I.
Hawes, Warren, Corp. Co. D 9th Batt. O. V. I.
Hawley, Frank, Pr. Co. D 9th Batt. O. V. I.
Hawkins, Wood B., Pr. Co. B 9th Batt. O. V. I.
Haycook, Homer I., Pr. Co. A 2nd U. S. V. E.
Hayes, Charles H., Pr. Co. B 9th Batt. O. V. I.
Haynes, Harry L., Pr. Co. C 4th O.V.I.
Hayenes, Lem., Pr. Co. F 10th O.V.I.
Hayo, Stewart W., Pr. Bat. H 1st O. V. A.
Hedges, Robert L., Pr. Co. B 4th O. V. I.
Heffernan, John J., Pr. Co. A 4th O. V. I.
Hegie, Wiley, Pr. Co. D 9th Batt. O. V. I.
Heiman, Simon, Pr. Co. B 4th O. V. I.
Helwagen, Henry F., Pr. Co. C 4th O. V. I.
Hemming, Robert X., Pr. Co. F 4th O. V. I.
Henderson, Charles O., Pr. Co. F 7th O. V. I.
Hensel, Hugh, Pr. Co. B 5th O. V. I.
Hensel, Raymond C., Pr. Tr. D 1st O. V. C.

Hentershed, Allen, Pr. Tr. D 1st O.V.C.
Herbert, Charles T., Pr. Bat. H 1st O. V. A.
Herrell, Richard E., Pr. Co. B 9th Batt. O. V. I.
Hesley, Frederick, Pr. Co. C 4th O.V.I.
Hess, Edward, Pr. Co. F 4th O. V. I.
Hickey, Aaron J., Pr. Co. C 4th O.V.I.
Higdon, John, Pr. Co. D 9th Batt. O. V. I.
Hill, Charles F., Pr. Co. F 4th O. V. I.
Hilles, William N., Corp. Tr. D 1st O. V. C.
Hitchcock, Almonta R., Pr. Co. G 10th O. V. I.
Hodge, George, Pr. Co. B 9th Batt. O. V. I.
Hofman, Jay B., Pr. Bat. H 1st O.V.A.
Hoglen, John J., Corp. Bat. H 1st O. V. A.
Holmes, Archie J., Pr. Co. F 6th O.V.I.
Hook, John, Pr. Co. C 4th O. V. I.
Hosfield, Edwin Judson, Pr. Co. B 4th O. V. I.
Hoster, Louis P., Pr. Bat. H 1st O. V. A.
Huddle, Charley, Pr. Co. K 10th O.V.I.
Hughey, Charles F., Pr. Co. A 4th O. V. I.
Hull, Richard E., Sergt. Co. F 4th O. V. I.
Hummel, Charles E., Pr. Co. A 4th O. V. I.
Hunt, Charles A., Sergt. Co. B 4th O. V. I.
Ingersol, Charles G., Pr. Co. C 4th O. V. I.
Ingraham, Robert Benjamin, Pr. Co. B 4th O. V. I.
Ismon, Ralph E., Pr. Co. F 4th O. V. I.
Jackson, Aleck, Pr. U. R. 9th Batt. O. V. I.
Jacokes, Frank G., Sergt. Co. B 4th O. V. I.
James, Frank, Pr. Co. B 9th Batt. O. V. I.
James, Ripley C., Pr. U. R. 4th O. V. I.
Jaspersen, William, Pr. Bat. H 1st O. V. A.
Jefferson, Charles, Pr. Co. D 9th Batt. O. V. I.
Jenkins, Robert, Pr. U. R. 9th Batt. O. V. I.
Jenkins, Robert V., Corp. Bat. H 1st O. V. A.
Johnson, George M., Pr. Bat. H 1st O. V. A.
Johnston, Irvin R., Pr. U. R. 9th Batt. O. V. I.
Johnson, Robert J., Pr. Co. D 9th Batt. O. V. I.
Johnson, William E., Pr. Tr. D 1st O. V. C.
Johnson, William G., Pr. U. R. 9th Batt. O. V. I.

Johnson, William H., Pr. Co. D 9th Batt. O. V. I.
Jones, Charles Fred, Pr. Co. B 9th Batt. O. V. I.
Jones, Charles O., Pr. Co. B 9th Batt. O. V. I.
Jones, Elijah P., Pr. Co. B 9th Batt. O. V. I.
Jones, Tilden T., Sergt. Co. B 4th O. V. I.
Jorner, Fred, Pr. Co. B 9th Batt. O. V. I.
Judkins, William T., Pr. U. R. 4th O. V. I.
Kaine, James A., Pr. Co. B 9th Batt. O. V. I.
Kaiser, Frank J., Pr. Co. E 10th O.V.I.
Kaiser, Henry, Pr. Co. B 4th O. V. I.
Karshner, Malcolm A., Pr. Bat. H 1st O. V. A.
Keith, John, Musician Co. F 4th O.V.I.
Kelley, Charles E., Pr. Bat. H 1st O. V. A.
Kelly, John M., Pr. U. R. 4th O. V. I.
Keppler, Edward A., Pr. Co. C 10th O. V. I.
Kipp, Fremont, 1st Sergt. Tr. D 1st O. V. C.
Kirk, Charles W., Pr. Bat. H 1st O. V. A.
Kirkpatrick, Wordon, Pr. Co. F 4th O. V. I.
Kirschner, Charles, Pr. Co. C 10th O. V. I.
Klotts, Edwin P., Pr. Co. A 4th O. V. I.
Knouff, Oliver M., Pr. Co. A 4th O.V.I.
Koehler, Malcolm H., Pr. Co. F 7th O. V. I.
Krumm, Herbert Z., Pr. Bat. H 1st O. V. A.
Kuhn, George A., Pr. Co. B 4th O.V.I.
La Boyteaux, Maitland V., Pr. Bat. H 1st O. V. A.
Lanckton, Edward G., Pr. Co. B 5th O. V. I.
Lang, Edward J., Corp. Co. F 4th O. V. I.
Lansing, Horace C., Musician Co. H 7th O. V. I.
Lawrence, Arthur K., Hospital Steward 9th Batt. O. V. I.
Laws, William A., Corp. Co. D 9th Batt. O. V. I.
Lee, John, Pr. U. R. 9th Batt. O.V.I.
Lemon, Albert B., Pr. Bat. H 1st O. V. A.
Leonard, Andrew, Pr. Co. F 10th O. V. I.
Leonard, Francis A., Pr. Bat. H 1st O. V. A.
Leonard, Wellington T., Pr. Bat. H 1st O. V. A.
Leonhardt, Albert C., Pr. Co. E 10th O. V. I.
Lewis, Charles, Sergt. Co. B 9th Batt. O. V. I.
Lewis, Frank B., Pr. Co. C 4th O. V. I.

Lockhart, Frederick C., Pr. Co. A 4th O. V. I.
Long, Wilson G., Pr. Co. L 4th O.V.I.
Long, Beverly, Pr. Co. D 9th Batt. O. V. I.
Longenecker, Albert D., Pr. Bat. C 1s; O. V. A.
Longenecker, Orrin J., Pr. Bat. H 1st O. V. A.
Loos, Charles L., Pr. Bat. H 1st O. V. A.
Losek, Joseph, Pr. Co. C 4th O. V. I.
Loudenslager, Charles S., Musician Co. B 4th O. V. I.
Love, Harry F., Pr. U. R. 4th O. V. I.
Lucks, Albert, Pr. Co. C 10th O. V. I.
Lytle, Andrew G., Pr. Co. B 4th O.V.I.
Lytle, Lewis F., Prin. Musician 4th O. V. I.
MacDonald, James D., Sergt. Co. G 7th O. V. I.
Mack, Thomas, Pr. Co. D 9th Batt. O. V. I.
Madden, John W., Pr. U. R. 4th O.V.I.
Magly, Robert A., Pr. Co. H 7th O.V.I.
Manly, Walter, Pr. U. R. 9th Batt. O. V. I.
Mann, Allen D., Pr. Co. C 4th O. V. I.
Manning, James, Pr. Co. A 3rd O. V. I.
March, Charles C., Pr. Bat. G 1st O. V. A.
Markeson, William P., Pr. Co. F 4th O. V. I.
Martin, Clinton C., Pr. Co. C 4th O. V. I.
Martin, Thomas, Pr. Co. D 9th Batt. O. V. I.
Mayfield, Victor H., Pr. U. R. 4th O V. I.
McClain, George W., Pr. Co. C 7th O. V. I.
McClain, Samuel, Pr. Co. A 4th O. V. I.
McClelland, Chalmer K., Corp. Co. A 4th O. V. I.
McConnell, William C., 1st Sergt. Co. A 4th O. V. I.
McCoy, Lorin, Pr. Co. C 4th O. V. I.
McDonald, James, Pr. Co. I 5th O.V.I.
McDonald, James E., Pr. Co. B 4th O. V. I.
McDowell, Rufus, Pr. U. R. 9th Batt. O. V. I.
McFarland, Joseph, Pr. Co. B 9th Batt. O. V. I.
McFarland, William Riley, Pr. Co. B 4th O. V. I.
McGuire, Arthur C., 2nd Sergt. Co. A 4th O. V. I.
McLeod, Albert E., Pr. Co. C 4th O. V. I.
McMeekin, Joseph, Pr. Co. A 4th O. V. I.
McMillen, Ellis, Pr. U. R. 9th Batt. O. V. I.
McNally, Frank, Pr. Co. C 10th O.V.I.
McNeer, Robert E. L., Pr. Co. G 7th O. V. I.

McRea, William C., Pr. Co. L 4th O. V. I.
Meads, Richard, Wagoner Co. B 9th Batt. O. V. I.
Meeker, William B., Pr. Co. F 4th O. V. I.
Megahan, Budd I., Pr. Tr. D 1st O. V. C.
Mellentree, Alfred, Pr. Co. B 9th Batt. O. V. I.
Meyer, Emil, Corp. Co. A 4th O. V. I.
Michel, Robert H., Pr. Co. F 4th O. V. I.
Mihan, William, Pr. Co. A 4th O. V. I.
Miller, Herbert A., Musician Co. B 4th O. V. I.
Miller, Floyd, Pr. Co. A 3rd O. V. I.
Miller, Louis J., Pr. Co. B 5th O. V. I.
Miles, Gordon F., Sergt. Tr. D 1st O. V. C.
Milligan, Elmer James, Pr. Co. B 4th O. V. I.
Minnick, Robert F., Pr. Co. C 4th O. V. I.
Mininger, David E., Pr. Co. A 3rd O. V. I.
Mitchell, John G., Corp. Tr. D 1st O. V. C.
Mock, Francis T., Pr. Bat. H 1st O. V. A.
Modie, James W., Pr. Co. F 4th O.V.I.
Molloy, Theophilus F., Pr. Co. C 4th O. V. I.
Monett, Frank E., Pr. Bat. H 1st O. V. A.
Monsarrat, Charles R., Pr. Tr. D 1st O. V. C.
Moore, Clifford L., Sergt. Tr. D 1st O. V. C.
Moore, John A., Pr. Co. B 9th Batt. O. V. I.
Moore, John H., Pr. Co. D 9th Batt. O. V. I.
Moore, Roscoe E., Musician Bat. G 1st O. V. A.
Moore, Wallace D., Pr. Co. F 6th O. V. I.
Morehead, Robert H., Pr. Bat. H 1st O. V. A.
Morgan, Edwin S., Pr. Co. A 2nd U. S. V. E.
Morrall, Willis A., Hospital Steward 1st O. V. A.
Morris, Benjamin F., Corp. Co. C 4th O. V. I.
Morris, John C., Pr. Co. B 4th O. V. I.
Morrison, William A., Pr. Tr. D 1st O. V. C.
Mowday, David T., Pr. Co. B 5th O. V. I.
Mundin, George A., Pr. Co. D 9th Batt. O. V. I.
Murphy, James E., Pr. Tr. D 1st O. V. I.
Murphy, William F., Pr. Co. A 3rd O. V. I.

6—R. O. V.

Murray, Charles A., Pr. Co. C 10th O. V. I.

Neer, Harry S., Pr. Co. A 3rd O. V. I.

Newby, Howard E., Pr. Co. D 9th Batt. O. V. I.

Newman, John, Pr. Co. K 3rd O. V. I.

Newson, Joshua, Pr. U. R. 9th Batt. O. V. I.

Nichols, Harry H., Corp. Co. C 4th O. V. I.

Nobb, John, Jr., Pr. Bat. H 1st O.V.A.

Noble, Otto, Pr. Co. A 4th O. V. I.

Norris, Delbert W., Pr. Co. E 10th O. V. I.

Nunamaker, Norman C., Pr. Co. B 4th O. V. I.

Oberlin, Edgar G., Pr. Tr. D 1st O. V. C.

Oglesby, Nicholas P., Pr. U. R. 4th O. V. I.

Ohlen, Guy J., Pr. Bat. H 1st O. V. A.

O'Kane, Walter C., Sergt. Maj. 10th O. V. I.

Olds, Joseph, Jr., Pr. Co. A 4th O. V. I.

Olds, Marshall, Sergt. Tr. D 1st O.V.C.

Osborn, Clyde, Pr. Co. F 4th O. V. I.

O'Shaughnessy, Joseph F., Pr. Co. A 4th O. V. I.

Ott, Odd F., Pr. U. R. 4th O. V. I.

Pangle, Don C., Pr. Co. A 4th O. V. I.

Paraday, Charles F., Pr. Co. F 4th O V. I.

Palmer, Guy H., Pr. Bat. H 1st O.V.A.

Parker, Frank W., Pr. Co. E 4th O.V.I.

Parrett, Harlan A., Pr. Co. K 7th O. V. I.

Parsons, George M., Sergt. Bat. H 1st O. V. A.

Peabody, Orland S., Musician Bat. H 1st O. V. A.

Peabody, William H., Pr. Bat. H 1st O. V. A.

Peake, Frank, Pr. Bat. H 1st O. V. A.

Pfaff, Walter A., Pr. Bat. H 1st O.V.A.

Philo, Louis F., Bat. Sergt. Maj. 4th O. V. I.

Pickering, Stephen G., Pr. Bat. H 1st O. V. A.

Pierce, James, Sergt. Co. B 9th Batt. O. V. I.

Pindall, Thomas J., Pr. Co. C 9th Batt. O. V. I.

Porter, Frank McI., Pr. Tr. D 1st O. V. C.

Potter, Lewis M. H., Pr. Bat. H 1st O. V. A.

Potter, Thomas D., Corp. Co. F 4th O. V. I.

Preston, William, Pr. Co. F 4th O.V.I.

Price, Francis C., Pr. Co. A 4th O. V. I.

Pride, James M., Pr. Co. E 10th O.V.I.

Prine, Anthony E., Wagoner Co. G 6th O. V. I.

Pringle, Leroy, Pr. U. R. 4th O. V. I.

Pritner, Horatio C., Artificer Co. F 4th O. V. I.

Pulpress, Charles, Corp. Co. B 9th Batt. O. V. I.

Quayle, Jack, Pr. Co. G 7th O. V. I.

Rabourn, Allen E., Pr. Tr. D 1st O.V.C.

Randolph, Robert, Pr. Co. D 9th Batt. O. V. I.

Rau, Harry, Pr. Co. E 10th O. V. I.

Rawland, Charles D., Corp. Co. C 4th O. V. I.

Rector, James M., Pr. Bat. H 1st O. V. A.

Redman, Willie, Pr. Co. B 9th Batt. O. V. I.

Reed, William, Pr. Co. D 9th Batt. O. V. I.

Reichard, George W., Pr. Co. A 4th O. V. I.

Reiger, Joseph M., Pr. Co. F 6th O.V.I.

Reinke, Gustav E., Pr. Co. F 10th O. V. I.

Renck, Adam T., Pr. Co. C 4th O. V. I.

Renck, Charles F., Pr. Co. C 4th O. V. I.

Reynolds, Frank Louis, Pr. Co. B 9th Batt. O. V. I.

Reynolds, William H., Pr. Co. A 10th O. V. I.

Rhodes, Lawrence, Pr. Co. F 4th O. V. I.

Rhodes, Simeon, Pr. Co. C 4th O. V. I.

Richard, Arby C., Pr. Bat. H 1st O. V. A.

Richards, George C., Pr. Co. A 3rd O. V. I.

Richards, John W., Hospital Steward 4th O. V. I.

Riddle, Carlton, Pr. Co. A 4th O. V. I.

Riddlesberger, William, Pr. Co. F 4th O. V. I.

Riley, J. Sherman, Corp. Tr. D 1st O. V. C.

Ritter, Louis F., Hospital Steward 4th O. V. I.

Ritzman, Carl, Pr. Co. I 10th O. V. I.

Roberts, Charles R., Pr. Co. F 4th O. V. I.

Roberts, Matthew S., Pr. Co. C 4th O. V. I.

Robinson, Frank, Pr. U. R. 9th Batt. O. V. I.

Rodgers, Archibold, Pr. Bat. H 1st O. V. A.

Rogers, James L., Pr. Co. C 4th O.V.I.

Romains, Edwin, Pr. Co. A 4th O. V. I.

Rorick, Jonas Martin, Pr. Co. L 4th O. V. I.

Rose, Charles E., Musician Co. B 9th Batt. O. V. I.

Ross, Frank, Pr. Co. F 10th O. V. I.

Ross, Robert M., Pr. Co. A 2nd U. S. V. E.

Ross, William, Pr. Co. C 4th O. V. I.

Rowe, William I., Pr. Co. C 4th O. V. I.

Roy, Charles F., Pr. Co. A 4th O. V. I.

Rulo, Charles J., Prin. Musician 4th O. V. I.

Ruple, Oscar E., Pr. Tr. D 1st O. V. C.

Ryans, John, Pr. Co. B 9th Batt. O. V. I.

Sackett, Lawrence A., Pr. Co. A 4th O. V. I.

Sage, Lewis F., Pr. Co. F 4th O. V. I.

Schomaker, Edward B., Pr. Co. C 4th O. V. I.

Schoonover, Charles O., Pr. Co. C 4th O. V. I.

Schwartz, Charles A., Pr. Bat. H 1st O. V. A.

Scott, Bertie, Sergt. Co. B 9th Batt. O. V. I.

Scott, Cyrus E., Sergt. Bat. H 1st O. V. A.

Scott, Dewey M., Sergt. Co. A 2nd U. S. V. E.

Scott, George F., Corp. Bat. H 1st O. V. A.

Scott, Lester, Pr. U. R. 9th Batt. O. V. I.

Seibert, Frederick J., Pr. Bat. H 1st O. V. A.

Seiders, John T., Pr. Co. F 4th O. V. I.

Sellers, Harry J., Pr. Bat. H 1st O.V.A.

Seward, Russell M., Pr. Co. C 10th O. V. I.

Seward, Walter B., Pr. Co. C 10th O. V. I.

Seymour, Truman G., Pr. Bat. H 1st O. V. A.

Shannon, Dwight, Pr. Tr. D 1st O. V. C.

Shannon, Raymond, Pr. Co. K 3rd O. V. I.

Sharp, Birdsell, Corp. Co. F 4th O.V.I.

Sharp, Edward, Pr. U. R. 9th Batt. O. V. I.

Sharp, James McD., Sergt. Tr. D 1st O. V. C.

Sharp, John R., Pr. U. R. 4th O. V. I.

Shasteen, William, Pr. Co. F 6th O.V.I.

Shaw, Leroy, Pr. Co. F 4th O. V. I.

Shea, William H., Pr. Co. A 2nd U. S. V. E.

Shell, Frank M., Pr. Co. C 3rd O. V. I.

Sherwood, Milton W., Pr. U. R. 4th O. V. I.

Shipley, Clarence James, Pr. Co. B 4th O. V. I.

Shipley, Fred F., Pr. Co. F 4th O. V. I.

Shirey, Burley M., Pr. Co. B 4th O.V.I.

Shook, Roy B., Pr. Co. B 4th O. V. I.

Showalter, Clarence E., Pr. Co. E 10th O. V. I.

Shullin, Harry Walter, Pr. Co. B 4th O. V. I.

Shumaker, Harry C., Pr. Tr. D 1st O. V. C.

Sigrist, Charles F., Pr. Co. A 4th O.V.I.

Simons, Arthur H., Corp. Co. F 4th O. V. I.

Sincoe, George, Pr. Bat. C 1st O.V.A.

Sines, James G., Pr. Co. B 4th O. V. I.

Slater, Ernest G., Pr. Tr. D 1st O. V. C.

Slemmons, Mendel E., Pr. U. R. 4th O. V. I.

Sloan, Henry, Pr. Co. G 7th O. V. I.

Smith, Arthur, Pr. Co. B 9th Batt. O. V. I.

Smith, Augustus G., Pr. Co. A 4th O. V. I.

Smith, Benjamin R., Pr. Co. C 4th O. V. I.

Smith, Charles A., Pr. Co. B 4th O. V. I.

Smith, Edward H., Corp. Co. B 4th O. V. I.

Smith, Jesse F., Pr. Co. C 4th O. V. I.

Smith, John, Blacksmith Tr. D 1st O. V. C.

Smith, Louis, Pr. U. R. 9th Batt. O. V. I.

Smith, Ralph, Pr. Co. F 4th O. V. I.

Smith, Starrett G., Pr. Bat. H 1st O. V. A.

Snider, John F., Pr. U. R. 4th O. V. I.

Snyder, Edward, Pr. Co. F 4th O. V. I.

Southcomb, Robert P., Pr. Co. C 4th O. V. I.

Sparks, Charles N., Musician Bat. H 1st O. V. A.

Sparke, Hart, Pr. U. R. 4th O. V. I.

Spenny, Charles O., Musician Co. H 10th O. V. I.

Spurgeon, Chester M., Corp. Co. F 4th O. V. I.

Spurlock, Frank, Pr. U. R. 9th Batt. O. V. I.

Spurlock, Rutherford B., Pr. U. R 9th Batt. O. V. I.

Stalter, Edward, 3rd Sergt. Co. A 4th O. V. I.

Steinbarger, Herbert N., Corp. Bat. H 1st O. V. A.

Steinel, Jacob, Wagoner Co. B 4th O. V. I.

Steele, William, Pr. U. R. 9th Batt. O. V. I.

Stephens, Lorin, Pr. Co. C 4th O. V. I.

Stevenson, Lewis Miller, Pr. Co. B 4th O. V. I.

Stevenson, William P., 1st Sergt. Co. B 4th O. V. I.

Stevison, Frank H., Corp. Co. A 4th O. V. I.

Stewart, Gilbert H., Jr., Pr. Bat. H 1st O. V. A.

Stimmel, William E., Sergt. Co. C 4th O. V. I.

Stoker, Jacob, Jr., Pr. Co. B 4th O.V.I.

Stoneburner, George A., Pr. Co. F 4th O. V. I.

Storm, George H., Musician Co. B 9th Batt. O. V. I.

Stout, Calvin H., Pr. Co. F 6th O.V.I.

Stout, Walter Claude, Pr. Co. B 4th O. V. I.

Strasser, Albert F., Pr. Co. K 10th O. V. I.

Strauder, Albert A., Pr. Co. D 9th Batt. O. V. I.

Struggles, Willis C., Hospital Steward 8th O. V. I.

Stubenrauch, Edwin. Pr. Co. C 4th O. V. I.

Summers, William, Pr. Co. D 9th Batt. O. V. I.

Summerville, Jacob. Pr. U. R. 9th Batt. O. V. I.

Sunker, Oscar J., Pr. Bat. II 1st O.V.A.

Swiger, William Spencer. Pr. Co. B 4th O. V. I.

Swigert, Robert, Sergt. Co. B 4th O. V. I.

Syfert, Harry, Corp. Co. A 4th O. V. I.

Tapsico, Charles W., Pr. Co. B 9th Batt. O. V. I.

Tate, Joseph F., Pr. Co. A 4th O. V. I.

Taylor, Benjamin, Pr. Co. B 9th Batt. O. V. I.

Taylor, Burton, Pr. Co. B 9th Batt. O. V. I.

Taylor, Charles K., Pr. Co. C 4th O. V. I.

Taylor, Charles L., 'Q. M. Sergt. 4th O. V. I.

Taylor, Eddie. Pr. Co. B 9th Batt. O. V. I.

Taylor, Frank S., Pr. Co. F 4th O.V.I.

Taylor, Thomas E., Jr., Sergt. Co. F 4th O. V. I.

Taylor, William J., Pr. Co. B 9th Batt. O. V. I.

Teeter, Charles K., Pr. Co. A 4th O. V. I.

Tessin, Harry, Pr. Co. K 3rd O. V. I.

Thomas, George E., Pr. Tr. D 1st O. V. C.

Thomas, Harry H., Pr. Co. G 4th O.V.I.

Thomas, John W., Pr. Co. B 9th Batt. O. V. I.

Thomas, Walter S., Pr. Co. B 9th Batt. O. V. I.

Thompson, Robert E., Pr. Co. B 4th O. V. I.

Thompson, William H., Artificer Co. A 4th O. V. I.

Thornton, Frank L., Sergt. Co. F 4th O. V. I.

Thrall, Frank R., Corp. Co. A 4th O. V. I.

Tietjius, John E., Musician Co. F 6th O. V. I.

Tucker, Harry A., Pr. Co. A 3rd O.V.I.

Tufts, Earl D., Pr. Co. E 10th O. V. I.

Twaddle, Richard A., Pr. Co. C 4th O. V. I.

Tyler, Maurice H., Pr. Co. B 9th Batt. O. V. I.

Tyler, William, Pr. U. R. 9th Batt. O. V. I.

Underwood, Harvey, Pr. U. R. 9th Batt. O. V. I.

Updyke, Lawrence S., Pr. U. R. 4th O. V. I.

Valentine, Frank, Pr. Co. D 9th Batt. O. V. I.

Van Gilder, Lewis, Pr. Co. B 4th O.V.I.

Van Pelt, Loring J., Pr. Co. B 4th O. V. I.

Vetter, John, Pr. Co. C 4th O. V. I.

Vogle, John G., Pr. Tr. D 1st O. V. C.

Waddell, William E., Pr. Tr. D 1st O. V. C.

Wagner, Charles R., Corp. Co. B 4th O. V. I.

Walcott, Joshua L., Pr. Co. F 6th O. V. I.

Walker, John W., Pr. Co. A 4th O.V. I.

Walker, Wallace S., Pr. Co. B 9th Batt. O. V. I.

Walker, William W., Pr. Bat. II 1st O. V. I.

Wallace, George C., 1st Sergt. Co. D 9th Batt. O. V. I.

Wallace, Harry D., Pr. Co. A 4th O.V.I.

Wallace, Isaac A., Pr. Co. B 9th Batt. O. V. I.

Walsh, George E., Pr. Co. A 4th O.V.I.

Walters, Charlie, Pr. Co. D 9th Batt. O. V. I.

Walters, John A., Pr. Bat. II 1st O. V. A.

Walzek, Adam E., Pr. Co. I 4th O.V.I.

Ward, Courtland, Pr. U. R. 9th Batt. O. V. I.

Ward, Willis, Pr. Co. D 9th Batt. O. V. I.

Washington, Fred C., Corp. Co. B 9th Batt. O. V. I.

Warman, John W., Artificer Co. B 4th O. V. I.

Watson, Alexander L., Pr. Bat. II 1st O. V. A.

Watson, Don E., Pr. Bat. H 1st O.V.A.

Watts, Charles D., Pr. Co. D 9th Batt. O. V. I.

Waugh, George A., 1st Sergt. Co. B 9th Batt. O. V. I.

Weadon, John S., Pr. Co. A 4th O. V. I.

Weare, Frank J., Pr. Co. B 9th Batt. O. V. I.

Webber, Karl T., Pr. Bat. H 1st O. V. A.

Webster, Daniel E., Pr. Co. A 4th O. V. I.

Webster, Walter J., Pr. Co. B 9th Batt. O. V. I.

Weinman, Glen., Corp. Co. C 4th O.V.I.

Welch, Woodson, Pr. U. R. 9th Batt. O. V. I.

Wells, Ellsworth, Pr. Co. A 4th O. V. I.

Wells, Ira E., Pr. Co. C 4th O. V. I.

Welty, Noah J., Pr. Tr. D 1st O. V. C.

Wertz, Edwin S., Pr. Bat. H 1st O.V.A.

Westerhaver, Jackson, Pr. Co. F 4th O. V. I.

Westwater, Mark G., Pr. Bat. II 1st O. V. A.

Westwater, William G., Sergt. Bat. II 1st O. V. A.

Whalan, William F., Pr. Tr. D 1st O. V. C.

Whaler, James, Pr. Co. D 9th Batt. O. V. I.

White, Daniel, Pr. Co. D 9th Batt. O. V. I.

White, Edgar H., Corp. Tr D 1st O. V. C.
White, John, Pr. Co. D 9th Batt. O. V. I.
Whip, Harry C., Pr. Co. C 4th O. V. I.
Whittendton, Bon, Pr. Co. D 9th Batt. O. V. I.
Wiebner, Henry, Pr. Bat. H 1st O.V.A.
Wilcox, Sherlock, Pr. Tr. D 1st O.V.C.
Willard, Ezra H., Pr. Co. A 4th O.V.I.
Williams, Albert, Pr. Co. D 9th Batt. O. V. I.
Williams, David M., Pr. Co. A 4th O. V. I.
Williams, Frank E., Pr. Co. B 4th O. V. I.
Williams, Joshua L., Pr. Co. B 4th O. V. I.
Williamson, Harry W., Pr. Co. F 4th O. V. I.
Willie, Harry W., Pr. Tr. D 1st O. V. C.
Wilson, Arthur, Pr. Co. D 9th Batt. O. V. I.
Wilson, Fred, Pr. Co. D 9th Batt. O. V. I.
Wilson, George B., Pr. Co. D 9th Batt. O. V. I.

Wirick, Thomas R., Corp. Co. A 4th O. V. I.
Withers, Austin A., Pr. Co. C 4th O. V. I.
Witter, Harry B., Musician Bat. G 1st O. V. A.
Wolfel, Arthur, Pr. Co. B 4th O. V. I.
Woodbury, Arthur, Pr. Tr. D 1st O. V. C.
Woolard, Asa, Pr. Co. B 4th O. V. I.
Worcester, Warner W., Sergt. Bat. H. 1st O. V. A.
Worcester, Wolsey G., Pr. Bat. H 1st O. V. A.
Worthington, Jesse, Chief Musician 4th O. V. I.
Wright, Charles E., Pr. U. R. 4th O.V.I.
Wright, Ralph, Pr. Co. F 6th O. V. I.
Yeiser, Harry E., Pr. U. R. 4th O.V.I.
Yoast, William A., Pr. Co. C 4th O.V.I.
Yourk, Mike, Pr. Co. F 4th O. V. I.
Zeisler, Valentine A., Pr. Co. D 4th O. V. I.
Zultz, Frederick H., Pr. Co. B 5th O. V. I.
Zwerner, George P., Pr. Co. D 4th O. V. I.

CONCORD

Adams, Wade E., Pr. Co. M 5th O.V.I.
Card, William R., Pr. Co. M 5th O.V.I.

West, John W., Pr. Co. M 5th O. V. I.

CONNEAUT

Appleby, Fred W., Pr. Co. E 5th O.V.I.
Baker, Claud S., Pr. Co. E 5th O. V. I.
Brooks, Edwin C., Pr. Co. E 5th O.V.I.
Erambert, George D., Pr. Co. E 5th O. V. I.
McKay, Ernest L., Pr. Co. E 5th O. V. I.

Miner, George S., Pr. Co. E 5th O.V.I.
Parker, Robert G., Pr. Co. E 5th O. V. I.
Randall, Arthur L., Pr. Co. E 5th O. V. I.

CONNELSVILLE

Pulver, John B., Pr. Co. A 2nd U. S. V. E.

CONOVOR

Johnson, William E., Pr. Co. C 3rd O. V. I.
Medaris, Percey H., Corp. Co. K 3rd O. V. I.

Throckmorton, George, Pr. Co. K 3rd O. V. I.

CONSTITUTION

Johnson, Irving J., Pr. Co. D 7th O. V. I.

CORA

Blair, Wiley G., Pr. Co. C 7th O. V. I.
Blair, Wiley G., Pr. Co. C 7th O. V. I.
Davis, John W., Corp. Co. B 2nd U. S. V. E.

Morgan, Everett H., 1st Sergt. Co. C 7th O. V. I.

COSHOCTON

Albert, John A., Pr. Co. F 7th O. V. I.

Aronhalt, Frank O., Pr. Co. B 7th O. V. I.

Bible, Adam, Pr. Co. F 7th O. V. I.

Callentine, Charles, Pr. Co. F 7th O. V. I.

Callentine, George, Corp. Co. F 7th O. V. I.

Carnes, Graiton, Pr. Co. F 7th O. V. I.

Carnes, Roy R., 2nd Sergt. Co. F 7th O. V. I.

Carpenter, Adolphus, Pr. Co. F 7th O. V. I.

Carpenter, Charles W., 3rd Sergt. Co. F 7th O. V. I.

Compton, William M., Pr. Co. F 7th O. V. I.

Courtright, Harvey, Pr. Co. F 7th O. V. I.

Crawford, John, Pr. Co. F 7th O.V.I.

Davis, Harvey B., 1st Sergt. Co. F 7th O. V. I.

Dawson, Carlos E., Pr. Co. F 7th O. V. I.

Dawson, William R., Pr. Co. F 7th O. V. I.

Dunmead, Archibald C., Pr. Co. F 7th O. V. I.

Edwards, William G., Pr. Co. G 7th O. V. I.

Everhart, James M., Pr. Co. B 7th O. V. I.

Fortune, James H., Pr. Co. F 7th O. V. I.

Hack, Harry D., 4th Sergt. Co. F 7th O. V. I.

Hayes, Stewart B., 5th Sergt. Co. F 7th O. V. I.

Hoelzel, William N., Hospital Steward 7th O. V. I.

House, Florus A., Pr. Co. F 7th O.V.I.

Howard, Harry H., Pr. Co. F 7th O. V. I.

Jackson, David, Corp. Co. F 7th O V. I.

Jones, Edward P. L., Pr. Co. F 7th O. V. I.

Kunnemund, William, Pr. Co. F 7th O. V. I.

Lang, John H., Q. M. Sergt. Co. F 7th O. V. I.

Linn, Franklin C., Corp. Co. F 7th O. V. I.

McClain, Noah I., Musician Co. F 7th O. V. I.

McMannis, Charles E., Pr. Co. F 7th O. V. I.

Miller, Claude Lida, Pr. Co. F 7th O. V. I.

Miller, Ernest C., Pr. Co. F 7th O.V.I.

Milligan, William C., Pr. Co. F 7th O. V. I.

Mills, Earl A., Pr. Co. F 7th O. V. I.

Moore, Harry D., Corp. Co. F 7th O. V. I.

Patton, Roy J., Pr. Co. F 7th O. V. I.

Phillips, William H., Pr. Co. F 7th O. V. I.

Platt, Albert M., Musician Co. F 7th O. V. I.

Poole, Charles, Pr. Co. F 7th O. V. I.

Richard, John A., Pr. Co. F 7th O.V.I.

Richard, Samuel T., Pr. Co. F 7th O. V. I.

Savery, Eugene L., Pr. Co. F 7th O. V. I.

Shaw, George, Pr. Co. F 7th O. V. I.

Smith, George S., Pr. Co. F 7th O.V.I.

Spahn, Thomas, Jr., Artificer Co. F 7th O. V. I.

Squire, James W., Pr. Co. F 7th O.V.I.

Stafford, William E., Pr. Co. F 7th O. V. I.

Talmadge, Grey, Pr. Co. F 7th O. V. I.

Temple, Robert, M., Jr., Corp. Co. F 7th O. V. I.

Terrell, George C., Wagoner Co. F 7th O. V. I.

Tripey, John, Pr. Co. F 7th O. V. I.

Webb, William J., Pr. Co. K 7th O.V.I.

Weller, Samuel A., Pr. Co. F 7th O. V. I.

Wells, James F., Pr. Co. F 7th O. V. I.

Williams, Asa C., Corp. Co. F 7th O. V. I.

Woods, Melville C., Pr. Co. F 7th O. V. I.

COTTAGE HILL

Weekly, Scott H., Pr. Co. G 7th O.V.I.

COY

French, Charles, Wagoner Co. C 7th O. V. I.

COVINGTON

Addington, Lawrence, Musician Co. A 3rd O. V. I.

Belser, William, Pr. Co. A 3rd O. V. I.

Blanke, William C., Pr. Co. A 3rd O. V. I.

Branson, John H., Corp. Co. A 3rd O. V. I.

Burns, Robert R., Pr. Co. A 3rd O.V.I.

Butt, Artie, Pr. Co. A 3rd O. V. I.

Carey, Joseph M., Pr. Co. A 3rd O.V.I.

Cole, Benjamin A., Musician Co. A 3rd O. V. I.

Cummings, Elmer, Pr. Co. A 3rd O. V. I.

Davenport, Charles, Pr. Co. A 3rd O. V. I.

Davis, William C., Pr. Co. A 3rd O. V. I.

Day, George, Pr. Co. A 3rd O. V. I.

Dickey, Stephen, Pr. Co. A 3rd O. V. I.

Diltz, Eugene C., Sergt. Co. A 3r1 O. V. I.

Ebberts, George, Pr. Co. A 3rd O.V.I.

Fagrie, Philip T., Pr. Co. A 3rd O.V.I.

Franz, Albin, Pr. Co. A 3rd O. V. I.

French, Frank, Pr. Co. A 3r1 O. V. I.

Furnas, Homer H., Pr. Co. A 3rd O. V. I.

Furnas, Howard E., Pr. Co. A 3rd O. V. I.

Furnas, William M., Pr. Co. A 3rd O. V. I.

Furlong, Hezekiah, Pr. Co. A 3rd O. V. I.

Garrett, Louis W., Corp. Co. A 3rd O. V. I.

Griner, Julius, Pr. Co. A 3rd O. V. I.

Harman, John C., Pr. Co. A 3rd O.V.I.

Hill, Charles S., Sergt. Co. A 3rd O. V. I.

Hoover, Isaac, Wago. e- Co. A 3rd O. V. I.

Jones, Charles M., Corp Co. A 3rd O. V. I.

Jones, Davis W., Pr. Co. A 3rd O.V.I.

Kaufman, David, Pr. Co. K 3r1 O.V.I.

Keck, William C., Pr. Co. A 3rd O.V.I.

Kenney, Thomas F., Pr. Co. A 3rd O. V. I.

Klepinger, Walter, Pr. Co. A 3rd O. V. I.

Langston, Luther, Artificer Co. A 3rd O. V. I.

Langston, Raymond, Sergt. Co. A 3rd O. V. I.

Lehman, John H., 1st Sergt. Co A 3rd O. V. I.

Mendenhall, Everett, Pr. Co. A 3rd O. V. I.

Nason, Perry, Pr. Co. A 3rd O. V. I.

Neth, Lester L., Pr. Co. A 3rd O. V. I.

Parker, Frank M., Pr. Co. A 3rd O.V.I.

Penny, Isaac W., Corp. Co. K 3rd O. V. I.

Perry, Alvin W., Pr. Co. A 3rd O.V.I.

Ramsey, Ziba L., Bat. Sergt. Maj. 3rd O. V. I.

Scheffbaugh, David H., Pr. Co. A 3rd O V. I.

Smith, Charles, Q. M. Sergt. Co. A 3rd O. V. I.

Smith, Edward J., Sergt. Co. K 3rd O. V. I.

Smith, Henry, Pr. Co. K 3rd O. V. I.

Smith, Israel F., Sergt. Co. A 3rd O. V. I.

Snell, Ernest F., Principal Musician 3rd O. V. I.

Spencer, Harold K., Corp. Co. A 3rd O. V. I.

Sweeney, Morgan, Pr. Co. A 3rd O. V. I.

Tenney, Arthur, Pr. Co. A 3rd O. V. I.

Trimbur, Robert, Pr. Co. A 3rd O.V.I.

Tucker, William N., Corp. Co. A 3rd O. V. I.

Wallace, Edgar F., Pr. Co. A 3rd O. V. I.

Whitacre, Juriah R., Pr. Co. A 3rd O. V. I.

Williams, Edward G., Pr. Co. A 3rd O. V. I.

Wright, Rolen E., Corp. Co. A 3rd O. V. I.

CRAYON

Bosler, Benjamin S., Pr. Co. D 3rd O. V. I.

McInturff, Charles F., Pr. Co. D 3rd O. V. I.

CRIDERSVILLE

Osenbaugh, Albert M., Pr. Co. L 2nd O. V. I.

Phillips, Morley F., Pr. Co. L 2nd O. V. I.

Red, Elza, Pr. Co. L 2nd O. V. I.

Terry, Charles A., Pr. Co. L 2nd O.V.I.

Terry, Clark W., Pr. Co. L 2nd O.V.I.

CROWN CITY

Trobridge, Jefferson D., Corp. Co. C 7th O. V. I.

White, George R., Pr. Co. C 7th O.V.I.

CRYSTAL SPRING

Hardgrove, Burton C., Pr. Co. 1 8th O. V. I.

CUBA

Miller, James H., Pr. Co. K 7th O.V.I.

CUSTAR

Wismar, Frank E., Pr. Co. H 10th O. V. I.

CUYAHOGA FALLS

Keeney, George, Pr. Co. B 5th O. V. I.
Morris, John M., Pr. Co. K 8th O.V.I.

Oberholser, William J., Pr. Co. K 8th O. V. I.

CYGNET

Chase, Cydney C., Pr. Co. K 2nd O. V. I.

DALLAS

Barnes, Reece E., Pr. Co. F 3rd O.V.I.
Holmes, Harley S., Pr. Co. F 3rd O. V. I.

Whitehead, William R., Pr. Co. F 3rd O. V. I.

DALZELL

Koon, Warren M., Pr. Co. D 7th O. V. I.

DANVILLE

Henegen, Frank M., Pr. Co. M 2nd O. V. I.

DAWN

Burtch, Rufus A., Pr. Co. C 3rd O.V.I.

DAYTON

Alexander, Miles M., Pr. Co. A 2nd U. S. V. E.
Anderson, Clinton, Corp. Co. I 3rd O. V. I.
Anderson, Davis, Pr. Co. I 3rd O. V. I.
Arnold, Carroll B., Pr. Tr. F 1st O. V. C.
Arnold, Edwin F., Pr. Co. A 2nd U. S. V. E.
Austin, Edwin, Pr. Co. A 2nd U. S. V. E.
Bacon, Joseph C., Pr. Tr. F 1st O.V.C.
Bader, George, Pr. Tr. F 1st O. V. C.
Barlow, Theodore A., Pr. Tr. G 1st O. V. C.
Bartel, Samuel W., Pr. Tr. F 1st O. V. C.
Bates, Jesse S., Pr. Tr. F 1st O. V. C.
Beard, Fred S., Pr. Tr. F 1st O. V. C.
Becker, Henry J., Pr. Co. I 3rd O.V.I.
Beeson, Theodore S., Musician Tr. F 1st O. V. C.
Benner, Warren T., Pr. Co. G 3rd O. V. I.
Benson, Bennett, Pr. Co. B 2nd U. S. V. E.
Blackburn, William, Pr. Tr. F 1st O. V. C.
Bickham, Charles G., Corp. Co. G 3rd O. V. I.
Blessing, Raleigh W., Pr. Co. I 3rd O. V. I.

Bortel, Harvey B., Pr. Co. M 3rd O. V. I.
Bowman, Ben. S., Pr. Tr. F 1st O.V.C.
Boyer, Joseph D., Pr. Co. G 3rd O.V.I.
Boyer, William E., Pr. Co. I 3rd O.V.I.
Braun, J. F., Pr. Co. I 3rd O. V. I.
Brien, Bernis, Pr. Co. G 3rd O. V. I.
Brusman, Harry M., Pr. Co. A 2nd U. S. V. E.
Bucher, Frank A., Pr. Tr. F 1st O.V.C.
Bull, Fred A., Pr. Tr. F 1st O. V. C.
Burris, John W., Musician Co. A 2nd U. S. V. E.
Butler, Harry, Pr. Tr. F 1st O. V. C.
Campbell, Harry C., Pr. Co. G 3rd O. V. I.
Campbell, Harry E., Pr. Tr. F 1st O. V. C.
Carr, Edward C., Pr. Co. G 3rd O.V.I.
Cassel, Oliver D., Pr. Co. G 3rd O.V.I.
Catterlin, Bert, Pr. Co. I 3rd O. V. I.
Catterlin, William, Pr. Co. I 3rd O.V.I.
Chaffin, Charles C., 1st Sergt. Co. G 3rd O. V. I.
Chapman, Ora B., Sergt. Co. G 3rd O. V. I.
Chryst, William A., Pr. Co. G 3rd O. V. I.
Clark, Charles E., Pr. Tr. F 1st O.V.C.
Cleaver, Frank L., Pr. Co. G 3rd O. V. I.
Cleaver, Lee L., Pr. Co. G 3rd O. V. I.

Clemens, Grant, Pr. Co. C 9th Batt. O. V. I.
Clevell, Ernest, Pr. Tr. F 1st O. V. C.
Clevell, James E., Pr. Tr. F 1st O.V.C.
Cochran, Clarence W., Pr. Co. I 3rd O. V. I.
Coghill, Robert E., Pr. Co. G 3rd O. V. I.
Collins, Samuel, Pr. Tr. F 1st O. V. C.
Cooper, William, Pr. Tr. F 1st O.V.C.
Coughenour, Jesse H., Pr. Co. I 3rd O. V. I.
Cowan, Beverly, Pr. Co. G 3rd O. V. I.
Crane, Weakley, Pr. Co. G 3rd O. V. I.
Croft, Clifford, Pr. Co. I 3rd O. V. I.
Crone, James L., Pr. Co. G 3rd O. V. I.
Crowe, Thomas E., Pr. Tr. F 1st O. V. C.
Crume, William H., Sergt. Tr. F 1st O. V. C.
Cusick, Warren R., Pr. Co. A 2nd U. S. V. E.
Davidson, Edwin S., Corp. Tr. F 1st O. V. C.
Davies, Edward W., 1st Sergt. Tr. F 1st O. V. C.
Davies, John H., Corp. Co. G 3rd O. V. I.
Davis, Elmer, Sergt. Co. I 3rd O. V. I.
Davis, Roll, Pr. Co. I 3rd O. V. I.
Dickey, James, Saddler Tr. F 1st O. V. C.
Dietz, Peter, Pr. Tr. F 1st O. V. C.
Donoghue, Frank, Pr. Tr. F 1st O.V.C.
Dryden, Clifford S., Pr. Co. G 3rd O. V. I.
Dubs, Frank A., Pr. Co. G 3rd O. V. I.
Duckson, Norval D., Corp. Co. G 3rd O. V. I.
Dyke, Alfred M., Sergt. Co. G 3rd O. V. I.
Dyke, Perrie R., Pr. Co. G 3rd O. V. I.
Epting, James H., Pr. Co. G 3rd O.V.I.
Ferneding, John C., Pr. Co. I 3rd O. V. I.
Fischer, John G., Pr. Tr. F 1st O.V.C.
Floyd, Charles A., Pr. Co. G 3rd O.V.I.
Fox, Harold L., Pr. Co. G 3rd O. V. I.
Frantz, George, Pr. Tr. F 1st O. V. C.
Gaines, Walter H., Pr. Co. G 3rd O. V. I.
Gardner, William, Corp. Tr. F 1st O. V. C.
Gebhart, Richard G., Q. M. Sergt. Tr. F 1st O. V. C.
Geiger, Frank L., Corp. Co. A 2nd U. S. V. E.
Gibson, William, Pr. Tr. F 1st O.V.C.
Gimperling, Thomas N., Sergt. Co. G 3rd O. V. I.
Gratsh, Robert, Pr. Tr. F 1st O. V. C.
Griffin, Edward, Sergt. Co. I 3rd O.V.I.
Gross, Louis B., Pr. Co. I 3rd O. V. I.
Gruey, John B., Pr. Co. A 2nd U. S. V. E.
Hallis, Isaiah J., Wagoner Co. I 3rd O. V. I.

Haskett, Henry J., Q. M. Sergt. Co. G 3rd O. V. I.
Hayes, Patrick, Pr. Co. A 2nd U. S. V. E.
Heil, John, Pr. Co. A 2nd U. S. V. E.
Hentz, Paul G., Pr. Tr. F 1st O. V. C.
Heywood, Arthur T., Sergt. Co. A 2nd U. S. V. E.
Himes, Harry W., Pr. Co. I 3rd O.V.I.
Hinchey, Patrick S., Pr. Co. A 2nd U. S. V. E.
Hoffman, John E., Pr. Co. A 2nd U. S. V. E.
Hoffman, Howard L., Artificer Co. G 3rd O. V. I.
Holzer, Ferdinand, Pr. Co. G 3rd O.V.I.
Horlacher, Adolph G., Pr. Co. A 2nd U. S. V. E.
Hosier, Claude W., Pr. Tr. F 1st O. V. C.
Hunnicutt, Mark H., Pr. Co. G 3rd O. V. I.
Huppert, Daniel, Pr. Co. C 6th O.V.I.
Jaques, Harry O., Pr. Co. I 3rd O.V.I.
Jones, Charley W., Pr. Co. G 3rd O.V.I.
Jones, Henry E., Pr. Co. I 3rd O. V. I.
Jones, Julius I., Pr. Co. I 3rd O. V. I.
Johnson, Washington I., Musician Co. G 3rd O. V. I.
Kelly, Harry, Pr. Co. A 2nd U.S.V.E.
Kemp, David F., Sergt. Co. I 3rd O. V. I.
Kenney, Arthur P., Corp. Co. I 3rd O. V. I.
Kenney, Harry, Pr. Co. I 3rd O. V. I.
Ketzel, Frank, Artificer Co. I 3rd O. V. I.
Kiefaber, Elmer, Pr. Co. I 3rd O. V. I.
Kiehl, Ira G., Pr. Tr. F 1st O. V. C.
Kingsbury, George O., Pr. Tr. F 1st O. V. C.
Kissinger, Walter C., Sergt. Tr. F 1st O. V. C.
Kline, Edward, Pr. Co. M 3rd O. V. I.
Kline, Irwin, Musician Co. M 3rd O. V. I.
Kline, Keiffer S., Pr. Tr. G 1st O.V.C.
Klinger, Lee, Pr. Co. I 3rd O. V. I.
Knox, John B., Pr. Tr. F 1st O. V. C.
Kramer, Edward D., Pr. Co. G 3rd O. V. I.
Kramer, Leonard, Pr. Co. G 3rd O.V.I.
Lamborn, George, Pr. Co. I 3rd O.V.I.
Landfried, Frank J., Pr. Tr. F 1st O. V. C.
Launsberry, Frank W., Pr. Tr. F 1st O. V. C.
La Porte, Charles E., Pr. Co. G 3rd O. V. I.
Largent, Harvey, Pr. Co. I 3rd O.V.I.
La Rose, Louis F., Pr. Co. I 3rd O.V.I.
Lawrence, Charles E., Corp. Co. I 3rd O. V. I.
Lawrence, Charles E., Pr. Co. I 3rd O. V. I.
Layman, Russell W., Pr. Co. G 3rd O. V. I.

Lint, Amos, Pr. Co. A 2nd U. S. V. E.
Livingston, Frederick H., Musician Co. I 3rd O. V. I.
Loehr, John, Pr. Tr. F 1st O. V. C.
Long, Chester C., Pr. Co. G 3rd O.V.I.
Longstreth, Irvin H., Pr. Tr. F 1st O. V. C.
Loucks, Nevin A., Pr. Co. D 3rd O.V.I.
Loy, Henry, Corp. Co. G 3rd O. V. I.
Marker, Everett R., Pr. Co. I 3rd O. V. I.
Mausch, Andrew, Farrier Tr. F 1st O. V. C.
Mayers, Horace F., Pr. Co. I 3rd O. V. I.
McCain, Arthur B., Pr. Co. G 3rd O. V. I.
McClung, David W., Pr. Co. G 3rd O. V. I.
McDonald, Harry, Pr. Co. I 3rd O.V.I.
McDonnell, Hugh, Corp. Co. G 3rd O. V. I.
McGraw, Charles E., Pr. Co. G 3rd O V. I
McGregor, William T., Pr. Co. G 3rd O. V. I.
McKee, William L., Pr. Co. I 3rd O. V. I.
McNair, Ward D., Pr. Co. G 3rd O.V.I.
Mead, Daniel E., Pr. Co. G 3rd O. V. I.
Mead, Joseph W., Pr. Co. G 3rd O.V.I.
Meyer, Gustave, Pr. Co. A 2nd U. S. V. E.
Meyer, Robert A., Pr. Co. G 3rd O.V.I.
Miller, August, Pr. Co. C 3rd O. V. I.
Mills, Edwarde C., Corp. Co. I 3r1 O. V. I.
Mills, Harry C., Pr. Tr. F 1st O. V. C.
Minnick, Joseph E., Pr. Co. G 3rd O. V. I.
Moehlman, Fred, Pr. Co. I 3rd O. V. I.
Mohler, William M., Pr. Co. A 2nd U. S. V. E.
Moore, Walter B., Corp. Tr. F 1s: O. V. C.
Morris, John, Pr. Co. I 3rd O. V. I.
Morris, Orville K., Pr. Co. G 3rd O.V.I.
Morrison, T. Edward, Pr. Co. I 3rd O. V. I.
Mueller, Henry F., Pr. Co. A 2nd U. S. V. E.
Myers, Howard M., Corp. Tr. F 1s. O. V. C.
Myers, Vi. H., Pr. Co. C 3rd O. V. I.
Neff, William F., Pr. Co. G 3rd O. V. I.
Nehrik, Louis H., Pr. Co. G 3rd O.V.I.
Nevin, Robert R., Corp. Tr. F 1st O. V. C.
Nicholas, George J., Corp. Co. G 3rd O. V. I.
Nusz, George W., Pr. Tr. F 1s: O.V.C.
O'Brien, Edward F., Pr. Co. A 2nd U. S. V. E.
O'Connor, Bernard, Pr. Co. I 3rd O. V. I.

Orr, Elijah P., Pr. Co. A 2nd U. S. V. E.
Owens, Charles, Q. M. Sergt. Co. I 3rd O. V. I.
Owings, Samuel D., Sergt. Tr. F 1st O. V. C.
Ozias, Ernest R., Pr. Co. C 3rd O. V. I.
Palfray, Samuel A., Pr. Co. A 2nd U. S. V. E.
Parish, Albert E., Pr. Co. I 3rd O.V.I.
Parratt, John E., Sergt. Tr. F 1st O. V. C.
Paul, George, Pr. Co. I 3rd O. V. I.
Paul, Robert J., Wagoner Co. G 3rd O. V. I.
Pease, Calvin E., Pr. U. R 3rd O. V. I.
Pease, Edward G., Pr. Tr. F 1st O.V.C.
Peck, Herbert M., Pr. Co. A 2nd U. S. V. E.
Peckolt, Frank, Pr. Co. A 2nd U. S. V. E.
Pfarrer, Matthew, Bat. Sergt. Maj. 3rd O. V. I.
Pfeifer, Arthur T., Pr. Co. G 3rd O.V.I.
Plance, Clem C., Pr. Co. I 3rd O.V.I.
Prentiss, Park B., Musician Co. G 3rd O. V. I.
Prentiss, Paul A., Sergt. Co. A 2nd U. S. V. E.
Putnam, Albert W., Sergt. Co. C 2nd U. S. V. E.
Rausch, George, 1st Sergt. Co. I 3rd O. V. I.
Real, John F., Wagoner Co. M 3rd O. V. I.
Rhodelhamel, Jesse E., Pr. Co. I 3rd O. V. I.
Rike, Fred, Pr. Co. I 3rd O. V. I.
Ringler, William, Pr. Tr. F 1st O.V.C.
Ritter, Walter C., Corp. Tr. F 1st O. V. C.
Robison, Frank J., Pr. Co. G 3rd O.V.I.
Robison, Wilson, Pr. Co. I 3rd O.V.I.
Roche, Joseph P., Corp. Co. A 2nd U. S. V. E.
Rockafeller, George, Pr. Co. I 3rd O. V. I.
Rosenthal, Israel, Pr. Tr. F 1s: O.V.C.
Roth, Jacob, Jr., Pr. Co. G 3rd O.V.I.
Scheibenzuber, Fred, Pr. Co. I 3rd O. V. I.
Scheibenzuber, Philip, Musician Co. I 3rd O. V. I.
Schell, William, Pr. Co. I 3rd O. V. I.
Schenck, Joseph, Pr. Co. A 2nd U. S. V. E.
Schiewets, Charles, Pr. Co. I 3rd O.V.I.
Schlagal, John, Corp. Co. I 3rd O.V.I.
Schneider, Charles, Pr. Co. G 3rd O. V. I.
Schulte, George, Pr. Tr. F 1st O. V. C.
Schultz, Andrew J., Pr. Tr. F 1st O. V. C.
Scott, Frank J., Pr. Tr. G 1st O. V. C.
Seehler, Lawrence H., Pr. Co. G 3rd O. V. I.
Shaw, Warren D., Pr. Tr. F 1st O.V.C.

Sherer, Ward, Pr. Co. I 3rd O. V. I.
Shuler, Carl F., Pr. Tr, F 1st O. V. C.
Sigler, George E., Pr. Co. G 3rd O.V.I.
Skinner, John R., Pr. Co. G 3rd O.V.I.
Small, Bert, Pr. Co. I 3rd O. V. I.
Smith, Charles E., Pr. Tr. F 1st O.V.C.
Smith, Herbert, Corp. Co. I 3rd O.V.I.
Snyder, Edward, Pr. Co. A 2nd U. S.
V. E.
Steinbach, William, Pr. Co. I 3rd O.
V. I.
Swadener, William, Pr. Co. I 3rd O.
V. I.
Tannreuther, Wilmer, Pr. Co. I 3rd O.
V. I.
Taylor, Peter, Pr. Co. I 3rd O. V. I.
Thirkield, Howard E., Pr. Tr. F 1st O.
V. C.
Thorne, Thomas, Pr. Tr. F 1st O.V.C.
Trout, Carl S., Musician Tr. F 1st O.
V. C.
Turton, George S., Pr. Co. A 2nd U.
S. V. E.
Tuthill, William, Pr. Co. I 3rd O. V. I.
Ullery, Walter S., Pr. Co. G 3rd O.V.I.
Vickroy, Edward S., Pr. Co. G 3rd O.
V. I.
Voerge, Ziba, Pr. Tr. F 1st O. V. C.
Wagner, Bradley, Pr. Tr. F 1s O.V.C.
Wagner, Charles W., Corp. Tr. F 1st
O. V. C.

Wagoner, Melvin C., Corp. Co. L 1st
O. V. I.
Wallace, Fred S., Pr. Tr. F 1st O.V.C.
Walz, Henry F., Pr. Co. I 3rd O. V. I.
Warner, John E., Pr. Co. A 2nd U.
S. V. E.
Washington, George V., Pr. Co. G 3rd
O. V. I.
Webb, Charles H., Pr. Co. G 3rd O.
V. I.
Webber, Charles, Pr. Co. I 3rd O. V. I.
Wheatley, John C., Pr. Co. A 2nd U.
S. V. E.
Wheaton, John C., Pr. Co. A 2nd U.
S. V. E.
Williams, Harvey L., Pr. Co. A 2nd
U. S. V. E.
Wilson, Verba E., Pr. Co. I 3rd O.V.I.
Winchet, Irvin, Corp. Tr. F 1st O.V.C.
Wittler, Ferdinand, Pr. Tr. F 1st O.
V. C.
Wood, Francis C., Pr. Tr. F 1st O.
V. C.
Woodruff, Charles H., Pr. Co. G 3rd
O. V. I.
Worman, Horace D., Pr. Tr. F 1st O.
V. C.
Wuichet, Alexander G., Sergt. Co. I
3rd O. V. I.
Zellers, Ira R., Pr. Co. I 3rd O. V. I.

DEFIANCE

Abell, Ben. E., Corp. Co. M 6th O.V.I.
Ash, William O., Corp. Co. M 6th O.
V. I.
Barbillion, Frank, Pr. Co. M 6th O.
V. I.
Barr, Arthur J., Pr. Co. M 6th O.V.I.
Bartels, Frederick L., Pr. Co. M 6th
O. V. I.
Bartels, Herman F., Pr. Co. M 6th O.
V. I.
Barth, August C., Pr. Co. M 6th O.V.I.
Beal, Charles C., Pr. Co. M 6th O.V.I.
Beardsley, Leroy E., Corp. Co. M 6th
O. V. I.
Beardsley, William D., Pr. Co. M 6th
O. V. I.
Birmingham, Jesse, Pr. Co. M 6th O.
V. I.
Bowen, Charley, Pr. Co. M 6th O.V.I.
Bowers, William H., Corp. Co. M 6th
O. V. I.
Carpenter, Lewis L., Pr. Co. M 6th
O. V. I.
Clark, Frank, Pr. Co. M 6th O. V. I.
Clark, Frank M., Pr. Co. M 6th O.V.I.
Connors, William, Pr. Co. M 6th O.
V. I.
Conway, Edward W., Pr. Co. M 6th
O. V. I.
Corcellious, Louis, Pr. Co. M 6th O.
V. I.
Daniels, Edwin B., Pr. Co. M 6th O.
V. I.

Davis, Clyde E., Pr. Co. M 6th O. V. I.
Dils, Albert R., Artificer Co. M 6th O.
V. I.
Ellsworth, James J., Pr. Co. M 6th O.
V. I.
Gardner, Joseph, Pr. Co. M 6th O.V.I.
Garver, Sylvis, 1st Sergt. Co. M 6th O.
V. I.
Gilmore, Frank L., Musician Co. M 6th
O. V. I.
Glassmire, Alva G., Wagoner Co. M
6th O. V. I.
Gorman, Frank B., Sergt. Co. M 6th
O. V. I.
Hale, Gale E., Pr. Co. M 6th O. V. I.
Harper, James J., Pr. Co. M 6th O.V.I.
Hatfield, Irwin C., Pr. Co. M 6th O.
V. I.
Hawk, James, Pr. Co. M 6th O. V. I.
Hawkins, John, Pr. Co. M 6th O. V. I.
Hilton, Brice, Pr. Co. M 6th O. V. I.
Hoover, Max, Pr. Co. M 6th O. V. I.
Houck, William E., Pr. Co. M 6th O.
V. I
Keffer, Theodore, Pr. Co. M 6th O.V.I.
Kindig, Edward, Pr. Co. M 6th O.V.I.
Korn, Frank G., Pr. Co. M 6th O.V.I.
Koup, Miley B., Pr. Co. M 6th O. V. I.
Krabach, Christ. Pr. Co. M 6th O. V. I.
Ledyard, Clinton, Pr. Co. M 6th O.V.I.
Lee, George, Pr. Co. M 6th O. V. I.
Lewis, Henry C., Pr. Co. M 6th O.V.I.

Luken, Herman J., Pr. Co. M 6th O. V. I.
Mann, Charles, Pr. Co. M 6th O. V. I.
McCauley, Howard, Pr. Co. M 6th O. V. I.
McCullough, Robert, Pr. Co. M 6th O. V. I.
Miller, Clem S., Pr. Co. M 6th O.V.I.
Mills, Fred A., Pr. Co. M 6th O. V. I.
Mink, Fred N., Pr. Co. M 6th O. V. I.
Motter, Wilson, Pr. Co. M 6th O. V. I.
Neaderhauser, John H., Pr. Co. M 6th O. V. I.
Newill, Willis A., Pr. Co. M 6th O.V.I.
Noe, Arlo J., Pr. Co. M 6th O. V. I.
Parmer, Volney A., Pr. Co. M 6th O. V. I.
Partee, Milow W., Corp. Co. M 6th O. V. I.
Patton, J. Fred, Pr. Co. M 6th O.V.I.
Philips, David, Sergt. Co. M 6th O.V.I.
Powell, Bertram, Pr. Co. M 6th O.V.I.
Prosser, William M., Musician Co. M 6th O. V. I.
Ralston, Karl K., Pr. Co. M 6th O.V.I.
Rath, George M., Pr. Co. M 6th O.V.I.
Richardson, Merle, Pr. Co. M 6th O. V. I.
Rollins, Albert L., Pr. Co. M 6th O. V. I.
Root, Fred G., Corp. Co. M 6th O.V.I.
Rowan, John E., Pr. Co. M 6th O.V.I.
Sapp, Lem., Corp. Co. M 6th O. V. I.
Schmick, Carl H., Sergt. Co. M., 6th O. V. I

Schultz, Edward A., Pr. Co. M 6th O. V. I.
Scott, John, Pr. Co. M 6th O. V. I.
Sieren, Albert V., Corp. Co. M 6th O. V. I.
Spangler, Herman A., Corp. Co. M 6th O. V. I.
Switzer, Charles M., Pr. Co. M 6th O. V. I.
Tiller, Charles, Pr. Co. M 6th O. V. I.
Travers, Norton R., Pr. Co. M 6th O. V. I.
Tuttle, John C., Sergt. Co. M 6th O. V. I.
Ulrich, Alfred, Pr. Co. M 6th O. V. I.
Van Horn, Harry H., Sergt. Co. M 6th O. V. I.
Warren, Haddix M., Pr. Co. M 6th O. V. I.
Weaver, Robert R., Corp. Co. M 6th O. V. I.
Weisenberger, Earl, Corp. Co. M 6th O. V. I.
White, Charles, Pr. Co. M 6th O. V. I.
Whitney, Harry M., Pr. Co. M 6th O. V. I.
Williamson, Joseph, Pr. Co. M 6th O. V. I.
Wirock, John T., Pr. Co. M 6th O.V.I.
Wisda, Michael A., Pr. Co. M 6th O. V. I.
Wolf, Joseph, Pr. Co. M 6th O. V. I.
Wolf, Otto B., Pr. Co. M 6th O. V. I.
Wood, Web, Corp. Co. M 6th O. V. I.
Zoller, Fred H., Pr. Co. M 6th O.V.I.

DEGRAFF

Berndt, Edward, Pr. Co. F 2nd O. V. I.
Doan, Charles E., Pr. Co. F 2nd O.V.I.
Doan, Homer D., Pr. Co. F 2nd O.V.I.
Hess, B. F., Pr. Co. F 2nd O. V. I.
Martin, Forrest, Pr. Co. F 2nd O. V. I.
Matthews, Ralph N., Pr. Co. F 2nd O. V. I.

Rairdon, Clifford J., Pr. Co. F 2nd O. V. I.
Richardson, Harry C., Pr. Co. F 2nd O. V. I.
Spellman, Earl M., Pr. Co. F 2nd O. V. I.
Taylor, Harry, Pr. Co. F 2nd O. V. I.
Valentine, Elmer, Pr. Co. F 2nd O.V.I.

DELAWARE

Anderson, William, Pr. U. R. 3rd O. V. I.
Beitler, Claud M., Pr. Co. K 4th O.V.I.
Billig, Clinton E., Pr. Co. K 4th O.V.I.
Browning, Sherman W., Pr. Co. K 4th O. V. I.
Brugh, Earl E., Pr. Co. K 4th O. V. I.
Brunn, Harry C., Pr. Co. K 4th O.V.I.
Butt, Andrew M., Pr. Co. K 4th O.V.I.
Campbell, Herman R., Pr. Co. K 4th O. V. I.
Coleman, William E., Pr. Co. B 9th Batt. O. V. I.
Cosler, Harry A., Sergt. Co. K 4th O. V. I.
Cratty, Carl T., Sergt. Co. K 4th O.V.I.

Cruikshank, Alwood, Pr. Co. K 4th O. V. I.
Dall, Clive K., Pr. Co. K 4th O. V. I.
Davis, Horace W., Pr. Co. K 4th O. V. I.
Doke, Albert H., Pr. Co. F 4th O. V. I.
Dove, T. Clark, Pr. Co. K 4th O. V. I.
Dunham, Sturges S., Pr. Co. K 4th O. V. I.
Enright, Francis H., Pr. Co. K 4th O. V. I.
Finley, Charles W., Bat. Sergt. Maj. 4th O. V. I.
Ford, Willie R., Pr. Co. K 4th O. V. I.
France, Clyde O., Pr. Co. K 4th O.V.I.
Glaze, Thomas, Pr. Co. K 4th O. V. I.

Greible, George A., Sergt. Co. K 4th
O. V. I.
Greiner, John R., Pr. Co. K 4th O.V.I.
Grove, Thomas V., Pr. Co. K 4th O.
V. I.
Harmount, Alexander K., Corp. Co. K
4th O. V. I.
Harmount, William H., Pr. Co. K 4th
O. V. I.
Hills, Louis C., Pr. Co. K 4th O. V. I.
Hodges, Stanley M., Pr. Co. K 4th O.
V. I.
Housley, Edwin L., Pr. Co. K 4th O.
V. I.
Howald, William A., Pr. Co. K 4th O.
V. I.
Inscho, Albert D., Pr. Co. K 4th O.
V. I.
Inscho, Charles L., Artificer Co. K 4th
O. V. I.
Jones, Clarence L., Pr. Co. K 4th O.
V. I.
Koeppel, Oscar O., 1st Sergt. Co. K 4th
O. V. I.
Lawson, Charles E., Pr. Co. K 4th O.
V. I.
Longwell, John W., Pr. Co. K 4th O.
V. I.
Longwell, Ray, Pr. Co. K 4th O. V. I.
Marriott, John M., Pr. Co. K 4th O.
V. I.
McNaughton, Thomas R., Pr. Co. K
4th O. V. I.
Miller, Charles C., Pr. Co. K 4th O.
V. I.
Miller, Charley H., Pr. Tr. D 1st O.
V. C.
Miller, Harry A., Pr. Co. K 4th O.V.I.
Montane, Edward B., Pr. Co. K 4th O.
V. I.
Nelson, Elbert J., Corp. Co. K 4th O.
V. I.
Norton, William L., Sergt. Co. K 4th
O. V. I.
Osborn, Brice, Pr. Co. K 4th O. V. I.
Patrick, Orisan W., Pr. Co. K 4th O.
V. I.

Platz, George, Pr. Co. K 4th O. V. I.
Powell, Alexander B., Pr. Co. K 4th
O. V. I.
Read, Robert W., Pr. Co. K 4th O.V.I.
Reed, William, Pr. Co. K 4th O. V. I.
Riddle, Charles W., Sergt Co. K 4th
O. V. I.
Riddle, Lester C., Pr. Co. K 4th O.V.I.
Riddle, Roy R., Pr. Co. K 4th O.V.I.
Rider, Walter R., Wagoner Co. K 4th
O. V. I.
Robinson, Frank A., Pr. U. R. 3rd O.
V. I.
Rose, Henry E., Pr. Co. K 4th O. V. I.
Said, Frank M., Corp. Co. K 4th O.V.I.
Said, Presley, Pr. Co. K 4th O. V. I.
Sanger, Ulysses G., Pr. Co. K 4th O.
V. I.
Schneider, Bernhardt J., Pr. Co. K 4th
O. V. I.
Shank, John W., Pr. Co. K 4th O.V.I.
Sheldon, Henry E., Corp. Co. K 4th
V. I.
Shults, Joshua S., Musician Co. K 4th
O. V. I.
Sloop, Arthur, Pr. Co. D 4th O. V. I.
Smith, Robert B., Hospital Steward
10th O. V. I.
Spain, Lewis R., Pr. Co. K 4th O. V. I.
Standish, Phi H., Pr. Co. M 2nd O.V.I.
Starr, Merton S., Corp. Co. K 4th O.
V. I.
Thompson, Ed. O., Corp. Co. K 4th
O. V. I.
Thrall, Charles E., Pr. Co. K 4th O.
V. I.
Thrall, George W., Pr. Co. K 4th O.
V. I.
Vertner, Avery L., Pr. Co. K 4th O.
V. I.
Watkins, Frank, Pr. Co. K 4th O. V. I.
Wells, Rex Warren, Pr. Co. K 4th O.
V. I.
Windham, Roy A., Pr. Co. K 4th O.
V. I.
Wohleater, William Z., Pr. Co. K 4th
O. V. I.

DELMOUNT

Neal, William E., Pr. Co. 4th O.V.I.

DELPHOS

Hoelzer, John F., Pr. Co. D 2nd O.V.I.
Kroeger, Frank, Pr. Co. K 3rd O.V.I.
Krutsch, David O., Pr. Co. K 2nd O.
V. I.

Kundert, Henry C., Pr. Co. D 2nd O.
V. I.

DELTA

Gandy, Clyde M., Pr. Co. G 6th O.V.I.
Gehring, George W., Pr. Co. G 6th O.
V. I.
Isbell, Edward E., Pr. Co. G 6th O.
V. I.

Johnson, Charles P., Pr. Co. G 6th O.
V. I.
Kennedy, James E., Pr. Co. G 6th O.
V. I.

Kenyon, Frank C., Pr. Co. G 6th O.
V. I.
Lawrence, Walter, Pr. Co. G 6th O.V.I.
Miley, Ernest, Pr. Co. G 6th O. V. I.

Moyer, Ralph F., Pr. Co. G 6th O.V.I.
Planson, Frank M., Pr. Co. G 6th O.
V. I.

DENNISON

Barnes, Edwin P., Musician Co. M 7th
O. V. I.
Beck, Henry E., Wagoner Co. M 7th
O. V. I.
Bell, Howard D., Pr. Co. M 7th O.V.I.
Berton, James E., Sergt. Co. M 7th O.
V. I.
Bolter, William T., Pr. Co. M 7th O.
V. I.
Brown, Alvin H., Q. M. Sergt. Co. M
7th O. V. I.
Brown, Oliver S., Pr. Co. M 7th O.V.I.
Cappel, Theodore G., Sergt. Co. M 7th
O. V. I.
Castle, John H., Corp. Co. M 7th O.
V. I.
Converse, Jay F., 1st Sergt. Co. M 7th
O. V. I.
Cope, Clarence E., Pr. Co. M 7th O.
V. I.
Criss, William C., Pr. Co. M 7th O.V.I.
Davis, Francis M., Pr. Co. M 7th O.
V. I.
Davis, Rollo R., Pr. Co. M 7th O.V.I.
Devine, Walter, Corp. Co. M 7th O.
V. I.
Elson, David C., Musician Co. M 7th
O. V. I.
Fearon, Merrill G., Pr. Co. M 7th O.
V. I.
Feekey, John W., Pr. Co. M 7th O.V.I.
Gudgen, Lanie, Pr. Co. M 7th O.V.I.
Hanna, Albert D., Pr. Co. M 7th O.
V. I.
Harris, Claude E., Pr. Co. M 7th O.
V. I.
Havnar, William H., Pr. Co. M 7th
O. V. I.
Hillyer, George E., Pr. Co. M 7th O.
V. I.
Holbrook, Stewart A., Pr. Co. M 7th
O. V. I.
Johnson, Charles A., Pr. Co. M 7th
O. V. I.
Jones, Charles A., Pr. Co. M 7th O.V.I.
Julien, Otto, Sergt. Co. M 7th O. V. I.
Keesey, Edwin B., Pr. Co. M 7th O.
V. I.
Kennedy John H., Pr. Co. M 7th O.
V. I.

Kothe, Daniel C., Corp. Co. M 7th
O. V. I.
Kothe, Fred A., Pr. Co. M 7th O. V. I.
Lewis, John E., Pr. Co. M 7th O. V. I.
Lewis, Sherman D., Corp. Co. M 7th
O. V. I.
Lewis, William E., Pr. Co. M 7th O.
V. I.
Ludwig, Clarence, Pr. Co. M 7th O.
V. I.
Luttrell, Arthur S., Pr. Co. M 7th O.
V. I.
Luttrell, Walter B., Pr. Co. M 7th O.
V. I.
Marshall, William O., Pr. Co. M 7th
O. V. I.
McConn, Aaron E., Pr. Co. M 7th O.
V. I.
McCullough, George L., Pr. Co. M 7th
O. V. I.
McGuire, John, Pr. Co. M 7th O. V. I.
Murray, Wheeler S., Pr. Co. M 7th O.
V. I.
Norris, William S., Pr. Co. M 7th O.
V. I.
Parks, Charles H., Pr. Co. M 7th O.
V. I.
Polen, Lewis E., Pr. Co. M 7th O.V.I.
Randall, William E., Pr. Co. M 7th O.
V. I.
Rogers, Thomas C., Pr. Co. M 7th O.
V. I.
Roney, Charley A., Pr. Co. M 7th O.
V. I.
Row, Arthur D., Pr. Co. M 7th O.V.I.
Schambra, Charles C., Hospital Steward
7th O. V. I.
Stewart, George H., Pr. Co. M 7th O.
V. I.
Stewart, William W., Pr. Co. M 7th
O. V. I.
Storing, Henry W., Pr. Co. M 7th O.
V. I.
Thompson, Charles B., Corp. Co. M
7th O. V. I.
Tweed, Frank B., Pr. Co. M 7th O.V.I.
Tweed, Harry J., Pr. Co. M 7th O.V.I.
Umpleby, Arthur, Sergt. Co. M 7th O.
V. I.

DESHLER

Collins, Tad C., Pr. Co. K 2nd O.V.I.

O'Hearn, Edward P., Pr. Co. H 10th
O. V. I.

DETROIT, MICH

Armstrong, Edward, Pr. Co. I 5th O.
V. I.

Gerhke, August, Pr. Co. C 10th O.V.I.

DOVER

Shuler, John, Pr. Co. D 4th O. V. I.

DRESDEN

Adams, Herbert, Pr. Co. I 10th O.V.I.
Black, Arthur R., Pr. Tr. D 1st O.V.C.

Gould, Melvin O., Pr. Co. I 10th O. V. I.
Spicer, Ora T., Pr. Co. I 10th O. V. I.

DUNCAN'S FALLS

Wolfe, Alfred K., Pr. Co. L 10th O.V.I.

DUNDEE, MICH.

Zeluff, Clifton D., Pr. Tr E 1st O.V.C.

DUNKIRK

Arn, Lawrence V., Pr. Co. E 2nd O. V. I.
Bender, George W., Pr. Co. I 2nd O. V. I.
Gauch, Frank, Pr. Co. I 2nd O. V. I.
Haldeman, James B., Jr., Pr. Co. K 2nd O. V. I.
Helms, William H., Pr. Co. I 2nd O. V. I.

Kisting, Joseph B., Pr. Tr. D 1st O. V. C.
Obenour, Charlie A., Pr. Co. G 2nd O. V. I.
Wedertz, George, Pr. Co. I 2nd O.V.I.
Williamson, Harlie, Pr. Co. G 2nd O. V. I.

DURBIN

Jenkins, John, Pr. Co. B 3rd O. V. I.

EAST CLEVELAND

Bowman, Walter E., Jr., Corp. Co. K 10th O. V. I.

EAST LIVERPOOL

Anderson, Baird N., Pr. Co. E 8th O. V. I.
Beatty, Thomas J., Pr. Co. E 8th O. V. I.
Blake, George T., Pr. U. R. 8th O.V.I.
Campbell, George W., Pr. Co. E 8th O. V. I.
Carnahan, Morris J., Pr. Co. E 8th O. V. I.
Cook, Walter S., Pr. Co. E 8th O.V.I.
Cox, Charles C., Pr. Co. E 8th O. V. I.
Crewson, Walter S., Pr. Co. E 8th O. V I.
Davis, Harry K., Pr. Co. E 8th O.V.I.
Davis, Joseph C., Corp. Co. E 8th O. V. I.
Dewar, James H., Musician Co. E 8th O. V. I.
Dodd, Carrol L., Pr. Co. E 8th O.V.I.
Dye, Frank S., Pr. Co. E 8th O. V. I.
Eaton, Harry A., Pr. Co. E 8th O.V.I.
Eoff, William M., Pr. Co. E 8th O.V.I.
Gibson, John R., Wagoner Co. E 8th O. V. I.

Hackworth, William G., Corp. Co. E 8th O. V. I.
Hanley, William F., 1st Sergt. Co. E 8th O. V. I.
Harvey, Joseph B., Pr. Co. E 8th O. V. I.
Hayden, Harry, Pr. Co. E 8th O. V. I.
Heddleson, Lawrence E., Pr. Co. E 8th O. V. I.
Hedley, John C., Pr. Co. E 8th O.V.I.
Howard, John A., Pr. Co. E 8th O.V.I.
Hoyt, Joel W., Pr Co. E 8th O. V. I.
Hughes, John H., Pr. Co. E 8th O.V.I.
Kerr, Harry G., Pr. Co. E 8th O. V. I.
Kinsey, William H., Sergt. Co. E 8th O. V. I.
Kirkwood, Allie M., Pr. Co. E 8th O. V. I.
Lucas, Isaac, Pr. Co. E 8th O. V. I.
Martin, Frederick A., Pr. Co. E 8th O. V. I.
McCord, William R., Corp. Co. E 8th O. V. I.

McCurran, Dennis M., Pr. Co. E 8th O. V. I.
McGill, Thomas G., Pr. Co. E 8th O. V. I.
McIntosh, John P., Pr. Co. E 8th O. V. I.
McKinney, William H., Pr. Co. E 8th O. V. I.
McKinnon, John C. D., Pr. Co. E 8th O. V. I.
McKinnon, Orville J., Pr. Co. E 8th O. V. I.
Miller, William J., Corp. Co. 8th O. V. I.
Mite, Raymond L., Pr. Co. E 8th O. V. I.
Moon, Samuel, Pr. Co. E 8th O. V. I.
Moore, Philip, Pr. Co. E 8th O. V. I.
Morley, Edwin S., Pr. Co. E 8th O.V.I.
Murray, John W., Pr. Co. E 8th O.V.I.
Oschman, Fred G., Pr. Co. E 8th O. V. I.
Pool, Lewis M., Pr. Co. E 8th O. V. I.
Purinton, Charles A., Sergt. Co. E 8th O. V. I.
Rahon, James D., Pr. Co. E 8 h O.V.I.
Reniker, Alfred W., Pr. Co. E 8th O. V. I.

Reynolds, Oliver C., Pr. Co. E 8th O. V. I.
Robinson, John, Pr. Co. E 8th O.V.I.
Simms, Ezra H., Pr. Co. E 8th O.V.I.
Smith, Fred A., Pr. Co. E 8th O. V. I.
Smith, Harry E., Pr. Co. E 8th O.V.I.
Smith, Thomas C., Sergt. Co. E 8th O. V. I.
Steine, Albert M., Pr. Co. E 8th O.V.I.
Swingwood, George, Pr. Co. E 8th O. V. I.
Switzer, Charles W., Pr. Co. E 8th O. V. I.
Trump, Frank L., Sergt. Co. E 8th O. V. I.
Ward, James E., Pr. Co. E 8th O. V. I.
Weaver, Vaughn P., Corp. Co. E 8th O. V. I.
Wilkinson, George A., Pr. Co. E 8th O. V. I.
Williams, Timothy, Pr. Co. E 8th O. V. I.
Wilson, William D., Pr. Co. E 8 h O. V. I.
Wood, Ralph A., Pr. Co. E 8th O.V.I.
Wyman, George E., Corp. Co. E 8th O. V. I.

EAST NORWALK

Dunick, Thiers J., Pr. Co. G 5th O.V.I.

EAST TOLEDO

Reinhart, Albert G., Pr. Co. C 10th O. V. I.

Skidmore, Earl R., Pr. Co. G 10th O. V. I.

EAST TOWNSEND

Austin, Edgar D., Pr. Co. G 5th O.V.I.
Fox, Alvin E., Pr. Co. G 5th O. V. I.

Stacey, Charles L., Pr. Co. G 5th O. V. I.

EDWARDS STATION

Larrimer, Frank O., Pr. Bat. H 1st O. V. A.

ELBA

Alban, Rees A., 3rd Sergt. Co. D 7th O. V. I.
Ball, Allan, Pr. Co. D 7th O. V. I.

Miracle, Wade, Pr. Co. D 7th O. V. I.
Smith, Emery F., Pr. Co. D 7th O.V.I.

ELKHART, IND.

Drapert, Fred, Pr. Co. G 7th O. V. I.

ELMORE

Allyn, Andrew F., Pr. Co. H 10th O. V. I.
Boggs, Brazilla, Pr. Co. H 10th O.V.I.
Bothe, August J., Pr. Co. G 10th O.V.I.
Crozier, Wesley E., Pr. Co. H 10th O. V. I.

Damschroder, Charlie F., Pr. Co. H 10th O. V. I.
Edinger, John, Pr. Co. H 10th O. V. I.
Egert, George, Pr. Co. H 10th O. V. I.
Fought, Bert E., Pr. Tr. E 1st O. V. C.

Fredrich, Gustav C., Pr. Co. H 10th O. V. I.

Hunter, William E., Pr. Co. H 10th O. V. I.

Logan, Flevious, Pr. Co. H 10th O.V.I.
Logan, Isaac, Pr. Co. H 10th O. V. I.
Logan, Theodore, Pr. Co. H 10th O. V. I.

McGowin, Harry H., Pr. Tr. E 1st O. V. C.

Meyers, Charles F., Pr. Co. G 10th O. V. I.

Pafenbach, John E., Pr. Co. H 10th O. V. I.

Rapole, Charlie G., Pr. Tr. E 1st O. V. C.

Reese, Wortha L., Pr. Tr. E 1s' O.V.C.

Rothert, Charles, Pr. Co. G 10th O.V.I.

Sarnes, Eugene R., Pr. Co. H 10th O. V. I.

Shepardson, Charles M., Pr. Co. H 10th O. V. I.

Webb, Roy E., Pr. Co. G 5th O. V. I.

Willey, Fred W., Pr. Co. H 10th O.V.I.

Winn, Addison G., Pr. Co. H 10th O. V. I.

Wood, James L., Pr. Tr. E 1s O.V.C.

ELYRIA

Berry, Ernest A., Wagoner Co. H 8th O. V. I.

Caldwell, Lawrence, Pr. Co. A 10th O. V. I.

Hallenberger, J. Henry, Pr. Tr. G 1st O. V. C.

Paulson, Joseph V., Pr. Tr. B 1st O. V. C.

EMMETT

Votrie, Albert B., Pr. Co. M 6th O.V.I.

ENO

Gould, John W., Pr. Co. C 7th O. V. I.

ERIS

Howard, Harry H., Pr. Co. D 3rd O. V. I.

ERLANGER, KY.

Kreher, Peter, Pr. Co. B 2nd U.S.V.E.

ETNA

Balthaser, Frank, P. Co. K 3rd O. V. I.

EUREKA

Hazlette, Print, Pr. Co. C 7th O. V. I.
Holston, William, Pr. Co. C 7th O.V.I.
Kinder, Charles R., 4th Sergt. Co. C 7th O. V. I.

Martindill, Millard L., Corp. Co. C 7th O. V. I.

Roach, Samuel, Pr. Co. C 7th O. V. I.

Wright, Clarence E., Pr. Co. C 7th O. V. I.

EVANSTON P. O.

Evans, Charles H., Pr. Bat. H 1st O. V. A.

FAIRFIELD CO.

Hansley, Seymore E., Pr. Co. I 4th O. V. I.

FAIRMOUNT

Bittner, Gust. P., Pr. Tr. B 1st O. V. C.

FAIRPORT

Congos, Victor, Pr. Co. M 5th O.V.I.
Hissa, Herman, Pr. Co. M 5th O.V.I.
Kaukonen, Anton, Pr. Co. M 5th O. V. I

Markko, John Eddie, Pr. Co. M 5th O. V. I.

Mattson, Emil A., Pr. Co. M 5th O.V.I.

Takala, Thomas V., Pr. Co. M 5th O. V. I.

FARGO

Parks, Frank, Pr. Co. C 3rd O. V. I.

FAYETTE

Wilson, George C., Pr. Co. G 6th O. V. I.

FINDLAY

Arnold, Clarence W., Pr. Co. A 2nd O. V. I.

Arnold, John H., Pr. Co. A 2nd O.V.I.

Barnd, Jean O., Q. M. Sergt. Co. A 2nd O. V. I.

Berthuarne, Hardin W., Pr. Co. A 2nd O. V. I.

Biery, John Jay, Pr. Co. A 2nd O.V.I.

Biggs, Charles R., Pr. Co. A 2nd O.V.I.

Biggs, Frank M., Bat. Sergt. Maj. 2nd O. V. I.

Biggs, Harry, Pr. Co. A 2nd O. V. I.

Boyd, Albert, Pr. Co. H 3rd O. V. I.

Burlingham, Charles, Pr. Co. A 2nd O. V. I.

Carlin, Rawson K., Pr. Co. A 2nd O. V. I.

Carter, Walter C., Pr. Co. A 2nd O. V. I.

Chance, Wilbur, Pr. Co. A 2nd O. V. I.

Chase, Edro S., Pr. Co. A 2nd O. V. I.

Cherry, John P., Pr. Co. A 2nd O.V.I.

Clark, Preston J., Pr. Co. A 2nd O.V.I.

Curry John D., 2nd Sergt. Co. A 2nd O. V. I.

Darling, Foust R., Pr. Co. A 2nd O. V. I.

Dempsey, John, 1st Sergt. Co. A 2nd O. V. I.

Dennison, Harry I., 5th Corp. Co. A 2nd O. V. I.

Dennison, James, Jr., Pr. Co. A 2nd O. V. I.

Dennison, Remus C., 5th Sergt. Co. A 2nd O. V. I.

Desprez, Owen S., Pr. Co. A 2nd O. V. I.

Dittman, William E., Pr. Co. A 2nd O. V. I.

Dukes, Burton L., Pr. Tr. G 1st O.V.C.

Dukes, Paul W., Pr. Co. A 2nd O.V.I.

Dye, Charles, Pr. Co. A 2nd O. V. I.

Dye, James, Wagoner Co. A 2nd O.V.I.

Dye, Louis, Pr. Co. A 2nd O. V. I.

Dye, Monroe, Pr. Co. A 2nd O. V. I.

Eisenstein, William W., Artificer Co. A 2nd O. V. I.

Farling, John W., 2nd Corp. Co. A 2nd O. V. I.

Farquhar, Harry H., Pr. Tr. G 1st O. V. C.

Fellebaum, Jason, Pr. Co. A 2nd O.V.I.

Franks, Clinton V., 3rd Sergt. Co. A 2nd O. V. I.

Furgeson, John F., Pr. Co. A 2nd O. V. I.

Gallaway, William B., Pr. Co. A 2nd O. V. I.

Galloway, Samuel, Pr. Co. A 2nd O. V. I.

Gardner, James B., Pr. Co. A 2nd O. V. I.

George, Elliott C., Pr. Co. A 2nd O. V. I.

Geyer, William, Pr. Co. A 2nd O. V. I.

Gilbert, Claude M. C., Pr. Co. A 2nd O. V. I.

Gilbert, Logan M., Pr. Co. A 2nd O. V. I.

Glathart, Rolland, Pr. Co. A 2nd O.V.I.

Good, Charles F., Pr. Co. A 2nd O.V.I.

Greene, Charles, Pr. Co. A 2nd O. V. I.

Greer, Jesse N., Pr. Co. A 2nd O.V.I.

Groves, Richard R., Pr. Co. A 2nd O. V. I.

Grubb, Aurora Del., 1st Corp. Co. A 2nd O. V. I.

Grubb, Y. J., Pr. Co. A 2nd O. V. I.

Hammond, Burt, Pr. Co. A 2nd O.V.I.

Harris, Burt, Pr. Co. A 2nd O. V. I.

Hayse, Andrew J., Pr. Co. A 2nd O.V.I.

Hendricks, Charles, Pr. Co. A 2nd O. V. I.

Hendricks, Milton, Pr. Co. A 2nd O. V. I.

Henry, Claude A., Pr. Co. A 2nd O. V. I.

Hollowell, C. L., Pr. Tr. G 1st O.V.C.

Karg, Henry W., Pr. Co. A 2nd O.V.I.

Keller, Robert C., Pr. Co. A 2nd O.V.I.

Klentsche, Reg., Pr. Co. A 2nd O. V. I.

Lafferty, P. J., 4th Sergt. Co. A 2nd O. V. I.

Long, Otis A., Pr. Co. A 2nd O. V. I.

Martin, Charles W., Pr. Co. A 2nd O. V. I.

Maxwell, John, Pr. Co. A 2nd O. V. I.

McFarland, Charles, Pr. Co. A 2nd O. V. I.

McGinnis, Charles, Pr. Co. A 2nd O. V. I.

McVey, Harry, Pr. Co. A 2nd O. V. I.

Mellott, Charles E., Pr. Co. A 2nd O. V. I.

Miles, Robert I., Pr. Co. A 2nd O.V.I.

Montgomery, Elmer, Pr. Co. A 2nd O. V. I.

Morrison, Fred H., Pr. Co. A 2nd O. V. I.

Moyer, Frank J., Pr. Co. A 2nd O.V.I.

Myers, Curtis, Pr. Co. A 2nd O. V. I.

Neff, Joseph C., Pr. Co. A 2nd O. V. I.

O'Harra, Thomas J., Principal Musician 2nd O. V. I.
Parr, Charles, Pr. Co. A 2nd O. V. I.
Peet, Wilbur A., Pr. Co. A 2nd O.V.I.
Pennington, James E., Pr. Co. A 2nd O. V. I.
Perry, Charles, Pr. Co. A 2nd O. V. I.
Powell, Edwin Otto, Pr. Co. A 2nd O. V. I.
Perry, Lewis E., Musician Co. A 2nd O. V. I.
Price, William A., Pr. Co. A 2nd O.V.I.
Pugh, Ralph I., Pr. Co. A 2nd O. V. I.
Radebough, William M., Pr. Co. A 2nd O. V. I.
Rex, John D., 3rd Corp. Co. A 2nd O. V. I.
Ronk, William Henry, Pr. Co. A 2nd O. V. I.
Saunders, Merle, Pr. Co. A 2nd O.V.I.
Sealy, Frank N., Pr. Co. A 2nd O.V.I.
Seymour, Charles, Pr. Co. A 2nd O. V. I.
Sharpe, Robert G., Pr. Co. A 2nd O. V. I.
Sherwood, Frank E., Pr. Co. A 2nd O. V. I.
Shuler, John, Pr. Co. A 2nd O. V. I.
Siegfried, George F., Pr. Co. A 2nd O. V. I.

Snyder, Charles, Pr. Co. A 2nd O. V. I.
Spangler, Joe A., Pr. Co. A 2nd O.V.I.
Stiles, Donald Egar, Pr. Co. A 2nd O. V. I.
Stockton, William H., 4th Corp. Co. A 2nd O. V. I.
Sweeney, Lawrence M., Pr. Co. A 2nd O. V. I.
Taylor, William W., Pr. Co. A 2nd O. V. I.
Taylor, William W., Pr. Co. A 2nd O. V. I.
Thomas, Albert, Pr. Co. A 2nd O. V. I.
Todd, Murell, Pr. Co. A 2nd O. V. I.
Vernon, Jesse O., Pr. Co. A 2nd O.V.I.
Warnock, Arthur J., Pr. Co. A 2nd O. V. I.
Watt, Frank, Pr. Co. A 2nd O. V. I.
Watt, Lerow W., Pr. Co. A 2nd O.V.I.
Wayt, Charles T., 6th Corp. Co. A 2nd O. V. I.
Wheeler, James R., Pr. Co. A 2nd O. V. I.
Wilson, Eberson P., Pr. Co. A 2nd O. V. I.
Wilson, Edward D., Pr. Co. A 2nd O. V. I.
Westenbarger, Urbana V., Pr. Co. K 2nd O. V. I.
Wolfe, Cliffe, Pr. Co. A 2nd O. V. I.

FLAT ROCK

Snyder, John, Pr. Co. F 8th O. V. I.

FLETCHER

Sullenberger, Ora, Pr. Co. K 3rd O. V. I.

FLINT

Arnold, Robert M., Pr. Co. F 7th O. V. I.

FLORIDA

Brubaker, Rush, Pr. Co. M 6th O.V.I.
Emmel, William H., Pr. Co. M 6th O. V. I.

Hughy, Charles V., Pr. Co. M 2nd O. V. I.

FORAKER

Barry, Dine, Pr. Co. G 2nd O. V. I.

Ross, Charles, Pr. Co. K 3rd O. V. I.

FOREST

Doster, William S., Pr. Co. I 2nd O. V. I.

Dycus, William W., Pr. Co. I 2nd O. V. I.

FORESTDALE

Patterson, Carl G., Pr. Co. I 7th O.V.I.

FOSTORIA

Adams, George E., Pr. Co. D 6th O. V. I.

Alley, Lafer J., Pr. Co. D 6th O. V. I.

Andes, William D., Sergt. Co. D 6th O. V. I.

Bachar, Opha, Corp. Co. D 6th O.V.I.

Ball, William C., Pr. Co. D 6th O.V.I.

Blosser, Harvey T., Musician Co. D 6th O. V. I.

Bly, Louis, Pr. Co. D 6th O. V. I.

Both, Charles W., Pr. Co. D 6th O.V.I.

Bowe, John A., Pr. Co. D 6th O. V. I.

Bricker, Edward A., Pr. Co. D 6th O. V. I.

Briner, Louis A., Corp. Co. D 6th O. V. I.

Class, Louis J., Pr. Co. D 6th O. V. I.

Coil, Curtis, Pr. Co. D 6th O. V. I.

Cook, William E., Pr. Co. D 6th O.V.I.

Culbertson, John F., Corp. Co. D 6th O. V. I.

Culp, Albert M., Corp. Co. D 6th O. V. I.

Cunningham, Charles G., Pr. Co. D 6th O. V. I.

Cupps, Thomas A., Pr. Co. D 6th O. V. I.

Dale, Will W., Pr. Co. D 6th O. V. I.

Davis, Paul W., Pr. Co. D 6th O. V. I.

Doe, Cecil G., Pr. Co. D 6th O. V. I.

Dutcher, Frank, Pr. Co. D 6th O.V.I.

Engstrom, Earle E., Pr. Co. D 6th O. V. I.

Ernest, Ralph C., Pr. Co. D 6th O.V.I.

Fletcher, Arthur J., Pr. Co. D 6th O. V. I.

Gamer, Everett E., Sergt. Co. D 6th O. V. I.

Gleason, Jacob, Pr. Co. D 6th O. V. I.

Gollmer, Joseph K., Pr. Co. D 6th O. V. I.

Green, Frank E., Pr. Co. D 6th O.V.I.

Grubb, Frank R., Pr. Co. D 6th O.V.I.

Hagemeyer, Charley H., Pr. Co. D 6th O. V. I.

Haughey, Edward, Pr. Co. D 6th O. V. I.

Hazen, Neri E., Pr. Co. D 6th O. V. I.

Heacox, Roscoe D., Pr. Co. D 6th O. V. I.

Hollopeter, Clayton E., Sergt. Co. D 6th O. V. I.

Hooper, Arthur G., Pr. Co. D 6th O. V. I.

Jones, Louis, Pr. Co. D 6th O. V. I.

Jones, Thomas L., Pr. Co. D 6th O.V.I.

Kistner, Rawson J., Pr. Co. D 6th O. V. I.

Lancaster, Eugene J., Wagoner Co. D 6th O. V. I.

Lancaster, William H., Musician Co. D 6th O. V. I.

Lance, Ray M., Pr. Co. D 6th O. V. I.

Lea, Thomas M., Corp. Co. D 6th O. V. I.

Lee, William M., Pr. Co. D 6th O.V.I.

Lynch, D. A., Hospital Steward 6th O. V. I.

McClead, Alfred C., Pr. Co. D 6th O. V. I.

McMeen, James B., 1st Sergt. Co. D 6th O. V. I.

Newcomb, Clark N., Pr. Co. D 6th O. V. I.

Nichols, Roldon O., Corp. Co. D 6th O. V. I.

Overmyer, Oliver L., Pr. Co. D 6th O. V. I.

Ransbottom, Charles W., Pr. Co. D 6th O. V. I.

Riedel, William L., Pr. Co. D 6th O. V. I.

Schlatter, Daniel D., Pr. Co. D 6th O. V. I.

Shoemaker, Mervil M., Pr. Co. D 6th O. V. I.

Short, Lloyd L., Pr. Co. D 6th O.V.I.

Sinclair, Warren H., Pr. Co. D 6th O. V. I.

Smith, Aaron R., Pr. Co. D 6th O.V.I.

Smith, Carl, Pr. Co. D 6th O. V. I.

Smith, Robert Lee, Pr. Co. D 6th O. V. I.

Smith, Rollie W., Pr. Co. D 6th O.V.I.

Steingraber, Gust, Pr. Co. D 6th O.V.I.

Stewart, Victor W., Pr. Co. D 6th O. V. I.

Tallman, William A., Artificer Co. D 6th O. V. I.

Troutman, Frank J., Sergt. Co. D 6th O. V. I.

Vosburg, Frederick A., Sergt. Co. D 6th O. V. I.

Webber, Otto B., Pr. Co. D 6th O.V.I.

Wickerd, Otis D., Pr. Co. D 6th O.V.I.

Wilson, Orlo C., Pr. Co. D 6th O.V.I.

Wolf, Cyrus A., Pr. Co. D 6th O.V.I.

Zuern, Frank J., Pr. Co. D 6th O. V. I.

FOUBLESBURG

Harris, Wilbert S., Pr. Co. K 7th O. V. I.

FRANKFORT

Abernathy, Charles W., Pr. Co. K 7th O. V. I.

Wisehart, Neal P., Pr. Co. K 7th O.V.I...

FRANKLIN

Anderson, Daniel C., Musician Co. C
2nd U. S. V. E.
Bridge, Carl, Pr. Co. C 2nd U.S.V.E.

O'Kett, Oscar O., Pr. Co. C 10th O.
V. I.

FREDERICKTOWN

Newton, John, Pr. U. R. 8th O. V. I.

FREMONT

Anderson, William, Pr. Co. K 6th O.
V. I.
Bellinger, Charley H., Pr. Co. K 6th
O. V. I.
Boop, Irwin, Pr. Co. K 6th O. V. I.
Buckland, Stephen, Sergt. Co. K 6th
O. V. I.
Campbell, Ralph, Pr. Co. K 6th O.V.I.
Childs, Clarence C., Musician Co. K 6th
O. V. I.
Cook, George H., Pr. Co. K 6th O.V.I.
Cooley, William F., Pr. Co. K 6th O.
V. I.
Dickinson, James A., Pr. Co. K 6th O.
V. I.
Ehmann, George, Artificer Co. K 6th
O. V. I.
Emerson, Frank W., Pr. Co. K 6th O.
V. I.
Emerson, Guy G., Corp. Co. K 6th O.
V. I.
Ferrenberg, Bert H., Pr. Co. K 6th O.
V. I.
Fisher, Harry F., Pr. Co. K 6th O.V.I.
Florkowski, John, Pr. Co. K 6th O.V.I.
Foley, Patrick M., Pr. Co. K 6th O.
V. I.
Fouke, John W., Sergt. Co. K 6th O.
V. I.
Fry, Roscoe A., 1st Sergt. Co. K 6th
O. V. I.
Garn, William A., Pr. Co. K 6th O.V.I.
Gilmore, Rutherford H., Pr. Co. K 6th
O. V. I.
Goebel, Louis A., Pr. Co. K 6th O.V.I.
Hague, Irwin F., Pr. Co. K 6th O.V.I.
Halter, David F., Pr. Co. K 6th O.V.I.
Hanawalt, Arthur, Pr. Co. K 6th O.
V. I.
Harrington, Consider A., Pr. Co. K 6th
O. V. I.
Hayman, Guy C., Pr. Co. K 6th O.V.I.
Hazel, Harry R., Corp. Co. K 6th O.
V. I.
Heider, Edward H., Musician Co. K
6th O. V. I.
Levy, Albert A., Pr. Co. K 6th O.V.I.
Long, Howard H., Jr., Pr. Co. K 6th
O. V. I.
Michaels, Burton O., Corp. Co. K 6th
O. V. I.
Mierka, Amos, Pr. Co. C 6th O. V. I.

Mills, Bert M., Pr. Co. K 6th O. V. I.
Mish, David M., Pr. Co. K 6th O.V.I.
Morgan, Harry J., Pr. Co. K 6th O.
V. I.
Myers, Charles, Corp. Co. K 6th O.
V. I.
Myers, Henry C., Pr. Co. K 6th O.V.I.
Nickel, Ed., Pr. Co. K 6th O. V. I.
Nickel, Leonard W., Pr. Co. K 6th O.
V. I.
Over, Clarence, Pr. Co. K 6th O. V. I.
Overmeyer, George H., Pr. Co. K 6th
O. V. I.
Park, James W., Pr. Co. K 6th O.V.I.
Patterson, Fred R., Pr. Co. K 6th O.
V. I.
Proctor, Shorley A., Corp. Co. K 6th
O. V. I.
Proctor, William E., Jr., Pr. Co. K 6th
O. V. I.
Ransauer, Charles R., Pr. Co. K 6th O.
V. I.
Ransauer, William F., Pr. Co. K 6th O.
V. I.
Reamer, William A., Pr. Co. K 6th O.
V. I.
Rearick, J. Arthur, Pr. Co. K 6th O.
V. I.
Reinick, Al. A., Pr. Co. K 6th O. V. I.
Renshler, William, Pr. Co. K 6th O.
V. I.
Rhodes, Edgar A., Pr. Co. K 6th O.
V. I.
Rice, J. Wilson, Pr. Co. K 6th O.V.I.
Russell, Judson G., Pr. Co. K 6th O.
V. I.
Slessman, Allen E., Pr. Tr. D 1st O.
V. C.
Smith, Homer, Pr. Co. K 6th O. V. I.
Snyder, Hugh A., Pr. Co. K 6th O.V.I.
Stine, Frank C., Sergt. Co. K 6th O.
V. I.
Stine, Wallace R., Sergt. Co. K 6th O.
V. I.
Strohl, Myrle D., Pr. Co. K 6th O.V.I.
Terry, Guy D., Pr. Co. K 6th O. V. I.
Veith, William, Pr. Co. K 6th O. V. I.
Welker, George H., Pr. Co. K 6th O.
V. I.
Wickert, Guy G., Corp. Co. K 6th O.
V. I.
Wickert, Ralph, Wagoner Co. K 6th
O. V. I.

FREEDOM

Masters, Frank L., Pr. Co. K 10th O. V. I.

FRUIT HILL

Doty, Charles E., Pr. Co. C 2nd U. S. V. E.

FUNK

Anderson, Bert A., Pr. Co. H 8th O. V. I.

Kuhn, Edward G., Pr. Co. H 8th O. V. I.

GALION

Beck, Ora R., Pr. Bat. C 1st O. V. A.
Hayes, Morton H., Pr. Bat. H 1st O. V. A.

Mackey, Guy A., Pr. Co. I 10th O.V.I.
Sheridan, Jack F., Pr. Co. B 10th O. V. I.

GALLIPOLIS

Angell, Henry I., Pr. Co. C 7th O. V. I.
Angell, Lewis R., Pr. Co. C 7th O.V.I.
Bird, William G., Pr. Co. B 2nd U. S. V. E.
Bratt, Howard H., Pr. Co. B 2nd U. S. V. E.
Carter, Will W., Pr. Co. C 7th O.V.I.
Chick, Berry, Pr. Co. C 7th O. V. I.
Coulson, Bruce, Pr. Co. C 7th O. V. I.
Coulson, Harry, Pr. Co. C 7th O.V.I.
Dale, Thomas C., Pr. Co. C 7th O.V.I.
Dawson, Arthur C., Pr. Co. C 7th O. V. I.
Dugan, Dennis, Corp. Co. C 7th O.V.I.
Durkee, Will, Corp. Co. C 7th O. V. I.
Dyer, Luther O., Pr. Co. C 7th O.V.I.
Eads, John W., Pr. Co. C 7th O. V. I.
Edwards, Newton, Pr. Co. C 7th O.V.I.
Ghrist, Millard C., 2nd Sergt. Co. C 7th O. V. I.
Glenn, Andrew J., Pr. Co. C 7th O.V.I.
Haley, David L., Pr. Co. C 7th O.V.I.
Hall, John, Pr. Co. C 7th O. V. I.
Hamilton, Frank D., Pr. Co. B 2nd U. S. V. E.
Hamlin, John T., Pr. Co. C 7th O.V.I.
Hunnel, George D., Corp. Co. C 7th O. V. I.
Jacox, John L., Pr. Co. C 7th O. V. I.
Jenks, Earl R., Pr. Co. C 7th O. V. I.
Karr, Horace W., Pr. Co. C 7th O.V.I.

Karr, Irving R., 3rd Sergt. Co. C 7th O. V. I.
Kinder, Frank A., Pr. Co. C 7th O.V.I.
Knuckles, William, Pr. Co. C 7th O. V. I.
Kuhn, William S., Pr. Co. C 7th O.V.I.
Long, Albert, Pr. Co. C 7th O. V. I.
Mathena, John H., Pr. Co. C 7th O. V. I.
McConnell, Morris C., Pr. Co. C 7th O. V. I.
McCune, Jerome, Pr. Co. C 7th O.V.I.
Moats, Frank, Pr. Co. C 7th O. V. I.
Mullineaux, Harry G., Corp. Co. B 2nd U. S. V. E.
Nanna, Lee W., Pr. Co. C 7th O. V. I.
Owens, Will M., Corp. Co. C 7th O. V. I.
Petry, August, Pr. Co. F 4th O. V. I.
Phillips, Rome, Pr. Co. C 7th O. V. I.
Ray, Peter G., Corp. Co. C 7th O. V. I.
Rusk, Charley, Pr. Co. C 7th O. V. I.
Safford, Thomas C., Corp. Co. C 7th O. V. I.
Small, Charles W., Corp. Co. C 7th O. V. I.
Sutherland, Alex. T., Q. M. Sergt. Co. C 7th O. V. I.
Taylor, John R., Pr. Co. C 7th O. V. I.
Wall, Carl M., Pr. Co. C 7th O. V. I.
Williams, Arius K., Pr. Co. B 2nd U. S. V. E.

GALLOWAY

Gregory, Charles F., Pr. Co. B 4th O. V. I.

Wolff, Oliver, Pr. Co. E 3rd O. V. I.

GAMBIER

Bigler, Eugene F., Pr. Co. L 4th O.V.I.

GARRETTSVILLE

Streator, Charles P., Pr. Co. K 10th O. V. I.

Talcott, Earl R., Pr. Co. K 10th O.V.I.

GATH

Jodry, C. Eugene, Pr. Co. F 3rd O. V. I.

GEARY, MICH.

Myers, Henry A., Pr. Tr. G 1st O.V.C.

GENEVA

Ackerman, Roy R., Pr. Co. E 5th O. V. I.
Albert, Franklin R., Pr. Co. E 5th O. V. I.
Barnes, Hugh W., Sergt. Co. E 5th O. V. I.
Bartholomew, Lucius M., Pr. Co. E 5th O. V. I.
Bartholomew, William E., Pr. Co. E 5th O. V. I.
Beattie, Ray C., Corp. Co. E 5th O. V. I.
Brown, Lawrence J., Pr. Co. E 5th O. V. I.
Brown, William H., Q. M. Sergt. Co. E 5th O. V. I.
Buff, Harry, Corp. Co. E 5th O. V. I.
Burdon, Eugene R., Pr. Co. E 5th O. V. I.
Cowles, Fred L., Pr. Co. E 5th O.V.I.
Foster, Elbert R., Musician Co. E 5th O. V. I.
Hecker, Harvey H., Sergt. Co. E 5th O. V. I.
Hewitt, Charles F., Sergt. Co. E 5th O. V. I.
Hileman, Cleveland H., Corp. Co. E 5th O. V. I.
Hubbard, Walter M., Pr. Co. E 5th O. V. I.
Mason, Jessa G., Pr. Co. E 5th O.V.I.

McGregor, Ambrose M., Pr. Co. E 5th O. V. I.
Miner, Rolla A., Pr. Co. E 5th O. V. I.
Montgomery, Fred, Pr. Co. E 5th O. V. I.
Norton, Emry B., Corp. Co. E 5th O. V. I.
Pancost, Ernest D., Pr. Co. E 5th O. V. I.
Perry, Fred, 1st Sergt. Co. E 5th O. V. I.
Pratt, Howard U., Pr. Co. E 5th O. V. I.
Prevost, Edward W., Pr. Co. E 5th O. V. I.
Russell, Charles H., Pr. Co. E 5th O. V. I.
Scott, Henry T., Pr. Co. E 5th O.V.I.
Smith, Herbert R., Pr. Co. K 10th O. V. I.
Sperry, Merle P., Pr. Co. E 5th O.V.I.
Sprague, Harry W., Corp. Co. E 5th O. V. I.
Spring, Richard D., Pr. Co. E 5th O. V. I.
Stone, Darwin, Pr. Co. E 5th O. V. I.
Talcott, Ernest G., Corp. Co. E 5th O. V. I.
Turner, Charles F., Pr. Co. E 5th O. V. I.

GEORGETOWN

Bradford, W. Parker, Pr. Co. H 3rd O. V. I.
Burger, Peter C., Pr. Co. H 3rd O.V.I.
Campbell, William D., Pr. Co. H 3rd O. V. I.
Manning, Milo, Pr. Co. H 3rd O. V. I.

Misner, Frank, Pr. Co. H 3rd O. V. I.
Parker, George A., Corp. Co. H 3rd O. V. I.
Purdon, Tom E., Pr. Co. H 3rd O.V.I.
Robinson, Charles, Pr. Co. H 3rd O. V. I.

GETTYSBURG

Bell, Edgar, Corp. Co. C 3rd O. V. I.
Brandon, Clifford, Musician Co. C 3rd O. V. I.
Clark, Joseph W., Sergt. Co. C 3rd O. V. I.
Esky, Richard, Pr. Co. C 3rd O. V. I.
Gottschall, Lionelle, Q. M. Sergt. Co. C 3rd O. V. I.
Hahn, Samuel N., Sergt. Co. C 3rd O. V. I.
Hahn, William, Pr. Co. C 3rd O. V. I.
Hathaway, Frank, Pr. Co. C 3rd O.V.I.

Kent, Augustus, Pr. Co. C 3rd O. V. I.
Miller, John C., Pr. Co. C 3rd O. V. I.
Moore, John T., 1st Sergt. Co. C 3rd O. V. I.
Moul, Artimas A., Musician Co. C 3rd O. V. I.
Moul, Charles P., Sergt. Co. C 3rd O. V. I.
Moul, John M., Corp. Co. C 3rd O.V.I.
Myers, Ortha H., Corp. Co. C 3rd O. V. I.

Myers, Zachary T., Pr. Co. C 3rd O. V. I.
Palmer, Percy F., Sergt. Co. C 3rd O. V. I.
Paulin, Amos, Pr. Co. C 3rd O. V. I.
Pfoutz, Daniel W., Artificer Co. C 3rd O. V. I.

Russell, William E., Pr. Co. C 3rd O. V. I.
Seman, Emanuel I., Corp. Co. C 3rd O. V. I.
Smith, Harry G., Corp. Co. C 3rd O. V. I.
Wion, David F., Pr. Co. C 3rd O. V. I.

GEYER

McClellan, Rollie, Pr. Co. L 2nd O.V.I.

GIBSONBURG

Fowler, Elmer H., Pr. Tr. E 1st O.V.C.   Vogeli, John, Pr. Co. C 10th O. V. I.

GILLESPIEVILLE

Ray, Victor L., Pr. Co. H 7th O. V. I.

GLENDALE

Arms, Harry M., Pr. Co. I 1st O. V. I.   Keyes, William H., Pr. Co. I 1st O.V.I.

GLENN

Hanger, David J., Corp. Co. C 7th O. V. I.

McCarley, Frank P., Pr. Co. C 7th O. V. I.

GLENVILLE

Armstrong, Arthur C., Pr. Co. F 5th O. V. I.
Eastman, Frank R., Pr. Co. I 10th O. V. I.
Farley, Thomas S., Jr., Pr. Co. K 10th O. V. I.
Foster, William R., Corp. Co. K 10th O. V. I.
Gerber, Frank, Pr. Co. K 10th O. V. I.

Horn, Adam, Artificer Co. F 5th O.V.I.
Johnson, Frank P., Pr. Co. I 10th O. V. I.
Merseburg, Henry A., Pr. Co. I 10th O. V. I.
Van Ornum, Arthur P., Wagoner Co. B 10th O. V. I.
Winter, Calvert J., Pr. Co. I 10th O. V. I.

GLYNNWOOD

O'Connell, John, Pr. Co. L 2nd O.V.I.

GRAND RAPIDS, MICH.

McCarthy, Frank P., Pr. Co. H 10th O. V. I.

GRANGER

Levette, Leonard W., Pr. Co. C 5th O. V. I.

GRANVILLE

Brown, N. Worth, Sergt. Co. B 5th O. V. I.
Courtney, John B., Corp. Co. K 7th O. V. I.
Daniels, Walter V., Pr. Co. K 7th O. V. I.
Deeds, Alva S., Pr. Co. K 7th O. V. I.

Haynes, Arthur, Pr. Co. K 7th O. V. I.
Jackson, Charles A., Pr. Co. A 9th Batt. O. V. I.
Jones, Cary W., Q. M. Sergt. Co. K 7th O. V. I.
Lake, Charles H., Corp. Co. K 7th O. V. I.

Moore, Fred D., Corp. Co. I 5th O.
V. I.
Munson, Morton M., 1st Sergt. Co. K
7th O. V. I.
Sample, Herbert L., Sergt. Co. I 5th
O. V. I.

Shepardson, John Ernest, 2nd Sergt.
Co. K 7th O. V. I.
Wagner, Harry S., Corp. Co. B 5th O.
V. I.

GRATIOT

Gard, John H., Pr. Bat. C 1st O. V. A.

Nash, Oliver N., Pr. Bat. C 1st O.V.A.

GRAYTOWN

Lenz, Henry C., Pr. Co. G 10th O.V.I.
Pickard, George F., Pr. Co. G 10th O.
V. I.

Rehfeldt, Otto H., Pr. Co. G 10th O.
V. I.

GREENFIELD

Strobel, Carl A., Pr. Co. C 7th O. V. I.

Watkins, Ison, Corp. Co. D 9th Batt.
O. V. I.

GREENVILLE·

Weaver, Daniel J., Pr. Co. C 3rd O. V. I.

GREENWICH

Shriner, John Ph., Artificer Co. G 5th O. V. I.

GROGAN

Faller, Samuel V., Pr. Co. A 2nd U. S. V. E.

GROVE CITY

Alkire, Jesse, Pr. Co. A 2nd U.S.V.E.

Hampshire, Davis M., Pr. Bat. H 1st
O. V. A.

GROVEPORT

Heise, Thomas K., Pr. Tr. D 1st O.
V. C.

Powell, William L., Pr. Tr. D 1st O.
V. C.
Simms, Edwin M., Pr. Co. F 4th O.V.I.

GROVER HILL

Campbell, Russell D., Pr. Co. M 2nd
O. V. I.

Mansfield, George A., Pr. Co. M 2nd
O. V. I.

HALLEY

Martin, James V., Pr. Co. C 7th O.V.I.

HAMERSVILLE

Carow, Starling N., Pr. Co. F 3rd O. V. I.

HAMILTON

Allen, Cornelius A., Wagoner Co. E 1st
O. V. I.
Allen, Theodore, Pr. Co. E 1st O.V.I.
Anderson, Rolla E., Pr. Co. E 1st O.
V. I.

Bantham, Daniel R., Pr. Co. E 1st
O. V. I.
Barnes, Abraham H., Pr. Co. E 1st O.
V. I.
Berk, Fred T., Pr. Co. E 1st O. V. I.

Bernard, Arthur C., Pr. Co. E 1st O. V. I.

Berry, Charles B., Pr. Co. E 1st O.V.I.

Berry, Peter Lewis, Pr. Co. E 1st O. V. I.

Bogaske, John, Pr. Co. E 1st O. V. I.

Brown, Anzie M., Pr. Co. E 1st O.V.I.

Buckner, Frank B., Pr. Co. E 1st O. V. I.

Buell, Israel E., Pr. Co. E 1st O. V. I.

Carroll, Thomas R., Sergt. Co. E 1st O. V. I.

Castator, Charles E., Artificer Co. E 1st O. V. I.

Cawley, James T., Pr. Co. E 1st O.V.I.

Chadwick, Harry R., Musician Co. E 1st O. V. I.

Cook, Frank G., Pr. Co. E 1st O. V. I.

Cox, Charles H., Sergt. Co. E 1st O. V. I.

Davis, Elmer F., Corp. Co. E 1st O. V. I.

Dully, Henry A., Pr. Co. E 1st O. V. I.

Dunbar, William H., Pr. Co. E 1st O. V. I.

Durkin, John S., Pr. Co. E 1st O.V.I.

Elkins, Albert F., Musician Co. E 1st O. V. I.

Elkins, Authur, Pr. Co. E 1st O. V. I.

Engler, Julius, Pr. Co. E 1st O. V. I.

French, Linus H., Sergt. Co. E 1st O. V. I.

Gailey, Charles Von, Pr. Co. E 1st O. V. I.

Gerhard, Fred, Corp. Co. E 1st O.V.I.

Hanrahan, Edward, Pr. Co. E 1st O. V. I.

Hartman, William J., Pr. Co. E 1st O. V. I.

Harvey, Elmer G., Pr. Co. E 1st O.V.I.

Henninger, Raymond, Corp. Co. E 1st O. V. I.

Howard, George, Corp. Co. E 1st O. V. I.

Hyman, William, Pr. Co. E 1st O.V.I.

Jones, John, Pr. Co. E 1st O. V. I.

Jones, Leslie, Pr. Co. E 1st O. V. I.

King, William C., Pr. Co. E 1st O.V.I.

Kinser, Otto A., Pr. Co. E 1st O.V.I.

Kurtz, John A., Pr. Co. E 1st O. V. I.

Lambertson, John, Pr. Co. E 1st O. V. I.

Lancaster, Harry, Pr. Co. E 1st O.V.I.

Leroy, Hugh, Pr. Co. E 1st O. V. I.

Letsche, Charles, Pr. Co. E 1st O.V.I.

Littlejohn, James D., Pr. Co. E 1st O. V. I.

Lutterman, Christopher W., Pr. Co. E 1st O. V. I.

Manifold, Wilson H., Pr. Co. E 1st O. V. I.

Marshall, Jesse H., Pr. Co. E 1st O. V. I.

McCollum, Thomas, Pr. Co. E 1st O. V. I.

McDonald, Amasa C., Corp. Co. E 1st O. V. I.

O'Brian, Walter B., Pr. Co. E 1st O. V. I.

O'Keefe, William C., Pr. Co. E 1st O. V. I.

Reynolds, William E., Pr. Co. E 1st O. V. I.

Roll, Jacob M., Q. M. Sergt. Co. E 1st O. V. I.

Ross, Charles E., Sergt. Co. E 1st O. V. I.

Schwenk, Fred W., Pr. Co. E 1st O. V. I.

Shafer, Charles R., Pr. Co. E 1st O. V. I.

Sims, Arthur W., 1st Sergt. Co. E 1st O. V. I.

Sommers, Harry J., Pr. Co. E 1st O. V. I.

Spanner, Henry J., Pr. Co. E 1st O. V. I.

Stone, Thomas A., Pr. Co. E 1st O.V.I.

Thompson, John, Pr. Co. E 1st O.V.I.

Walter, Frank E., Pr. Co. E 1st O.V.I.

Wellinghoff, Frank, Pr. Co. E 1st O. V. I.

Wilcox, Daniel J., Pr. Co. E 1st O.V.I.

Wilson, Fred R., Pr. Co. E 1st O.V.I.

Werbel, Joseph L., Pr. Co. E 1st O. V. I.

Young, Theodore, Corp. Co. E 1st O. V. I.

HAMLER

Durham, John W., Pr. Co. K 2nd O. V. I.

HANGING ROCK

Berridge, Alonzo, Pr. Co. I 7th O.V.I.

Farmer, Thomas B., Pr. Co. I 7th O. V. I.

Gibbons, Arnold E., Pr. Co. I 7th O. V. I.

Trumbo, Lester A., Pr. Co. B 2nd U. S. V. E.

HANOVER

Johnston, Ernest E., Pr. Co. G 7th O. V. I.

Ritchey, Harry J., Pr. Co. G 7th O.V.I.

Williams, Rollin F., Pr. Co. K 7th O. V. I.

HARDIN

Price, Morenes H., Pr. Co. L 3rd O.   Vogler, Elmer E., Pr. Co. L 3rd O.V.I.
V. I.

HARPESFIELD

Judd, Percy A., Pr. Co. E 5th O. V. I.   Paugburn, Carl E., Pr. Co. E 5th O.
Jerome, John J., Pr. Co. E 5th O. V. I.   V. I.

HARPERSFIELD

Poeppel, Gustave, Pr. Co. M 5th O.V.I.

HARRISONVILLE

Lee, Loren P., Pr. Tr. G 1st O. V. C.

HAYESVILLE

Armstrong, Thomas R., Pr. Co. C 8th   McQuillin, Willard, Pr. Co. C 8th O.
O. V. I.   V. I.

HEBRON

Atwood, Septimus, 1st Sergt. Co. K 7th   Jury, Ross W., Pr. Co. K 7th O. V. I.
O. V. I.   Lafollett, John, Pr. Co. K 7th O. V. I.
Baker, Benjamin F., Corp. Co. K 7th   Price, Nicholas E., Pr. Co. K 7th O.
O. V. I.   V. I.
Burch, Charles H., Musician Co. K 7th   Tygard, Chas. F., Pr. Co. K 7th O.V.I.
O. V. I.

HEDGES

McLaughlin, Webster L., Pr. Co. M 2nd O. V. I.

HELENA

Hoffman, Harry, Pr. Co. K 6th O.V.I.

HENRY CO.

Beaverson, Walter, Pr. Co. M 6th O.   Hasselschwardt, Joseph, Pr. Co. M 6th
V. I.   O. V. I.

HEPBURN

Vanatta, Grant, Pr. Co. I 2nd O. V. I.   Vanatta, Philip, Pr. Co. I 2nd O. V. I.

HICKSVILLE

Armstrong, Ernest F., Pr. Co. M 2nd   Martin, Ottiemer, Pr. Co. M 2nd O.
O. V. I.   V. I.
Biggs, Orvill L., Pr. Co. M 2nd O.V.I.   Pittman, Clement J., Pr. Co. M 2nd O.
Edgerton, Benjamin B., Pr. Co. M 2nd   V. I.
O. V. I.   Rockwood, Bert B., Corp. Co. M 2nd
Gillespie, Dean C., Musician Co. M   O. V. I.
2nd O. V. I.   Ryan, Otis, Pr. Co. M 2nd O. V. I.
Keefer, Charles A., Pr. Co. M 2nd O.
V. I.

HILLSBOROUGH

Barrere, Geo. W., Jr., Pr. Co. F 3rd O. V. I.
Beecher, Hyman O'H., Pr. Bat. H 1st O. V. A.
Brabson, Fred C., Pr. Co. F 3rd O.V.I.
Butler, Harry, Pr. Co. F 3rd O. V. I.
Carow, James, Pr. Co. F 3rd O. V. I.
Carroll, William, Pr. Co. F 3rd O.V.I.
Colburn, Otway B., Pr. Co. F 3rd O. V. I.
Day, Harry L., Corp. Co. F 3rd O.V.I.
Duffey, Charles, Pr. Co. F 3rd O. V. I.
Duncan, Lee, Pr. Co. F 3rd O. V. I.
Dryden, William H., Sergt. Co. F 3rd O. V. I.
Eggeling, William, Pr. Co. F 3rd O. V. I.
Fahrlender, Louis, Pr. Co. F 3rd O.V.I.
Fahrlender, Walter, Pr. Co. F 3rd O. V. I.
Fleming, W. D., Pr. Co. F 3rd O.V.I.
Fullerton, Ralph N., Pr. Co. F 3rd O. V. I.
Gaines, Arch., Pr. Co. F 3rd O. V. I.
Gorman, Charles, Pr. Co. F 3rd O.V.I.
Gorman, James J., Pr. U. R. 3rd O. V. I.
Henderly, John A., Pr. Co. F 3rd O. V. I.
Hilton, Greenbury W., Pr. Co. F 3rd O. V. I.
Holladay, Charlie, Pr. Co. F 3rd O.V.I.
Hughey, Claire, Pr. Co. F 3rd O. V. I.
Jolly, David S., Pr. Co. F 3rd O. V. I.
Lyle, Albert J., Pr. Co. F 3rd O. V. I.

Lyle, Harry H., Pr. Co. F 3rd O. V. I.
Mackerley, Roy S., Pr. Co. F 3rd O. V. I.
Martin, Emmet R., Pr. Co. F 3rd O. V. I.
Miller, Burch, Pr. U. R. 3rd O. V. I.
Miller, L. Vernon, Pr. Co. F 3rd O.V.I.
Morgan, Walter, Pr. Co. F 3rd O.V.I.
Mullenix, Charles L., Pr. Co. F 3rd O. V. I.
Mullenix, Henry Mid., Pr. U. R. 3rd O. V. I.
Neal, Nathan, Pr. Co. F 3rd O. V. I.
Neal, Walter P., Pr. Co. F 3rd O. V. I.
Newby, Wilbur, Corp. Co. F 3rd O.V.I.
Orr, Charlie S., Pr. Co. F 3rd O. V. I.
Pence, Charles W., Pr. Co. F 3rd O. V. I.
Phibbs, David A., Pr. Co. F 3rd O.V.I.
Raines, Kirby, Pr. Co. F 3rd O. V. I.
Reinbold, Louis C., Pr. Co. F 3rd O. V. I.
Rockel, William, Pr. Co. F 3rd O.V.I.
Smith, Lyne S., Jr., Pr. Co. F 3rd O. V. I.
Stratton, Charles N., Pr. Co. F 3rd O. V. I.
Uhrig, Walter, Pr. Co. F 3rd O. V. I.
Utman, James E., Pr. Co. F 3rd O.V.I.
Wilkins, William S., Pr. Co. F 3rd O. V. I.
Willett, Stephen W., Pr. Co. F 3rd O. V. I.
Woods, David, Pr. Co. F 3rd O. V. I.

HINCKLEY

Riley, James, Pr. Co. L 5th O. V. I.

HIRAM

Shupe, Charles A., Pr. Co. K 10th O. V. I.

HOCKING TOWNSHIP

Clark, Henry C., Corp. Co. I 4th O. V. I.

HOLGATE

Britegam, Url, Pr. Co. M 6th O. V. I.
Fast, Edward M., Pr. Co. M 6th O.V.I.
McCabe, Peter D., Pr. Co. G 7th O. V. I.
McCabe, William T., Pr. Co. G 7th O. V. I.

Meyers, Charles F., Pr. Co. M 6th O. V. I.
Myers, Edson E., Pr. Co. M 6th O.V.I.
Shuman, Claud, Pr. Co. M 6th O. V. I.

HOLLAND

Gunn, Frank A., Pr. Co. H 10th O.V.I.

HOLMESVILLE

Hudnet, Charles W., Pr. Co. H 8th O. V. I.
Kidd, Samuel M., Pr. Co. H 8th O.V.I.
Loller, Harry D., Pr. Co. H 8th O.V.I.

Skelley, Alfred M., Pr. Co. H 8th O. V. I.
Switzer, David O., Pr. Co. H 8th O. V. I.

HOMERVILLE

Kerr, Lewis J., Pr. Tr. B 1st O. V. C.

HOOKSBURG

Hambleton, Benjamin F., Pr. Co. B 7th O. V. I.

HOUCKTOWN

Waltimere, Harvey T., Pr. Co. K 2nd O. V. I.

HOWENSTINE

Shew, Orrin P., Pr. Co. I 8th O. V. I.   Shew, Samuel J., Pr. Co. I 8th O. V. I.

HOYTVILLE

Baker, William, Pr. Co. K 2nd O. V.I.
Copus, James C., Pr. Co. K 2nd O.V.I.
Copus, Prenton O., Pr. Co. K 2nd O. V. I.
Dermer, Simon W., Pr. Co. K 2nd O. V. I.
Marshall, Gideon B., Pr. Co. K 2nd O. V. I.
McHenry, Earl O., Pr. Co. K 2nd O. V. I.
Taylor, Elmer W., Corp. Co. K 2nd O. V. I.
Whitney, William E., Pr. Co. K 2nd O. V. I.

HUDSON

Axtell, Louis B., Pr. Co. A 10th O.V.I.
Buss, John C., Pr. Co. A 10th O. V. I.
Fuller, Albert L., Pr. Co. C 10th O.V.I.
Lewis, Raymond E., Pr. Co. B 8th O. V. I.
Long, Frank, Pr. Co. A 10th O. V. I.

HUMBOLDT

Buck, David O., Pr. Tr. M 1st O.V.C.

HUNTINGTON

Jones, Albert H., Wagoner Co. C 8th O. V. I.
Leininger, William, Pr. Co. C 8th O. V. I.

HUNTINGTON, W. VA.

Faggan, Acan C., Sergt. Co. B 2nd U. S. V. E.
Fierburg, Jacob E., Pr. Co. C 7th O. V. I.
Roach, Douglas, Pr. Co. C 7th O. V. I.

HUNTSVILLE

Harrod, Jay S., Pr. Co. F 2nd O. V. I.   Miller, Robert E., Pr. Co. F 2nd O.V.I.

HURON

Day, Edward R., Pr. Tr. B 1st O.V.C.
Fisher, Edward A., Pr. Tr. B 1st O. V. C.

INDEPENDENCE

McGregor, George, Pr. Co. B 10th O. V. I.

IRONTON

Arbaugh, Charles T., Corp. Co. B 2nd U. S. V. E.
Blackwell, Ross R., Pr. Co. I 7th O. V. I.
Breece, Elza E., Pr. Co. I 7th O. V. I.
Brown, John C., Pr. Co. G 7th O. V. I.
Burwell, William, Pr. Co. I 7th O.V.I.
Clark, Harry L., Pr. Co. I 7th O. V. I.
Clarke, William J., Pr. Co. I 7th O.V.I.
Coates, Thomas, Pr. Co. B 2nd U. S. V. E.
Coffman, Martin V. B., Pr. Co. I 7th O. V. I.
Corns, Walter C., Pr. Co. I 7th O.V.I.
Courtney, Willis C., Pr. Co. I 7th O. V. I
Cox, Harry G., Pr. Co. I 7th O. V. I.
Dolin, Thomas M., Band Leader 7th O. V. I.
Ellsberry, Benjamin Frank, Pr. Co. I 7th O. V. I.
Felldre, Curtis, Pr. Co. I 7th O. V. I.
Feuchter, Leo A., Pr. Co. II 7th O.V.I.
Gates, Edwin F., Pr. Co. I 7th O. V. I.
George, Fred W., Pr. Co. I 7th O.V.I.
Golden, Newton, Pr. Co. I 7th O. V. I.
Gray, Charles S., Pr. Co. I 7th O. V. I.
Gray, George H., Pr. Co. I 7th O.V.I.
Hart, Harry C., Pr. Co. I 7th O. V. I.
Heidorn, Willard, Pr. Co. I 7th O. V. I.
Hunter, Henry, Pr. Co. I 7th O. V. I.
Kemp, Carl C., Artificer Co. I 7th O. V. I.
Lander, George C., Pr. Co. I 7th O. V. I.
Libbee, Edward M., Corp. Co. I 7th O V. I.
Leighty, Percy J., Pr. Co. I 7th O.V.I.
Lynd, Fred D., Pr. Co. I 7th O. V. I.
Mack, Thomas M., Pr. Co. I 7th O.V.I.
Martin, Byard D., Musician Co. I 7th O. V. I.
Martin, Fred, Wagoner Co. I 7th O. V. I.
McGowan, John F., Pr. Co. H 7th O. V. I.
Meyers, William H., Pr. Co. I 7th O. V. I.
Miller, George M., Pr. Co. I 7th O. V. I.

Mountain, Ralph W., Pr. Co. I 7th O. V. I.
Murdock, Clarence K., Corp. Co. I 7th O. V. I.
Murdock, Thomas H., Pr. Co. I 7th O. V. I.
Myers Joshua H., Pr. Co. I 7th O.V.I.
Pilcher, David, Pr. Co. I 7th O. V. I.
Pratt, Charles Edward, Principal Musician 7th O. V. I.
Pratt, Eugene L., Q. M. Sergt. Co. I 7th O. V. I.
Rodgers, Charles, Pr. Co. I 7th O.V.I.
Sample, Aaron C., Corp. Co. I 7th O. V. I.
Schweninger, Frank, Pr. Co. I 7th O. V. I.
Sheldon, Howard, Pr. Co. I 7th O.V.I.
Selb, Emery A., Pr. Co. I 7th O. V. I.
Sheridan, Frank, Pr. Co. B 2nd U. S. V. E.
Smith, Carey L., Sergt. Co. I 7th O. V. I.
Smith, Edward C., Sergt. Co. I 7th O. V. I.
Spencer, George, Corp. Co. I 7th O. V. I.
Sperry, Chas M., Pr. Co. A 7th O.V.I.
Thompson, William E., Sergt. Co. I 7th O. V. I.
Thuma, Allen L., Corp. Co. I 7th O. V. I.
Turney, Edward C., Pr. Co. I 7th O. V. I.
Vaughn, Joseph, Pr. Co. I 7th O. V. I.
Vogelsong, Henry A., 1st Sergt. Co. I 7th O. V. I.
Warfule, Frank H., Pr. Co. A 7th O. V. I.
Wayne, Charles A., Pr. Co. G 7th O. V. I.
Wilson, Frank W., Pr. Co. I 7th O.V.I.
Winkler, George C., Pr. Co. B 2nd U. S. V. E.
Wolie, Cecil O., Pr. Co. I 7th O. V. I.
Wright, George E., Sergt. Co. I 7th O. V. I.
Young, Joseph A., Corp. Co. I 7th O. V. I.

IRWIN

Brake, Allie, Pr. Co. D 3rd O. V. I.
Farrington, William L., Pr. Co. D 3rd O. V. I.
Kees, Isaac, Pr. Co. D 4th O. V. I
Lower, Clifton, Pr. Co. D 4th O. V. I.

JACKSON

Jones, Lloyd T., Pr. Co. F 7th O.V.I.
Monahan, Wm. H., Jr., Pr. Co. F 7th O. V. I.

JACKSON CO.

Reeves, James J., Pr. Co. I 10th O.V.I.

JACKSONTOWN

Davis, Foster, Pr. Co. K 7th O. V. I.

JACKSONVILLE

Koch, John R., Pr. Co. K 7th O. V. I.

JAMESTOWN

Larkin, John F., Pr. Co. H 10th O.V.I.

JEFFERSON

Bucher, William H., Jr., Pr. Co. D 8th O. V. I.
Howells, Joseph A., Jr., Pr. Co. E 5th O. V. I.
Newman, Earnest J., Pr. Co. E 5th O. V. I.
Pease, Pearl N., Pr. Co. E 5th O. V. I.
Pennicks, Sinclair J., Pr. Co. D 8th O. V. I.
Simmons, Wayland A., Pr. Co. E 5th O. V. I.
Udell, Henry B., Pr. Co. E 5th O.V.I.

JEROMEVILLE

Harpster, F. Burt, Pr. Co. C 8th O.V.I.
Hosler, Elza. Pr. Co. C 8th O. V. I.
Maxwell, Curtis B., Pr. U. R. 8th O. V. I.
Wilson, Jay B., Corp. Co. C 8th O.V.I.

JERRY CITY

Miller, Emery A., Pr. Co. K 2nd O.V.I.
Palmerton, James, Pr. Co. K 2nd O. V. I.
Thompson, Rush B., Pr. Co. K 2nd O. V. I.

JEWELL

Young, Martin O., Pr. Co. M 6th O. V. I.

JOBS

Snedden, William A., Pr. Co. C 2nd U. S. V. E.

JOHN'S CREEK

Neal, Robert, Pr. Co. I 7th O. V. I.

JOHNSON

Dickson, Robert T., Pr. Co. B 8th O. V. I.

JOHNSTOWN

Belt, Oscar C., Pr. Co. K 7th O. V. I.
Bishop, Harry A., Pr. Co. K 7th O. V. I.
Scovell, David W., Corp. Co. K 7th O. V. I.

JUMBO

Burris, Eyler C., Pr. Co. G 2nd O.V.I.
Collins, Orvil, Pr. Co. I 2nd O. V. I.

JUNCTION

Marlett, Justin A., Pr. Co. M 2nd O. V. I.
Sage, Marion, Pr. Co. M 2nd O. V. I.

KANSAS CITY, MO.

Manning. Charles G., Corp. Co. A 2nd U. S. V. E.

KENT

Bly, John J., Pr. Co. B 10th O. V. I.
Brown, Clifton S., Corp. Co. B 10th O. V. I.
Caris. Charley H., Pr. Co. C 10th O. V. I.
Cull, Thomas, Pr. Co. B 10th O. V. I.
Gardner, Howard J., Pr. Co. H 10th O. V. I.
Gressard, Frank A., Pr. Co. C 10th O. V. I.
Hodges, Harry W., Pr. Co. K 10th O. V. I.

Mellin, Vernon A., Pr. Co. K 10th O. V. I.
Price, Walter W., Pr. Co. C 10th O. V. I.
Reynolds, Francis T., Pr. Co. B 10th O. V. I.
Rooney, Thomas, Pr. Co. B 10th O. V. I.
Sanford, Selden M., Pr. Co. B 10th O. V. I.

KENTON

Ackerman, Thurman, Pr. Co. G 2nd O. V. I.
Allen, George W., Pr. Co. I 2nd O.V.I.
Ansley, Frank S., Pr. Co. I 2nd O.V.I.
Bailey, Charles R., Pr. Co. I 2nd O. V. I.
Baldwin, Charles E., 1st Sergt. Co. G 2nd O. V. I.
Benjamin, Jesse W., Pr. Co. I 2nd O. V. I.
Biggs, Charles L., Pr. Co. I 2n I O.V.I.
Bloom, William H., Pr. Co. G 2nd O. V. I.
Bogardus, Frank H., Corp. Co. I 2nd O. V. I.
Bolenbaugh, Asna G., Pr. Co. G 2nd O. V. I.
Bolenbaugh, Henry W., Pr. Co. G 2nd O. V. I.
Bowman, Tellie J., Pr. Co. G 2nd O. V. I.
Briggs, Raymond D., Pr. Co. G 2nd O. V. I.
Bryant, Tod, Pr. Co. I 2nd O. V. I.
Burger, Louis, Hospital Steward 2nd O. V. I.
Canaan, Emmit E., Pr. Co. G 2nd O. V. I.
Cessna, Ray H., Pr. Co. G 2nd O. V. I.
Clements, Hugh, Pr. Co. I 2nd O.V.I.
Clucker, Fred A., Pr. Co. G 2nd O.V.I.
Coats, Robert Ed., Pr. Co. I 2nd O. V. I.
Cook, John J., Pr. Co. I 2nd O. V. I.
Cook, Lewis R., Corp. Co. G 2nd O. V. I.
Cook, Nathaniel, Pr. Co. I 2nd O.V.I.
Collins, James W., Pr. Co. I 2nd O. V. I.
Collins, John H., Pr. Co. G 2nd O.V.I.
Corey, C. Clay, Pr. Co. I 2nd O. V. I.
Corey, John L., Pr. Co. I 2nd O. V. I.
Crum, Charles, Pr. Co. I 2nd O. V. I.
Dickinson, Charles, Pr. Co. I 2nd O. V. I.

Dinehart, William, Pr. Co. I 2nd O. V. I.
Dorn, Carl, Sergt. Co. I 2nd O. V. I.
Dorn, Harry A., Q. M. Sergt. Co. G 2nd O. V. I.
Dunham, Robert, Pr. Co. I 2nd O.V.I.
Dunson, Edward W., Pr. Co. G 2nd O. V. I.
Eddy, Ora, Pr. Co. I 2nd O. V. I.
Ellis, Meade E., Pr. Co. I 2nd O. V. I.
Evans, Charles E., Pr. Co. G 2nd O. V. I.
Ewing, Epp E., Pr. Co. G 2nd O. V. I.
Fink, Edward W., Pr. Co. G 2nd O. V. I.
Fink, William, Pr. Co. I 2nd O. V. I.
Fisher, Claud, Pr. Co. G 2nd O. V. I.
Gauch, Fred, Pr. Co. I 2nd O. V. I.
Gerlach, Alpha, Corp. Co. I 2nd O.V.I.
Gerlach, Arthur, Pr. Co. I 2nd O. V. I.
Gill, Floyd A., Pr. Co. G 2nd O. V. I.
Given, Robert A., Pr. Co. I 2nd O.V.I.
Glenn, John T., Reg. Sergt. Maj. 2nd O. V. I.
Golden, Ernest P., Pr. Co. G 2nd O. V. I.
Goodwin, Elsie B., Pr. Co. G 2nd O. V. I.
Goodwin, Frank, Pr. Co. G 2nd O.V.I.
Gordon, Oliver P., Jr., Corp. Co. I 2nd O. V. I.
Gottier, Thomas R. L., Pr. Co. G 2nd O. V. I.
Grady, Harry, Pr. Co. G 2nd O. V. I.
Haley, Charles E., Pr. Co. G 5th O. V. I.
Harper, Earl V., Corp. Co. G 2nd O. V. I.
Harrod, E. Earl, Corp. Co. G 2nd O. V. I.
Harshman, Clyde, Pr. Co. I 2nd O.V.I.
Hart, Edward D., Pr. Co. G 2nd O.V.I.
Hatcher, Harry O., Pr. Co. G 2nd O. V. I.
Helfinstine, Simon P., Pr. Co. I 2nd O. V. I.

Upmeyer, William, Musician Co. I 2nd O. V. I.
Vorpe, Charles, Pr. Co. I 2nd O. V. I.
Ward, Samuel W., Pr. Co. G 2nd O. V. I.
Wagner, Carrol H., Pr. Co. G 2nd O. V. I.
Wagner, William D., Pr. Co. G 2nd O. V. I.
Weber, Earnest, Pr. Co. I 2nd O. V. I.
Wells, Clint M., Sergt. Co. G 2nd O. V. I.
Wells, Denton S., Pr. Co I 2nd O.V.I.
Wells, Frank, Pr. Co. G 2nd O. V. I.
Wells, James H., Pr. Co. G 2nd O.V.I.
Wheeler, Vernie, Pr. Co. I 2nd O. V. I.
Wilkin, Harry D., Corp. Co. G 2nd O. V. I.
Wilkin, Perle H., Principal Musician 2nd O. V. I.
Williams, Albert B., Sergt. Co. G 2nd O. V. I.

Williams, Clarence, Pr. Co. G 2nd O. V. I.
Williams, Fred G., Pr. Co. G 2nd O. V. I.
Williams, Paul. Pr. Co. G 2nd O. V. I.
Wilmarth, Charles J., Pr. Co. G 2nd O. V. I.
Wilson, Edward L., Pr. Co. I 2nd O. V. I.
Wilson, Harry R., Pr. Co. G 2nd O. V. I.
Wilson, Newton, Pr. Co. I 2nd O. V. I.
Wilson, Willis H., Pr. Co. I 2nd O.V.I.
Wolke, Henry F., Pr. Co. I 2nd O.V.I.
Wooley, Frank M., Pr. Co. I 2nd O. V. I.
Worthington, Bert. J., Pr. Co. I 2nd O. V. I.
Wright, James E., Pr. Co. I 2nd O.V.I.
Yost, Charles, Pr. Co. G 2nd O. V. I.
Young, Robert, Pr. Co. I 2nd O. V. I.
Young, Scott, Pr. Co. I 2nd O. V. I.

KILMER

Craig, Elsworth, Pr. Co. D 7th O.V.I.

KILLBUCK

Brink, Harold S., Pr. Co. H 8th O.V.I.
Burklew, Sewell R., Musician Co. H 8th O. V. I.

Patterson, Thomas C., Pr. Co. H 8th O. V. I.

KINSMAN

Root, Ralph, Pr. Co. C 10th O. V. I.

KIRKERSVILLE

Finkbone, Allen T., Pr. Co. K 7th O. V. I.

Wells, Charles N., Pr. Co. K 7th O. V. I.

KIRKWOOD

Eldredge, Clyde, Pr. Co. K 3rd O.V.I.

Havescher, Fred W., Pr. Co. L 3rd O. V. I.

KIRTLAND

Allen, David L., Pr. Co. M 5th O.V.I.
Morse, Frank W., Pr. Co. M 5th O. V. I.

Thompson, Clive W., Pr. Co. M 5th O. V. I.

KLOTTER RAVINE

Hoeltzel, George, Pr. Co. I 1st O.V.I.

KNOXVILLE, TENN.

Clay, Samuel E., Pr. Co. D 9th Batt. O. V. I.

Gallagher, Dennis F., Wagoner Co. K 7th O. V. I.

KRAVENSVILLE, TENN.

Dry, William, Pr. Co. D 9th Batt. O. V. I.

LAFAYETTE

Booth, John R., Pr. Co. E 3rd O. V. I.
Dillow, Earnest G., Pr. Co. E 3rd O. V. I.
Dulaney, Denton, Pr. Co. E 3rd O.V.I.
Flemming, Louis, Pr. Co. E 3rd O.V.I.

Jones. George W., Artificer Co. E 3rd O. V. I.
Minter, John W., Pr. Co. E 3rd O.V.I.
Peel, Charles T., Pr. Co. E 3rd O.V.I.
Volka, John C., Corp. Co. E 3rd O. V. I.

LAFERGEVILLE, N. Y.

Vogt, Andrew F., Pr. Co. A 2nd U. S. V. E.

LAKE ODESSA, MICH.

Gates, Edward D., Pr. Co. A 10th O. V. I.

LAKEWOOD

Bates, Frank S., Pr. Co. F 5th O. V. I.
Boedewig, Louis F., Pr. Co. B 10th O. V. I.

Haake, Albert H., Pr. Co. B 10th O. V. I.

LANCASTER

Arnold, Jesse W., Pr. Co. I 4th O.V.I.
Beery, Frank E., Pr. Co. I 4th O.V.I.
Bentrup, Charles F., Pr. Co. I 4th O. V. I.
Bope, Charles B., Pr. Co. Y 4th O.V.I.
Brainard, Willie J., Pr. Co. I 4th O. V. I.
Buckley, William J., Pr. Co. I 4th O. V. I.
Clifton, George, Pr. Co. I 4th O. V. I.
Cook, Irving A., Musician Co. I 4th O. V. I.
Deer, Charles E., Pr. Co. I 4th O.V.I.
Fishbaugh, Charley, Corp. Co. I 4th O. V. I.
Flood, William H., Pr. Co. I 4th O. V. I.
Gantz, John G., Pr. Co. I 4th O. V. I.
Getz, Oscar D., Musician Co. I 4th O. V. I.
Green, Lester O., Pr. Co. I 4th O.V.I.
Greentree, James, Pr. Co. I 4th O.V.I.
Hart, George B., Pr. Co. C 5th O.V.I.
Herman, Henry, Pr. Co. I 4th O. V. I.
Hooker, William M., Sergt. Co. I 4th O. V. I.
Jeffries, George T., Pr. Co. I 4th O. V. I.
Justice, George L., Pr. Co. I 4th O. V. I.
Keller, William U., Pr. Co. I 4th O. V. I.
Kindler, William S., 1st Sergt. Co. I 4th O. V. I.
Knotts, Charles, Pr. Co. I 4th O. V. I.
Leeper, Clarence Le, Pr. Co. I 4th O. V. I.

Littrell, John W., Corp. Co. I 4th O. V. I.
Lowry, Warren A., Pr. Co. I 4th O. V. I.
McClain, Clifford C., Pr. Co. I 4th O. V. I.
McSweeney, James F., Pr. Co. I 4th O. V. I.
Moore, Charles R., Pr. Co. I 4th O. V. I.
Murphy, Frank M., Sergt. Co. I 4th O. V. I.
Nisley, Harry J., Pr. Co. I 4th O. V. I.
Peters, Gaylord C., Sergt. Co. I 4th O. V. I.
Phillips, Arthur J., Corp. Co. I 4th O. V. I.
Proctor, Harry E., Pr. Co. I 4th O. V. I.
Reed, Charles G., Pr. Co. I 4th O.V.I.
Robinson, Amos W., Pr. Co. I 4th O. V. I.
Robinson, Robert B., Pr. Co. I 4th O. V. I.
Roskovencky, Lewis S., Pr. Co. I 4th O. V. I.
Seifert, Abe, Pr. Co. I 4th O. V. I.
Thomas, John E., Sergt. Co. I 4th O. V. I.
Todhunter, Reese B., Pr. Co. I 4th O. V. I.
Walters, Perrie, Pr. Co. I 4th O. V. I.
White, John E., Pr. Co. I 4th O. V. I.
Williams, Howard A., Pr. Co. I 4th O. V. I.
Zimmerman, John D., Pr. Co. I 4th O. V. I.

LARUE

Barron, James, Corp. Co. B 10th O. V. I.
McConnell, Charles, Pr. Co. G 4th O. V. I.

Swallem, Harry, Pr. Co. G 4th O.V.I.
Thomas, John O., Pr. Co. I 2nd O.V.I.

LATTASBURG

Brownson, Charles W., Pr. Co. C 8th O. V. I.

LATTY

Adams, Henry, Musician Co. M 2nd O. V. I.

Cook, Edwin A., Pr. Co. M 2nd O.V.I.

Flory, Benjamin F., Pr. Co. M 2nd O. V. I.

LAURA

Carey, Thomas A., Pr. Co. C 3rd O. V. I.

LEAPER

Frownfeltor, Otto, Pr. Co. C 7th O. V. I.

LEAVITTSBURG,

Garrard, Charles H., Wagoner Co. C 5th O. V. I.

LEBANON

Brant, Clifford, Pr. Co. C 2nd U. S. V. E.

Ross, Charles J., Pr. Co. A 1st O.V.I.

Wright, Clint E., Pr. Co. A 1st O.V.I.

LEESBURG

Covan, William C., Pr. Co. C 7th O. V. I.

LEIPSIC

Bright, Walter D., Pr. Co. D 10th O. V. I.

Mapel, Mack, Pr. Co. D 10th O. V. I.

Nutter, Ory C., Pr. Co. D 10th O.V.I.

Sherman, Frank, Pr. Co. D 10th O. V. I.

LEONARD

Kiefhaber, Edward C., Pr. Co. A 2nd U. S. V. E.

LEVANNA

Heinz, George R., Pr. Co. H 3rd O. V. I.

Hunneman, Julius, Pr. Co. H 3rd O. V. I.

LEXINGTON, VA.

McManamay, James H., Pr. Co. B 7th O. V. I.

LIMA

Allen, Carey C., Corp. Co. C 2nd O. V. I.

Applas, Brice B., Pr. Co. C 2nd O.V.I.

Armstrong, James D., Sergt. Co. C 2nd O. V. I.

Ashton, Paul R., Pr. Co. C 2nd O.V.I.

Atha, John, Pr. Co. C 2nd O. V. I.

Barnes, Roy, Pr. Co. C 2nd O. V. I.

Baum, Charles W., Pr. Co. C 2nd O. V. I.

Berney, Edward P., Wagoner Co. C 2nd O. V. I.

Betz, Henry A., Pr. Co. C 2nd O. V. I.

Breese, Clarence, Pr. Co. C 2nd O.V.I.

Brown, Charles J., Pr. Co. C 2nd O. V. I.

Bussert, Earl D., Pr. Co. C 2nd O.V.I.

Campbell, Walter K., Pr. Co. C 2nd O. V. I.

Cantieny, Dominic R., Sergt. Co. C 2nd O. V. I.

Carter, Frank, Q. M. Sergt. Co. C 2nd O. V. I.

Collahan, Cornelius P., Pr. Co. C 2nd O. V. I.

Davis, Donald N., Pr. Co. C 2nd O. V. I.

Davis, Foster B., Pr. Co. C 2nd O.V.I.

Doan, Carey S., Pr. Co. C 2nd O.V.I.

Faurot, George, Pr. Co. C 2nd O.V.I.

Ferguson, Walter G., Pr. Co. C 2nd O. V. I.

Ferrall, James L., Artificer Co. C 2nd O. V. I.

Freeman, Winfield, Pr. Co. C 2nd O. V. I.

Gale, Albert E., Sergt. Co. C 2nd O. V. I.

Gorman, Harry J., Pr. Co. C 2nd O. V. I.

Gottfield, John, Pr. Co. C 2nd O. V. I.

Graham, Howard, Pr. Co. C 2nd O. V. I.

Griebling, Carl, Pr. Co. C 2nd O. V. I.

Harley, John, Pr. Co. C 2nd O. V. I.

Harper, Oscar, Pr. Co. C 2nd O. V. I.

Harrison, William F., Pr. Co. D 9th Batt. O. V. I.

Heffner, James I., Pr. Co. C 2nd O. V. I.

Herman, Homer D., Corp. Co. C 2nd O. V. I.

Hofmann, Lewis J., Pr. Co. C 2nd O. V. I.

Holbrook, Samuel A., Pr. Co. C 2nd O. V. I.

Hughes, Kent W., Sergt. Co. C 2nd O. V. I.

Kelley, Charles H., Pr. Co. C 2nd O. V. I.

Keys, David F., Corp. Co. B 10th O. V. I.

Killian, Floyd, Pr. Co. C 2nd O. V. I.

Lawlor, Edward P., Pr. Co. C 2nd O. V. I.

Link, Frank, Pr. Co. C 2nd O. V. I.

Lutz, John W., Pr. Co. C 2nd O. V. I.

Mahon, James A., Pr. Co. C 2nd O. V. I.

McGinnis, Harry W., Pr. Co. C 2nd O. V. I.

McKinney, Rolla, Pr. Co. C 2nd O. V. I.

McPeak, Robert, Pr. Co. C 2nd O. V. I.

Miller, John D., Pr. Co. C 2nd O.V.I.

Myers, William P., Pr. Co. C 2nd O. V. I.

Naylor, Charles, Pr. Co. C 2nd O.V.I.

Neely, Loren E., Pr. Co. C 2nd O. V. I.

Neise, James H., Pr. Co. C 2nd O.V.I.

Norton, Rolland A., Pr. Tr. G 1st O. V. C.

O'Brien, Henry, Jr., Pr. Co. C 2nd O. V. I.

Odell, Omer H., Jr., Pr. Co. L 3rd O. V. I.

Parmenter, Walter, Pr. Co. C 2nd O. V. I.

Porter, John E., 1st Sergt. Co. C 2nd O. V. I.

Quail, George H., Pr. Co. C 2nd O. V. I.

Remackel, Nick, Pr. Co. C 2nd O.V.I.

Reynolds, Charles F., Pr. Co. C 2nd O. V. I.

Robinson, James H., Pr. Co. C 2nd O. V. I.

Sellers, Roy V., Corp. Co. C 2nd O. V. I.

Smith, George A., Pr. Co. C 2nd O. V. I.

Stager, Jahn A., Pr. Co. C 2nd O.V.I.

Standish, Harold S., Corp. Co. C 2nd O V. I.

Stemen, John E., Pr. Co. C 2nd O.V.I.

Stephens, Lou P., Corp. Co. C 2nd O. V. I.

Swift, John W., Pr. Tr. G 1st O. V. C.

Thomas, Fred B., Sergt. Co. C 2nd O. V. I.

Tibbot, George, Pr. Co. C 2nd O. V. I.

Watts, Alexander H., Pr. Co. C 2nd O. V. I.

Welty, Albert B., Pr. Co. C 2nd O.V.I.

Welty, Benjamin F., Pr. Co. C 2nd O. V. I.

Wood, George W., Pr. Co. C 2nd O. V. I.

Zeits, Fred W., Pr. Co. C 2nd O. V. I.

LIMAVILLE

Reynolds, Eugene, Pr. Co. K 8th O. V. I.

LINDSEY

Boyer, Alton A., Pr. Co. K 6th O.V.I.

Richards, William C., Pr. Co. K 6th O. V. I.

LIVERPOOL

Miller, Bert, Pr. Co. C 8th O. V. I.

LLOYD

Hutson, Jesse P., Pr. Co. K 8th O.V.I.

LOCUST GROVE

Ault, Charles L., Pr. Co. B 3rd O.V.I.

LODI

Carr, Sherman H., Pr. Co. D 8th O. V. I.

Plank, Harry F., Pr. Co. D 8th O.V.I.

LOGAN COUNTY

McClure, Frank W., Pr. Co. F 2nd O. V. I.

LOOKOUT

Chapman, Walter, Pr. Co. K 3rd O. V. I.

LOUDONVILLE

Beeman, Earl T., Pr. Co. H 8th O.V.I.
Bird, Charles E., Pr. Co. H 8th O.V.I.
Campbell, Walter, Sergt. Co. H 8th O. V. I.
Carpenter, John F., Pr. Co. C 8th O. V. I.

Critchfield, Benjamin H., Pr. Co. H 8th O. V. I.
Eberly, George, Pr. Co. H 8th O. V. I.
Getz, John W., Pr. Co. H 8th O. V. I.

LOUISVILLE

Cunin, Austin, Pr. Co. F 8th O. V. I.
Myers, William, Pr. Co. F 8th O. V. I.
Slusser, Lincoln A., Pr. Co. L 8th O. V. I.

Westenberger, William H., Pr. Co. L 8th O. V. I.

LOWELL

Biehl, Frank H., Pr. Co. D 7th O.V.I.

LOWER SALEM

Blake, Edward S., 1st Sergt. Co. D 7th O. V. I.
Boeshaar, Fred C., 2nd Corp. Co. D 7th O. V. I.
Broome, Henry, Pr. Co. D 7th O.V.I.
Hardy, Maurice L., Pr. Co. D 7th O. V. I.
Hartshorn, Elum D., 5th Corp. Co. D 7th O. V. I.
Hartshorn, Joseph P., 5th Sergt. Co. D 7th O. V. I.
Hockenberry, Clinton, 3rd Corp. Co. D 7th O. V. I.

Jacobs, William H., Pr. Co. D 7th O. V. I.
Kehl, Henry, Pr. Co. D 7th O. V. I.
Rhodes, Charles, Pr. Co. D 7th O.V.I.
Twiggs, Warren A., Pr. Co. D 7th O. V. I.
Watkins, Harry T., 1st Corp. Co. D 7th O. V. I.
Whetstone, Allan M., 2nd Sergt. Co. D 7th O. V. I.
Whetstone, Frederick, Pr. Co. D 7th O. V. I.
Zumbro, George F., 4th Sergt. Co. D 7th O. V. I.

LONDON

Anderson, Charles, Pr. Co. E 3rd O. V. I.
Armstrong, Harry H., Sergt. Co. E 3rd O. V. I.
Baker, John H., Pr. Co. E 3rd O.V.I.
Betts, Edward, Pr. Co. E 3rd O. V. I.

Bradley, James L., Pr. Co. E 3rd O. V. I.
Bunnemeyer, Henry, Pr. Co. E 3rd O. V. I.
Burt, Ernest, Pr. Co. E 3rd O. V. I.
Cain, Charles W., Pr. Co. A 9th Batt., O. V. I.

Cavanaugh, Richard, Pr. Co. E 3rd O.
V. I.
Chandler, Wright D., Pr. Co. G 10th
O. V. I.
Chenoweth, Rea, 1st Sergt. Co. E 3rd
O. V. I.
Coleman, Thomas, Sergt. Co. E 3r I
O. V. I.
Corbitt, Frank, Pr. Co. E 3rd O.V.I.
Davidson, George W., Musician Co. E
3rd O. V. I.
Davidson, William Mac, Pr. Co. E 3rd
O. V. I.
Dwyer, Patrick, Pr. Co. E 3rd O.V.I.
Fisher, Howard E., Pr. Co. A 9th Batt.
O. V. I.
Freeman, Fremont, Pr. Co. E 3rd O.
V. I.
Gallagher, Harry B., Corp. Co. E 3rd
O. V. I.
Graham, Toland J., Pr. Co. E 3rd O.
V. I.
Griffith, Albert, Pr. Co. E 3rd O. V. I.
Gulcher, Harry, Pr. Co. E 3rd O. V. I.
Haithcock, Archelaus, Pr. U. R. 9th
Batt. O. V. I.
Harding, Elijah, Pr. Co. E 3rd O.V.I.
Heilman, Peter, Pr. Co. E 3rd O. V. I.
Henderson, Joseph, Pr. Co. A 9th
Batt. O. V. I.
Herdman, James, Pr. Co. E 3rd O.V.I.
Hickey, Michael, Pr. Co. E 3rd O.V.I.
Holt, Howard, Pr. Co. E. 3rd O. V. I.
Hunt, Arnold G. W., Pr. Co. A 9th
Batt. O. V. I.
Jack, Charles, Pr. Co. E 3rd O. V. I.
Keefer, Thaddeus, Pr. Co. E 3rd O.
V. I.
Kinner, William, Pr. Co. E 3rd O.V.I.
Kulp, Charles S., Pr. Co. E 3rd O.V.I.
Legge, Drill B., Corp. Co. E 3rd O.
V. I.
Liller, Lonzo, Pr. Co. E 3rd O. V. I.
Long, Leroy, Pr. Co. E 3rd O. V. I.
Manrel, Thomas, Pr. Co. E 3rd O.V.I.
McCollum, Reed, Pr. Co. E 3rd O.V.I.
McCormack, Ernest W., Sergt. Co. E
3rd O. V. I.

McCormack, Thomas H., Corp. Co. E
3rd O. V. I.
Murlett, Clifford, Pr. Co. E 3rd O.V.I.
Norris, James Bryan, Pr. Co. B 9th
Batt. O. V. I.
Norris, William H., Pr. Co. A 9th
Batt. O., V. I.
O'Brien, John, Pr. Co. E 3rd O. V. I.
Prentergast, Richard D., Pr. Co. E 3rd
O. V. I.
Robey, William J., Corp. Co. E 3rd
O. V. I.
Robinson, Samuel, Pr. Co. A 9th Batt.
O. V. I.
Ryan, Harry, Pr. Co. E 3rd O. V. I.
Sharp, Leighton F., Pr. Co. E 3rd O.
V. I.
Sidner, Earnest L., Pr. Co. E 3rd O.
V. I.
Skeels, Charles W., Musician Co. E 3rd
O. V. I.
Smith, George, Pr. Co. E 3rd O. V. I.
Snyder, Claude, Wagoner Co. E 3rd
O. V. I.
Stahl, Walter J., Corp. Co. E 3rd O.
V. I.
Timmons, Emmett, Pr. Co. E 3rd O.
V. I.
Toland, Harford A., Sergt. Co. E 3rd
O. V. I.
Trehearne, William S., Sergt. Co. E
3rd O. V. I.
Tumbleson, Charles, Pr. Co. E 3rd O.
V. I.
Webb, Howard N., Pr. Co. E 3rd O.
V. I
Wicker, Clarence S., Pr. Co. A 9th
Batt. O. V. I.
Winans, William E., Corp. Co. E 3rd
O. V. I.
Winslow, Charles, Pr. Co. A 9th Batt.
O. V. I.
Winslow, Nelson R., Pr. Co. A 9th
Batt. O. V. I.
Wolfe, Walter W., Pr. Co. E 3rd O.
V. I.
Young, Charles, Pr. Co. E 3rd O.V.I.

LORAIN

Adams, Charles, Pr. Co. A 5th O.V.I.
Adams, Frank A., Pr. Co. A 5th O.
V. I.
Bailing, Arthur W., Pr. Co. A 5th O.
V. I.
Barnes, Theodore M., Wagoner Co. A
5th O. V. I.
Becker, Charles F., Pr. Co. A 5th O.
V. I.
Bergner, Edward G., Pr. Co. A 5th O.
V. I.
Berkline, Jake, Pr. Co. A 5th O. V. I.
Blaine, David M., Pr. Co. A 5th O.V.I.
Brown, Harvey T., Pr. Co. A 5th O.
V. I.

Cobb, John Jay, Pr. Co. A 5th O. V. I.
Earl, Arthur J., Pr. Co. A 5th O. V. I.
Eddy, Arthur L., 3rd Sergt. Co. A 5th
O. V. I.
Finnegan, Hugh A., Pr. Co. A 5th O.
V. I.
George, William, Musician Co. A 5th
O. V. I.
Gove, Adelbert F., Pr. Co. A 5th O.
V. I.
Gove, Roy M., Pr. Co. A 5th O. V. I.
Hakes, Robert E., Pr. Co. A 5th O.
V. I.
Haupt, Edward H., Pr. Co. A 5th O.
V. I.

Hinman, Scott, 4th Corp. Co. A 5th
O. V. I.
Hobbs, Abner, Pr. Co. A 5th O. V. I.
Hoffman, George J., 2nd Sergt. Co. A
5th O. V. I.
Holbrook, Clyde W., Pr. Co. A 5th O.
V. I.
Hudson, Harry H., Pr. Co. A 5th O.
V. I.
Hurd, Elbridge H., Pr. Co. A 5th O.
V. I.
Jessie, Charles H., Pr. Co. A 5th O.
V. I.
Jones, Harry H., Musician Co. A 5th
O. V. I.
Jaycox, Lewis H., Pr. Co. A 5th O.
V. I.
Jones, Rupert H., Pr. Co. A 5th O.V.I.
Koehler, Charles V., 5th Sergt. Co. A
5th O. V. I.
Koehler, Joseph L., Pr. Co. A 5th O.
V. I.
Ledyard, Clarence E., 5th Corp. Co. A
5th O. V. I.
Leinbos, George, Pr. Co. A 5th O.V.I.
Loofborrow, Ellery C., Pr. Co. A 5th
O. V. I.
McGrady, John, Pr. Co. A 5th O. V. I.
McMasters, Robert E., Pr. Co. A 5th
O. V. I.
Mead, Richard B., 4th Sergt. Co. A
5th O. V. I.
Miller, John E., Artificer Co. A 5th O.
V. I.
Moore, Frank W., Pr. Co. A 5th O.
V. I.
Murbach, John F., 1st Corp. Co. A 5th
O. V. I.
Parks, Edward F., Pr. Co. A 5th O.
V. I.
Patton, Glenn R., Q. M. Sergt. Co. A
5th O. V. I.
Penrod, Howard T., Pr. Co. A 5th O.
V. I.

Raymond, Charles O., Pr. Co. A 5th
O. V. I.
Reedy, Alfred J., Pr. Co. A 5th O.V.I.
Reichert, John S., Pr. Co. A 5th O.
V. I.
Reininger, William, Pr. Co. A 5th O.
V. I.
Rice, Harry L., Pr. Co. A 5th O. V. I.
Richardson, Ralph M., Pr. Co. A 5th
O. V. I.
Rickard, Samuel, Pr. Co. A 5th O.V.I.
Sachmann, Fred E., Pr. Co. A 5th O.
V. I.
Sanford, James S., Pr. Co. A 5th O.
V. I.
Schrock, John G., Pr. Co. A 5th O.
V. I.
Shaw, Harry L., Pr. Co. A 5th O. V. I.
Shuman, William E., Pr. Co. A 5th O.
V. I.
Smith, Charles L., Pr. Co. A 5th O.
V. I.
Strike, William R., 3rd Corp. Co. A
5th O. V. I.
Titus, Clarence H., Pr. Co. A 5th O.
V. I.
Traxler, Peter J., Pr. Co. A 5th O.V.I.
Vehlber, William, Pr. Co. A 5th O.V.I.
Warburton, Lewis, Pr. Co. A 5th O.
V. I.
Washburn, Lewis H., 2nd Corp. Co. A
5th O. V. I.
Washburn, Walter H., Pr. Co. A 5th
O. V. I.
Webber, Gilbert G., Pr. Co. A 5th O.
V. I.
Whitby, George P., Pr. Co. A 5th O.
V. I.
Wiegand, Fred H., 6th Corp. Co. A 5th
O. V. I.
Wilder, Moses G., Pr. Co. A 5th O.
V. I.
Wright, Joseph R., 1st Sergt. Co. A
5th O. V. I.

LUDLOW, KY.

Ehrlich, Edward F., Corp. Co. B 2nd U. S. V. E.

LUDWICK

Frost, Seaver, Pr. Co. F 3rd O. V. I.

LYONS, N. Y.

Bear, Clifford L., Pr. Tr. G 1st O.V.C.

MACEDONIA

Mack, George J., Pr. Tr. B 1st O.V.C.

MADISON

Hunter, Joseph R., Pr. Co. E 5th O. V. I.
Randall, William A., Pr. Co. E 5th O. V. I.

Vrooman, Charlie H., Pr. Co. E 5th O. V. I.
Waterbury, Robert J., Pr. Co. E 5th O. V. I.
Wolfe, Fred B., Pr. Co. E 5th O.V.I.

MADISONVILLE

Meinhardt, Frank R., Pr. Co. C 2nd U. S. V. E.

MALTA

Fouts, William, Pr. Co. L 10th O.V.I.
Hughes, George M., Pr. Bat. C 1st O. V. A.

Rothrock, James A., Pr. Co. L 10th O. V. I.

MALVERN

Deckman, Arthur W., Pr. Co. F 8th O. V. I.

Hewitt, Herb., Pr. Co. F 8th O. V. I.

MANARA

Shepard, Clarence, Pr. Co. F 7th O. V. I.

Shumate, Guy O., Pr. Co. F 7th O.V.I.

MANDALE

Protzman, Edward A., Pr. Co. M 2nd O. V. I.

MANSFIELD

Alvord, Joseph Grant, Sergt. Co. M 8th O. V. I.
Beelman, Charles C., Corp. Co. M 8th O. V. I.
Bell, Tom M., Corp. Co. M 8th O.V.I.
Beverstock, Frank, Pr. Co. M 8th O. V. I.
Bloom, Geoffry J., Pr. Co. M 8th O. V. I.
Bride, Harry M., Pr. Co. M 8th O.V.I.
Bride, Theodore, Sergt. Co. M 8th O. V. I.
Byrd, Fred, Pr. Co. M 8th O. V. I.
Carrick, Thomas A., Pr. U. R. 8th O. V. I.
Chatlain, Charles E., Pr. Co. M 8th O. V. I.
Coleman, George W., Pr. Co. M 8th O. V. I.
Colesworthy, William J., Pr. Co. M 8th O. V. I.
Connelly, Freeman E., Pr. Co. M 8th O. V. I.
Craig, Frank B., Pr. Co. M 8th O.V.I.
Culp, William A., Artificer Co. M 8th O. V. I.
Daugherty, Harry F., Pr. Co. M 8th O. V. I.
Day, Charles W., Pr. Co. M 8th O.V.I.
Day, Ralph B., Q. M. Sergt. 1st O. V. C.
Eckis, Ezra L., Pr. Co. M 8th O. V. I.
Fisher, Elmer D., Pr. Co. M 8th O.V.I.

Frankeberger, William F., Corp. Co. M 8th O. V. I.
Gailey, John B., Sergt. Co. M 8th O. V. I.
Gandert, John W., Corp. Co. M 8th O. V. I.
Gates, Charles A., Pr. Co. M 8th O. V. I.
Hall, Charles R., Pr. Co. M 8th O V.I.
Harbaugh, Wade, Pr. Co. M 8th O. V. I.
Harrington, Alfred I., Pr. Co. M 8th O. V. I.
Hartman, William V., Pr. Co. M 8th O. V. I.
Hastings, Thomas F., Pr. Co. M 8th O. V. I.
Hayner, George J., Pr. Co. M 8th O. V. I.
Hiltabidle, Guy P., Pr. Co. M 8th O. V. I.
Hine, Peter V., Sergt. Co. M 8th O. V. I.
Hoyer, Harvey B., Pr. Co. M 8th O. V. I.
Huggins, John B., 1st Sergt. Co. M 8th O. V. I.
Hull, Hugh B., Pr. Co. M 8th O. V. I.
Huston, Charles H., Pr. Co. M 8th O. V. I.
Irvin, Charles F., Pr. Co. M 8th O.V.I.
Johnson, William C., Pr. Co. M 8th O. V. I.

Johnston, Charles R., Pr. Co. M 8th O. V. I.
Kanary, Pat., Pr. Co. M 8th O. V. I.
Karg, William, Pr. Co. M 8th O. V. I.
Kasler, George, Pr. Co. M 8th O. V. I.
King, Rufus, Corp. Co. M 8th O.V.I.
Koons, Harry J., Pr. Co. M 8th O.V.I.
Kraska, August, Pr. Co. M 8th O.V.I.
Lamberton, James C., Pr. Co. M 8th O. V. I.
Lowry, Robert, Pr. Co. M 8th O. V. I.
Maguire, Joseph, Pr. Co. M 8th O.V.I.
Massa, Albert H., Pr. Co. M 8th O. V. I.
McFarland, Harry W., Pr. Co. M 8th O. V. I.
McKay, William K., Pr. Co. M 8th O. V. I.
McPerren, James W., Pr. Co. M 8th O. V. I.
Miller, Ralph C., Pr. Co. M 8th O.V.I.
Nichols, Arthur J., Pr. Co. M 8th O. V. I.
Overholt, Frank, Pr. Co. M 8th O.V.I.
Phipps, Elda L., Pr. Co. M 8th O.V.I.

Porch, Roscoe E., Corp. Co. M 8th O. V. I.
Reed, William W., Pr. Co. M 8th O. V. I.
Sawhill, Edward J., Pr. Co. M 8th O. V. I.
Seymour, Joseph D., Pr. Co. M 8th O. V. I.
Shade, Warren S., Pr. Co. M 8th O. V. I.
Shea, Charles E., Pr. Co. M 8th O.V.I.
Smith, Anson H., Wagoner Co. M 8th O. V. I.
Spittler, Durbin W., Pr. Co. M 8th O. V. I.
Starrett, Jesse A., Sergt. Co. M 8th O. V. I.
Summerville, B. Carl, Pr. Co. M 8th O. V. I.
Teeple, Ralph S., Pr. Tr. B 1st O.V.C.
Trease, Davis, Pr. Co. M 8th O. V. I.
Warner, Joy W., Pr. Co. M 8th O.V.I.
Wolff, Will B., Pr. Co. M 8th O. V. I.
Young, Charles R., Pr. Co. M 8th O. V. I.

MARIETTA

Baker, John, Pr. Co. D 7th O. V. I.
Chapman, Albert E., Pr. Co. D 7th O. V. I.
Chapman, Elmer S., Pr. Co. D 7th O. V. I.
Davidson, Elias E., Pr. Co. D 7th O. V. I.
Dutton, Walter F., Corp. Co. B 5th O. V. I.
Folger, Theodore, 4th Corp. Co. D 7th O. V. I.
Foraker, Richard E., Pr. Co. D 7th O. V. I.
Geren, Walter F., Pr. Co. D 7th O.V.I.
Hart, Thomas W., Pr. Co. D 7th O. V. I.
Heydrick, Gilbert T., Pr. Co. D 7th O. V. I.
Hoffman, Edward, Pr. Co. D 7th O. V. I.

Leeper, John R., Pr. Co. M 10th O. V. I.
Mattern, William G., Pr. Co. D 7th O. V. I.
Miller, John, Pr. Co. D 7th O. V. I.
Minor, Samuel, Pr. Co. D 7th O. V. I.
Miraben, Lee, Q. M. Sergt. Co. D 7th O. V. I.
Nott, Oscar, Pr. Co. D 7th O. V. I.
Posey, Alexander, Pr. Co. D 7th O. V. I.
Ritchey, Pete, Pr. Co. D 7th O. V. I.
Semon, Alfred H., Pr. Co. D 7th O. V. I.
Smith, Enoch F., Pr. Co. D 7th O.V.I.
Stover, George W., Pr. Co. D 7th O. V. I.
Suder, Jacob, Artificer Co. D 7th O. V. I.
Trein, Frank E., Pr. Co. D 7th O.V.I.
Wilking, Earnest, Pr. Co. D 7th O.V.I.

MARION

Alexander, Arthur G., Pr. Co. G 4th O. V. I.
Anderson, Neal J., Pr. Co. G 4th O. V. I.
Berry, Frank C., Pr. Co. G 4th O.V.I.
Biechler, Albert, Pr. Co. G 4th O.V.I.
Boyer, Ernst, Pr. Co. G 4th O. V. I.
Bryan, Harry F., Pr. Co. G 4th O.V.I.
Carey, Howard E., Pr. Co. G 4th O. V. I.
Carroll, Harry G., Pr. Co. G 4th O. V. I.
Chapman, Ross, Pr. Co. G 4th Q. V. I.

Clapper, Nathaniel J., Pr. Co. G 4th O. V. I.
Cleveland, William E., Pr. Co. G 4th O. V. I.
Copeland, Charles F., Pr. Co. G 4th O. V. I.
Day, Louis E., Pr. Co. G 4th O. V. I.
Doke, Charles H., Pr. Co. G 4th O. V. I.
Elliott, Ulysses G., Pr. Co. G 4th O. V. I.
Evans, Edward C., Corp. Co. G 4th O. V. I.

French, Arthur J., Pr. Co. G 4th O. V. I.
Gunder, Zed E., 1st Sergt. Co. G 4th O. V. I.
Hessong, Charles E., Pr. Co. G 4th O. V. I.
Hill, George W., Pr. Co. G 4th O.V.I.
Hinklin, Howard A., Pr. Co. G 4th O. V. I.
Hubby, Earl E., Pr. Co. G 4th O. V. I.
Hull, Hollis H., Pr. Co. G 4th O. V. I.
Hunt, Will H., Corp. Co. G 4th O.V.I.
Irey, Harley O., Pr. Co. G 4th O.V.I.
Irvin, George E., Corp. Co. G 4th O. V. I.
Jordon, Frank L., Pr. Co. G 4th O.V.I.
Latimore, Charles R., Sergt. Co. G 4th O. V. I.
Latimore, Frank E., Sergt. Co. G 4th O. V. I.
Little, Frank M., Pr. Co. G 4th O.V.I.
Livingston, A. Ray, Pr. Co. K 2nd O. V. I.
Maag, William A., Corp. Co. G 4th O. V. I.
Madden, John W., Pr. Co. G 4th O. V. I.
McFadden, Edward S., Sergt. Co. G 4th O. V. I.
McMurray, James W., Sergt. Co. G 4th O. V. I.
Messenger, Harry T., Pr. Co. G 4th O. V. I.
Messinger, James E., Corp. Co. G 4th O. V. I.
Midlam, Carl O., Pr. Co. G 4th O.V.I.

Monnette, Arthur A., Pr. Co. G 4th O. V. I.
O'Brien, Thomas J., Pr. Co. G 4th O. V. I.
Padgett, Frank O., Pr. Co. G 4th O. V. I.
Pierce, Daniel B., Pr. Co. G 4th O.V.I.
Purkey, George A., Pr. Co. G 4th O. V. I.
Rathel, Robert L., Pr. Co. G 4th O. V. I.
Riddle, William W., Pr. Co. G 4th O. V. I.
Scott, John W., Pr. Co. G 4th O. V. I.
Shaffer, Frank E., Pr. Co. G 4th O. V. I.
Simpson, John W. W., Pr. Co. G 4th O. V. I.
Snider, John F., Musician Co. G 4th O. V. I.
Spring Harry L., Pr. Co. G 4th O.V.I.
Stevenson, Frank C., Pr. Co. G 4th O. V. I.
Stone, William, Pr. Co. G 4th O. V. I.
Strump, Frederick Charles, Pr. Co. G 4th O. V. I.
Thomas, Lloyd W., Pr. Co. G 4th O. V. I.
Thompson, Robert, Pr. Co. G 4th O. V. I.
Ward, Omie P., Pr. Co. G 4th O. V. I.
Wickers, John L., Pr. Co. G 4th O. V. I.
Wilson, John R., Pr. Co. G 4th O.V.I.
Winter, Wesley C., Pr. Co. G 4th O. V. I.
Wolfe, Finley M., Corp. Co. G 4th O. V. I.

MARLBORO

Hissner, Elmer A., Pr. Co. K 8th O. V. I.

MARCHAND

Stormfeltz, Charles, Pr. Co. F 8th O. V. I.

MARROW

Miranda, Thomas N., Pr. Co. C 10th O. V. I.

MARS, PA. BUTLER CO.

Weaver, Collins A., Pr. Co. G 7th O. V. I.

MARSEILLES

Hensel, Orlando, Pr. Co. I 2nd O.V.I.   Willey, Ernest, Pr. Co. I 2nd O. V. I.

MARTEL

Sharrock, James, Pr. Co. G 4th O.V.I.

MARYSVILLE

Adams, Charles, Pr. Tr. G 1st O.V.C.
Alexander, Thomas J., Sergt. Co. D 4th O. V. I.
Amrine, Arthur H., Pr. Co. D 4th O. V. I.
Amrine, Harry G., Pr. Co. D 4th O. V. I.
Amrine, Lutrelle, Pr. Tr. G 1st O.V.C.
Beck, James, Pr. Co. D 4th O. V. I.
Bishop, Newton Otto, Pr. Co. D 4th O. V. I.
Brown, George E., Pr. Co. D 4th O. V. I.
Cavis, Frederick L., Pr. Tr. G 1st Q. V. C.
Clapham, Frank, Pr. Co. D 4th O.V.I.
Connell, Will E., Pr. Co. D 4th O.V.I.
Cramer, Edward L., Pr. Tr. G 1st O. V. C.
Daugherty, Benjamin A., Pr. Co. D 4th O. V. I.
Donohoe, Frederick B., Pr. Co. D 4th O. V. I.
Edson, Allen C., Sergt. Co. D 4th O. V. I.
Evans, Frederick E., Pr. Tr. G 1st O. V. C.
Finley, David, Pr. Tr. G 1st O. V. C.
Ford, Charles D., Corp. Co. D 4th O. V. I.
Fox, Philip M., Pr. Tr. G 1st O.V.C.
Gregg, Walter P., Corp. Co. D 4th O. V. I.
Green, Charles, Sergt. Co. D 4th O. V. I.
Gosnell, Jasper O., Pr. Co. D 4th O. V. I.
Hedges, Elmer C., Pr. Co. D 4th O. V. I.
Henry, William S., Pr. Tr. G 1st O. V. C.
Hill, Samuel L., Pr. Co. D 4th O.V.I.
Horr, Elijah A., Corp. Co. D 4th O. V. I.
Johnson, Alla D., Pr. Co. D 4th O.V.I.
Johnson, Joseph A., Pr. Co. D 4th O. V. I.
Johnson, William C., Corp. Co. D 4th O. V. I.
Jones, Allen, Pr. Co. D 4th O. V. I.
Jones, George H., Pr. Tr. G 1st O. V. C.
Kennedy, William R., Sergt. Co. D 4th O. V. I.
Kinnear, Theodore E., Pr. Tr. G 1st O. V. C.
Kirchner, Conrad, Pr. Co. D 4th O. V. I.
Laird, Charles M., Pr. Co. D 4th O. V. I.
Lansdour, John M., Artificer Co. D 4th O. V. I.
Lauer, Stace R., Pr. Tr. G 1st O.V.C.

Lockwood, Orville A., Pr. Tr. G 1st O. V. C.
Maris, Bertram G., Musician Co. D 4th O. V. I.
Maris, Harry, Pr. Co. D 4th O. V. I.
Martin, William S., Pr. Co. D 4th O. V. I.
Mills, Charles D., Pr. Co. D 4th O.V.I.
Mills, Frank, Sergt. Co. D 4th O. V. I.
Mills, Joseph, Pr. Co. D 4th O. V. I.
Montgomery, Elmer E., Pr. Tr. G 1st O. V. C.
Moore, Spencer B., Pr. Co. D 4th O. V. I.
Mullen, George, Pr. Co. D 4th O.V.I.
Mullen, Joseph S., Pr. Co. D 4th O. V. I.
Newlove, Abe, 1st Sergt. Co. D 4th O. V. I.
Newlove, Lute J., Pr. Co. D 4th O. V. I.
Orahood, Charles W., Corp. Co. D 4th O. V. I.
Orahood, James Guy, Pr. Tr. G 1st O. V. C.
Orahood, Lewis F., Corp. Co. D 4th O. V. I.
Orr, Noah L., Pr. Co. D 4th O. V. I.
Otte, Louis F., Pr. Co. D 4th O.V.I.
Parmenter, John, Pr. Tr. G 1st O.V.C.
Parmenter, Thomas, Pr. Tr. G 1st O. V. C.
Plotner, Albert A., Pr. Co. D 4th O. V. I.
Patch, Delmore D., Pr. Tr. G 1st O. V. C.
Patch, Irvin, Pr. Tr. G 1st O. V. C.
Patch, Mathew, Pr. Tr. G 1st O. V. C.
Randall, Edward, Pr. Co. D 4th O.V.I.
Rausch, William L., Pr. Co. D 4th O. V. I.
Saygrover, Will, Pr. Co. D 4th O.V.I
Schlegel, George, Pr. Co. D 4th O. V. I.
Shetterby, Carson B., Pr. Co. D 4th O. V. I.
Shetterby, Joseph E., Pr. Co. D 4th O. V. I.
Smith, Albert J., Pr. Co. D 4th O.V.I.
Taylor, Clayton, Pr. Tr. G 1st O.V.C.
Taylor, Frank P., Musician Co. D 4th O. V. I.
Turner, Edmund, Pr. Tr. G 1st O.V.C.
Tway, Carl W., Pr. Co. D 4th O. V. I.
Vail, Reuben R., Pr. Co. D 4th O.V.I.
Weber, Walter J., Pr. Co. D 4th O. V. I.
Williams, Anderson L., Wagoner Co. D 4th O. V. I.
Williams, William C., Pr. Co. D 4th O. V. I.
Zimmerman, Charles, Pr. Tr. G 1st O. V. C.

MASSILLON

Aldrich, Bert. Pr. Co. K 8th O. V. I.
Breckenridge, William, Pr. Co. F 8th O. V. I.
Clark, William A., Corp. Co. L 8th O. V. I.
Curley, Harry O., Pr. Co. L 8th O. V. I.
Dulabahm, Henry K., Pr. Co. L 8th O. V. I.
Hagan, Henry H., Pr. Co. L 8th O. V. I.

Renie, George, Pr. Co. L 8th O. V. I.
Thoman, William B., Pr. Co. L 8th O. V. I.
Tobin, Joseph P., Pr. Co. L 8th O. V. I.
Van Dervort, Carl R., Pr. Co. F 8th O. V. I.
Voght, Walton T. M., Pr. Co. C 10th O. V. I.
Witt, Louis G., Pr. Co. I 8th O. V. I.

MASTERTON

Evans, James F., Pr. Co. D 7th O. V. I.

MATAMORAS

Hall, Ira, Pr. Co. E 7th O. V. I.
Irwin, Melvin O., Pr. Co. E 7th O. V. I.
Kaster, Benjamin W., Pr. Co. E 7th O. V. I.
Kirkbride, Henry M., Pr. Co. E 7th O. V. I.
Lentz, Harry A., Pr. Co. E 7th O.V.I.
Mason, Charley F., Pr. Co. E 7th O. V. I.
McBee, Charles W., Pr. Co. E 7th O. V. I.
McCool, Samuel A., Pr. Co. E 7th O. V. I.
Miracle, Forest H., Pr. Co. E 7th O. V. I.

Murphy, Herbert, Pr. Co. E 7th O. V. I.
Neely, George E., Pr. Co. E 7th O. V. I.
Ribb, Hiram, Pr. Co. E 7th O. V. I.
Ridgeway, William D., Pr. Co. E 7th O. V. I.
Riley, Charlie, Pr. Co. E 7th O. V. I.
Sibson, William, Pr. Co. E 7th O.V.I.
Smith, Howard, Pr. Co. E 7th O.V.I.
Stickel, Alexander S., Pr. Co. E 7th O. V. I.
Stone, Ralph D., Pr. Co. E 7th O.V.I.
Thompson, George B., Pr. Co. E 7th O. V. I.
Travis, Robert, Pr. Co. E 7th O.V.I.
Wheeler, Frank, Pr. Co. E 7th O.V.I.

MAUMEE

Cambric, John, Pr. Co. H 10th O.V.I.
Gessner, George L., Pr. Co. H 10th O. V. I.
Glemon, Willie J., Pr. Co. C 10th O. V. I.
Hall, John, Pr. Co. H 10th O. V. I.
Helsly, Thomas H., Pr. Co. C 10th O. V. I.
Keil, John A., Pr. Co. H 10th O.V.I.

Kelley, Ernest R., Pr. Co. C 10th O. V. I.
Lapoint, George J., Pr. Co. H 10th O. V. I.
Perrin, Charles L., Corp. Co. H 10th O. V. I.
Rodd, Charles O., Pr. Co. C 10th O. V. I.

MACKSBURG

Davis, Richard, Pr. Co. D 7th O.V.I.

MAXIMO

Treuthardt, John G., Pr. Co. K 8th O. V. I.

McARTHUR

Barnes, George H., Pr. Co. D 7th O. V. I.
Carnal, Jesse W., Pr. Co. L 7th O.V.I.
Gorsuch, William T., Pr. Co. L 7th O. V. I.

Horten, Fred C., Pr. Co. A 7th O.V.I.
Morris, Edgar M., Pr. Co. L 7th O. V. I.
Murphy, Joseph L., Pr. Co. B 7th O. V. I.

Pearce, Milton S., Pr. Co. L 7th O. V. I.

Redd, Greely, Pr. Co. L 7th O. V. I.

Reynolds, Ernest E., Pr. Co. L 7th O. V. I.

Shockey, Chauncey P., Pr. Co. D 7th O. V. I.

Shockey, George W., Pr. Co. B 7th O. V. I.

Shockey, Joseph A., Pr. Co. B 7th O. V. I.

Steel, John L., Pr. Co. L 7th O. V. I.

Winters, Lane H., Pr. Co. L 7th O. V. I.

McCOMB

Groff, Leonard O., Pr. Co. I 2nd O. V. I.

McCONNELSVILLE

Bain, Sylvester J., Pr. Co. L 10th O. V. I.

Farris, William A., Pr. Bat. C 1st O. V. A.

Harris, Charles L., Pr. Co. L 10th O. V. I.

Ramsey, Carl E., Pr. Co. L 10th O. V. I.

Tomson, Forest, Pr. Co. L 10th O. V. I.

McDANIEL

Eakins, Bert W., 5th Sergt. Co. C 7th O. V. I.

MECHANICSBURG

Craig, Griffith E., Pr. Co. D 3rd O. V. I.

Fisher, Summer J., Pr. Co. D 3rd O. V. I.

Fout, Joseph F., Pr. Co. D 3rd O.V.I.

Garratt, Ray M., Pr. Co. E 3rd O.V.I.

Holycross, Thomas J., Pr. Co. D 3rd O. V. I.

Lannon, John W., Pr. Co. D 3rd O. V. I.

Lewis, Thomas O., Pr. Co. D 3rd O. V. I.

Mattox, William R., Pr. Co. D 3rd O. V. I.

McIlvaine, Robert B., Pr. Co. D 3rd O. V. I.

McKinney, Forest O., Pr. Co. D 3rd O. V. I.

Shaffer, John S., Sergt. Co. D 3rd O. V. I.

MEDINA

Weinschenker, Henry, Pr. Co. B 10th O. V. I.

MELROSE

Shriver, Horace G., Pr. Co. C 6th O. V. I.

MEMPHIS

Canter, Oscar, Pr. Co. M 3rd O. V. I.

MENTOR

Conkling, Elmer A., Corp. Co. M 5th O. V. I.

Davis, William F., Pr. Co. M 5th O. V. I.

Hart, Ralph T., Pr. Co. M 5th O.V.I.

Lapham, Owen W., Sergt. Co. M 5th O. V. I.

Lett, Peter Allen, Pr. Co. M 5th O. V. I.

MERCERVILLE

Cofer, Francis, Pr. Co. C 7th O. V. I.

MERMILL

Luce, Joseph, Pr. Co. H 10th O. V. I.

MIDDLEFIELD

Artman, Charles C., Pr. Co. M 5th O. V. I.

Brown, John E., Pr. Co. M 5th O.V.I.

MIDDLEPORT

Allen, Lewis J., Pr. Co. L 7th O.V.I.
Anderson, Edward, Wagoner, Co. L 7th O. V. I.
Barrett, Wallace A., Batt. Sergt. Maj. 7th O. V. I.
Barrett, William H., 1st Sergt. Co. L 7th O. V. I.
Beaver, Albert J., 5th Corp. Co. I. 7th O.. V. I.
Bowman, Carlos H., Pr. Co. L 7th O. V. I.
Bunce, Frank H., 5th Sergt. Co. L 7th O. V. I.
Bryan, Earl F., Pr. Co. L 7th O. V. I.
Cady, Willie B., Pr. Co. L 7th O.V.I.
Cotterill, Elantheno C., Pr. Co. L 7th O. V. I.
Dealrymple, Bradford K., Pr. Co. C 7th O. V. I.
Dewees, Henry S. H., Pr. Co. L 7th O. V. I.
Dickson, James H., Pr. Co. L 7th O. V. I.
Downing, Earl, 2nd Corp. Co. L 7th O. V. I.
Duffy, Thomas, Pr. Co. L 7th O.V.I.
Dumble, Fred M., Pr. Co. L 7th O. V. I.
Ebersbach, William H., Pr. Co. L 7th O. V. I.
Encinlier, Joseph, Pr. Co. L 7th O. V. I.
Estep, Jacob, Pr. Co. L 7th O. V. I.
Farmer, Orval D., Pr. Co. L 7th O. V. I.
Hartinger, Merrill J., Pr. Co. L 7th O. V. I.

Hobbs, Samuel, Pr. Co. L 7th O.V.I.
Jarvis, William H., Pr. Co. L 7th O. V. I.
Kepler, Charles, Pr. Co. L 7th O.V.I.
Koester, Wesley S., Pr. Co. L 7th O. V. I.
Laird, David C., Musician Co. L 7th O. V. I.
McCracken, Herbert L., 1st Corp. Co. L 7th O. V. I.
Mercer, Leslie L., Pr. Co. L 7th O. V. I.
Murray, James E., Pr. Co. L 7th O V. I.
Nast, Otto B., Pr. Co. L 7th O. V. I.
Nichols, Ira, 3rd Corp. Co. L 7th O. V. I.
Parker, Harry C., Musician Co. L 7th O. V. I.
Parsons, Charley, Pr. Co. L 7th O. V. I.
Parsons, J. Edward, Q. M. Sergt. Co. L 7th O. V. I.
Petty, Fred C., Pr. Co. L 7th O.V.I.
Rice, Charles E., Pr. Co. L 7th O.V.I.
Root, Hezzie S., Pr. Co. L 7th O.V.I.
Root, Sarnie, 4th Corp. Co. L 7th O. V. I.
Russell, Winfred L., Pr. Co. L 7th O. V. I.
Schreiner, Frederick W., 4th Sergt. Co. L 7th O. V. I.
Skinner, Liston A., 2nd Sergt. Co. L 7th O. V. I.
Willock, Jurell A., 6th Corp. Co. L 7th O. V. I.
Zins, Julian, 3rd Sergt. Co. L 7th O. V. I.

MIDDLETOWN

Ayres, John, Pr. Co. L 1st O. V. I.
Bailey, Earl J., Pr. Co. L 1st O.V.I.
Bailey, Sylvester, Sergt. Co. L 1st O. V. I.
Barnett, Joseph C., Pr. Co. L 1st O. V. I.
Barnitz, Charles G., Pr. Co. L 1st O. V. I.
Barratt, Edward J., Pr. Co. L 1st O. V. I.
Barry, John E., Pr. Co. L 1st O.V.I.
Behrens, Henry G., Corp. Co. L 1st O. V. I.
Blemmer, Lee, Pr. Co. L 1st O. V. I.
Bolser, James, Jr., Pr. Co. L 1st O. V. I.
Boyd, William, Sergt. Co. L 1st O. V. I.

Brookover, Andrew J., Corp. Co. L 1st O. V. I.
Brown, Charles, Pr. Co. L 1st O.V.I.
Busey, John P., Pr. Co. L 1st O. V. I.
Byrd, Frank, Sergt. Co. L 1st O.V.I.
Carr, Sidney S., Pr. Co. L 1st O.V.I.
Catterlin, Elmer, Pr. Co. L 1st O.V.I.
Clise, George, Pr. Co. L 1st O. V. I.
Coate, Gilbert, Pr. Co. L 1st O. V. I.
Collins, Arthur M., Corp. Co. L 1st O. V. I.
Conarroe, Charley E., Musician Co. L 1st O. V. I.
Dougherty, Solomon, Pr. Co. L 1st O. V. I.
Gillespie, Frank P., Pr. Co. L 1st O. V. I.

Gillespie, Robert T., Pr. Co. L 1st O. V. I.

Haigh, Albert E., Pr. Co. L 1st O. V. I.

Hansel, Charles, Corp. Co. L 1st O. V. I.

Harkrader, Wallace, Pr. Co. L 1st O. V. I.

Harrison, Albert, Pr. Co. L 1st O.V.I.

Hawthorne, Mortimer T., Pr. Co. L 1st O. V. I.

Henderson, James T., Pr. Co. L 1st O. V. I.

Hoover, Wilbert E., 1st Sergt. Co. L 1st O. V. I.

Hower, Frank, Wagoner Co. L 1st O. V. I.

Iutzi, Louis, Pr. Co. L 1st O. V. I.

Jennings, Andrew, Corp. Co. L 1st O. V. I.

Kelly, Frank, Pr. Co. L 1st O. V. I.

Knowlton, Herman, Pr. Co. L 1st O. V. I.

Leonard, Harry W., Pr. Co. L 1st O. V. I.

Leslie, Howard L., Pr. Co. L 1st O. V. I.

Lloyd, Benjamin F., Pr. Co. L 1st O. V. I.

Long, Charles, Pr. Co. L 1st O. V. I.

Lorenz, Henry A., Corp. Co. L 1st O. V. I.

Lucas, Harry W., Pr. Co. L 1st O. V. I.

Marts, Arthur, Q. M. Sergt. Co. L 1st O. V. I.

Marts, Dem., Pr. Co. L 1st O. V. I.

Marts, John C., Pr. Co. L 1st O.V.I.

McGee, Elvmas, Pr. Co. L 1st O.V.I.

Minch, Frank, Pr. Co. L 1st O. V. I.

Moon, Frank, Pr. Co. L 1st O. V. I.

Moren, Murray P., Pr. Co. L 1st O. V. I.

Muthert, Charles, Pr. Co. L 1st O. V. I.

Nuss, George, Artificer Co. L 1st O. V. I.

Ogle, Hiram, Pr. Co. L 1st O. V. I.

Orr, William, Sergt. Co. L 1st O.V.I.

Palmer, Hugh D., Corp. Co. L 1st O. V. I.

Plack, John J., Pr. Co. L 1st O. V. I.

Primley, Worthington, Pr. Co. L 1st O. V. I.

Riley, Michael, Pr. Co. L 1st O. V. I.

Snider, Edward, Pr. Co. L 1st O.V.I.

Staigbrook, Daniel, Pr. Co. L 1st O. V. I.

Stieg, John H., Pr. Co. L 1st O. V. I.

Stauder, Nicholas, Musician Co. L 1st O. V. I.

Tebo, Albert H., Pr. Co. L 1st O.V.I.

Williams, Elmer, Pr. Co. L 1st O.V.I.

Wilson, William, Pr. Co. L 1st O.V.I.

Yeakle, Christ, Corp. Co. L 1st O.V.I.

MILFORD CENTRE

Fisher, Victor H., Pr. Co. D 4th O. V. I.

Lyons, Charles, Pr. Co. D 4th O.V.I.

MILFORD, CONN.

Sullivan, Edward J., Pr. Co. C 10th O. V. I.

MILLBROOK

Hensel, Rollen, Pr. Co. H 8th O.V.I.

Kister, Melville S., Pr. Co. H 8th O. V. I.

Leeper, William H., Pr. Co. H 8th O. V. I.

Wyre, Orphanas F., Pr. Co. H 8th O. V. I.

Wyre, Sherman, Pr. Co. H 8th O.V.I.

MILLER CITY

McCoy, Charles A., Pr. Co. I 8th O. V. I.

MILLERSBURG

Allmeroth, Elsworth E., Pr. Co. H 8th O. V. I.

Armstrong, Robert L., Pr. Co. H 8th O. V. I.

Brown, Harry B., Pr. Co. H 8th O. V. I.

Close, William M., Pr. Co. H 8th O. V. I.

Dix, Martin W., Pr. Co. H 8th O. V. I.

Douglas, Harvey C., Pr. Co. H 8th O. V. I.

Douglas, William H., Pr. Co. H 8th O. V. I.

Duer, Joseph D., Pr. Co. H 8th O. V. I.

Farver, Cyrus W., Pr. Co. H 8th O. V. I.

Genet, Edward, Pr. Co. H 8th O.V.I.

Hanna, Robert H., Pr. Co. H 8th O.
V. I.
Hopper, George L., Pr. Co. H 8th O.
V. I.
Jones, Samuel T., Pr. Co. H 8th O.
V. I.

McNamara, Herbert V., Pr. Co. H 8th
O. V. I.
Stuber, George W., Pr. Co. H 8th O.
V. I.
White, Harry B., Pr. Co. H 8th O.
V. I.

MILLERSPORT

Brison, Joseph Franklin, 3rd Sergt. Co.
K 7th O. V. I.
Castle, William L., Prin. Musician 7th
O. V. I.
Critton, Gabriel M., Jr., Pr. Co. K 7th
O. V. I.
Fetters, George C., Corp. Co. K 7th
O. V. I.
Geil, Orrin G., Pr. Co. K 7th O.V.I.

Harlow, William F., Pr. Co. K 7th
O. V. I.
Shellenberger, Reuben R., Artificer Co.
K 7th O. V. I.
Smith, Wilfred C., Musician Co. K 7th
O. V. I.
Thompson, John A., Pr. Co K 7th
O. V. I.
White, John F., Pr. Co. K 7th O.V.I.

MILO

Kriel, George, Pr. Co. F 4th O. V. I.

MILROY

Ennis, Robert L., Pr. Co. G 6th O.V.I.

MILWAUKEE, WIS.

Meyer, Alwin J., Pr. Co. G 10th O. V. I.

MINERAL

King, Hoyt S., Pr. Co. B 7th O.V.I.   Lowry, Don B., Pr. Co. B 7th O.V.I.

MINERAL RIDGE

Thomas, William R., Pr. Co. K 10th
O. V. I.

Wentz, B. Herbert, Pr. Co. K 10th O.
V. I.

MINGO

Reed, Edgar J., Pr. Co. D 3rd O.V.I.

MONCLOVA

Frankin, Melvin, Pr. Tr. E 1st O.V.C.   Jackson, Percy C., Pr. Tr. E 1st O.
V. C.

MONROE, MICH.

Alford, Hobart W., Pr. Co. G 10th O. V. I.

MONROE FALLS

Castle, Howard T., Pr. Co. A 3rd O. V. I.

MONROEVILLE

Myers, William J., Pr. Co. G 5th O.
V. I.
Powley, George S., Corp. Co. G 5th
O. V. I.

Shibley, Joseph E., Corp. Co. B 10th
O. V. I.

9—R. O. V.

MONTPELIER

Fox, Charles F., Pr. Co. E 6th O.V.I.   Kelly, Jacob P., Pr. Co. E 6th O.V.I.

MOODY

Neal, Thomas J., Pr. Co. C 7th O.V.I.

MORTIMER

Van Keuren, Wade, Musician Co. K 2nd O. V. I.

MOUNT CORY

Reiter, Frank B., Pr. Co. A 2nd O. V. I.

MOUNT ORAB

Harris, Henry, Pr. Co. H 3rd O. V. I.

Honaker, William, Pr. Co. H 3rd O. V. I.

Long, Charles C., Pr. Co. H 3rd O. V. I.

Malott, Joseph S., Pr. Co. H 3rd O. V. I.

Pickering, Charles L., Pr. Co. H 3rd O. V. I.

Power, James C., Pr. Co. H 3rd O. V. I.

Randall, John C., Corp. Co. H 3rd O. V. I.

Remley, Walter L., Corp. Co. H 3rd O. V. I.

Stroup, Charles W., Pr. Co. H 3rd O. V. I.

Vance, Lafayette S., Pr. Co. H 3rd O. V. I.

Van Delft, John H., Pr. Co. H 3rd O. V. I.

Wilson, William, Pr. Co. H 3rd O. V. I.

MOUNT VICTORY

Bowen, Charles L., Pr. Co. G 2nd O. V. I.

Golden, Edward R., Pr. Co. G 2nd O. V. I.

Powelson, Albert A., Pr. Co. G 2nd O. V. I.

Wagner, Louis J., Pr. Co. G 2nd O. V. I.

MT. VERNON

Adams, Oscar S., Pr. Co. I, 4th O. V. I.

Armentrout, L. Vance, Pr. Co. L 4th O. V. I.

Ashton, Walter G., Pr. Co. L 4th O. V. I.

Banbury, Charles K., Pr. Co. L 4th O. V. I.

Bigler, Arthur L., Pr. Co. L 4th O. V. I.

Birmingham, Harry L., Pr. Co. L 4th O. V. I.

Brentlinger, Claud L., Pr. Co. L 4th O. V. I.

Buckner, George K., Pr. Co. L 4th O. V. I.

Cochran, John M., Pr. Co. L 4th O. V. I.

Cochran, Walter, Pr. Co. L 4th O. V. I.

Cochran, Ward B., Pr. Co. L 4th O. V. I.

Coile, Ollie E., Pr. Co. L 4th O.V.I.

Davis, Charles E., Pr. Co. L 4th O. V. I.

Davis, Jacie J., Pr. Co. L 4th O. V. I.

Davis, John K., Wagoner Co. L 4th O. V. I.

Edwards, William S., Corp. Co. L 4th O. V. I.

Ewalt, John Lewis, Corp. Co. L 4th O. V. I.

Graff, George, Pr. Co. L 4th O. V. I.

Graff, James H., Sergt. Co. L 4th O. V. I.

Gregory, William, Artificer Co. L 4th O. V. I.

Harker, William H., Pr. Co. L 4th O. V. I.

Hayes, James M., Pr. Co. L 4th O. V. I.

Headington, John L., Pr. Co. L 4th O. V. I.

Hissong, John R., Pr. Co. L 4th O. V. I.

Jackson, Carroll R., Corp. Co. L 4th O. V. I.

Jacobs, John D., Corp. Co. L 4th O. V. I.

Jacobus, Harry M., Pr. Co. L 4th O. V. I.

Kirby, Alva S., Pr. Co. L 4th O.V.I.

Lane, George M., Pr. Co. L 4th O. V. I.

Lee, John T., Pr. Co. L 4th O. V. I.

Lewis, George D., Sergt. Co. L 4th O. V. I.

Loose, Jacob L., Pr. Co. L 4th O.V.I.

Magill, John S., Pr. Co. L 4th O.V.I.

Mendenhall, Elbert L., Corp. Co. L 4th O. V. I.

Morey, Roy C., Pr. Co. L 4th O.V.I.

Murphy, Willie, Pr. Co. B 5th O.V.I.

Osborn, Timothy G., Pr. Co. L 4th O. V. I.

Porter, Orrin C., Pr. Co. L 4th O.V.I.

Purdy, Walter S., Corp. Co. L 4th O. V. I.

Sapp, Frank W., Pr. Co. L 4th O. V. I.

Scott, Edwin J., Sergt. Co. L 4th O. V. I.

Sherman, Rupert L., Pr Co. L 4th O. V. I.

Shetler, Walter S., Pr. Co. L 4th O. V. I.

Simpson, Otis A., Pr. Co. L 4th O. V. I.

Smith, Oliver H., Pr. Co. L 4th O. V. I.

Thuma, Earl F., 1st Sergt. Co. L 4th O. V. I.

Thuma, Harry L., Pr. Co. L 4th O. V. I.

Wade, Bruce M., Pr. Co. L 4th O. V. I.

Weider, Will F., Pr. Co. L 4th O.V.I.

Welchymer, Charles B., Pr. Co. L 4th O. V. I.

Westlake, Robert H., Sergt. Co. L 4th O. V. I.

White, David Horton, Pr. Co. L 4th O. V. I.

Whitney, William M., Pr. Co. L 4th O. V. I.

Wolfe, Fred W., Pr. Co. L 4th O.V.I.

Wood, Charles W., Musician Co. L 4th O. V. I.

Wood, Herbert C., Pr. Co. L 4th O. V. I.

Wright, Clinton, Pr. Co. L 4th O.V.I.

Wright, Frank D., Pr. Co. L 4th O. V. I.

Wyant, Burr A., Sergt. Co. L 4th O. V. I.

MUTUAL

Fay, William H., Pr. Co. D 3rd O. V. I.

Redman, William L., Pr. Co. D 3rd O. V. I.

NAPOLEON

Babcock, Charles H., Pr. Co. F 6th O. V. I.

Babcock, Jesse L., Pr. Co. F 6th O. V. I.

Baker, Orville H., Pr. Co. F 6th O. V. I.

Baldwin, Albert G., Pr. Co. F 6th O. V. I.

Balsinger, Milton H., Pr. Co. F 6th O. V. I.

Bauman, Calib, Pr. Co. F 6th O. V. I.

Benskin, Sherman, Pr. Co. F 6th O. V. I.

Brownell, Frank E., Corp. Co. F 6th O. V. I.

Callendine, Charles, Pr. Co. F 6th O. V. I.

Cameron, Charles A., Corp. Co. F 6th O. V. I.

Cameron, Will S., Pr. Co. F 6th O. V. I.

Carroll, Alonzo, Pr. Co. F 6th O.V.I.

Carroll, Jacob, Pr. Co. F 6th O. V. I.

Carter, Albert G., Pr. Co. F 6th O. V. I.

Crockett, William E., Sergt. Co. F 6th O. V. I.

Eby, Frank A., Pr. Co. F 6th O. V. I.

Edwards, William S., Corp. Co. F 6th O. V. I.

Fisk, Forst F., Sergt. Co. F 6th O. V. I.

Gardner, Cecil L., Pr. Co. F 6th O. V. I.

Gleason, Clarence E., Pr. Co. F 6th O. V. I.

Gunn, George H., Corp. Co. F 6th O. V. I.

Haly, Adam A., Pr. Co. F 6th O.V.I.

Hartman, Wilbur B., Corp. Co. F 6th O. V. I.

Hiser, George T., Pr. Co. F 6th O.V.I.

Hughes, Harley W., Pr. Co. F 6th O. V. I.

Kanney, William C., Pr. Co. F 6th O. V. I.

Lazenby, Grant, Pr. Co. F 6th O.V.I.

McGill, Charles M., Pr. Co. F 6th O. V. I.

McGill, Welton A., Pr. Co. F 6th O. V. I.

Meekison, Malcolm V., Pr. Co. F 6th O. V. I.

Middleton, Preston B., Pr. Co. F 6th
O. V. I.
Minche, George H., Pr. Co. F 6th O.
V. I.
Riggs, Frederick W., Sergt. Co. F 6th
O. V. I.
Robinson, Cassius M. C., Pr. Co. F
6th O. V. I.
Shook, Lea M., Pr. Co. F 6th O.V.I.
Snyder, Leo A., Corp. Co. F 6th O.
V. I.
Swin, Rollie T., Pr. Co. F 6th O.V.I.
Teeple, Berton, Pr. Co. F 6th O. V. I.
Teeple, Charles, Pr. Co. F 6th O.V.I.
Thompson, Edward, Pr. Co. F 6th O.
V. I.
Trumble, Charles R., Pr. Co. F 6th O.
V. I.

Tuttle, Harry T., Pr. Co. F 6th O.V.I.
Van Ness, Wilson A., Wagoner Co. F
6th O. V. I.
Vanpelt, George W., Artificer Co. F
6th O. V. I.
Vocke, Joseph B., Jr., Sergt. Co. F 6th
O. V. I.
Wadams, George W., Pr. Co. F 6th
O. V. I.
Walcott, Austin S., 1st Sergt. Co. F
6th O. V. I.
Walker, Cloyce, Musician Co. F 6th
O. V. I.
Webb, Ross J., Sergt. Co. F 6th O.
V. I.
Zenz, John, Pr. Co. F 6th O. V. I.

NELSONVILLE

Gilmore, Edward F., Pr. Co. C 2nd U.
S. V. E.
Goodspeed, William A., Sergt. Co. C
2nd U. S. V. E.
Hughes, John, Pr. Co. C 2nd U. S.
V. E.
Keasey, Sherman, Pr. Co. C 2nd U.
S. V. E.
Kelch, Lawrence R., Pr. Co. C 2nd
U. S. V. E.
Scott, Clarence, Pr. Co. C 2nd U. S.
V. E.

Scott, Earl L., Pr. Co. C 2nd U. S.
V. E.
Sloane, William, Pr. Co. C 2nd U. S.
V. E.
Sweany, John E., Pr. Co. C 2nd U. S.
V. E.
Warner, Walter H., Pr. Co. C 2nd U.
S. V. E.
Wickham, Patrick W., Pr. Co. C 2nd
U. S. V. E.
Woody, Everett, Sergt. Co. C 2nd U.
S. V. E.

NEW ANTIOCH

James, Everett, Pr. Co. M 3rd O.V.I.

NEWARK

Abernathy, Arthur V., Pr. Bat. G 1st
O. V. A.
Ackerman, James S., Pr. Bat. G 1st
O. V. A.
Adams, Charles S., Pr. Bat. G 1st O.
V. A.
Alexander, Frank M., Pr. Bat. G 1st
O. V. A.
Allbaugh, Steve, Pr. Co. G 7th O.V.I.
Allen, Homer W., Corp. Bat. G 1st
O. V. A.
Alward, James N., Pr. Bat. G 1st O.
V. A.
Armstrong, M. W., Pr. Co. G 7th O.
V. I.
Bacon, Edward O., Pr. Co. G 7th O.
V. I.
Beadle, Sylvester H., Sergt. Co. G 7th
O. V. I.
Beaumont, Daniel, Pr. Bat. G 1st O.
V. A.
Beaumont, Louis D., Pr. Bat. G 1st
O. V. A.
Bernard, Jonas M., Pr. Bat. G 1st O.
V. A.

Brooke, Frederick L., Corp. Bat. G
1st O. V. A.
Brubaker, William E., Pr. Co. G 7th
O. V. I.
Burke, Michael J., Pr. Co. G 7th O.
V. I.
Copeland, William W., Pr. Bat. G 1st
O. V. A.
Coulter, Horace B., Pr. Bat. G 1st O.
V. A.
Craig, Walter E., Pr. Co. G 7th O.
V. I.
Dailey, Edward G., Corp. Bat. G 1st
O. V. A.
Damuth, Jason L., Pr. Co. G 7th O.
V. I.
Davis, William, Pr. Co. G 7th O.V.I.
Deedim, George, Corp. Co. G 7th O.
Dickinson, Edward R., Corp. Bat. G
1st O. V. A.
Dille, Fred E., Corp. Co. G 7th O.
V. I.
Donahey, Howard W., Pr. Bat. G 1st.
O. V. A.

Dush, Frank D., Pr. Bat. G 1st O. V. A.

Eben, Arthur D., Pr. Bat. G 1st O. V. A.

Edington, William D., Pr. Bat. G 1st O. V. A.

Edwards, Albert, Pr. Bat. G 1st O. V. A.

Elsner, Richard E., Pr. Co. G 7th O. V. I.

Evans, Franklin D., Pr. Bat. G 1st O. V. A.

Evans, William B., Sergt. Bat. G 1st O. V. A.

Farmer, Melvin D., Corp. Bat. G 1st O. V. A.

Foster, John H., Pr. Bat. G 1st O. V. A.

George, Harry F., Pr. Bat. G 1st O. V. A.

Glass, Charles, Pr. Bat. G 1st O.V.A.

Glass, Frank, Pr. Bat. G 1st O. V. A.

Gooch, Harry L., Corp. Co. G 7th O. V. I.

Graff, Charles F., Pr. Bat. G 1st O. V. A.

Grasser, James E., Pr. Bat. G 1st O. V. A.

Guckert, Harry L., Pr. Bat. G 1st O. V. A.

Haag, Frank E., Pr. Bat. G 1st O. V. A.

Hamilton, Charles C., 1st Sergt. Co. G 7th O. V. I.

Harris, James P., Pr. Bat. G 1st O. V. A.

Hawley, Wilber L., Pr. Bat. G 1st O. V. A.

Headley, Frank B., Pr. Bat. G 1st O. V. A.

Heidy, Reno, Pr. Bat. G 1st O. V. A.

Hickey, Dennis J., Pr. Co. G 7th O. V. I.

Hill, George O., Pr. Bat. G 1st O.V.A.

Hoenig, Charles J., Pr. Bat. G 1st O. V. A.

Hower, John, Pr. Bat. G 1st O. V. A.

Irwin, Frederick H., Pr. Co. G 7th O. V. I.

Jones, Arthur W., Pr. Bat. G 1st O. V. A.

Jones, Frederick E., Sergt. Bat. G 1st O. V. A.

Jones, Simon P., Sergt. Bat. G 1st O. V. A.

Keller, John W., Pr. Bat. G 1st O. V. A.

Kimbark, Albert H., Wagoner Co. G 7th O. V. I.

Kneeland, William R., Pr. Bat. G 1st O. V. A.

Lohaas, Frederick W., Pr. Bat. G 1st O. V. A.

Loughery, William, Pr. Bat. G 1st O. V. A.

MacCracken, Samuel F., Pr. Bat. G 1st O. V. A.

Magill, David H., Pr. Co. G 7th O. V. I.

Mauger, Edward E., Pr. Bat. G 1st O. V. A.

Mauger, Fern C., Pr. Bat. G 1st O. V. A.

Marlow, Wayland C., Sergt. Bat. G 1st O. V. A.

Martindale, Fred, Pr. Bat. G 1st O. V. A.

Marvin, Frederick T., Musician Co. G 7th O. V. I.

Mason, George H., Pr. Co. G 7th O. V. I.

Matthews, Charles E., Musician Co. G 7th O. V. I.

McFarland, William, Pr. Bat. G 1st O. V. A.

McGowan, Sterling, Pr. Bat. G 1st O. V. A.

McManus, Samuel, Pr. Bat. G 1st O. V. A.

McNeal, Charles A., Artificer Co. G 7th O. V. I.

Meeks, William L., Pr. Bat. G 1st O. V. A.

Millinger, Arthur C., Pr. Bat. G 1st O. V. A.

Moore, John W., Pr. Bat. G 1st O. V. A.

Moore, Samuel, Pr. Co. G 7th O.V.I.

Morris, Burton L., Pr. Bat. G 1st O. V. A.

Myer, Arthur C., Pr. Bat. G 1st O. V. A.

Myers, Pearl E., Pr. Bat. G 1st O. V. A.

Naylor, Charles W., Pr. Bat. G 1st O. V. A.

Nehls, William F., Pr. Co. G 7th O. V. I.

Oakleaf, Albert N., Pr. Co. G 7th O. V. I.

O'Neill, Albert D., Pr. Co. G 7th O. V. I.

O'Neill, Joseph B., Pr. Co. G 7th O. V. I.

Pence, Burrell H., Pr. Bat. G 1st O. V. A.

Peeper, Hiram D., Pr. Bat. G 1st O. V. A.

Petrey, Charles C., Sergt. Co. G 7th O. V. I.

Price, Edgar, Pr. Co. G 7th O. V. I.

Procter, William H., Pr. Bat. G 1st O. V. A.

Reese, Jesse T., Pr. Co. G 7th O.V.I.

Reichert, William, Pr. Bat. G 1st O. V. A.

Reynolds, Edgar H., Pr. Bat. G 1st O. V. A.

Rodgers, Austin, Pr. Bat. G 1st O. V. A.

Roe, Edward, Pr. Bat. G 1st O. V. A.

Rosebrough, Clifton H., Pr. Co. G 7th O. V. I.
Showman. John H., Pr. Bat. G 1st O. V. A.
Shutts, Harry N., Pr. Bat. G 1st O. V. A.
Smith, Allen W., Pr. Bat. G 1st O. V. A.
Smith, Horace W., Pr. Bat. G 1st O. V. A.
Snider. Mark B., Pr. Co. G 7th O.V.I.
Speer, Roderick I.. 1st Sergt. Bat. G 1st O. V. A.
Stafford, Ollie E., Pr. Co. G 7th O. V. I.
Staugh, William H., Corp. Co. G 7th O. V. I.
Stouffer, Mine Bert. Pr. Co. G 7th O. V. I.
Styron, Frederick J., Corp. Bat. G 1st O. V. A.
Sutor, Charles W., Pr. Bat. G 1st O. V. A.
Thompson, Clarence R., Corp. Bat. G 1st O. V. A.
Thompson. Harry H., Pr. Co. G 7th O. V. I.
Thompson, James G., Pr. Co. G 7th O. V. I.

Thrapp. Ward G., Pr. Bat. G 1st O. V. A.
Vanatta, Frank. Pr. Co. G 7th O.V.I.
Walton, Charles F., Sergt. Co. G 7th O. V. I.
Watkins, Guy H., Corp. Bat. G 1st O. V. A.
Webb, Albert R., Sergt. Bat. G 1st O. V. A.
Welsh. Charles R., Pr. Bat. G 1st O. V. A.
Weston, Charles W., Pr. Bat. G 1st O. V. A.
White, Robert A., Pr. Bat. G 1st O. V. A.
Wood. Horatio C., Pr. Bat. G 1st O. V. A.
Woolway, Reginald, Sergt. Co. G 1st O. V. A.
Wright, Thomas J., Pr. Bat. G 1st O. V. A.
Wyley. John W., Pr. Bat. G 1st O. V. A.
Youse, Charles W., Pr. Bat. G 1st O. V. A.
Youse, William G., Pr. Bat. G 1st O. V. A.

NEW BALTIMORE

Bryan, John L., Pr. Co. K 8th O. V. I.

NEW BERLIN

Willaman, C. H., Pr. Co. F 8th O. V. I.

NEW BREMEN

Hering, Henry, Pr. Co. L 2nd O. V. I.
Ivins, William E., Pr. Co. L 2nd O. V. I.
Kettler, Clarence B., Pr. Co. L 2nd O. V. I.

Steinebrey, Otta A., Pr. Co. L 2nd O. V. I.
Tombafe, William, Pr. Co. L 2nd O.V.I.

NEWBURGH

Buchman, Wilhelm, Pr. Co. B 10th O. V. I.

McIntyre, Arthur G., Pr. Co. L 5th O. V. I.

NEW CARLISLE

King. Charles, Pr. Co. B 3rd O. V. I.

NEWCOMERSTOWN

Benton, George L., Artificer. Co. M 7th O. V. I.
Booth, Daniel F., Pr. Co. M. 7th O. V. I.
Cook, Joe D., Pr. Co. M 7th O. V. I.
Duff. Roland O., Pr. Co. M 7th O. V. I.
Graham, William, Pr Co. M 7th O. V. I.
Harbolt, Clark P., Pr. Co. M 7th O.V.I.
Miskimen, Frank S., Corp. Co. M 7th O. V. I.

Miskimen, John S., Pr. Co. M 7th O. V. I.
Sells, Bert F., Pr. Co M 7th O. V. I.
Shurtz. Millie A., Pr. Co M 7th O. V. I.
Shurtz, William S., Pr. Co. M 7th O. V. I.
Speers, J. Waldo, Pr. Co. M 7th O.V.I.
Stitt. David G., Pr. Co. M 7th O. V. I.

NEW HAVEN

Dawson, Harry S., Corp. Co. G 5th O. V. I.

Layer, William A., Pr. Co. G 5th O. V. I.

NEW KNOXVILLE

Steinecker, George C., Pr. Co. L 2nd O. V. I.

NEW LEXINGTON

Adams, Charles E., Pr. Co. A 7th O. V. I.

Allen, Martin H., Pr. Co. A. 7th O. V. I.

Bland, Septimus, Pr. Co. A 7th O. V. I.

Blair, Charles D., Pr. Co. A 7th O. V. I.

Boring, Guy A., Pr. Co. A 7th O. V. I.

Bowman, Charles R., Corp. Co. A 7th O. V. I.

Bowman, Edward H., Musician Co. A 7th O. V. I.

Braddock, Frank M., Pr. Co. A 7th O V. I.

Brown, Charles, Pr. Co. A 7th O. V. I.

Brown, Harry Lee, Pr. Co. A 7th O. V. I.

Carroll, Whitney P., Sergt. Co. A. 7th O. V. I.

Carson, Clarence C., Pr. Co. A 7th O. V. I.

Carson, Ira Herbert, Pr. Co. A 7th O. V. I.

Colborn, Charles E., Pr. Co. A 7th O. V. I.

Compton, Fred W., Pr. Co. A 7th O. V. I.

Connor, Paul M., Pr. Co. A 7th O. V. I.

Crawford, Charles, Pr. Co. A 7th O.V.I.

Davis, Marcellus D., Pr. Co. A 7th O. V. I.

Emrich, John H., Q. M. Sergt. Co. A 7th O. V. I.

Ferriter, Richard, Pr. Co. A 7th O. V. I.

Funk, Charlie A., Pr. Co. A 7th O.V.I.

Gaver, Earle E., Pr. Co. A 7th O. V. I.

Goodin, George B., Pr. Co. A 7th O. V. I.

Graves, Benjamin B., Pr. Co. A 7th O. V. I.

Hankinson, Worle Howard, Pr. Co A 7th O. V. I.

Harper, Harvey H., Pr. Co. A 7th O. V. I.

Hitchcock, John W., Corp. Co. A 7th O. V. I.

Holcomb, Ephraim K., Pr. Co. A 7th O. V. I.

Irvin, Harvey L., Sergt. Co. A 7th O. V. I.

James, Edward, Wagoner Co. A 7th O. V. I.

Keck, Jacob W., Pr. Co. A 7th O. V. I

Kelley, Joseph A., Pr. Co. A 7th O.V.I.

Kelley, Thomas Ross, Musician Co. A 7th O. V. I.

Lewis, Schuyler C., Pr. Co. A 7th O. V. I

Mason, Rufus S., Corp. Co. A 7th O. V. I.

Mason, Weaver E., Pr. Co. A 7th O. V. I.

Minor, Fred L., Pr. Co. A 7th O. V. I.

Patton, James W., 1st Sergt. Co. A 7th O. V. I.

Penrod, Cyrus F., Pr. Co. A 7th O.V.I.

Puterbaugh, Robert W., Pr. Co. A 7th O. V. I.

Quest, Frank P., Pr. Co. A 7th O. V. I.

Rarick, Samuel A., Pr. Co. A 7th O.V.I.

Ricket, Howard S., Pr. Co. A 7th O.V.I.

Rinehart, James C., Corp. Co. A 7th O. V. I.

Rinker, Samuel, Pr Co. A 7th O. V. I.

Rowe, Lee, Pr. Co. A 7th O. V. I.

Seifert, Birchard R. H., Pr. Co. A 7th O. V. I.

Shepperd, Howard E., Pr. Co. A 7th O. V. I.

Shepperd, Thomas D., Pr. Co. A 7th O. V. I.

Siemer, John H., Corp. Co. A 7th O.V.I.

Slioher, Harry R., Pr. Co. A 7th O.V.I.

Sowers, Marvin L., Pr. Co. A 7th O.V.I.

Spencer, Charles J., Pr. Co. A 7th O. V. I.

Spencer, Paul R., Pr. Co. A 7th O. V. I.

Steels, Charles W., Pr. Co. A 7th O.V.I.

Stine, Forest R., Pr. Co. A 7th O. V. I.

Stowe, Samuel E., Pr. Co. A 7th O.V.I.

Stull, Rhey, Pr. Co. L 10th O. V. I.

Watkins, Edward M., Artificer Co. A 7th O. V. I.

Wallace, Edmund S., Pr. Co. A 7th O. V. I.

Whitaker, Carlos A., Pr. Co. A 7th O. V. I.

Whitmen, Charles E., Pr. Co. A 7th O. V. I.

Williams, Thomas B., Pr. Co. A 7th O. V. I.

Wilson, Victor, Corp. Co. A 7th O.V.I.

NEW MATAMORAS

Andrews, Charles G., Pr. Co. E 7th O. V. I.

Armstrong, Clarence S., Pr. Co E 7th O. V. I.

Barnhart, Harry, Pr. Co. E 7th O. V. I.

Bennett, Homer L., Pr. Co. E 7th O. V. I.

Bond, William J., Pr. Co. E 7th O.V.I.

Bratton, Edward A., Pr. Co. E 7th O. V. I.

Campbell, Carl T., Pr. Co. E 7th O. V. I.

Cline, Llewellyn J., Pr. Co. E 7th O.V.I

Cunningham, Charles J., Pr. Co. E 7th O. V. I.

Cunningham, Frank, Q. M. Sergt. Co. E 7th O. V. I.

Cunningham, Harry, Pr. Co. E 7th O. V. I.

Cunningham, John, Pr. Co. E 7th O. V. I.

Davis, James, Pr. Co. E 7th O. V. I.

Dippel, Theodore, Pr. Co. E 7th O.V.I.

Eaton, George W., Pr. Co. E 7th O.V.I.

Elrod, William E., Pr. Co. E 7th O.V.I.

Ferry, James W., Pr. Co. E 7th O. V. I.

Fox, Charles W., Pr. Co. E 7th O. V. I.

Galbraith, William P., Pr. Co. E 7th O. V. I.

Gillespie, John C., Pr. Co. E 7th O. V. I.

Green, Thomas B., Pr. Co. E 7th O.V.I.

Greenwood, Homer L., Pr. Co. E 7th O. V. I.

Griffin, Perry O., Pr. Co. E 7th O. V. I.

Griffin, Robert W., Pr. Co. E 7th O.V.I.

Grubbs, William J., Musician Co. E 7th O. V. I.

Gautschi, Otto, Pr. Co. E 7th O. V. I.

Hare, Charles W., Sergt. Co. E 7th O. V. I.

Hare, Frank, Sergt. Co. E 7th O. V. I.

Hanshumaker, Louis, Sergt. Co. E 7th O. V. I.

Hubbard, Frank S., Pr. Co. E 7th O. V. I.

Kane, Hugh B., Corp. Co. E 7th O.V.I.

Kerr, Patrick M., Corp. Co. E 7th O. V. I.

Martin, Frank W., Corp. Co. E 7th O. V. I.

Miller, William C., Sergt. Co. E 7th O. V. I.

Morrison, Simeon D., Corp. Co. E 7th O. V. I.

Nikolaus, Forrest C., Corp. Co. E 7th O. V. I.

Powell, George C. W., Corp. Co. E 7th O. V. I.

Rupp, Harry P., Musician Co. E 7th O. V. I.

Stewart, William J., Sergt. Co. E 7th O. V. I.

Watson, George D., Artificer Co. E 7th O. V. I.

Way, Thomas F., Pr. Co. E 7th O. V. I.

Way, William S., Jr., Pr. Co. E 7th O. V. I.

Wisecup, Clarence E., Pr. Co. E 7th O. V. I.

Woods, Harry, Pr. Co. E 7th O. V. I.

Woods, John C., Wagoner Co. E 7th O. V. I.

NEWPORT

Hanna, Frank L., Pr. Co. E 7th O. V. I.

NEW SALEM

Dupler, Murry C., Pr. Co. I 4th O. V. I.   Jordan, Samuel, Pr. Co. K 7th O. V. I.

NEWTON TOWNSHIP, LICKING COUNTY

Roe, George E., Corp. Co. G 7th O.V.I.

Van Wey, Calvin M., Pr. Co. G 7th O. V. I.

Williams, Samuel, Pr Co. G 7th O. V. I

Wright, Mertis L., Pr. Co. G 7th O. V. I.

NEW WASHINGTON

Donnenworth, Clarence F., Pr. Co. A 8th O. V. I.

Huber, Jacob, Pr. Co. A 8th O. V. I.

NEW YORK CITY

Bailey, William E., Pr. Co. A 10th O. V. I.

Johnson, William A., Artificer Co. D 9th Batt. O. V. I.

Pierce, Eugene, Pr. Co. D 9th Batt. O. V. I.

NEY

Goller, Charles R., Pr. Co. E 6th O.V.I.

NORTH BALTIMORE

Archambeault, Clem, Corp. Co. K 2nd O. V. I.

Atkins, Charles E., Pr. Co. K 2nd O.V.I.

Adams, Frank L., Pr. Co. K 2nd O.V.I.

Bender, Peter M., Pr. Co. K 2nd O. V. I.

Billhamer, Charles A., Pr. Co. K 2nd, O. V. I.

Bowman, Claud H., Pr. Co. K 2nd O. V. I.

Crann, Hiram G., Q. M. Sergt. Co. K 2nd O. V. I.

Downs, Edward J., Sergt. Co. K 2nd O V. I.

Downs, Ephriam H., Sergt. Co. K 2nd O. V. I.

Eiting, Jacob, Sergt. Co. K 2nd O. V. I.

Flaherty, James S., Pr. Co. K 2nd O. V .I.

Hale, George W., Pr. Co. K 2nd O.V.I.

Heminger, Mark A., Pr. Co. K 2nd O. V. I.

Heverly, Paul D., Pr. Co.K 2nd O. V. I

Locy, James F., Pr. Co. K 2nd O. V. I

Longan, Bennie C., Pr. Co. K 2nd O. V. I.

McFall, George C., Pr. Co. K 2nd O. V. I.

McNamara, Edward, Pr. Co. K 2nd O. V. I.

Mock, Ebbert A., Corp. Co. K 2nd O. V. I.

Osterholt, Fred, Pr. Co. K. 2nd O.V.I.

Osterholt, Perry E., Pr. Co. K 2nd O. V. I.

Partlow, Wilson R., Corp. Co. K 2nd O. V. I.

Quigley, William F., Musician Co. K 2nd O. V. I.

Rickard, Hayes, Pr. Co. K 2nd O. V. I.

Rogers, James R., Pr. Co. K 2nd O.V.I.

Sennet, William H., Pr. Co. K 2nd O. V. I.

Shuler, Jesse A., Pr. Co. K 2nd O.V.I.

Slaughterbeck, George E., Pr. Co. K 2nd O. V. I.

Sprague, William, Pr. Co. K 2nd O. V. I.

Steel, Charley, Pr Co. K 2nd O. V. I.

Steel, Jay, Pr. Co. K 2nd O. V. I.

Stevens, Milton, Pr. Co. K 2nd O.V.I.

Trout, William H., Sergt. Co. K 2nd O. V. I.

Updyke, Daniel R., Pr. Co..K 2nd O. V. I.

Warner, Sylvester E., Pr. Co. K 2nd O. V. I.

White, Fred W., Corp. Co. K 2nd O. O. V. I.

Wilson, Frank L., 1st Sergt. Co. K 2nd O. V. I.

NORTH BENTON

Hutson, George, Pr. Co. K 8th O. V. I.

NORTHFIELD

McConnell, Charles, Pr. Tr. B 1st O. V. C.

NORTH HAMPTON

Prior, George A., Pr. Co. B 8th O.V.I.

NORTH LEWISBURG

Austin, Earnest, Pr. Co. D 3rd O. V. I.

Heston, Frank F., Pr. Co. K 7th O. V. I.

Heston, William B., Pr. Co. K 7th O. V. I.

NORTH ROBINSON

Deam, William C., Pr. Co. A 8th O. V. I.

Stanley, Edgar A., Pr. Co. A 8th O. V. I.

Warden, Albert E., Pr. Co. A 8th O. V. I.

NORTHUP

Thivener, John W., Pr. Co. C 7th O. V. I.

NORTH GREENFIELD

Smith, Banner A., Pr. Co. I 2nd O.V.I.

NORTH TOLEDO

Shantean, David, Pr. Co. G 10th O. V. I.

NORTH VERNON, IND.

Boyer, James M., Corp. Co. B 2nd U. S. V. E.

NORWALK

Aldrich, Albert E., Q. M. Sergt. Co. G 5th O. V. I.

Beeman, Frank P., Pr. Co. G 5th O. V. I.

Bell, Charles G., Pr. Co. G 5th O.V.I.

Boalt, Frederick L., Pr. Co. G 5th O. V. I.

Butt, Frank H., Pr. Co. G 5th O.V.I.

Cartwright, Oliver M., Pr. Co. G 5th O. V. I.

Castle, Olin C., Batt. Sergt. Maj. 7th O. V. I.

Chaffee, Burt M., Pr. Co. G 5th O.V.I.

Cunningham, Samuel A., Pr. Co. G 5th O. V. I.

De La Mater, Bennie E., Pr. Tr. B 1st O. V. C.

Filson, Frank P., Pr. Co. G 5th O.V.I.

Finch, James A., Pr. Co. G 5th O. V. I.

Fisher, Alfred B., Pr. Co. G 5th O V. I.

Gorham, Aaron B., Corp. Co. G 5th O. V. I.

Hallett, George W., Pr. Co. G 5th O. V. I.

Hartline, Fred O., Pr. Co. G 5th O.V.I.

Hearson, Albert L., Corp. Co. G 5th O. V. I.

Humbel, Charles F., Pr. Co. G 5th O. V. I.

Hunt, William H., Wagoner. Co. G 5th O. V. I.

Kean, William C., Pr. Co. G 5th O.V.I.

Keller, Fred W., Pr. Co. G 5th O. V. I.

King, Theodore, Pr. Co. G 5th O. V. I

Koppleman, Marcus, Pr. Co. M 5th O. V. I.

Laning, Ford H., Batt. Sergt. Maj. 5th O. V. I.

Lawrence, Ralph E., Pr. Co. G 5th O. V. I.

Manahan, Merritt M., Sergt. Co. G 5th O. V. I.

Martin, George, Pr. Co. G 5th O. V. I.

Mason, Arthur K., Pr. Co. G 5th O. V. I.

Mesnard, Ralph E., Sergt. Co. G 5th O. V. I.

Moore, Frank P., Pr. Co. G 5th O. V. I.

Morrill, Dee E., Pr. Co. G 5th O. V. I.

Myers, Joshua M, Pr. Co. G 5th O.V.I.

Osborn, Walter H., Pr. Co. G 5th O. V. I.

Patrick, George S., Pr. Co. G 5th O. V. I.

Peck, Walter H., Pr. Co. G 5th O.V.I.

Plount, Edward, Pr. Co. G 5th O. V. I.

Schafer, William P., Pr. Co. G 5th O. V. I.

Schucerer, Fred B., Pr. Co. B 6th O. V. I.

Sheldon, Albert R., Pr. Co. A 5th O. V. I.

Snable, William, Pr. Co. G 5th O.V.I.

Snyder, Frank J., Pr. Co. G 5th O.V.I.

Stafford, George E., Pr. Co. G 5th O. V. I.

Stoughton, George H., Pr. Co. G 5th O. V. I.

Suhrer, Frank J., Pr. Co. G 5th O.V.I.

Thorley, Harry S., Pr. Co. G 5th O. V. I.

Trumble, Arthur J., Corp. Co. G 5th O. V. I.

Van Dusen, James W., 1st Sergt. Co. G 5th O. V. I.

Ward, Clarence F., Pr. Co. B 6th O. V. I.

Wilson, Frank A., Pr. Co. G 5th O.V.I.

Wilcox, Frank T., Corp. Co. G 5th O V. I.

Wilkinson, Samuel A., Pr. Co. G 5th O. V. I.

Williams, David A., Sergt. Co. G 5th O. V. I.

Williams, John H., Pr. Co. G 5th O. V. I.

Willsey, Joseph H., Pr. Co. G 5th O. V. I.

NORWICH

Border, Rupert L., Pr. Bat. C 1st O. V. A.

NORWOOD

Gibson, William J., Pr. Co. C 2nd U.   Richards, Albert, Sergt. Co. C 2nd U.
S. V. E.   S. V. E.

NOVA

Nolan, David H., Corp. Co. C 8th O.   Nolan, Frank J., Pr. Co. C 8th O.V.I.
V. I.

OBAL

Calhoun, Ira E., Pr. Co. C 7th O. V. I.   Deckard, Randall, Pr. Co. C 7th O.
V. I.

OBERLIN

Davidson, Eugene, Pr. Co. D 9th Batt.   Dietrick, Will A., Corp. Co. F 5th O.
O. V. I.   V. I.
     Halley, Albert S., Pr. Co. F 5th O.V.I.

OAK SHADE

Ferry, Ellis, Pr. Co. G 6th O. V. I.   Lee, Bertram E., Pr. Co. G 6th O. V. I.

OLENA

Webb, Burt T., Pr. Co. G 5th O. V. I.

OAK HARBOR

McGrath, Charles, Pr. Co. H 10th O.   Rafferty, Bert Y., Pr. Co. C 10th O.
V. I.   V. I.

OTTAKER

Verity, James L., Pr. Co. G 6th O. V. I.

OTTOVILLE

Durck, Edward, Pr. Co. C 10th O. V. I.

OTHO

Hahn, David H., Pr. Bat. C 1st O.V.A.

OREGONIA

Roberson, Byron G., Pr. Co. C 9th Batt. O. V. I.

ORRVILLE

Goodrich, Harry S., Pr. Co. I 10th O.   Mish, Guy E., Pr. Co. I 10th O. V. I.
V. I.   Newcomer, William H., Pr. Co. L 8th
McMillin, Clyde B., Pr. Co. I 10th O.   O. V. I.
V. I.

ORCHARD

Holt, Frank, Pr. Co. E 3rd O. V. I.

OSWEGO, N. Y.

Young, William H., Pr. Co. C 10th O. V. I.

PAINESVILLE

Aults, Henry H., Corp. Co. M 5th O. V. I.
Baldwin, Henry Leslie, Musician Co. M 5th O. V. I.
Belden, Burr T., 1st Sergt. Co. M 5th O. V. I.
Bottin, Fred T., Pr. Co. M 5th O. V. I.
Brainard, Hubert Z., Sergt. Co. M 5th O. V. I.
Burns, Frederick T., Pr. Co. M 5th O. V. I.
Card, Burton E., Corp. Co. M 5th O. V. I.
Carter, Hubert E., Corp. Co. M 5th O. V. I.
Chapman, Fred, Pr. Co. M 5th O. V. I
Cleveland,, Owen R., Sergt. Co. M 5th O. V. I.
Cone, Salmon Earl, Q. M. Sergt. Co. M 5th O. V. I.
Eaton, Milton Hugh, Pr. Co. M 5th O V I

Gill, Clayton L., Pr. Co. M 5th O. V. I
Grauel, Clifton M., Principal Musician 5th O. V. I.
Hart, John C., Pr. Co. M 5th O. V. I.
Herroon, William C., Corp. Co. M 5th O. V. I.
Howlett, Halstead J., Pr. Co. M 5th O. V. I.
Huntington, Edwin G., Sergt. Co. M 5th O. V. I.
Kiernan, John S., Wagoner Co. M 5th O. V. I.
Minick, Arthur E., Pr. Co. M 5th O. V. I.
Price, George H., Corp. Co. C 10th O. V. I.
Sheldin, Hile G., Pr. Co. M 5th O. V. I.
Shepard, Ray P., Artificer, Co. M 5th O. V. I.
Trulsen, Carl O., Pr. Co. M 5th O.V.I.
West, Charley C., Pr. Co. M 5th O. V. I

PAINT VALLEY

Jarvis, Arthur, Pr. Co. H 8th O. V. I.

PASCO

Willoughby, Franklin T., Pr. Co. L 3rd O. V. I.

PATTERSON

Webb, Ezro M., Pr. Co. I 2nd O. V. I.

Webb, Schuyler S., Pr. Co. I 2nd O. V. I.

PATRIOT

Jones, Garfield, Pr. Co. C 7th O. V. I.

Myers, John, Pr. Co. C 7th O. V. I.

PAULDING

Ausman, Charles E., Pr. Co. M 2nd O. V. I.
Ausman, Francis M., Pr. Co. M 2nd O. V. I.
Barber, Edgar M., Pr. Co. M 2nd O. V. I.
Barnard, William S., Pr. Co. M 2nd O. V. I.
Barrick, Joshua C., Corp. Co. M 2nd O. V. I.

Biglow, William M., Pr. Co. M 2nd O. V. I.
Bland, Caleb, Pr. Co. M 2nd O. V. I.
Brown, Walter S., Pr. Co. M 2nd O V. I.
Buck, Edward, Corp. Co. M. 2nd O. V. I.
Carter, Joseph L., Pr. Co. M 2nd O.V.I.
Clous, George, Pr. Co. M 2nd O. V. I.
Cramer, George C., Pr. Co. M 2nd O. V. I.

Cromley, Victor E., Pr. Co. M 2nd O. V. I.

DeWitt, John S., Sergt. Co. M 2nd O. V. I.

Douart, Orin W., Sergt. Co. M 2nd O. V. I.

Elder, Jefferson, Pr. Co. M 2nd O.V.I.

Englehart, Ernest E., Pr. Co. M 2nd O. V. I.

Fellers, Roy, Pr. Co. M 2nd O. V. I.

Funk, David, Pr. Co. M 2nd O. V. I.

Gasser, Harold F., **Corp. Co. M 2nd** O. V. I.

Hardesty, Elijah R., Pr. Co. M 6th O V. I.

Heater, Edward R., Pr. Co. M 2nd O. V. I.

Hiester, Edward, Corp. Co. M 2nd O. V. I.

Hoover, Joseph, Pr. Co. M 2nd O.V.I.

Ice, Henry J., Pr. Co. M 2nd O. V. I.

Jackson, Coe G., Pr. Co. M 2nd O.V.I.

Jackson, Jesse B., Q. M. Sergt. Co. M 2nd O. V. I.

Kirk, John S., Pr. Co. M 2nd O. V. I.

Kirk, William H., Sergt. Co. M 2nd O. V. I.

Lawrence, William A., Pr. Co. M 2nd O. V. I.

Martin, Jacob F., Pr. Co. M 2nd O. V. I.

Mathers, Seth, Pr. Co. M 2nd O. V. I.

McCaffrey, George E., Pr. Co. M 2nd O. V. I.

McConnell, Edwin B., Corp., Co. M 2nd O. V. I.

Myers, David R., Corp. Co. M 2nd O. V. I.

Newton, Roy H., Corp. Co. M 2nd O. V. I.

Parker, Arthur, Pr. Co. M 2nd O. V. I.

Patton, John M., Pr. Co. M 2nd O.V.I.

Pursel, Carl, 1st Sergt. Co. M 2nd O. V. I.

Rodenbaugh, Adam, Pr. Co. M 2nd O. V. I.

Russell, Edward J., Artificer Co. M 2nd O. V. I.

Thompson, Loran J., Corp. Co. M 2nd O. V. I.

Wood, Charles, Pr. Co. M 2nd O. V. I.

PAYNE

Pease, Willard N., Pr. Co. M 2nd O. V. I.

Pease, Willis N., Pr. Co. M 2nd O.V.I.

PEEBLES

Wickerham, Peter A., Pr. Co. C 2nd U. S. V. E.

PENIEL

Wood, Thomas W., Pr. Co. M 2nd O. V. I.

PENINSULA

Martin, Charles, Pr. Co. F 10th O.V.I.

PENNSVILLE

Hollett, Clarence L., Pr. Co. B 7th O. V. I.

PERRY.

Mallory, Henry H., Pr. Co. E 5th O. V. I.

Winter, Fred, Pr. Co. E 5th O. V. I.

PERRYSBURG

Berger, Carl R., Pr. U. R. 2nd O.V.I.

Bruce, Eugene R., Pr. Co. H 10th O. V. I.

Chappell, Chester A., Pr. Co. H 10th O. V. I.

Ford, Walter, Pr. Co. D 9th Batt. O. V. I.

McAllister, Henry A., Pr. Co. H 10th O. V. I.

Peck, Augustus H., Pr. Co. G 10th O. V. I.

Scott, William P., Corp. Co. H 10th O. V. I.

PERRYSVILLE

Linton, William H., Pr. Co. H 8th O. V. I.

PETERSBURG, W. VA.

Welton, Maurice Seymour, Pr. Co. I 5th O. V. I.

PHILO

Brown, Bert A., Pr. Co. L 10th O.V.I.   Longley, Carlos E., Pr. Co. L 10th O. V. I

PIERCE

Buchman, John, Pr. Co. I 8th O.V.I.

PIKE RUN

Crosby, Cyrus S., Pr. Co. L 7th O. V. I.

PIONEER

Doolittle, Orrin J., Pr. Co. E 6th O. V. I.   Riley, William J., Pr. Co. E 6th O. V. I.

PIQUA

Allen, Joel R., Sergt. Co. K 3rd O.V.I.
Alley, Harry, Pr. Co. C 3rd O. V. I.
Anthony, Clarence, Pr. Co. K 3rd O. V. I.
Bain, Charles, Pr. Co. K 3rd O. V. I.
Baker, Martin R., Corp. Co. K 3rd O. V. I.
Baldock, Lafie, Pr. Co. K 3rd O.V.I.
Beckenbaugh, John, Pr. Co. K 3rd O. V. I.
Bowdle, Charles W., 1st Sergt. Co. K 3rd O. V. I.
Bowdle, George F., Sergt. Co. K 3rd O. V. I.
Brant, David, Sergt. Co. K 3rd O.V.I.
Brookman, John, Pr. Co. K 3rd O. V. I.
Brooks, Clifford, Pr. Co. K 3rd O.V.I.
Brooks, Edward, Pr. Co. K 3rd O. V. I.
Carter, Charles, Pr. Co. K 3rd O.V.I.
Clouse, William B., Pr. Co. C 3rd O. V. I.
Cron, James, Pr. Co. K 3rd O. V. I.
Drake, Ben. S., Pr. Co. C 3rd O.V.I.
Draper, Rial, Pr. Co. K 3rd O. V. I.
Dunkle, Rolla R., Pr. U. R. 3rd O. V. I.
Feaster, William, Pr. Co. K 3rd O. V. I.
Ficken, Willie, Pr. Co. K 3rd O. V. I.
Frank, Andrew, Pr. Co. K 3rd O.V.I.
Geist, Edward, Pr. Co. K 3rd O. V. I.
Genslinger, Steven, Corp. Co. K 3rd O. V. I.
George, Robert, Pr. Co. K 3rd O.V.I.
Gorrell, George W., Pr. Co. K 3rd O. V. I.
Gorrell, Wesley, Pr. Co. K 3rd O.V.I.
Greene, Edward R., Pr. Co. C 3rd O. V. I.

Grosvenor, Charles, Pr. Co. K 3rd O. V. I.
Hall, Charles H., Sergt. Co. K 3rd O. V. I.
Hardesty, Walker, Corp. Co. K 3rd O. V. I.
Henning, Harry F., Pr. Co. F 8th O. V. I.
Higgins, Ben. D., Pr. Co. K 3rd O. V. I.
Houck, Louis, Pr. Co. K 3rd O. V. I.
Houser, Edward, Pr. Co. K 3rd O.V.I.
Hubbard, John, Pr. Co. K 3rd O.V.I.
Huffman, Harry, Pr. Co. K 3rd O.V.I.
Hughes, Charles, Pr. Co. K 3rd O.V.I.
Jay, Frank P., Pr. Co. K 3rd O. V. I.
Jessup, Frank, Pr. Co. K 3rd O. V. I.
Johnson, Marion, Pr. Co. K 3rd O. V. I.
Karnehem, Ollie, Pr. Co. K 3rd O. V. I.
Kipp, Charles, Pr. Co. K 3rd O. V. I.
Kouz, Henry, Pr. Co. K 3rd O. V. I.
Leedom, Chester B., Corp. Co. K 3rd O. V. I.
Lindsay, Eugene, Pr. Co. K 3rd O. V. I.
Link, John S., Pr. Co. K 3rd O. V. I.
Loeffler, Chryst H., Corp. Co. K 3rd O. V. I.
Lyman, Timothy, Pr. Co. K 3rd O. V. I.
McCloud, Joseph, Pr. Co. K 3rd O. V. I.
Mikles, James, Pr. Co. K 3rd O. V. I.
Nolan, John E., Pr. Co. K 3rd O. V. I.
Noland, Melvin, Pr. Co. K 3rd O.V.I.
Peck, Cezelo, Corp. Co. K 3rd O.V.I.
Peterson, Harry G., Sergt. Maj. 3rd O. V. I.

Piel, Fred W., Sergt. Co. C 2nd U. S. V. E.
Plumb, King, Pr. Co. K 3rd O. V. I.
Prosser, Arthur, Pr. Co. K 3rd O.V.I.
Reamer, George, Musician Co. K 3rd O. V. I.
Reedy, Charles F., Pr. U. R. 3rd O. V. I.
Reimiller, Henry, Pr. Co. K 3rd O. V. I.
Roberts, Lou, Wagoner Co. K 3rd O. V. I.
Ross, Arthur, Pr. Co. K 3rd O. V. I.
Sachs, William, Pr. Co. K 3rd O.V.I.
Safford, Clarence, Pr. Co. K 3rd O. V. I.
Schneider, August, Pr. Co. K 3rd O. V. I.
Shafer, William, Musician Co. K 3rd O. V. I.
Smith, William S., Pr. Tr. E 1st O. V. C.
Souders, Claude, Corp. Co. K 3rd O. V. I.
Spencer, Frank, Pr. Co. K 3rd O.V.I.

Stevens, Ross, Pr. Co. K 3rd O. V. I.
Stein, John, Pr. Co. K 3rd O. V. I.
Stillwell, Charles, Corp. Co. K 3rd O. V. I.
Stilwell, Clifford, Pr. Co. K 3rd O. V. I.
Street, Robert, Artificer Co. K 3rd O. V. I.
Strome, Charles, Pr. Co. C 3rd O.V.I.
Strome, Frank, Pr. Co. K 3rd O.V.I.
Toonney, James, Pr. Co. K 3rd O.V.I.
Trexler, Robert, Pr. Co. K 3rd O.V.I.
Trummel, Albert, Pr. Co. K 3rd O. V. I.
Uhry, Joseph, Pr. Co. K 3rd O. V. I.
Vantilburg, Ben., Pr. Co. K 3rd O. V. I.
Warner, Edward, Pr. Co. K 3rd O. V. I.
White, George, Pr. Co. K 3rd O. V. I.
Wirick, William, Pr. Co. K 3rd O.V.I.
Wright, Enos, Corp. Co. K 3rd O. V. I.
Yumey, William, Pr. Co. K 3rd O. V. I.

PITCHIN

Dunworth, Samuel A., Pr. Co. B 3rd O. V. I

Littler, Clyde E., Pr. Co. B 3rd O.V.I.

PITTSBURG, PA.

Burns, John A., Pr. Bat. C 1st O.V.A.

Campbell, Robert I., Pr. Co. C 10th O. V. I.

PLAIN CITY

Ballinger, Samuel T., Pr. Tr. M 1st O. V. C.

Kilbury, Claude, Pr. Co. K 3rd O.V.I.
Sandahl, Eugene, Pr. Co. K 3rd O. V. I.

PLAINVILLE

Oaks, Charles N., Corp. Co. C 2nd U. S. V. E.

PLEASANT BEND

Lantz, Jesse, Pr. Co. M 6th O. V. I.

PLEASANT HILL

Reed, Alonzo C., Corp. Co. C 2nd U. S. V. E.

PLEASANT HOME

Warner, Charles E., Pr. Co. C 8th O. V. I.

PLEASANTVILLE

Brooke, Philo R., Pr. Co. I 4th O.V.I.
Bush, Samuel L., Artificer Co. I 4th O. V. I.
Curtiss, Ernest I., Corp. Co. I 4th O. V. I.

Dyarman, Charles L., Pr. Co. I 4th O. V. I.
England, Benjamin J., Pr. Co. I 4th O. V. I.

Gebhardt, William H., Pr. Co. I 4th
O. V. I.
Keller, James O., Pr. Co. I 4th O.V.I.
Love, Hugh S., Pr. Co. I 4th O. V. I.
McNaughten, Roy T., Sergt. Co. I 4th
O. V. I.

Mertz, Jacob J., Pr. Co. I 4th O. V. I.
Nickurn, Thomas Wray, Pr. Co. I 4th
O. V. I.
Spitler, David L., Pr. Co. I 4th O.V.I.
Stewart, Elmer E., Pr. Co. B 4th O.
V. I.

PLIMPTON

Croker, John W., Pr. Co. H 8th O. V. I.

PLUMWOOD

Cowgill, Frank, Corp. Co. E 3rd O. V. I.

PRICETOWN

Chaney, Alex. S., Pr. Co. F 3rd O. V. I.

POLK

Auhl, Fred, Pr. Co. C 8th O. V. I.
Barrick, Jacob, Artificer Co. C 8th O.
V. I.
Bryan, Joseph C., Sergt. Co. C 8th O.
V. I.
Diveler, Amos M., Pr. Co. C 8th O.
V. I.
Eidt, John M., Sergt. Co. C 8th O.V.I.
Glessner, Eugene, Sergt. Co. C 8th O.
V. I.
Griner, Grant S., Corp. Co. C 8th O.
V. I.

Hartsel, Frank L., Sergt. Co. C 8th
O. V. I.
Hess, James, 1st Sergt. Co. C 8th O.
V. I.
Kiplinger, Don T., Pr. Co. C 8th O.
V. I.
Marks, William, Corp. Co. C 8th O.
V. I.
Millar, Denton J., Pr. Co. C 8th O.
V. I.

POMEROY

Ament, Joseph, Pr. Co. L 7th O. V. I.
Arnold, Gustav, Pr. Co. L 7th O.V.I.
Baber, George H., Artificer Co. L 7th
O. V. I.
Bengel, Harry T., Pr. Co. L 7th O.
V. I.
Hartley, Aaron W., Pr. Co. L 7th O.
V. I.
Hartley, Charles A., Pr. Co. L 7th O.
V. I.

Harvey, Walter, Pr. Co. L 7th O.V.I.
Hovey, Gilbert A., Pr. Co. L 7th O.
V. I.
Jones, Floyd B., Pr. Co. L 7th O.V.I.
Osborn, Henry L., Pr. Co. B 10th O.
V. I.
Sauer, Edward, Pr. Co. L 7th O. V. I.
Shaver, Orville O., Pr. Co. L 7th O.
V. I.
White, Evert F., Pr. Co. L 7th O.V.I.

PONTIAC, ILL.

Boller, Vernon W., Pr. Tr. G 1st O. V. C.

POPLAR RIDGE

Robinson, Alexander N., Pr. Co. C 3rd O. V. I.

PORTAGE

Mears, James F., Pr. Co. C 10th O. V. I.

PORT CLINTON

Meyer, Gerhard H., Pr. Co. A 10th O.
V. I.

Smith, Rolland D., Pr. Co. A 10th O.
V. I.

PORT JEFFERSON

Apgar, William, Pr. Co. L 3rd O.V.I.
Burton, Daniel W., Pr. Co. L 3rd O.
V. I.

Hussey, Clem L., Pr. Co. L 3rd O.
V. I.
Ruff, George P., Pr. Co. L 3rd O.V.I.

PORTLAND

Wheeler, Newberry W., Pr. Co. G 4th O. V. I.

PORTSMOUTH

Alger, Frank H., Corp. Co. H 4th O.
V. I.
Alger, J. Barry, Pr. Co. H 4th O.V.I.
Anderson, Preston H., Pr. Co. H 4th
O. V. I.
Armstrong, Fred M., Pr. Co. H 4th
O. V. I.
Barber, Albert M., Pr. Co. H 4th O.
V. I.
Batterson, George A., Pr. Co. H 4th
O. V. I.
Bratt, Joseph C., Corp. Co. H 4th O.
V. I.
Briggs, Forest C., 1st Sergt. Co. H
4th O. V. I.
Brooks, Frank, Corp. Co. D 9th Batt.
O. V. I.
Bumgardner, Elton M., Pr. Co. H 4th
O. V. I.
Bybee, Mont. G., Pr. Co. H 4th O.
V. I.
Calvert, Ralph W., Pr. Co. H 4th O.
V. I.
Carroll, George S., Corp. Co. H 7th
O. V. I.
Cole, Charles C., Pr. Tr. D 1st O.V.C.
Cole, William L., Pr. Co. H 4th O.
V. I.
Cooper, Milton J., Pr. Co. H 4th O.
V. I.
Crull, Demer, Pr. Co. H 4th O. V. I.
Davidson, Asbury W., Corp. Co. H 4th
O. V. I.
Davidson, Reed M., Pr. Co. H 4th O.
V. I.
Davies, Alexander B., Pr. Co. A 10th
O. V. I.
Distel, Louis E., Pr. Co. H 4th O.V.I.
Dodge, Daniel H., Pr. Co. H 4th O.
V. I.
Donaldson, Harry W., Artificer Co. H
4th O. V. I.
Douglas, Duncan M., Pr. Co. H 4th
O. V. I.
Evans, Mitchell H., Pr. Co. H 4th O.
V. I.
Foster, Andrew B., Sergt. Co. H 4th
O. V. I.
Funk, Kinney P., Pr. Co. H 4th O.
V. I.
George, Robert M., Pr. Co. H 4th O.
V. I.
Getz, John F., Pr. Co. H 4th O. V. I.
Herms, Albert G., Pr. Co. H 4th O.
V. I.

Hicks, Edward B., Pr. Co. H 4th O.
V. I.
Jackson, Andrew B., Pr. Co. H 3rd
O. V. I.
Kelley, William H., Pr. Co. H 4th O.
V. I.
Kinney, Clifford M., Pr. Co. H 4th O.
V. I.
Kinney, J. Wesley, Pr. Co. H 4th O.
V. I.
Kitt, Nicholas, Jr., Pr. Co. K 3rd O.
V. I.
Maguire, Charles H., Corp. Co. H 4th
O. V. I.
Masters, William A., Pr. Co. H 4th O.
V. I.
McDonald, George F., Sergt. Co. H
4th O. V. I.
McGonigle, William D., Wagoner Co.
H 4th O. V. I.
McGuire, Eddie M., Jr., Pr. Co. H 4th
O. V. I.
McKeown, Emmett K., Pr. Co. H 4th
O. V. I.
McMonigle, John L., Pr. Co. H 4th
O. V. I.
Mohl, Harry U., Pr. Co. H 4th O.V.I.
Morrison, Harry M., Pr. Co. H 4th
O. V. I.
Muecklheim, Leo C., Pr. Co. H 4th O.
V. I.
Newman, Russell C., Sergt. Co. H 4th
O. V. I.
Noel, Charles S., Pr. Co. H 4th O.V.I.
Oldfield, George G., Corp. Co. H 4th
O. V. I.
Patterson, Elbert L., Corp. Co. H 4th
O. V. I.
Peebles, William M., Pr. Co. H 4th O.
V. I.
Redman, Joseph A., Pr. Co. H 4th O.
V. I.
Reed, Charles H., Corp. Co. H 4th O.
V. I.
Reed, William P., Pr. Co. H 4th O.
V. I.
Reinert, Adolph G., Pr. Co. H 4th O.
V. I.
Reinhardt, Edward J., Pr. Co. H 4th
O. V. I.
Searl, Clinton M., Pr. Co. H 4th O.
V. I.
Shriver, Byron D., Pr. Co. H 4th O.
V. I.

Stewart, James F., Pr. Co. H 4th O. V. I.

Stone, Walter, Pr. Co. H 4th O. V. I.

Sturgill, William C., Pr. Co H 4th O. V. I.

Taylor, Charles C., Pr. Co. H 4th O. V. I.

Thompson, Matthew W., Pr. Co. H 4th O. V. I.

Thurman, Floyd E., Pr. Co. H 4th O. V. I.

Trimmer, Walter H., Sergt. Co. H 4th O. V. I.

Welch, Arthur, Pr. Co. H 4th O.V.I.

Wells, Edgar S., Pr. Co. H 4th O. V. I.

Whitman, Charles R., Pr. Co. H 4th O. V. I.

Wilhelm, Charles C., Sergt. Co. H 4th O. V. I.

Will, Harvey M., Corp. Co. H 4th O. V. I.

Williams, Samuel A., Pr. Co. H 4th O. V. I.

Winter, Henry H., Pr. Co. H 4th O. V. I.

Zeek, Edward, Pr. Co. H 4th O. V. I

PORT WILLIAM

Arnold, Frank E., Pr. U. R. 3rd O. V. I.

PRAIRIE DEPOT

Dern, Charles W., Pr. Co. G 2nd O. V. I.

PROSPECT

Boudley, Charles J., Pr. Co. G 2nd O. V. I.

Bondley, Elmer R., Pr. Co. G 2nd O. V. I.

PULASKI

Ames, Bert W., Pr. Co. E 6th O. V. I.

Shankster, George H., Pr. Co. E 6th O. V. I.

Stoner, Williard, Pr. Co. E 6th O.V.I.

Wyatt, Oscar W., Pr. Co. E 6th O. V. I.

RAINBOW

Cline, George T., Pr. Co. D 7th O. V. I.

Schofield, Carl S., Pr. Co. D 7th O. V. I.

RANDOLPH

Austin, Montgomery O., Pr. Co. A 10th O. V. I.

RANGE

Londergan, Cornelius, Pr. Co. E 3rd O. V. I.

Ross, William W., Pr. Co. E 3rd O. V. I.

Ward, Jacob E., Corp. Co. E 3rd O. V. I.

RAVENNA

Bittner, Edward A., Pr. Co. B 10th O. V. I.

Bosgra, Henry, Pr. Co. C 10th O.V.I.

Clements, Eugene G., Pr. Co. B 10th O. V. I.

Collins, Thad, Pr. Co. B 10th O. V. I.

French, Emmer M., Artificer Co. B 10th O. V. I.

Hart, Joseph D., Pr. Co. C 10th O. V. I.

Knapp, Martin, Pr. Co. B 10th O.V.I.

Knapp, Phillip W., Pr. Co. B 10th O. V. I.

Laubert, Fred S., Pr. Co. B 10th O. V. I.

Philpott, Percy J., Pr. Co. C 10th O. V. I.

RAYMOND

Dawson, Frank, Pr. Tr. G 1st O.V.C.
Dillon, Okey D., Pr. Tr. G 1st O.V.C.
Green, Hewit H., Pr. Co. D 4th O.
V. I.

Myers, Orrin D., Pr. Tr. G 1st O.V.C.
Simmons, Charles C., Pr. Tr. G 1st
O. V. C.

REDFIELD

Ferguson, John M., Pr. Co. L 10th O. V. I.

RED HAW.

Fahr, Ilger C., Corp. Co. C 8th O.V.I.
Kopp, Clarence E., Pr. Co. C 8th O.
V. I.

Wise, Tilden, Pr. Co. C 8th O. V. I.

REED URBAN

Lippoldt, Charles H., Pr. Co. L 8th O. V. I.

RENDVILLE

Brooks, Charles E., Pr. Co. D 9th Batt
O. V. I.

Clark, Spencer, Pr. Co. D 9th Batt. O.
V. I.

RENO

Amos, Elmer E., Pr. Co. D 7th O. V. I.

Sarver, Earnest L., Pr. Co. D 7th O.
V. I.

REPUBLIC

Anway, Frank L., Pr. Co. E 2nd O.
V. I.
Hisey, Elvin A., Pr. Co. E 2nd O. V. I.
Rakestraw, George L., Pr. Co. E 2nd
O. V. I.

Smith, Frederick W., Pr. Co. E 2nd O.
V. I.
Way, Frank P., Pr. Co. E 2nd O. V. I.

REYNOLDS

Ayers, Ralph L., Musician Co. D 3rd
O. V. I.
Goul, William H., Pr. Co. D 3rd O.V.I.

Lyons, Charles E., Sergt. Co. D 3rd
O. V. I.
Vermillion, Evan S., Corp. Co. D 3rd
O. V. I.

REYNOLDSBURG

Rodebaugh, Ernst M., Pr. Bat. H 1st O. V. A.

RICHVILLE

Wingard, John L., Pr. Co. L 8th O. V. I.

RIGEWAY

Grimes, George L., Pr. Co. I 2nd O. V. I.

RIO GRANDE

Wood, Clyde A., Musician Co. C 7th O. V. I.

RIPLEY.

Behymer, Elbert. Pr. Co. H 3rd O.V.I.
Brown, Clifford, Pr. Co. H 3rd O.V.I.
Campbell, Benjamin A., Corp. Co. H 3rd O. V. I.
Coburn, Spencer S.. Pr. Co. H 3rd O. V. I.
Cochran. George H.. Pr. Co. H 3rd O. .V. I.
Cook. Milton, Pr. Co. H 3rd O. V. I.
Culter, Charles L., Sergt. Co. H 3rd O. V. I.
Davis, Thomas F., Pr. Co. H 3rd O. V. I.
Dunham. Edward. Pr. Co. H 3rd O. V. I.
Fleig. Harry, Sergt. Co. H 3rd O. V. I
Fulton, Nelson B.. Corp. Co. H 3rd O. V. I.
Fussnecker. William. Pr. Co. H 3rd O. V. I.
Hughes, Harry. Pr. Co. H 3rd O.V.I.
Jones, Joseph E., Pr. Co. H 3rd O.V.I.
Jones. Sam. H.. Pr. Co. H 3rd O.V.I.
Jones, Thomas, Pr. Co. H 3rd O. V. I.
Kinkead, Ed. Pr. Co. H 3rd O. V. I.
Kinkead, Hamer C., Pr. Co. H 3rd O. V. I.
Koob, George, Pr. Co. H 3rd O. V. I.

List, Otto J., Pr. Co. H 3rd O. V. I.
Martin. George W., Pr. Co. H 3rd O. V. I.
Mauser, Oswald. Pr. Co. H 3rd O.V.I.
Mitchell, John J.. Pr. Co. H 3rd O.V.I.
Mussinon, Joseph, Pr. Co H 3rd O.V.I.
Richards. Charles J., Q. M. Sergt. Co. H. 3rd O. V. I.
Rockwell, Frank. Pr. Co. H 3rd O.V I.
Rubenaker, John, Pr Co. H 3rd O V I
Senteney, Welda S., 1st Sergt. Co. H 3rd O. V. I.
Shafer, Nicklous, Pr. Co. H 3rd O.V.I.
Sutherland, Charles A., Corp. Co. H. 3rd O. V. I.
Stephenson, Pearl. Pr. Co. H 3rd O V. I.
Swisher, Walter S.. Pr. Co. H 3rd O. V. I.
Thompson. John W., Pr. Co. H 3rd O. V. I.
Wagner, John E., Pr. Co. H 3rd O. V. I.
Watters. Charles M., Sergt. Co. H 3rd O. V. I.
Webster, Arthur, Pr. Co. H 3rd O.V.I.
Yearsley. Lawrence B., Pr. Co. H 3rd O. V. I.

RISING SUN

Bates, Sardis W., Pr. Co. K 2nd O. V. I.

ROACHTON

Fachelmann. George, Pr. Co. H 10th O. V. I.

Hoffman, George J., Pr. Co. H 10th O. V. I.

ROCHESTER, N. Y.

Cauley. Charles F.. Pr. Co. G 10th O. V. I.

Loftus. John W.. Pr. Co. K 10th O. V. I.

ROCKPORT

Alexander. Albert F.. Pr. Co. H 10th O. V. I.
Bassett. Russell W., Pr. Co. F 5th O. V. I.

Potter, Burton J., Pr. Co. F 5th O.V.I.
Spencer, Roy P.. Wagoner Co. F 5th O. V. I.

RODNEY

Mossman, William H., Pr. Co. C 7th O. V. I.

Waddell, George E., Corp. Co. C 7th O. V. I.

ROSCOE

Burchfield, David. Pr. Co. F 7th O.V.I.

ROSEVILLE

Kildow, Clarence N., Pr. Co. L 10th O. V. I.

Veyon, Harry, Pr. Co. L 10th O. V. I..

ROLLERSVILLE

Peterson, Ernest H., Pr. Co. K 2nd O. V. I.

ROUNDHEAD

Butler, Earnest M., Pr. Co. I 2nd O.   Moore, James D., Pr. Co. I 2nd O.V.I.
V. I.

ROXABELL

Whaley, Fred L., Pr. Co. K 7th O.V.I.

RUPERT

Connor, Hugh F., Pr. Co. E 3rd O.V.I.   Dewey, Birnum H., Corp. Co. E 3rd
                                            O. V. I.

RUSHVILLE

Shaw, Robert, Pr. Co. I 4th O. V. I.

RUSSELL

Barnes, Charles E., Pr. Co. F 3rd O.   Brewer, Louis, Pr. Co. F 3rd O. V. I.
V. I.   Britton, James P., Pr. Co. F 3rd O.V.I.
Bish, James O., Pr Co. F 3rd O. V. I.   Hart, Charlie S., Pr. Co. F 3rd O. V. I.

RUSSELVILLE

Edwards, Arthur, Pr. Co. H 3rd O.V.I.   Zurcher, John W., Pr. Co. H 3rd O.
                                            V. I.

RUTLAND

Chase, Frank E., Pr. Co. L 7th O.V.I.   Pullins, Charles W., Pr. Co. L 7th O.
                                            V. I.

SABINA

Alexander, Charles B., 5th Corp. Co.   Cherryhomes, George, 1st Sergt. Co. M
M 3rd O. V. I.   3rd O. V. I.
Anderson, Parker T., Pr. Co. M 3rd O.   Crisenbery, Luther J., Pr. Co. M 3rd
V. I.   O. V. I.
Ansbaugh, Thomas, 3rd Sergt. Co. M   Dawson, Hinton, Pr. Co. M 3rd O.
3rd O. V. I.   V. I.
Bantz, Otto, Pr. Co. M 3rd O. V. I.   Donohoe, James, Pr. Co. M 3rd O.V.I.
Barlow, Hoye, 3rd Corp. Co. M 3rd O.   Driscoll, William T., Pr. Co. M 3rd
V. I.   O. V. I.
Barlow, Marshall, Pr. Co. M 3rd O.V.I.   Duke, Grant, Pr. Co. M 3rd O. V. I.
Bayless, Norman, Pr. Co. M 3rd O.V.I.   Dunham, John, Musician Co. M 3rd O.
Beard, Joseph W., Pr. Co. M 3rd O.   V. I.
V. I.   Ferguson, Samuel S., Pr. Co. M 3rd
Beckett, Edd, Pr. Co. M 3rd O. V. I.   O. V. I.
Beckett, James, Pr. Co. M 3rd O. V. I.   Flint, James O., Pr. Co. M 3rd O. V. I.
Bence, William, 4th Sergt. Co. M 3rd   Garrison, Andrew, Pr. Co. M 3rd O.
O. V. I.   V. I.
Bennett, Thomas, Pr. Co. M 3rd O.V.I.   Graybill, John, Pr Co. M 3rd O. V. I.
Bogan, Franklin, Pr. Co. M 3rd O.   James, Ulysses C., 6th Corp. Co. M 3rd
V. I.   O. V. I.
Burl, William H., Q. M. Sergt. Co. M   Johnson, Clinton, Pr. Co. M 3rd O.V.I.
3rd O. V. I.   Johnson, Lang, Pr. Co. M 3rd O. V. I.
Butterfield, Burt, 1st Corp. Co. M 3rd   Kelso, Harry L., 6th Sergt. Co. M 3rd
O. V. I.   O. V. I.

Keyle, Ormond, 4th Corp. Co. M 3rd O. V. I.
Koch, John V., Pr. Co. M 3rd O. V. I.
Lowenshimer, Bert, Pr. Co. M 3rd O. V. I.
McFadden, Hugh, Pr. Co. M 3rd O. V. I.
Michael, William, Pr. Co. M 3rd O. V. I.
Mitchell, Elsworth, Pr. Co. M 3rd O. V. I.
Moon, Alonzo, Pr. Co. M 3rd O. V. I.
Parker, John A., Pr. Co. M 3rd O.V.I.
Patton, William, Pr. Co. M 3rd O.V.I.
Pearson, George, Pr. Co. M 3rd O.V.I.
Plott, Herbert, Pr. Co. M 3rd O. V. I.
Robuck, Alonzo, Pr. Co. M 3rd O.V.I.
Roush, Charles A., Pr. Co. M 3rd O. V. I.
Runnels, John, Pr. Co. M 3rd O. V. I.
Schindler, Albert, Artificer Co. M 3rd O. V. I.

Scott, Forest M., 2nd Corp. Co. M 3rd O. V. I.
Shank, Frederick A., Pr. Co. M 3rd O. V. I.
Stivers, Allen, Pr. Co. M 3rd O. V. I.
Swindler, Emmett, Pr. Co. M 3rd O. V. I.
Syferd, Louis, Pr. Co. M 3rd O. V. I.
Taylor, Samuel L., Pr. Co. M 3rd O. V. I.
VanPelt, Charles W., 5th Sergt. Co. M 3rd O. V. I.
Wade, Cyrus, Pr. Co. M 3rd O. V. I.
Ward, Ernest, Pr. Co. M 3rd O. V. I.
Warren, Samuel, Pr. Co. M 3rd O.V.I.
West, James, Pr. Co. M 3rd O. V. I.
Williams, Horace, Pr. Co. M 3rd O. V. I.
Zimmerman, Allen, Pr. Co. M 3rd O. V. I.

SALEM

Frescott, Ernest, Wagoner, Co. K 8th O. V. I.
Lawrence, Harry B., Pr. Co. E 5th O. V. I.

SANDUSKY

Atwood, Guy W., Pr. Co. B 6th O.V.I.
Baker, George C., Pr. Co. B 6th O.V.I.
Bamberl, John A., Pr. Co. B 6th O.V.I.
Biemeller, Andrew F., Pr. Co. B 6th O. V. I.
Blatt, William, Pr Co. B 6th O. V. I.
Brown, Charles G., Pr. Co. B 6th O. V. I.
Brown, Julius, Pr. Co. B 6th O. V. I.
Buyer, Robert G., Pr. Co. B 6th O. V. I.
Carpenter, Jesse, Pr. Co. B 6th O. V. I.
Cogswell, Frederick R., Pr. Co. B 6th O. V. I.
DeWitt, Rufus, Pr. Co. B 6th O. V. I.
Dick, Carl A., Pr. Co. B 6th O. V. I.
Donovan, William F., Pr. Co. B 6th O. V. I.
Eberl, Christian F., Pr. Co. B 6th O. V. I.
Egger, Fedal, Pr. Co. B 6th O. V. I.
Englert, Joseph, Corp. Co. B 6th O. V. I.
Ernst, Albert H., Pr. Co. B 6th O. V. I.
Gaw, William C., Sergt. Co. B 6th O. V. I.
Gilbert, William H., Pr. Co. B 6th O. V. I.
Grathwol, William F., Pr. Co. B 6th O. V. I.
Groch, Robert A., Musician Co. B 6th O. V. I.
Haines, John W., Pr. Co. B 6th O.V.I.
Halladay, Frederick T., Pr. Co. B 6th O V. I.

Hartwell, Othniel Carl, Pr Co. B 6th O. V. I.
Haase, Diedrick, Pr. Co. B 6th O.V.I.
Henry, Herbert H., Sergt. Co. B 6th O. V. I.
Henry, Leroy, Pr. Co. B 6th O. V. I.
Holland, Harry A., Pr. Co. B 6th O. V. I.
Hubbard, Alex M, Pr. Co. B 6th O. V. I.
Hull, George W., Pr. Co. B 6th O.V.I.
Huntington, Warner D., Sergt. Co. B 6th O. V. I.
Irwine, Justin S., Corp. Co. B 6th O. V. I.
King, Clifford M., Sergt. Maj. 6th Θ. V. I.
Kramer, William, Pr. Co. B 6th O. V. I.
Lang, Frederick, Pr. Co. B 6th O. V. I.
Lea, James D., Sergt. Co. B 6th O. V. I.
Lunceford, George W., Wagoner Co. B 6th O. V. I.
MacAaron, Walter S., Pr. Co. B 6th O. V. I.
McMorris, Charles A., Corp. Co. B 6th O. V. I.
Meyer, Joseph A., Pr. Co. B 6th O. V. I.
Miller, John M., Pr. Co. B 6th O. V. I.
Mitchell, Sylvester A, Pr. Co. B 6th O. V. I.
Mulheim, William F., Pr. Co. C 6th O V. I.

Nolan, John E., Pr. Co. B 6th O. V. I.
Peckham, Charlie M., Pr. Co. B 6th O. V. I.
Philby, Alfred W., Corp. Co. B 6th O. V. I.
Philby, Frederick J., Jr., Pr. Co. B 6th O. V. I.
Porter, Charles V., Pr. Co. B 6th O. V. I.
Rhonehouse, George L., Corp. Co. B 6th O. V. I.
Rogers, Roy T., Pr. Co. B 6th O. V. I.
Rude, Benjamin C., Sergt. Co. B 6th O. V. I.
Schiller, George S., Artificer Co. B 6th O. V. I.
Schnorr, John A., Pr. Co. B 6th O. V. I.
Schultz, August C., Pr. Co. B 6th O. V. I.
Sedgwick, Harry F., Pr. Co. B 6th O. V. I.

Sinderwald, Albert F., Pr. Co. B 6th O. V. I.
Sinderwald, John, Pr. Co. B 6th O. V. I.
Smith, Charles T., Pr. Co. B 6th O. V. I.
Spencer, Paul R., Pr. Co. B 6th O.V.I.
Stawetzki, Rudolph W., Pr. Co. B 6th O. V. I.
Thorn, William, Corp. Co. B 6th O. V. I.
Upp, Edwin L., Pr. Co. B 6th O. V. I.
Upp, William C., Pr. Co. B 6th O.V.I.
Weber, Edward G., Pr. Co. B 6th O. V. I.
Weber, Russell L., Musician Co. B 6th O. V. I.
Wiesner, Frank, Pr. Co. B 6th O. V. I.
Wurm, John C., Sergt. Co. B 6th O. V. I.
Zurhorst, William K., Pr. Co. B 6th O. V. I.

SAYBROOK

Creter, Herman F., Pr. Co. E 5th O. V. I.
Forbes, Parmer E., Pr. Co. E 5th O. V. I.

Lombard, Leon H., Pr. Co. E 5th O. V. I.

SCIO

Barnes, Fred M., Pr. Co. B 7th O.V.I.

SCOTT

Williams, Andrew M., Pr. Co. M 2nd O. V. I.

SEDALIA

Haynes, George N., Pr. Co. E 3rd O. V. I.
Heath, William, Pr. Co. E 3rd O.V.I.
Howard, Arthur, Pr. Co. E 3rd O.V.I.
Nicely, Thomas J., Pr. Co. E 3rd O. V. I.

Taylor, Chancie, Pr. Co. E 3rd O.V.I.
Taylor, John, Pr. Co. E 3rd O. V. I.
Washington, Ed., Pr. Co. E 3rd O. V. I.

SHADEVILLE

Dennis, William, Pr. Bat. H 1st O. V. A.
Loos, Conrad, Pr. Bat. H 1st O. V. A.

Tucker, Albert E., Pr. Co. F 4th O. V. I.

SHAMOKIN, PA.

Jones, William R., Pr. Co. G 7th O. V. I.

SHELBY

Sutten, Harry, Pr. Tr. G 1st O. V. C.

Whityer, Arby V., Pr. Bat. C 1st O. V. A.

SHELL KNOT, MO.

Monson, Hugh J., Pr. Tr. G 1st O. V. C.

SHERWOOD

Marlett. Edward F., Pr. Co. M 2nd O. V. I.

SHREVE

Airhart, Charles, Sergt. Co. H 8th O.
V. I.
Airhart, Harley H., Corp. Co. H 8th
O. V. I.
Barry, William E., Pr. Co. II 8th O.
V. I.
Bedford, Frank, Pr. Co. II 8th O.V.I.
Bricker, Altie L., Pr. Co. H 8th O.V.I.
Brown. Thomas B., Pr. Co. H 8th O.
V. I.
Burnett, William, Pr. Co. II 8th O.
V. I.
Campbell, Robert J., Sergt. Co. H 8th
O. V. I.
Cole, James R., Corp. Co. H 8th O.
V. I.
Eberhart, Galilian C., Pr. Co. H 8th
O. V. I.
Hague, Harry G., Pr. Co. H 8th O.
V. I.
Hoover, Harold, Pr. Co. H 8th O.V.I.

Manson, John C., Corp. Co. H 8th O.
V. I.
Manson, Samuel, Sergt. Co. H 8th O.
V. I.
Miller, Bert, Pr. Co. H 8th O. V. I.
Miller, Henry N., Corp. Co. H 8th O.
V. I.
Miller, Peter E., 1st Sergt. Co. H 8th
O. V. I.
Mohn, Alva V., Corp. Co. H 8th O.
V. I.
Morrison, Herbert, Corp. Co. H 8th
O. V. I.
Robison, Bert D., Sergt. Co. H 8th
O. V. I.
Robison, Walter, Pr. Co. H 8th O.V.I.
Smith, William F., Pr. Co. H 8th O.
V. I.
Weiker, Leonard L., Artificer Co. H
8th O. V. I.
Young, John A., Artificer Co. L 8th
O. V. I.

SIDNEY

Ackerly, George, Pr. Co L 3rd O.V.I.
Bush, DeWitt S., Pr. Co. L 3rd O.V.I.
Carey, Jason, Pr. Co. L 3rd O. V. I.
Deveny, William B., Pr. Co. L 3rd O.
V. I.
Dunnavant, William T., Pr. Co. L 3rd
O. V. I.
Eberle, William F., Pr. Co. L 3rd O.
V. I.
Edgar, Ferd. S., Pr. Co. L 3rd O.V.I.
Elliott, Ervin A., Pr. Co. L 3rd O.
V. I.
Flinn, Eayre D., Pr. Co. L 3rd O.V.I.
Frazier. Jesse L., 3rd Sergt. Co. L 3rd
O. V. I.
Frey, Chris. J., Pr. Co. L 3rd O.V.I.
Gilfillan, William W., Pr. Co. L 3rd
O. V. I.
Ginn, Robert W., Pr. Co. L 3rd O.
V. I.
Haines, Eayre R., Pr. Co. L 3rd O.
V. I.
Haines, George D., Pr. Co. L 3rd O.
V. I.
Heiges, Ralph S., Pr. Co. I 3rd O.
V. I.
Huffman, Albert B., Pr. Co. L 3rd O.
V. I.
Hussey, Frank M., 4th Sergt. Co. L
3rd O. V. I.
Hussey, Weber A., Pr. Co. L 3rd O.
V. I.
Kah, Arthur W., 5th Sergt. Co. L 3rd
O. V. I.

Kah, Harland E., Musician Co L 3rd
O. V. I.
Kendall, Elmer R., Corp. Co. L 3rd
O. V. I.
Kraft, Louis P., Corp. Co. L 3rd O.
V. I.
Lewis, George W., Pr. Co. L 3rd O.
V. I.
Longanecker, John, Pr. Co. L 3rd O.
V. I.
McCullough, Benjamin, 2nd Sergt. Co.
L 3rd O. V. I.
McHenry, John R., Pr. Co. L 3rd O.
V. I.
McVay, Frank, Pr. Co. L 3rd O. V. I.
Miller, Harry J., Pr. Co. L 3rd O.V.I.
Morton, George H., Pr. Co. L 3rd O.
V. I.
Motsinger, Roy B., Pr. Co. L 3rd O.
V. I.
Neal, Harry S., Pr. Co. L 3rd O.V.I.
Orbison, James, Corp. Co. L 3rd O.
V. I.
Parcher, Walter H., Pr. Co. L 3rd O.
V. I.
Reiger, Joseph, Pr. Co. L 3rd O. V. I.
Rostron, William R., Pr Co. L 3rd O.
V. I.
Royon, J. Charles, Musician Co. L 3rd
O. V. I.
Sarver, Emery C., Pr. Co. L 3rd O.
V. I.
Sarver, William G., Wagoner Co. L
3rd O. V. I.

Stang, John, Pr. Co. L 3rd O. V. I.
Struckmann, Julius W., Pr. Co. L 3rd
O. V. I.
Talbot, Asby G., Artificer Co. L 3rd
O. V. I.
Toller, John, Jr., Pr. Co. L 3rd O.V.I.
Van DeGrift, Robert C., Corp. Co. L
3rd O. V. I.
Wagner, Albert W., Pr. Co. L 3rd O.
V. I.
Weaver, A. Todd, Pr. Co. L 3rd O.
V. I.
Wikoff, Dan B., Pr. Co. L 3rd O.V.I.

Wiley, Benjamin C., Pr. Co. L 3rd O.
V. I.
Williams, Adolphus O., Pr. Co. L 3rd
O. V. I.
Williams, Melvin T., Corp. Co. L 3rd
O. V. I.
Wilson, J. Cliffe, Q. M. Sergt. Co. L
3rd O. V. I.
Wilson, Jesse C., 1st Sergt. Co. L 3rd
O. V. I.
Wright, Freeman, Pr. Co. L 3rd O.
V. I.

SMITHS FERRY, PA.

Hamilton, Clyde S., Pr. Co. B 10th O. V. I.

SMITHVILLE

Starn, Homer H., Pr. Co. G 2nd O. V. I.

SONORA

Doty, Thomas W., Pr. Co. L 10th O.
V. I.
Hina, Charles A., Pr. Co. L 10th O.
V. I.

Varner, Otto B., Pr. Co. L 10th O.
V. I.

SOUTH BEND, IND.

Henderson, William E., Pr. Co. D 9th Batt. O. V. I.

SOUTH BLOOMINGVILLE

Rose, William W., Pr. Co. K 7th O. V. I.

SOUTH CHARLESTON

Florence, William J., Corp. Co. E 3rd
O. V. I.
Moorman, Wilbur M., Pr. Co. A 2nd
U. S. V. E.

Penny, Samuel H., Pr. Co. D 3rd O.
V. I.
Scarff, James C., Pr. Co. A 2nd U. S.
V. E.

SOUTH POINT

Hastings, Lawson D., Pr. Co. I 7th O. V. I.

SOUTH SALEM

Duggleby, John W., Pr. Co. K 7th O.
V. I.

Lumbeck, Frank R., Pr. Co. K 7th O.
V. I.

SOUTH SOLON

Curry, Benjamin F., Pr. Co. E 3rd O.
V. I.
Fout, Zeph, Pr. Co. E 3rd O. V. I.
Hartman, George, Pr. Co. E 3rd O.
V. I

Moon, Morgan, Pr. Co. E 3rd O. V. I.
Morris, Samuel A., Pr. Co. E 3rd O.
V. I.
Richardson, James H., Pr. Co. E 3rd
O. V. I.

SOUTH ZANESVILLE

Pearson, Frank, Pr. Co. L 10th O.V.I.

SPARTA

Dyer, Ward B., Pr. Co. I 8th O. V. I.
Orshorn, David Grant, Pr. Co. B 4th
O. V. I.

White, Cary B., Pr. Co. B 4th O. V. I.

SPICY

Blake, Ansel T., Pr. Co. C 7th O.V.I.

Mooney, William H., Pr. Co. C 7th
O. V. I.

SPRINGFIELD

Addelsberger, Bernard, Pr. Co. E 10th
O. V. I.
Allen, Pearl, Musician Co. B 3rd O.
V. I.
Alexander, Elmer, Pr. Co. E 10th O.
V. I.
Alexander, Louis B., Pr. Co. B 3rd
O. V. I.
Amos, James E., Pr. Co. A 2nd U. S.
V. E.
Anderson, Henry Pr. Co. A 9th Batt.
O. V. I.
Atkinson, Charles, Pr. Co. E 10th O.
V. I.
Bahin, James F., Pr. Co. B 3rd O.V.I.
Baker, John H., Pr. Co. E 10th O.V.I.
Bakhaus, Carl V., Pr. Co. E 10th O.
V. I.
Bakhaus, Eugene B., Corp. Co. A 2nd
U. S. V. E.
Bakhaus, William C., Sergt. Co. A 2nd
U. S. V. E.
Bailey, William M., Pr. Co. A 9th Batt.
O. V. I.
Ballentine, Richard W., Pr. Co. A 2nd
U. S. V. E.
Bateman, Brer. O., Corp. Co. A 2nd
U. S. V. E.
Benfold, John C., Pr. U. R. 3rd O.V.I.
Berkshire, William A., Pr. Co. A 9th
Batt. O. V. I.
Bevitt, Edwin D., Pr. Co. E 10th O.V.I.
Bevitt, Sidney H., Q. M. Sergt. Co. E
10th O. V. I.
Black, Joseph W., Pr. Co. B 3rd O.
V. I.
Boland, Frank, Pr. Co. E 10th O. V. I.
Bonnsler, Curvil, Corp. Co. A 9th Batt.
O. V. I.
Bowman, Leo F., Pr. Co. A 9th Batt.
O. V. I.
Brautner, Thaddeus H., Corp. Co. B
3rd O. V. I.
Bratton, Edward A., Musician Co. B
3rd O. V. I.
Bright, Wilson, Pr. Co. A 9th Batt.
O. V. I.
Brown, John, Pr. Co. E 10th O. V. I.
Bryan, John B., Pr. Co. E 10th O.V.I.
Budd, Bert M., Artificer Co. B 3rd
O. V. I.
Budd, Charles F., Pr. Co. E 10th O.
V. I.

Bumgardner, Clifford H., Pr. Co. H
3rd O. V. I.
Burton, Curtis J., Hospital Steward
3rd O. V. I.
Cadugan, Clarence, Pr. Co. B 3rd O.
V. I.
Caliman, Aloah Moses, Pr. Co. A 9th
Batt. O. V. I.
Carpenter, Albert H., Pr. Co. E 10th
O. V. I.
Carr, Harry E., Pr. Co. B 3rd O.V.I.
Castin, John, Pr. Co. A 2nd U.S.V.E.
Castle, Orie O., Corp. Co. E 10th O.
V. I.
Clair, Phillip, Pr. Co. E 10th O. V. I.
Clark, Ezra T., Corp. Co. B 3rd O.
V. I.
Clark, John W., Pr. Co. E 10th O.V.I.
Clark, Samuel B., Pr. Co. B 3rd O.
V. I.
Clark, William H., Pr. Co. E 10th O.
V. I.
Clayton, James D., Pr. Co. A 2nd U.
S. V. E.
Clouse, George W., Pr. Co. E 10th O.
V. I.
Collier, Daniel Clyde, Pr. Co. A 9th
Batt. O. V. I.
Compton, Earl E., Pr. U. R. 3rd O.
V. I.
Conley, George A., Pr. Co. A 9th Batt.
O. V. I.
Cook, Charles, Pr. Co. E 10th O. V. I.
Conrad, Charles V., Pr. Co. B 3rd O.
V. I.
Conrad, Hollis C., Pr. Co. B 3rd O.
V. I.
Craig, Samuel S., Pr Co. A 9th Batt.
O. V. I.
Craver, Paul G., Pr. Tr. D 1st O.V.C.
Crouder, Harry, Pr. Co. A 9th Batt.
O. V. I.
Curry, Clarence, Corp. Co. A 9th Batt.
O. V. I.
Curry, Newton H., Pr. Co. A 9th Batt.
O. V. I.
Dalrymple, Charles E., Pr. Co. E 10th
O. V. I.
Day, William, Pr. Co. B 3rd O. V. I.
Dillahunt, Charles A., Corp. Co. E 10th
O. V. I.
Dillow, James F., Pr. Co. E 10th O.
V. I.

Dudley, William, Pr. Co. A 9th Batt. O. V. I.
Earnest, Robert A., Corp. Co. E 10th O. V. I.
Eaton, William H., Pr. Co. E 10th O. V. I.
Ebert, Frank P., Pr. Co. C 3rd O.V.I.
Eccles, William, Corp. Co. E 10th O. V. I.
Ecton, Charles, Pr. Co. A 9th Batt. O. V. I.
Ely, John S., Sergt. Co. A 2nd U. S. V. E.
Ernest, Fred. Pr. Co. D 3rd O. V. I.
Eslick, Pearl, Pr. Co. A 9th Batt. O. V. I.
Evans, Thomas J., Pr. Co. H 3rd O. V. I.
Fanning, Alfred M., Corp. Co. E 10th O. V. I.
Fay, Charles A., Bat. Sergt. Maj. 3rd O. V. I.
Fields, Julius, Corp. Co. A 9th Batt. O. V. I.
Filbert, Ezra K., Sergt. Co. B 3rd O. V. I.
Finney, Samuel, Pr. Co. E 10th O.V.I.
Fleming, John H., Pr. Co. E 10th O. V. I.
Folk, Charles, Corp. Co. E 10th O. V. I.
Folk, Herbert M., Pr. Co. E 10th O. V. I.
Frantz, Dore M., Pr. Co. E 10th O. V. I.
Frey, Edward, Corp. Co. A 9th Batt. O. V. I.
Frye, Charles E., 1st Sergt. Co. A 9th Batt. O. V. I.
Fulmer, Walter S., Pr. Co. E 10th O. V. I.
Gable, Roy F., Corp. Co. E 10th O. V. I.
Gebhardt, Edward, Pr. Co. B 3rd O. V. I.
Grant, Harry G., Pr. Co. A 3rd O.V.I.
Green, John W., Artificer Co. A 9th Batt. O. V. I.
Greene, Edwin C., Pr. Co. G 3rd O. V. I.
Grinnell, Bernard, Pr. Co. E 10th O. V. I.
Gurnell, John W., Pr. Co. A 9th Batt. O. V. I.
Hall, William, Sergt. Co. A 9th Batt. O. V. I.
Harley, William G., Pr. Co. E 10th O. V. I.
Harphant, William A., Pr. Co. B 3rd O. V. I.
Harrison, Edward, Pr. Co. A 9th Batt. O. V. I.
Harvey, Solomon A., Sergt. Co. A 9th Batt. O. V. I.
Harwood, Fred H., Q. M. Sergt. 10th O. V. I.

Hayward, Pearl P., Q. M. Sergt. Co. A 3rd O. V. I.
Henderson, Clifford, Pr. Co. A 9th Batt. O. V. I.
Hensel, John H., Pr. Tr. D 1st O V.C.
Henthorn, Charles F., Corp. Co. E 10th O. V. I.
Herzog, Peter, Musician, Co. E 10th O. V. I.
Hill, Harry E., Pr. Co. A 2nd U. S. V. E.
Hildebrandt, Guy, Pr. Co. B 3rd O. V. I.
Hoffer, Frank L., Pr. Co. B 3rd O. V. I.
Hohl, Wilbur John, Corp. Co. E 10th O. V. I.
Hollenbeck, Clarence M., Pr. Co. H 3rd O. V. I.
Hoover, James, Pr. Co. E 10th O.V.I.
Hoppings, James, Pr. Co. E 10th O. V. I.
Huffman, George W., Pr. Co. B 3rd O. V. I.
Hughes, Milton, Pr. Co. E 10th O.V.I.
Humbarger, Edgar M., Corp. Co. E 10th O. V. I.
Humphrey, Arthur N., Musician Co. E 10th O. V. I.
Hunt, Frank R., Pr. Co. B 3rd O. V. I.
Hupman, Harry R., Corp. Co. D 3rd O. V. I.
Iliff, Harry S., Pr. Co. A 2nd U. S. V. E.
Jackson, David, Musician Co. A 9th Batt. O. V. I.
Jackson, Henry L., Corp. Co. A 9th Batt. O. V. I.
Jackson, William A., Sergt. Co. A 9th Batt. O. V. I.
James, Oakley, Pr. Co. B 3rd O. V. I.
Jones, William A., Pr. Co. E 10th O. V. I.
Kauffman, Owen A., Corp. Co. F 3rd O. V. I.
Kennedy, Charles E., Sergt. Co. B 3rd O. V. I.
King, Lester, Pr. Co. E 10th O. V. I.
King, Oliver J., Pr. Co. B 3rd O V.I.
King, Wesley E., Pr. Co. E 10th O. V. I.
Kitchen, Zade E., Pr. Co. B 3rd O. V. I.
Knecht, Walter P., Corp. Co. B 3rd O. V. I.
Kruft, Benjamin A., Pr. Co. E 10th O. V. I.
Laine, Thomas J., Pr. Co. B 3rd O. V. I.
Lattridge, George M., Pr. Co. A 2nd U. S. V. E.
Lee, Samuel R. W., Corp. Co. A 9th Batt. O. V. I.
Little, Daniel E., Pr. Co. E 10th O.V.I.
Liverpool, Lincoln, Pr. Co. A 9th Batt. O. V. I.

Livingston, Mark M., Hospital Steward 3rd O. V. I.
Lock, Samuel M., Pr. Co. E 10th O.V.I.
Logan, James W., Pr. Co. A 9th Batt. O. V. I.
Long, Aaron H., Pr. Co. E 10th O. V. I.
Luce, William, Pr. Co. E 10th O.V.I.
Magnett, William, Pr. Co. E 10th O. V. I.
Martin, Emmit L., Pr. Co. A 9th Batt. O. V. I.
Martin, Henry, Pr. Co. E 10th O. V. I.
Maxwell, James F., Pr. Co. B 3rd O. V. I.
McAdoo, Victor W., Pr. Co. A 9th Batt. O. V. I.
McCollum, Lester, Pr. Co. B 3rd O. V. I.
McConnell, James N., Sergt. Co. E 10th O. V. I.
McCuddy, James W., 1st Sergt. Co. B 3rd O. V. I.
Meisner, Fred C., Pr. Co. B 3rd O. V. I.
Mitchell, Harry K., Pr. Co. E 10th O. V. I.
Mitman, Reuben A., Corp. Co. E 10th O. V. I.
Moody, William, Pr. Co. A 9th Batt. O. V. I.
Moffett, Howard, Pr. Co. B 3rd O. V. I.
Moore, Earl A., Wagoner Co. B 3rd O. V. I.
Moore, Robert T., Pr. Co. B 3rd O. V. I.
Morris, Henry K., Corp. Co. E 10th O. V. I.
Myers, George W., Pr. Co. A 9th Batt. O. V. I.
Myers, William M., Pr. Co. B 3rd O. V. I
Nagel, Larry, Wagoner Co. E 10th O. V. I.
Neeley, Peter W., Musician Co. A 2nd U. S. V. E.
Neill, Frank W., Pr. Co. A 2nd U. S. V. E.
Netts, Charles L., Sergt. Co. E 10th O. V. I.
Netts, Robert I., Sergt. Co. E 10th O. V. I.
Odenthal, Albert, Pr. Co. A 2nd U. S. V. E.
Osborn, Charles R., Pr. Tr. D 1st O. V. C.
Pensinger, Daniel S., Pr. Co. B 3rd O. V. I.
Perry, John S., Pr. Co. E 10th O. V. I.
Powell, James, Pr. Co. A 9th Batt. O. V. I.
Powell, John M., Sergt. Co. B 3rd O. V. I.
Puckridge, Bert, Pr. Co. E 10th O. V. I.

Randall, Charles E., Sergt. Co. E 10th O. V. I.
Reynolds, Grant, Pr. Co. B 3rd O.V.I.
Rhodes, Irvin A., Pr. Co. E 10th O. V. I.
Richardson, John D., Pr. Co. A 9th Batt. O. V. I.
Ridgely, F. Byron, Pr. Co. B 3rd O. V. I.
Riebold, Louis R., Pr. Co. B 3rd O. V. I.
Riley, William, Pr. Co. E 10th O.V.I.
Rinehart, David C., Pr. Co. B 3rd O. V. I.
Roberts, Gracen, Pr. Co. A 9th Batt. O. V. I.
Robinson, Joseph, Pr. Co. E 10th O. V. I.
Robinson, Robert, Pr. Co. A 9th Batt. O. V. I.
Rogers, Thomas J., Pr. Co. A 9th Batt. O. V. I.
Roller, Oliver I., Pr. Co. E 10th O. V. I.
Rotsel, Fred C., Pr. Co. B 3rd O.V.I.
Rudd, Benjamin F., Sergt. Co. A 9th Batt. O. V. I.
Russell, John S., Pr. Co. C 3rd O.V.I.
Russell, Joseph K., Pr. Co. E 10th O. V. I.
Rust, William F., Pr. Co. E 10th O. V. I.
Scherschmidt, Charley, Pr. Co. E 10th O. V. I.
Schoenthal, Alexander J., Pr. Co. B 3rd O. V. I.
Scruggs, Charles J., Pr. Co. B 3rd O. V. I.
Serfass, Charles R., Pr. Co. B 8th O. V. I.
Shewalter, Wilbur E., Pr. U. R. 3rd O. V. I.
Shingledecker, Harry, Pr. Co. E 10th O. V. I.
Shultz, Elmer C., Pr. Co. E 10th O. V. I.
Skinner, Cornelius S., Pr. Co. E 10th O. V. I.
Simeral, William, Pr. Co. B 3rd O. V. I.
Singleton, Archie R., Pr. Co. A 9th Batt. O. V. I.
Small, Lester, Pr. Co. E 10th O. V. I.
Smith, Azel M., Pr. Co E 10th O. V. I.
Smith, Charles H., Pr. Co. A 9th Batt. O. V. I.
Smith, David W., Pr. Co E 10th O. V. I.
Smith, Elmer, Pr. Co. E 10th O. V. I.
Smith, George L., Sergt. Co. B 3rd O. V. I.
Smith, George S., Pr. Co. B 3rd O. V. I.
Smith, Henry D., 1st Sergt. Co. E 10th O. V. I.
Smith, John, Pr. Co. A 9th Batt. O.V.I.
Snyder, Fred, Pr. Co. M 3rd O. V. I.

Soliday, L. Harry, Pr. Co. B 3rd O. V. I.

Sommerville, Floyd E., Pr. Co. E 10th O. V. I.

Speaks, William, Pr. Co. A 9th Batt. O. V. I.

Spillman, James A., Wagoner Co. A 9th Batt. O. V. I.

Spitler, William E., Pr. Co. B 3rd O. V. I.

Stabner, George, Pr. Co. E 10th O.V.I.

Startzman, Harry R., Corp. Co. B 3rd O. V. I.

Stevens, Ernest, Pr. Co. E 10th O.V.I.

Stewart, Edmund W., Pr. Co. B 3rd O. V. I.

Stewart, James, Pr. Co A 9th Batt. O. V. I.

Stine, Harry W., Pr. Co. A 2nd U. S. V. E.

Stockle, Clarence, Pr. Co. E 10th O. V. I.

Stratthan, Frank L., Corp. Co. A 2nd U. S. V. E.

Swartz, Charles A., Pr. Co. B 3rd O. V. I.

Taylor, Edward B., Pr. Co. B 3rd O. V. I.

Taylor, Richard, Pr. Co. A 9th Batt. O. V. I.

Teach, Manford S., Artificer Co. E 10th O. V. I.

Temple, Calvin W., Q. M. Sergt. Co. B 3rd O. V. I.

Thalls, Clyde, Pr. Co. E 10th O. V. I.

Turner, Charles, Pr. Co. A 9th Batt. O. V. I.

Valentine, Henry B., Pr. Co. A 9th Batt. O. V. I.

Vester, Carl E., Pr. Co. E 10th O.V.I.

Ward, James E., Pr. Co. E 10th O. V. I.

Webb, J. Henry, Pr. Co. B 3rd O.V.I.

Weber, Edward A., Pr. Co. D 3rd O. V. I.

Webster, William A., Corp. Co. A 2nd U. S. V. E.

White, James M., Pr. Co. A 9th Batt. O. V. I.

Whetsel, William O., Pr. Co. A 9th Batt. O. V. I.

Wilborn, David, Sergt. Co. A 9th Batt. O. V. I.

Williams, Edward, Pr. Co. A 9th Batt. O. V. I.

Wilson, Robert G., Pr. Co. B 3rd O. V. I.

Wilson, Van C., Pr. Co. B 3rd O.V.I.

Wingert, Frank O., Pr. Co. E 10th O. V. I.

Wingert, Sidney, Pr. Co. E 10th O. V. I.

Winkey, William, Pr. Co. A 2nd U. S. V. E.

Wolf, Ottis E., Corp. Co. B 3rd O.V.I.

Wood, George McIntire, Pr Co. E 10th O. V. I.

Wright, Dennis, Pr. Co. B 3rd O.V.I.

Yeazel, Paul R., Pr. Co. E 10th O.V.I.

Zimmerman, Roy G., Pr. Co. L 3rd O. V. I.

SPRING HILL

Pheneger, Jeptha W., Pr. U. R. 3rd O. V. I.

STATE OF IOWA

Jones, Stephen, Pr. Co. D 9th Batt. O. V. I.

ST. BERNARD

Apking, Phillip, Pr. Co. C 2nd U. S. V. E.

STELVIDEO

Coppess, Ray, Pr. Co. C 3rd O. V. I.
Hayes, Elmer E., Pr. Co. C 3rd O.V.I.
Shafer, William, Pr. Co. C 3rd O.V.I.

Sheets, Hiram T., Pr. Co. C 3rd O. V. I.

STEUBEN

Hodges, Clinton C., Pr. Co. G 5th O. V. I.

ST. MARYS

Adams, Marion R., Pr. Co. L 2nd O. V. I.

Agenbroad, Henry M., Pr. Co. L 2nd O. V. I.

Aschoff, Max, Pr. Co. L 2nd O. V. I.

Buxton, Russel D., Pr. Co. L 2nd O. V. I.

Day, Roy, Pr. Co. L 2nd O. V. I.

Hollman, Ferdinand E., Pr. Co. L 2nd. O. V. I.

Kreutzman, Edward, Pr. Co. L 2nd O. V. I.
Peckham, William C., Pr. Co. L 2nd O. V. I.

Ruther, Tony, Pr. Co. L 2nd O. V. I.
Sifert, Henry B., Pr. Co. L 2nd O.V.I.
Stewart, William E., Pr. Co. L 2nd O. V. I.

STRASBURGH

Rearick, Rutherford B., Pr. Co. A 10th O. V. I.

STRYKER

Kennedy, Albert R., Pr. Co. E 6th O. V. I.

Taylor, Elwin E., Pr. Co. E 6th O. V. I.

SULLIVAN

Gibson, Louis R., Pr. Co. C 8th O. V. I.

Spencer, John E., Pr. Co. C 8th O. V. I.

SUMMERFORD

Cleary, John F., Pr. Co. E 3rd O.V.I.
Kelly, Eugene, Pr. Co. E 3rd O.V.I.

Markley, John A., Pr. Co. E 3rd O. V. I.

SUNBURY

Schrock, Fred C., Pr. Co. F 4th O. V. I.

SWANTON

Hood, Frederick, Pr. Co. E 6th O.V.I.

Scott, David A., Pr. Co. G 6th O. V. I.

SYRACUSE, N. Y.

Roe, Benjamin S., Pr. Co. K 10th O. V. I.

SYCAMORE

Brown, Fay W., Pr. Co. A 8th O.V.I.
Emerson, Guy P., Pr. Co. A 8th O. V. I.

Hayman, Roy H., Pr. Co. A 8th O. V. I.

SYRACUSE

* Bailey, Samuel E., Pr. Co. C 7th O. V. I.

THOMPSON

Whitney, Frank W., Pr. Co. M 5th O. V. I.

THIVENER

Notter, Lewis A., Pr. Co. C 7th O. V. I.

THORNPORT

McCandlish, William N., Pr. Co. K 7th O. V. I.

Welsh, James A., Pr. Co. K 7th O. V. I.

THORNVILLE

Baker, Edward G., Corp. Co. K 7th O. V. I.

Orr, Clarence E., Pr. Co. K 7th O. V. I.

Parrett, William A., Pr. Co. K 7th O. V. I.

Rousculp, Reno B., 4th Sergt. Co. K 7th O. V. I.

Spangler, Frank H., Pr. Co. K 7th O. V. I.

Witmer, Galenus D., Pr. Co. K 7th O. V. I.

THURMAN

· Morgon, Charlie R., Pr. Co. C 7th O. V. I.

TIFFIN

Abbott, William S., Pr. Co. E 2nd O. V. I.

Adams, Harry B., Pr. Co. E 2nd O. V. I.

Barbean, Louis G., Pr. Co. E 2nd O. V. I.

Benner, Ernest E., Pr. Co. E 2nd O. V. I.

Bigger, Paul B., Pr. Co. E 2nd O.V.I.

Brown, John C., 2nd Sergt. Co. E 2nd O. V. I.

Buell, Clark H., Pr. Co. E 2nd O.V.I.

Chandler, Myron H., Pr. Co. E 2nd O. V. I.

Clevidence, Claude C., Pr. Co. E 2nd O. V. I.

Crocker, Edward, Sergt. Co. E 2nd O. V. I.

Daywalt, William E., Corp. Co. E 2nd O. V. I.

Deisler, Harley M., Pr. Co. E 2nd O. V. I.

Demarest, Raymond E., Band Leader 2nd O. V. I.

Dildine, Charles G., Pr. Co. E 2nd O. V. I.

Drake, William R., Pr. Co. E 2nd O. V. I.

Faulkner, Charles L., Pr. Co. E 2nd O. V. I.

Flint, Frank, Pr. Co. E 2nd O. V. I.

Frost, Frank L., Pr. Co. E 2nd O.V.I.

Geyer, Arthur, Pr. Co. E 2nd O. V. I.

Grubb, Philip, Sergt. Co. E 2nd O.V.I.

Grummel, Frank J., Pr. Co. E 2nd O. O. V. I.

Guss, Frank W., Sergt. Co. E 2nd O. V. I.

Hammond, William B., Pr. Co. E 2nd O. V. I.

Harshman, Harvey N., Pr. Co. E 2nd O. V. I.

Hasson, Lee R., Pr. Co. E 2nd O.V.I.

Hoffman, Marion G., Pr. Co. E 2nd O. V. I.

Irwin, Charles R., Pr. Co. E 2nd O. V. I.

Jolley, Charles L., Pr. Co. E 2nd O. V. I.

Jones, Charles W., Jr., Corp. Co. E 2nd O. V. I.

Kemp, Loyd N., Pr. Co. E 2nd O. V. I.

Koff, Charles Jacob, Pr. Co. E 2nd O. V. I.

Lauer, Charles, Corp. Co. E 2nd O. V. I.

Lott, Howard A., Pr. Co. E 2nd O. V. I.

Magers, Joseph W., Pr. Co. E 2nd O. V. I.

McCluskey, Harry L., Pr. Co. E 2nd O. V. I.

McCormick, Carl P., Pr. Co. E 2nd O. V. I.

McCormick, Edward E., Pr. Co. E 2nd O. V. I.

McFarland, J. Barnum, Pr. Co. E 2nd O. V. I.

McManigal, Artie E., Pr. Co. E 2nd O. V. I.

Meligh, Harry N., Pr. Co. E 2nd O. V. I.

Messer, Parker W., Pr. Co. E 2nd O. V. I.

Pease, Ward T., Corp. Co. E 2nd O. V. I.

Perrine, Hugh R., Pr. Co. E 2nd O. V. I.

Plattenburg, Pearl, Pr. Co. E 2nd O. V. I.

Pope, Arthur E., Pr. Co. E 2nd O. V. I.

Ready, William E., Pr. Co. E 2nd O. V. I.

Rosenbarger, Elmer H., Pr. Co. E 2nd O. V. I.

Schumaker, Otto C., Pr. Co. E 2nd O. V. I.

Shankland, James W., Pr. Co. E 2nd O. V. I.

Smith, Charles J., Corp. Co. E 2nd O. V. I.

Smith, Herman N., Pr. Co. E 2nd O. V. I.

Stiner, Verne L., Hospital Steward 2nd O. V. I.

Strauss, Charles, Sergt. Co. E 2nd O. V. I.

Unger, Walter H., Pr. Co. E 2nd O. V. I.

Welter, Henry D., 1st Sergt. Co. E 2nd O. V. I.
Wengert, George F., Pr. Co. E 2nd O. V. I.
Wentz, Ralph B., Pr. Co. E 2nd O. V. I.

Woodward, Jay, Pr. Co. E 2nd O.V.I.
Yingling, Tobias R., Pr. Co. E 2nd O. V. I.
Yingst, Harry L., Corp. Co. E 2nd O. V. I.

TIMBERVILLE

Hill, Frank H., Pr. Co. A 8th O. V. I.

TIPTON

Lee, James W., Pr. Co. M 2nd O.V.I.

Sailor, Louis A., Pr. Co. M 2nd O. V. I.

TIRO

Coleman, George O., Pr. Co. A 8th O. V. I.
Davis, Avery E., Sergt. Co. G 5th O. V. I.

Lautsbaugh, Edward W., Pr. Co. G 5th O. V. I.
Trumbull, Roscoe A., Pr. Co. A 8th O. V. I.

TOBOSO

Baird, Grandason A., Pr. Co. G 7th O. V. I.
McFarland, Edward R., Q. M. Sergt. Co. G 7th O. V. I.

Shepherd, Orrie V., Pr. Co. G 7th O. V. I.

TOLEDO

Abraham, Harry, Pr. Co. H 6th O.V.I.
Abshire, Millard H., Pr. Co. C 6th O. V. I.
Achinger, George J., Pr. Co. C 6th O. V. I.
Albright, Harry L., Pr. Co. B 5th O. V. I.
Albritton, Fred L., Pr. Co. K 6th O. V. I.
Ammon, Henry W., Pr. Co. H 6th O. V. I.
Anderson, Phillip M., Pr. Co. H 6th O. V. I.
Ashley, Harry F., Pr. Co. I 6th O.V.I.
Ashley, John J., Pr. Co. H 10th O. V. I.
Austin, Harry R., Pr. Co. H 6th O. V. I.
Baker, Arthur L., Pr. Co. H 10th O. V. I.
Baker, Henry, Pr. Co. C 6th O. V. I.
Balbach, Henry, Pr. Co. C 6th O.V.I.
Barhite, Donald F., Pr. Co. D 10th O. V. I.
Barnhiser, Frank M., Pr. Tr. E 1st O. V. C.
Barnhiser, Robert C., Pr. Co. H 10th O. V. I.
Baron, Roger E., Pr. Co. C 6th O.V.I.
Barrett, Armon, Pr. Co. G 10th O.V.I.
Barror, Albert O., Pr. Co. H 10th O. V. I.
Bassett, William J., Pr. Tr. E 1st O. V. C.

Baumgardner, Frederick M., Sergt. Maj. 6th O. V. I.
Beat, John S., Sergt. Co. H 6th O. V. I.
Beck, George H., Pr. Co. L 6th O.V.I.
Beckman, John C., Corp. Co. C 6th O. V. I.
Beebe, Otto E., Artificer Co. A 6th O. V. I.
Beese, Fred, Corp. Co. C 6th O. V. I.
Beier, Albert, Wagoner Co. A 6th O. V. I.
Bell, Renick M., Pr. Co. L 6th O.V.I.
Bennett, Joseph C., Pr. Co. L 6th O. V. I.
Bigelow, Charles H., Pr. Tr. E 1st O. V. C.
Bigelow, John W., Pr. Tr. E 1st O. V. C.
Bigelow, Louis H., Pr. Co. D 10th O. V. I.
Bird, Henry T., Pr. Co. D 10th O.V.I.
Bishop, James A., Pr. Co. L 6th O. V. I.
Bissler, George L., Pr. Co. H 6th O. V. I.
Blackman, De Witt W., Pr. Co. G 10th O. V. I.
Blainey, James A., Corp. Co. D 10th O. V. I.
Blanchard, William P., Pr. Co. A 6th O. V. I.
Blankley, Andrew J., Artificer Co. H 6th O. V. I.

Bleher, John A., Pr. Co. A 6th O.V.I.
Blohm, John C., Corp. Co. D 10th O. V. I.
Bocck, Peter, Pr. Co. D 10th O. V. I.
Bonkuske, Keiser, Pr. Co. C 6th O. V. I.
Borchardt, Carl J., Pr. Co. A 6th O. V. I.
Bossard, Fred E., Sergt. Co. H 10th O. V. I.
Bott, Joseph G., Pr. Co. H 10th O.V.I.
Bowes, John, Pr. Co. D 10th O. V. I.
Bowman, George, Pr. Co. D 10th O. V. I.
Brandt, Oscar T. D., Pr. Co. G 6th O. V. I.
Bridenbaugh, George E., Pr. Tr. E 1st O. V. C.
Broer, Benjamin F., Pr. Co. D 10th O. V. I.
Brillmann, Frank J., Pr. Co. H 6th O. V. I.
Brower, Homer F., Pr. Co. H 6th O. V. I.
Brown, Dan. A., Pr. Tr. E 1st O.V.C.
Brown, Edward L., Pr. Tr. E 1st O. V C
Brown, Gordon L., Pr. Co. L 6th O. V. I.
Brown, Siloam G., Pr. Co. H 10th O. V. I.
Bryant, William L., Pr. Tr. E 1st O. V. C.
Buchert, Joseph C., Pr. Co. C 6th O. V. I.
Buck, Charles, Pr. Tr. E 1st O. V. C.
Burch, Arthur P., Corp. Co. H 10th O. V. I.
Burgess, Philip E., Corp. Co. L 6th O. V. I.
Burkard, Peter Lucas, Pr. Co. D 10th O. V. I.
Burry, Charles A., Pr. Co. C 6th O. V. I.
Burtless, Frank F., Pr. Co. A 6th O. V. I.
Burwick, John C., Pr. Co. A 6th O. V. I.
Butler, Carlton R., Corp. Co. G 10th O. V. I.
Caldwell, Charles C., Pr. Co. A 6th O. V. I.
Callahan, Cornelius J., Corp. Co. C 6th O. V. I.
Callard, Lyman W., Sergt. Co. G 10th O. V. I.
Campbell, Alexander D., 1st Sergt. Co. C 6th O. V. I.
Campbell, Charles, Pr. Co. G 10th O. V. I.
Canby, Ernest L., Pr. Co. G 10th O. V. I.
Carey, Elmer, Pr. Co. L 6th O. V. I.
Carragher, John, Artificer Co. D 10th O. V. I.
Carter, William, Pr. Co. D 9th Batt. O. V. I.

Cassaday, William N., Pr. Co. L 6th O. V. I.
Casseday, Albert J., Pr. Co. A 6th O. V. I.
Champion, Llewellyn E., Pr. Co. I 6th O. V. I.
Chandler, Orin M., Pr. Co. D 10th O. V. I.
Chapman, Thomas M., Pr. Co. L 6th O. V. I.
Chapman, William B., 1st Sergt. Co. G 10th O. V. I.
Chevalier, William W., Pr. Co. H 10th O. V. I.
Chirmer, Henry F., Pr. Co. G 10th O. V. I.
Chollett, Burt G., Pr. Co. A 6th O. V. I.
Christ, Frank A., Corp. Co. H 6th O. V. I.
Close, Lee M., Pr. Co. L 6th O. V. I.
Coakley, John J., Pr. Co. D 10th O. V. I.
Cohen, William R., Corp. Co. G 10th O. V. I.
Colcleugh, William J., Pr. Co. H 10th O. V. I.
Coldwell, James A., Pr. Co. A 6th O. V. I.
Connors, Michael J., Pr. Co. H 10th O. V. I.
Conrad, Ross E., Pr. Co. H 6th O.V.I.
Conroy, William J., Pr. Co. L 6th O. V. I.
Conway, John J., Pr. Co. H 6th O. V. I.
Cook, Lewis L., Pr. Co. C 6th O. V. I.
Cooke, Claude, Pr. Tr. E 1st O.V.C.
Cooley, William S., Pr. Co. H 6th O. V. I.
Copeland, Willie T., Pr. Co. C 6th O. V. I.
Corwin, Thomas E., Musician Co. L 6th O. V. I.
Crabbs, William E., Pr. Co. L 6th O. V. I.
Crandall, Hal. B., Pr. Co. D 10th O. V. I.
Crandall, Walter S., Corp. Co. D 10th O. V. I.
Crause, Walter H., Pr. Co. G 10th O. V. I.
Creighton, William F., Wagoner Co. H 6th O. V. I.
Croke, William C., Pr. Co. H 6th O. V. I.
Crosby, Owen, Pr. Co. C 6th O. V. I.
Crossmann, Benjamin F., Pr. Co. A 6th O. V. I.
Croy, Charles C., Pr. Co. G 10th O. V. I.
Cunningham, Frank, Pr. Co. G 10th O. V. I.
Cunningham, William R., Pr. Co. G 10th O. V. I.
Curtis, Edgar M., Corp. Co. A 6th O. V. I.

Cusick, Paul F., Pr. Co. G 10th O. V. I.

Daly, Edward D., Corp. Co. G 10th O. V. I.

D'Angelo, Romie, Pr. Co. A 6th O. V. I.

Daniels, George S., Pr. Co. A 6th O. V. I.

Day, Julian R., Pr. Co. H 10th O.V.I.

Day, Theodore W., Musician Co. G 10th O. V. I.

Deacon, Charles W., Pr. Tr. E 1st O. V. C.

DeBree, John B., Pr. Co. G 10th O. V. I.

Decker, Harvey C., Pr. Co. H 6th O. V. I.

Decker, Roland H., Pr. Co. L 6th O. V. I.

Delahanty, Clarence, Pr. Tr. E 1st O. V. C.

Delahanty, Joseph, Pr. Co. D 10th O. V. I.

Dennis, Harry O., Corp. Co. H 10th O. V. I.

Dennis, William S., Pr. Co. L 6th O. V. I.

Dent, Troy, Pr. Co. D 9th Batt. O.V.I.

Dettinger, Andrew, Jr., Pr. Co. A 6th O. V. I.

Dieball, Ernest E., Pr. Co. G 10th O. V. I.

Doan, Charles E., Pr. Co. C 6th O. V. I.

Dougheney, James J., Pr. Co. G 10th O. V. I.

Douglass, Clark E., Pr. Co. A 6th O. V. I.

Downer, Charles A., Pr. Co. H 6th O. V. I.

Downey, Thomas R., Pr. Co. H 6th O. V. I.

Dressor, Frank M., Pr. Tr. E 1st O. V. C.

Duffy, William H., Sergt. Co. H 6th O. V. I.

Durain, Louis E., Pr. Co. H 10th O. V. I.

Durivage, Emery J., Pr. Co. G 10th O. V. I.

Eagen, Harry M., Sergt. Co. G 10th O. V. I.

Eagen, John J., Pr. Co. L 6th O.V.I.

Earley, Edward J., Pr. Co. C 6th O. V. I.

Eastwood, Herbert G., Pr. Co. L 6th O. V. I.

Eastwood, William B., Pr. Co. L 6th O. V. I.

Eddy, Charles M., Corp. Co. H 10th O. V. I.

Eding, Gerrard J., Pr. Co. H 6th O. V. I.

Egelton, Clinton D., Pr. Co. L 6th O. V. I.

Egelton, Egbert William, Sergt. Co. L 6th O. V. I.

Ehlenfeldt, William F., Pr. Co. G 10th O. V. I.

Ehrbar, Charles, Pr. Co. G 10th O.V.I.

Eich, Matthias J., Pr. Co. G 10th O. V. I.

Elder, Roger B., Pr. Co. L 6th O.V.I.

Eldred, Rolland J., Pr. Co. C 6th O. V. I.

Elliott, Frank L., Pr. Co. D 10th O. V. I.

Ellis, Clarence, Pr. Co. D 10th O.V.I.

Embody, Thomas R., Pr. Co. C 6th O. V. I.

Emery, Edwin W., Pr. Tr. E 1st O. V. C.

Emmel, Arthur E., Corp. Co. H 10th O. V. I.

Englehart, Clark H., Pr. Co. H 6th O. V. I.

Enteman, Tony W., Pr. Co. L 6th O. V. I.

Eppstein, Isadore C., Pr. Co. G 10th O. V. I.

Espen, Michael S., Corp. Co. H 6th O. V. I.

Evans, Herbert L., Pr. Co. F 6th O. V. I.

Everett, William, Artificer Co. H 10th O. V. I.

Fallon, James D., Pr. Tr. E 1st O. V. C.

Fenstermaker, DeWitt C., Pr. Co. A 2nd U. S. V. E.

Ferrick, Thomas W., Pr. Tr. E 1st O. V. C.

Filson, Robert Kimber, Pr. Co. D 10th O. V. I.

Firth, George B., Pr. Co. L 6th O.V.I.

Fisher, Charles Albert, Pr. Co. B 10th O. V. I.

Fisk, Albert E., Pr. Co. L 6th O. V. I.

Fitch, Roy E., Pr. Co. G 10th O. V. I.

Fleig, Edward C., Pr. Co. G 10th O. V. I.

Flint, Herbert A., Pr. Co. D 10th O. V. I.

Fluckey, Ray E., Pr. Co. H 10th O. V. I.

Foley, William M., Corp. Co. G 10th O. V. I.

Fox, John B., Pr. Co. C 6th O. V. I.

Frank, Herman, Pr. Co. D 10th O. V. I.

Fraser, Edgar A., Pr. Co. H 10th O. V. I.

Fraser, William J., Sergt. Co. L 6th O. V. I.

Freilbach, Fred, Corp. Co. D 10th O. V. I.

Galbraith, Harvey, Pr. Tr. E 1st O. V. C.

Gallagher, Dennis, Pr. Tr. E 1st O. V. C.

Gamble, James B., Pr. Co. D 10th O. V. I.

Gates, Albert, Pr. Co. H 10th O. V. I.

Gerick, Frank, Pr. Co. C 6th O. V. I.

Geris, Gustave L., Sergt. Co. G 10th O. V. I.

Geris, Louis C., Q. M. Sergt. Co. G 10th O. V. I.

Gettnis, George F., Sergt. Co. I 6th O. V. I.

Gibb, Frank, Sergt. Co. A 6th O.V.I.

Gibson, Harry B., Pr. Co. A 6th O. V. I.

Goff, Pearl E., Pr. Co. A 6th O. V. I.

Goochee, Benjamin F., Pr. Co. A 6th O. V. I.

Good, Benjamin R., Musician Co. H 10th O. V. I.

Goodwin, Dwight H., Pr. Co. L 6th O. V. I.

Goodwin, Fred C., Corp. Co. L 6th O. V. I.

Gould, Alex. H., Pr. Co. D 10th O. V. I.

Gordon, James O., Pr. Co. L 6th O. V. I.

Gordon, John E., Pr. Co. G 10th O. V. I.

Gottschalk, John, Pr. Tr. E 1st O.V.C.

Grabelski, Frank S., Pr. Co. D 10th O. V. I.

Gradwohl, Charles A., Pr. Co. L 6th O. V. I.

Graham, Martin T., Pr. Co. H 6th O. V. I.

Graham, William, Pr. Tr. E 1st O. V. C.

Green, Amos R., Pr. Co. L 6th O.V.I.

Greening, Harlwell, Q. M. Sergt. Co. D 10th O. V. I.

Gregory, Arthur T., Pr. Co. A 6th O. V. I.

Gregory, Frank Q., Pr. Co. H 10th O. V. I.

Gregory, Fred H., Pr. Co. L 6th O. V. I.

Greiner, Arthur, Corp. Co. D 10th O. V. I.

Groenewold, Bernard, Pr. Co. L 6th O. V. I.

Hacker, John, Pr. Tr. E 1st O. V. C.

Hackett, James O., Pr. Co. H 6th O. V. I.

Hagner, Philip, Wagoner Co. C 6th O. V. I.

Halford, Fred D., Artificer Co. C 6th O. V. I.

Halford, Harry S., Pr. Co. G 10th O. V. I.

Hall, Thomas E., Pr. Tr. E 1st O.V.C.

Halsey, Dustin E., Chief Musician 10th O. V. I.

Hammond, Bert, Pr. Co. H 10th O. V. I.

Hampton, John D., Pr. Co. D 10th O. V. I.

Hankforth, Gust, Pr. Co. C 6th O.V.I.

Hanley, John, Pr. Co. D 10th O.V.I.

Harman, John J., Pr. Co. H 10th O. V. I.

Harmon, Harry D., Pr. Co. G 10th O. V. I.

Hart, Claude, Pr. Tr. E 1st O. V. C.

Hart, Harry H., Pr. Tr. E 1st O.V.C.

Hassenzahl, Albert, Pr. Tr. E 1st O. V. C.

Haughton, Frank R., Pr. Co. G 10th O. V. I.

Hauser, Gustav J., Corp. Co. A 6th O. V. I.

Hayden, Harry M., Corp. Co. G 10th O. V. I.

Haynes, William, Pr. Co. D 10th O. V. I.

Heany, Frank, Pr. Co. D 10th O.V.I.

Heidtke, Emil, Pr. Co. C 6th O. V. I.

Heim, Dean D., Pr. Co. H 6th O.V.I.

Heisey, Christian F., Artificer Co. G 10th O. V. I.

Hellfrisch, Osmann, Pr. Tr. E 1st O. V. C.

Henahan, Patrick, Pr. Co. A 6th O. V. I.

Henry, Charles E., Pr. Tr. E 1st O. V. C.

Henzler, William H., Sergt. Co. C 6th O. V. I.

Herling, Charles, Pr. Tr. E 1st O.V.C.

Herman, Fred, Pr. Tr. E 1st O. V. C.

Hero, Christ, Pr. Co. C 6th O. V. I.

Hill, Arthur D., Sergt. Maj. 6th O. V. I.

Hill, Roy H., Pr. Co. A 6th O. V. I.

Hinds, Robert L., Sergt. Co. H 6th O. V. I.

Hinkelman, Charles F., Corp. Co. C 6th O. V. I.

Hodge, Walter A., Pr. Co. L 6th O. V. I.

Hoehler, William, Pr. Co. G 10th O. V. I.

Hoffmann, George B., Corp. Co. H 10th O. V. I.

Holding, Richard N., Pr. Co. I 6th O. V. I.

Hollis, Fred M., Pr. Co. C 6th O.V.I.

Hollis, John A., Pr. Co. E 6th O.V.I.

Hoose, Allan B., Prin. Musician 10th O. V. I.

Hovey, John H., Pr. Tr. E 1st O.V.C.

Hubbell, Lyman J., Pr. Co. H 6th O. V. I.

Hudson, Henry A., Pr. Co. G 10th O. V. I.

Hunter, Charles H., Pr. Co. L 6th O. V. I.

Hunter, Gaylord L., Pr. Co. L 6th O. V. I.

Hunter, Thomas, Artificer Co. L 6th O. V. I.

Huppert, Daniel, Pr. Co. C 6th O.V.I.

Iford, Daniel W., Pr. Co. L 6th O.V.I.

Ingersoll, George W., Pr. Co. H 6th O. V. I.

Ingram, Edward, Pr. Tr. E 1st O.V.C.

Jardin, William T., Pr. Co. A 10th O. V. I.

Jeffry, Ernest M., Pr. Co. G 10th O. V. I.

Jennings, William F., Pr. Co. D 10th O. V. I.

Johnson, Eugene E., Pr. Co. F 6th O. V. I.

Johnson, Frank W., Pr. Co. A 6th O. V. I.

Johnson, Henry, Pr. Co. L 6th O.V.I.

Jones, George H., Hospital Steward 10th O. V. I.

Jones, Walter B., Pr. Co. D 9th Batt. O. V. I.

Jordan, Lee H., Pr. Co. H 6th O.V.I.

Julius, John M., Pr. Co. A 6th O.V.I.

Kane, John J., Pr. Co. C 6th O. V. I.

Kappler, Joseph W., Pr. Co. F 6th O. V. I.

Kappus, Justavus W., Pr. Co. A 6th O. V. I.

Kasdorf, Fred, 1st Sergt. Co. D 10th O. V. I.

Kelso, Roy M., Pr. Co. L 6th O.V.I.

Kelly, Roy H., Pr. Co. H 10th O.V.I.

Kelley, John I., Pr. Co. A 6th O.V.I.

Kemritz, Paul H., Pr. Co. A 6th O. V. I.

Kenson, William A., Pr. Co. C 6th O. V. I.

Kern, Harry E., Sergt. Co. D 10th O. V. I.

Kerr, John A., Pr. Tr. E 1st O. V. C.

Kerwin, James B., Pr. Co. G 10th O. V. I.

Kessler, Albert, Pr. Co. D 10th O.V.I.

Kessler, Edward, Wagoner Co. D 10th O. V. I.

Kettson, John C., Pr. Co. G 10th O. V. I.

Kewley, Thomas F., Pr. Co. G 10th O. V. I.

Kewley, William H., Musician Co. G 10th O. V. I.

Keys, John T., Pr. Co. C 6th O. V. I.

Kiger, William H., Hospital Steward 6th O. V. I.

King, Nelson B., Pr. Co. H 10th O. V. I.

Kinney, James B., Pr. Co. C 6th O. V. I.

Kirschner, Fred J., Pr. Co. D 10th O. V. I.

Kirtland, Leonard W., Pr. Co. H 6th O. V. I.

Knabenshue, Mark, Pr. Co. H 6th O. V. I.

Knights, Carl C., Corp. Co. H 6th O. V. I.

Koester, William, Pr. Co. G 10th O. V. I.

Krampe, Frederick R., Pr. Co. F 6th O. V. I.

Krebser, John S., Musician Co. C 6th O. V. I.

Kreling, Otto M., Pr. Co. L 6th O. V. I.

Krueger, Herman F., Pr. Co. C 6th O. V. I.

Kubitz, Albert W., Pr. Co. A 6th O. V. I.

Kuertin, Ewald, Pr. Co. L 6th O.V.I.

La Fountam, Fred S., Pr. Co. H 6th O. V. I.

Lamb, Allie J., Sergt. Co. G 6th O. V. I.

Lambert, Reinhart E., Pr. Co. A 6th O. V. I.

Lamme, H. Van, Pr. Co. D 10th O. V. I.

Lanfraw, Charles, Pr. Co. A 6th O. V. I.

Langenderfer, Lewis, Pr. Co. G 10th O. V. I.

Lantzenheiser, Jay H., Pr. Co. A 6th O. V. I.

Lardinais, Charles J., Pr. Co. A 6th O. V. I.

Larrow, Albert A., Pr. Co. C 6th O. V. I.

Larrow, Henry I., Pr. Co. C 6th O. V. I.

Lauffer, John, Pr. Co. G 10th O. V. I.

Law, Robert V., Sergt. Co. M 10th O. V. I.

Lawrence, George B., Pr. Tr. E 1st O. V. C.

Lawson, Harry C., Pr. Co. A 6th O. V. I.

Lawten, Harry W., Pr. Co. D 10th O. V. I.

Le Bold, Rolla W., Pr. Co. L 6th O. V. I.

Lehnertz, Jacob T., Corp. Co. C 6th O. V. I.

Lembke, Louis C., Pr. Co. H 10th O. V. I.

Leonard, George W., Pr. Co. D 10th O. V. I.

Le Seur, Frank Albert, Pr. Co. D 10th O. V. I.

Liebold, Albin E., Sergt. Co. D 10th O. V. I.

Limber, John M., Pr. Co. D 10th O. V. I.

Lindersmith, Robert E., Pr. Tr. E 1st O. V. C.

Link, Charles F., Pr. Co. H 6th O.V.I.

Linn, William, Pr. Tr. E 1st O. V. C.

Livers, Frank, Sergt. Co. C 6th O. V. I.

Logan, Walter J., Corp. Co. G 10th O. V. I.

Long, Fred E., Pr. Co. I 6th O. V. I.

Loomis, Homer W., 1st Sergt. Co. L. 6th O. V. I.

Luce, Charles B., Pr. Co. H 6th O. V. I.

Luckow, John, Jr., Pr. Co. H 6th O. V. I.

Ludwikoski, John, Pr. Co. H 10th O. V. I.

Lyke, Albert A., Pr. Tr. E 1st O.V.C.

Lyons, William E., 1st Sergt. Co. H 6th O. V. I.

Main, William L., Sergt. Co. A 6th O. V. I.
Mamerow, William J., Pr. Co. C 6th O. V. I.
Mangles, John H. F., Pr. Tr. E 1st O. V. C.
Marion, Edwin L., Pr. Co. L 6th O. V. I.
Marsh, Jacob M., Pr. Co. C 6th O.V.I.
Martin, Will C., Pr. Co. A 2nd U. S. V. E.
Maschler, Theodore, Corp. Co. H 10th O. V. I.
Mason, Daniel W., Corp. Co. H 10th O. V. I.
Mason, Fred M., Pr. Co. C 6th O.V.I.
Mattimore, John J., Pr. Co. C 10th O. V. I.
Mattimore, Joe P., Pr. Tr. E 1st O. V. C.
Mattimore, Thomas J., Pr. Tr. E 1st O. V. C.
May, Eugene, Pr. Co. L 6th O. V. I.
McAdams, Robert W., Pr. Co. L 6th O. V. I.
McDonald, Henry A., Pr. Tr. E 1st O. V. C.
McGrath, Frank, Pr. Co. A 2nd U. S. V. E.
McKenna, William E., Pr. Co. H 6th O. V. I.
McKinney, Thomas J., Pr. Co. C 6th O. V. I.
McLean, C. Herbert, Pr. Tr. E 1st O. V. C.
Meigs, Arch L., Q. M. Sergt. 6th O. V. I.
Meissner, Hugo F. W., Pr. Co. A 6th O. V. I.
Mescall, John, Pr. Co. C 10th O.V.I.
Meyers, Albert B., Corp. Co. G 10th O. V. I.
Meyers, Andrew P., Pr. Co. H 10th O. V. I.
Middaugh, Charlie, Pr. Co. C 10th O. V. I.
Mienka, William H., Sergt. Co. C 6th O. V. I.
Miller, George H., Pr. Co. C 6th O. V. I.
Miller, Henry Clay, Musician Co. D 10th O. V. I.
Mills, Harry A., Pr. Co. G 10th O.V.I.
Mock, James C., Pr. Tr. E 1st O.V.C.
Moffat, Dana C., Pr. Co. C 6th O.V.I.
Monnett, Richard, Pr. Co. C 10th O. V. I.
Moore, Charles H., Corp. Co. L 6th O. V. I.
Moore, Daniel C., Pr. Co. C 6th O. V. I.
Morgan, Harvey, Pr. Co. G 10th O. V. I.
Morgan, John L., Pr. Tr. E 1st O.V.C.
Morrissey, Timothy J., Pr. Co. G 10th O. V. I.

Motter, Frank C., Corp. Co. A 6th O. V. I.
Muehler, Fred, Pr. Co. A 6th O. V. I.
Mullen, John, Pr. Co. C 6th O. V. I.
Mullins, William, Pr. Co. C 10th O. V. I.
Munier, Eugene, Corp. Co. D 10th O. V. I.
Murphy, John P., Pr. Co. G 10th O. V. I.
Murphy, William H., Pr. Co. L 6th O. V. I.
Myers, Bernal, Pr. Co. C 10th O. V. I.
Myers, Earl R., Pr. Co. H 10th O.V.I.
Myers, William S., Pr. Co. H 6th O. V. I.
Nafus, Charles R., Pr. Co. H 10th O. V. I.
Nagle, James E., Pr. Co. C 6th O.V.I.
Neidhardt, Ernest E., Pr. Co. A 6th O. V. I.
Nester, Joseph T., Pr. Co. L 6th O. V. I.
Neubert, William F., Corp. Co. L 6th O. V. I.
Newberry, William H., Pr. Co. C 10th O. V. I.
Newman, Arthur B., Pr. Co. C 6th O. V. I.
Newton, John C., Corp. Co. L 6th O. V. I.
Nicewarner, James C., Pr. Co. H 6th O. V. I.
Nicholas, Frank L., Pr. Co. A 6th O. V. I.
Nicklet, Anthony F., Sergt. Co. G 10th O. V. I.
Nitschke, Arthur, Corp. Co. D 10th O. V. I.
Oatley, Robert O., Pr. Co. C 10th O. V. I.
O'Brien, Andrew F., Pr. Co. G 10th O. V. I.
O'Brien, Maurice, Pr. Co. H 10th O. V. I.
Odell, Roy T., Pr. Co. C 6th O. V. I.
O'Dwyer, Kevin, Pr. Co. G 10th O. V. I.
O'Konski, Peter, Pr. Co. C 10th O. V. I.
Oliver, Frank E., Sergt. Co. H 6th O. V. I.
Olsen, Barney, Pr. Tr. E 1st O. V. C.
O'Meara, Perry, Sergt. Co. C 6th O. V. I.
Ostrander, Claude H., Pr. Co. F 6th O. V. I.
Parker, Ross E., Sergt. Co. E 6th O. V. I.
Parker, Ross E., Sergt. Co. E 6th O. V. I.
Parsons, Eddie, Pr. Co. G 10th O.V.I.
Partland, Frank, Pr. Co. G 10th O. V. I.
Paterson, John A., Corp. Co. D 10th O. V. I.

Patterson, John A., Wagoner Co. H 10th O. V. I.
Pauken, Bert F., Prin. Musician 10th O. V. I.
Paxton, Edward, Pr. Co. D 9th Batt: O. V. I.
Pearson, William J., Pr. Co. H 10th O. V. I.
Pentz, George C., Pr. Co. G 10th O. V. I.
Peters, Frank H., Pr. Co. A 6th O. V. I.
Peters, Robert, Pr. Co. A 6th O. V. I.
Pew, John N., Pr. Co. H 6th O. V. I.
Phillips, McPherson, 1st Sergt. Co. A 6th O. V. I.
Pierce, Charles F., Corp. Co. G 10th O. V. I.
Pinkerton, James O., Pr. Co. H 6th O. V. I.
Pollock, Guy S., Corp. Co. G 10th O. V. I.
Porter, Harley D., Pr. Co. C 6th O. V. I.
Porter, James R., Pr. Co. C 10th O. V. I.
Price, C. Verne, Pr. Co. H 6th O.V.I.
Puder, Henry, Pr. Co. F 6th O. V. I.
Pugh, Martin Harold, Pr. Co. A 6th O. V. I.
Radunz, Emil A., Pr. Co. C 10th O. V. I.
Ray, Granville, Pr. Co. C 10th O.V.I.
Reagan, Arthur A., Corp. Co. D 10th O. V. I.
Rector, Cyrus H., Pr. Co. G 10th O. V. I.
Rector, John W., Pr. Co. G 10th O. V. I.
Reichard, George F., Pr. Co. C 10th O. V. I.
Reilly, Joseph, Corp. Co. D 10th O. V. I.
Reiniecke, Fred, Pr. Co. L 6th O.V.I.
Reynolds, Jason E., Pr. Tr. E 1st O. V. C.
Reynolds, Sherman G., Pr. Co. H 6th O. V. I.
Richardson, Fred A., Pr. Co. C 10th O. V. I.
Riechers, Fred G., Pr. Co. C 10th O. V. I.
Riess, Frank W., Pr. Co. C 10th O. V. I.
Robertson, Hollie P., Pr. Tr. E 1st O. V. C.
Robertson, John S., Pr. Co. H 10th O. V. I.
Robbins, James N., Corp. Co. H 6th O. V. I.
Rodenhauser, John, Pr. Co. G 10th O. V. I.
Rodgers, William H., Pr. Co. G 10th O. V. I.
Roethliesberger, Albert R., Pr. Co. G 10th O. V. I.

Rogers, Edwin H., Pr. Co. C 6th O. V. I.
Rohrs, Fred C., Pr. Co. C 6th O.V.I.
Roller, Louis E., Pr. Co. C 10th O. V. I.
Rook, Thomas, Pr. Co. H 10th O.V.I.
Rossman, Leon M., Pr. Co. H 6th O. V. I.
Roth, Rudolph F., Pr. Co. H 10th O. V. I.
Rouland, Alfred R., Pr. Co. L 6th O. V. I.
Rowe, Frank E., Corp. Co. A 6th O. V. I.
Rowley, Arthur F., Sergt. Co. L 6th O. V. I.
Rude, Richard R., Pr. Co. C 10th O. V. I.
Ruhl, Harry B., Pr. Co. G 10th O.V.I.
Ruhlin, Henry A., Pr. Co. C 6th O. V. I.
Russell, Joseph W., Corp. Co. E 6th O. V. I.
Russell, Joseph W., Corp. Co. E 6th O. V. I.
Salter, Julius C., Musician Co. H 6th O. V. I.
Sanborn, Orrie W., Corp. Co. H 6th O. V. I.
Sancke, John, Musician Co. A 6th O. V. I.
Sanzenbacher, William C., Pr. Co. G 10th O. V. I.
Samson, Henry C., Sergt. Co. C 6th O. V. I.
Schmidt, Willy, Pr. Co. A 6th O.V.I.
Schofield, Thomas, Pr. Co. A 6th O. V. I.
Schoedler, William C., Pr. Co. H 10th O. V. I.
Schrader, Frederick A., Corp. Co. D 10th O. V. I.
Schrag, John G., Corp. Co. G 10th O. V. I.
Schultz, Arthur F., Pr. Co. L 6th O. V. I.
Schwager, Edward A., Pr. Co. H 10th O. V. I.
Schwartz, William A., Pr. Co. C 10th O. V. I.
Scott, Alfred A., Sergt. Co. L 6th O. V. I.
Scott, Charles B., Pr. Co. H 10th O. V. I.
Scott, Lisle, Prin. Musician 6th O.V.I.
Seymour, William J., Pr. Co. A 6th O. V. I.
Shantean, William H., Wagoner Co. G 10th O. V. I.
Sheldon, George F., Corp. Co. D 10th O. V. I.
Shepard, William G., Corp. Co. L 6th O. V. I.
Shepler, Charles W., Sergt. Co. A 6th O. V. I.
Shepler, Harry L., Pr. Co. B 6th O. V. I.

Short, Henry F., Pr. Co. A 6th O.V.I.

Shroeder, Frank H., Pr. Co. C 6th O. V. I.

Simpson, George, Pr. Tr. E 1st O. V. C.

Singleton, Clarence C., Pr. Co. A 6th O. V. I.

Sisco, Arthur, Pr. Co. G 10th O. V. I.

Skelly, Clarence, Corp. Co. H 10th O. V. I.

Skinner, Newton E., Corp. Co. H 6th O. V. I.

Slattery, Matthew F., Pr. Co. C 10th O. V. I.

Smalley, Stanley B., Pr. Co. G 10th O. V. I.

Smith, Abie L., Pr. Co. G 10th O.V.I.

Smith, Austin I., Pr. Co. E 6th O.V.I.

Smith, Carl E., Pr. Co. C 10th O. V. I.

Smith, Charles M., Pr. Co. H 6th O. V I.

Smith, Clent, Pr. Co. G 10th O. V. I.

Smith, Felix M., Pr. Co. E 6th O.V.I.

Smith, John H., Pr. Co. H 6th O.V.I.

Smith, Joseph, Pr. Co. A 6th O. V. I.

Speice, Edward J., Hospital Steward 6th O. V. I.

Spohn, Howard L., Pr. Co. G 10th O. V. I.

Squires, Ira H., Pr. Co. H 6th O. V. I.

Squires, James E., Pr. Co. H 6th O. V. I.

Steger, Julius F., Sergt. Co. D 10th O. V. I.

Steig, Albert S., Pr. Co. L 6th O.V.I.

Steinmetz, Frank, Pr. Co. C 6th O. V. I.

Stevens, Carl A., Pr. Co. C 6th O.V.I.

Stewart, Ralph W., Sergt. Co. K 6th O. V. I.

Steele, Frank J., Pr. Co. G 10th O. V. I.

Stiegelmeyer, Fred H., Pr. Co. G 10th O. V. I.

St. John, Joseph D., Pr. Co. G 10th O. V. I.

Stock, Fred F., Pr. Co. H 6th O. V. I.

Stone, Fred, Pr. Co. C 10th O. V. I.

Stone, George F., Pr. Tr. E 1st O. V. C.

Stone, Louis, Pr. Tr. E 1st O. V. C.

Stratton, William W., Sergt. Co. H 6th O. V. I.

Strausz, Harry N., Pr. Co. L 6th O. V. I.

Strobel, Gotlieb R., Pr. Co. A 6th O. V. I.

Strouse, David O., Pr. Co. C 10th O. V. I.

Strub, Charles E., Pr. Co. H 10th O. V. I.

Stuart, Ray R., Pr. Co. L 6th O.V.I.

Sullivan, John J., Pr. Co. G 10th O. V. I.

Sullivan, Joseph, Pr. Tr. E 1st O.V.C.

Summerskill, Charlie J., Pr. Co. H 10th O. V. I.

Summerskill, William S., Sergt. Co. H 10th O. V. I.

Summerling, Charles, Pr. Co. A 6th O. V. I.

Sweeney, James, Pr. Co. H 6th O.V.I.

Switzer, Asa, Pr. Co. F 6th O. V. I.

Taraschke, August, Corp. Co. A 6th O. V. I.

Tattersall, John C., Pr. Tr. E 1st O. V. C.

Taylor, Earl W., Pr. Co. G 10th O. V. I.

Taylor, Hubert G., Pr. Co. H 6th O. V. I.

Taylor, Julius B., Musician Co. D 10th O. V. I.

Teatsworth, Reginald P., Pr. Co. G 10th O. V. I.

Terbille, Frank M., Pr. Co. H 6th O. V. I.

Thomas, Edward C., Pr. Co. C 10th O. V. I.

Thompson, Jay A., Pr. Co. L 6th O. V. I.

Thompson, Lucius E., Pr. Co. A 6th O. V. I.

Thurston, Wesley S., Jr., Corp. Co. H 10th O. V. I.

Towers, Frank William, Pr. Co. H 10th O. V. I.

Trueschel, Alfred C., Pr. Co. C 10th O. V. I.

Turner, Harry E., Corp. Co. G 10th O. V. I.

Tuttle, Cornelius, Pr. Co. G 10th O. V. I.

Unger, John C., Sergt. Co. A 6th O. V. I.

Upp, Clark W., Pr. Tr. E 1st O. V. C.

Vallette, James, Pr. Co. G 10th O.V.I.

Van Dusen, Menzies E., 1st Sergt. Co. H 10th O. V. I.

Van Karsen, John A., Pr. Co. G 10th O. V. I.

Vernier, Harmon G., Pr. Co. H 6th O. V. I.

Vighes, Peter A., Pr. Co. H 10th O. I.

Vogel, Peter, Pr. Co. C 10th O. V. I.

Vulver, Eli E., Pr. Co. D 10th O. V. I.

Wachter, Fred W., Musician Co. L 6th O. V. I.

Wagner, Fred A., Pr. Co. C 6th O.V.I.

Wagner, Walter O., Pr. Co. C 10th O. V. I.

Wahl, Frank W., Pr. Co. C 10th O. V. I.

Waite, Perry W., Q. M. Sergt. Co. H 10th O. V. I.

Wakefield, Fred, Corp. Co. H 10th O. V. I.

Waldvogel, Robert, Pr. Co. H 6th O. V. I.

Walter, Christian G., Pr. Co. C 10th O. V. I.

Walter, Frank A., Pr. Co. C 10th O. V. I.

Walsh, Frank P., Sergt. Co. L 6th O. V. I.

Wandtke, John, Musician Co. A 6th O. V. I.

Warner, Leigh H., Pr. Co. C 10th O. V. I.

Wasmund, William, Sergt. Co. A 6th O. V. I.

Watson, Harry L., Pr. Co. H 6th O. V. I.

Wavreck, Peter E., Pr. Co. H 6th O. V. I.

Weber, Thomas, Pr. Tr. E 1st O.V.C.

Weckerlin, Martin S., Pr. Co. H 6th O. V. I.

Weckle, Henry O., Pr. Co. C 6th O. V. I.

Weed, Sheldon C., Pr. Co. G 10th O. V. I.

Weidner, George, Pr. Tr. E 1st O. V. C.

Weier, Walter C., Pr. Co. A 6th O. V. I.

Welch, Thomas J., Pr. Tr. E 1st O. V. C.

Werner, Frank J., Pr. Co. L 6th O. V. I.

Wernert, Gregory H. A., Pr. Co. C 6th O. V. I.

Wernert, Edward J., Corp. Co. C 6th O. V. I.

Wertheim, Edward, Corp. Co. G 10th O. V. I.

West, Otto L., Corp. Co. A 6th O.V.I.

West, William H., Pr. Co. L 6th O. V. I.

Whipple, William H., Pr. Co. G 10th O. V. I.

Whitcomb, Lloyd O., Pr. Co. A 6th O. V. I.

White, Samuel, Pr. Co. D 9th Batt. O. V. I.

Whitney, Mark W., Pr. Co. A 6th O. V. I.

Wickenden, Leroy W., Sergt. Co. H 10th O. V. I.

Wilson, Charles E., Pr. Co. H 6th O. O. V. I.

Wilkinson, Charles R., Pr. Co. H 6th V. I.

Willets, George W., Pr. Tr. E 1st O. V. C.

Williams, Burcel E., Pr. Co. H 10th O. V. I.

Williamson, John F., Pr. Co. G 10th O. V. I.

Wilson, Dale, Pr. Co. L 6th O. V. I.

Wilson, William Albert, Pr. Co. A 6th O. V. I.

Wilson, William H., Pr. Co. G 10th O. V. I.

Williston, John C., Pr. Co. C 10th O. V. I.

Wirth, George W., Pr. Co. G 10th O. V. I.

Woggon, Ernest H. G., Pr. Co. A 6th O. V. I.

Woodmancy, William A., Pr. Co. H 6th O. V. I.

Woodworth, Alva E., Pr. Co. A 6th O. V. I.

Wortsmith, Henry G., Pr. Co. H 10th O. V. I.

Wragg, Charles S., Sergt. Co. D 10th O. V. I.

Wright, Lloyd, Wagoner Co. L 6th O. V. I.

Yoder, Charles, Pr. Co. L 6th O.V.I.

Young, John, Pr. Co. G 10th O. V. I.

Zeigler, Charles H., Musician Co. H 6th O. V. I.

Zeigler, Frank J., Pr. Co. L 6th O.V.I.

Zeluff, Sylvester S., Sergt. Tr. E 1st O .V .C.

TONTOGANY

Beaverstock, Clarence M., Pr. Co. K 2nd O. V. I.

Delano, Harry A., Pr. Co. B 5th O. V. I.

Weisweber, Lewis, Pr. Co. M 3rd O. V. I.

TOWNSEND

Tanner, Albert E., Pr. Co. H 10th O. V. I.

TREMONT CITY

Wilson, Harry, Corp. Co. B 3rd O.V.I.

TROBRIDGE

Martinson, Moris, Pr. Co. E 6th O.V.I.

TROY.

Collins, Albert G., Sergt. Co. B 2nd U. S. V. E.
Funderburg, James J., Pr. Co. A 3rd O. V. I.
Macy, Webster, Pr. Co. K 3rd O. V. I.
Owens, Amzi E., Pr. Co. C 3rd O. V. I.
Pontiss, Harvey, Pr. Co. K 3rd O.V.I.

Sterrett, Frank M., Jr., Pr. Co. C 3rd O. V. I.
Williams, H. L., Pr. Co. A 3rd O.V.I.
Wright, Thomas M., Pr. Tr. G 1st O. V. C.
Yest, Loren, Pr. Co. K 3rd O. V. I.

UNION COUNTY

Lee, Ell. M., Pr. Co. D 4th O. V. I.

Williams, Anderson L., Pr. Co. D 4th O. V. I.

UNION, MICHIGAN

Cronkwright, Albert, Pr., Co. B 3rd O. V. I.

UPPER SANDUSKY

Bolyard, Harry, Pr. Co. B 2nd O. V. I.
Brewer, Emmit W., Pr. Co. B 2nd O. V. I.
Brewer, James H., Pr. Co. B 2nd O. V. I.
Byers, Andrew V., Pr. Co. B 2nd O. V. I.
Byers, Winfield, Pr. Co. B 2nd O. V. I.
Cain, Andrew R., Sergt. Co. B 2nd O. V. I.
Cammain, Iren P., Pr. Co. B 2nd O. V. I.
Carpenter, John, Pr. Co. B 2nd O.V.I.
Clinger, Girden C., Pr. Co. B 2nd O. V. I.
Cole, Jessie R., Pr. Co. B 2nd O. V. I.
Cosgrove, James, Pr. Co. B 2nd O.V.I.
Diermeyer, Adolph, Pr. Co. B 2nd O. V. I.
Dow, David, Pr Co. B 2nd O. V. I.
Earp, Charles, Pr. Co. B 2nd O. V. I.
Ewing, William W., Pr. Co. B 2nd O. V. I.
Forney, George, Pr. Co. B 2nd O. V. I.
Frazier, Charles L., Sergt. Co. B 2nd O. V. I.
Garnsey, Edward W., Pr. Co. B 2nd O. V. I.
Gear, Frank, Sergt. Co. B 2nd O. V. I.
Ginsinger, Melville, Pr. Co. B 2nd O. V. I.
Gregg, Charles F., Pr. Co. B 2nd O. V. I.
Greek, George, Corp. Co. B 2nd O.V.I.
Greek, Samuel, Pr. Co. B 2nd O. V. I.
Grimes, William E., Pr. Co. B 2nd O. V. I.
Grundlisch, George, Wagoner Co. B 2nd O. V. I.
Halbedel, Carl F., Pr. Co. B 2nd O.V.I.
Harman, Charles, Artificer Co. B 2nd O. V. I.
Hawk, John, Pr. Co. B 2nd O. V. I.
Hewett, James C., Pr. Co. B 2nd O. V. I.

Hill, David N., Pr. Co. B 2nd O. V. I.
Holmes, John B., Pr. Co. B 2nd O.V.I.
Hornby, Roy W., Pr. Co. B 2nd O.V.I.
Ingard, Ralph W., Pr. Co. B 2nd O. V. I.
Kimmel, Charles G., Pr. Co. B 2nd O V. I.
King, Oscar T., Corp. Co. B 2nd O. V. I.
Keltner, Wayland, Pr Co. B 2nd O. V. I.
Kemerly, Charles G., Pr. Co. B 2nd O. V. I.
La Philliph, Jasper E., Corp. Co. B 2nd O. V. I.
Mann, George M., Pr. Co. B 2nd O. V. I.
McClain, Charles M., Corp. Co. B 2nd O. V. I.
McEvoy, John A. Pr. Co. B 2nd O. V. I.
McGugin, Harry, Pr. Co. B 2nd O.V.I.
Mears, John, Pr. Co. B 2nd O. V. I.
Metz, Clay C., Pr. Co. B 2nd O. V. I.
Miller, James D., 1st Sergt. Co. B 2nd O. V. I.
Miller, James G., Pr. Co. B 2nd O.V.I.
Mohr, Ray D., Musician Co. B 2nd O. V. I.
O'Donnell, Simon, Sergt. Co. B. 2nd O. V. I.
Ooley, Charles W., Pr. Co. B 2nd O. V. I.
Peters, Avery W., Q. M. Sergt. Co. B 2nd O. V. I.
Pool, George, Pr. Co. B 2nd O. V. I.
Ragon, Pliny M., Corp. Co. B 2nd O. V. I.
Rapp, George R., Pr. Co. B 2nd O.V.I.
Ritter, Otto F., Musician Co. B 2nd O. V. I.
Roseberry, Levi B., Pr. Co. B 2nd O. V. I.
Seebach, Clarence, Pr. Co. B 2nd O. V. I.

Sheets, Samuel, Pr. Co. B 2nd O. V. I.
Shorb, John, Pr. Co. B 2nd O. V. I.
Slemmer, George, Pr. Co. B 2nd O.V.I.
Stoneburner, Samuel H., Pr. Co. B 2nd O. V. I.
Stoner, Joseph, Pr. Co. B 2nd O. V. I.
Swartz, Harry E., Pr. Co. B 2nd O.V.I.
Ury, Clay, Pr. Co. B 2nd O. V. I.
Voelker, Louis, Pr. Co. B 2nd O. V. I.

Waggoner, Charles, Pr. Co. B 2nd O. V. I.
Weller, Ira A., Pr. Co. B 2nd O. V. I.
Wood, Ott, Pr. Co. B 2nd O. V. I.
Wurtz, Edward F., Pr. Co. B 2nd O. V. I.
Zimmerman, Bela, Corp. Co. B 2nd O. V. I.

URBANA

Bailey, Charles A., Corp. Co. D 3rd O. V. I.
Ball, Timothy O'Sullivan, Pr. Co. D 3rd O. V. I.
Barger, William L., Pr. Co. D 3rd O. V. I.
Bensing, Frank E., Pr. Co. D 3rd O. V. I.
Bosler, Frank M., Pr. Co. D 3rd O. V. I.
Brown, Edmund M., Q. M. Sergt. Co. D 3rd O. V. I.
Childs, Norman S., Pr. Co. D 3rd O. V. I.
Colwell, Frank F., Pr. Co. D 3rd O.V.I.
Colwell, Frank F., Pr. U. R. 3rd O.V.I.
Davis, Herbert C., Artificer Co. D 3rd O. V. I.
Ellis, Dallas P., Pr. Co. D 3rd O. V. I.
Gulick, Paul A., Pr. Co. D 3rd O. V. I.
Gumpert, William F., Pr. Co. D 3rd O. V. I.
James, Ernest E., Pr. Co. B 2nd U. S. V. E.
Lee, Frank N., Pr. Co. D 3rd O. V. I.
McClure, Andrew J., Pr. Co. D 3rd O. V. I.

Parrish, John R., Pr. Co. D 3rd O.V.I.
Redmond, Charles H., Pr. Co. D 3rd O. V. I.
Roberts, Edward D., Pr. Co. D 3rd O. V. I.
Romine, Annon W., Pr. Co. D 3rd O. V. I.
Sessions, Perry M., Pr. Co. D 3rd O. V. I.
Smith, Walter W., Corp. Co. D 3rd O. V. I.
Standish, Charles W., Pr. Co. D 3rd O. V. I.
Standish, Miles, Pr. Co. D 3rd O.V.I.
Stanley, Ross D., Pr. Co. D 3rd O.V.I.
Turner, Arthur, Pr. Co. D 3rd O. V. I.
Ullery, Edward H., 1st Sergt. Co. D 3rd O. V. I.
Ward, William E., Corp. Co. D 3rd O. V. I.
Weatherhead, Guy W., Pr. Co. D 3rd O. V. I.
White, Walter W., Pr. Co. D 3rd O. V. I.
Winder, Charles B., Pr. Co. D 3rd O. V. I.

VALLEY CROSSING

Kleinline, Charles F., Pr. Co. B 5th O. V. I.

VAN BUREN

Spitler, Clois, Pr. Co. K 2nd O. V. I.

Spitler, Samuel G., *Pr. Co. K 2nd O. V. I.

VAN WERT

Acheson, Ira L., Pr. Co. D 2nd O.V.I.
Andrews, Leon E., Pr. Co. D 2nd O. V. I.
Angevine, Richard, Pr. Co. D 2nd O. V. I.
Ball, William E., Pr. Co. D 2nd O.V.I.
Blake, Orville E., Corp. Co. D 2nd O. V. I.
Campbell, Charles W., Pr. Co. D 2nd O. V. I.
Campbell, Fred H., Pr. Co. D 2nd O. V. I.
Campbell, Thomas A., Pr. Co. D 2nd O. V. I.

Carnahan, George C., Pr. Co. D 2nd O. V. I.
Cole, Billie M., Pr. Co. D 2nd O. V. I.
Collett, Dan M., Pr. Co. D 2nd O. V. I.
Craig, James C., Pr. Co. D 2nd O. V. I.
Crone, Arthur S., Pr. Co. D 2nd O. V. I.
Crone, Edward F., Pr. Co. D 2nd O. V. I.
Conn, Curtis L., Pr. Co. D 2nd O. V. I
Daniels, Evan R., Pr. Co. D 2nd O. V. I.
Dasher, Charles O., Pr. Co. D 2nd O. V. I.

Davis, William L., Pr. Co. D 2nd O. V. I.

Davison, Guy P., Sergt. Co. D 2nd O. V. I.

Dippery, Manton E., Pr. Co. D 2nd O. V. I.

Dix, Ira J., Pr. Co. D 2nd O. V. I.

Doming, Oria, Pr. Co. D 2nd O. V. I.

Dunlap, Joe P., Corp. Co. D 2nd O. V. I.

Estell, Frank E., Corp. Co. D 2nd O. V. I.

Fair, Curtis E., Pr. Co. D 2nd O. V. I.

Fisher, Jacob, Pr. Co. D 2nd O. V. I.

Fritcher, Harry C., Pr. Co. D 2nd O. V. I.

Gilpin, Arthur C., 1st Sergt. Co. D 2nd O. V. I.

Glossett, George, Pr. Co. D 2nd O.V.I.

Gorman, Fred, Pr. Co. D 2nd O. V. I.

Griffith, William A., Pr. Co. D 2nd O. V. I.

Guinn, Charley H., Pr. Co. D 2nd O. V. I.

Guinn, David, Pr. Co. D 2nd O. V. I.

Hagerman, Harry G., Pr. Co. D 2nd O. V. I.

Harman, Harry S., Pr. Co. D 2nd O. V. I.

Hayler, George, Jr., Pr. Co. D 2nd O V. I.

Heinderleiter, George M., Pr. Co. D 2nd O. V. I.

Himmelreich, William F., Sergt. Co. D 2nd O. V. I.

Hyatt, Harry M., Pr. Co. D 2nd O.V.I.

Imbody, Charles N., Pr. Co. D 2nd O. V. I.

Johns, William T., Pr. Co. D 2nd O. V. I.

Johnson, Samuel, Pr. Co. D 2nd O.V.I.

Jones, Howard G., Pr. Co. D 2nd O. V. I.

Kear, Ernest W., Sergt. Co. D 2nd O. V. I.

Kimmel, Fred B., Pr. Co. D 2nd O. V. I.

Klein, Byron, Pr. Co. D 2nd O. V. I.

Klein, George W., Pr. Co. D 2nd O. V. I.

Knott, Pearl, Pr. Co. D 2nd O. V. I.

Krout, William C, Pr Co D 2nd O.V.I.

Le Hew, Wells W., Pr. Co. D 2nd O. V. I.

Lichty, Carey C., Pr. Co. D 2nd O.V.I.

Long, Harry C., Pr. Co. D 2nd O. V. I.

Louer, Garett, Pr. Co. D 2nd O.V.I.

Marker, Leonard J, Pr. Co. D 2nd O. V. I.

Martin, Adam C., Pr. Co. D 2nd O.V.I.

Martin, Frederick G., Pr. Co. D 2nd O. V. I.

Mathews, Albert T., Pr Co. D 2nd O. V. I.

McConahay, Verne B., Pr. Co. D 2nd O. V. I.

McFadden, Charles L., Pr. Co. H 10th O. V. I.

McIlvain, Glenn H., Pr. Co. D 2nd O. V. I.

McLaughlin, Cary C., Pr. Co. D 2nd O. V. I.

McPike, Ernest, Pr. Co. D 2nd O. V. I.

Michael, Carl C., Pr. Co. D 2nd O. V. I.

Miller, Arthur, Pr. Co. D 2nd O. V. I.

Miller, Clyde O., Pr. Co. D 2nd O.V.I.

Miller, Joe, Pr. Co. D 2nd O. V. I.

Moore, Roy J., Musician Co. D 2nd O. V. I.

Morgan, Hilas A., Pr. Co. D 2nd O. V. I.

Mullen, Charles W., Pr. Co. D 2nd O. V. I.

Mullen, Thomas E., Pr. Co. D 2nd O. V. I.

Murlin, Elmore K., Pr. Co. D 2nd O. V. I.

Neel, J. Sibley, Pr. Co. D 2nd O. V. I.

Norris, B. Frank, Pr. Co. D 2nd O. V. I.

Norris, Ben T., Pr. Co. D 2nd O. V. I.

Norris, James, Pr. Co. D 2nd O. V. I.

Parent, William M., Pr. Co. D 2nd O. V. I.

Pennell, Otto R., Pr. Co. D 2nd O.V.I.

Pennell, Robert L., Pr. Co. D 2nd O. V. I.

Potts, Doit, Pr. Co. D 2nd O. V. I.

Price, Charles H., Pr. Co. D 2nd O. V. I.

Raudebaugh, Earl, Pr. Co. D 2nd O. V. I.

Reese, William E., Pr. Co. D 2nd O. V. I.

Ricketts, Alonzo S., Pr. Co. D 2nd O. V. I.

Ross, Otis C., Corp. Co. D 2nd O. V. I.

Saltzgaber, William R., Pr. Co. D 2nd O. V. I.

Samsel, Henry, Pr. Co. D 2nd O. V. I.

Scott, Harry L., Sergt. Co. D 2nd O. V. I.

Schultz, Elmer, Pr. Co. D 2nd O. V. I.

Sheeter, William, Pr. Co. D 2nd O.V.I.

Siders, Charles M., Corp. Co. D 2nd O. V. I.

Siders, Foster, Pr. Co. D 2nd O. V. I.

Smith, Burton L., Corp. Co. D 2nd O. V. I.

Stanley, John, Pr. Co. D 2nd O. V. I.

Strohl, Amos P., Pr. Co. D 2nd O.V.I.

Swartz, Charles W., Pr. Co. D 2nd O. V. I

Trisler, George H., Pr. Co. D 2nd O. V. I.

Welker, John H., Pr. Co. D 2nd O.V.I.

West, Corwin S., Pr. Co. D 2nd O. V. I.

Wilson, Certeus W., Pr. Co. D 2nd O. Wiseman, George, Pr. Co. D 2nd O.V.I.
V. I. Zeigler, Ernest C., Pr. Co. D. 2nd O.
Wilson, Johnson, Pr. Co. D 2nd O.V.I. V. I.

VENNICE

Zehner, George B., Pr. Co. G 10th O. V. I.

VINTON

Lowe, Joseph R., Pr. Co. C 7th O.V.I. McMillen, Henry, Pr. Co. C 7th O.V.I.

VINTON COUNTY

Clark, Oscar, Pr. Co. K 3rd O. V. I.

WACO

Murphy, Marion M., Pr. Co. I 8th O. V. I.

WADE

Goodman, William J., Pr. Co. E 7th O. V. I.

WADSWORTH

Alexander, Herbert O., Pr. Co. G 8th
O. V. I.
Arick, Bert F., Pr. Co. G 8th O. V. I.
Baughman, Almon J., Pr. Co. G 8th
O. V. I.
Boden, Charles E., Pr. Co. G 8th O.
V. I.
Bolick, Herbert E., Sergt. Co. G 8th
O. V. I.
Bolick, William, Sergt. Co. G 8th O.
V. I.
Brumbaugh, George, Pr. Co. G 8th O.
V. I.
Campbell, Lowell, Pr. Co. G 8th O.V.I.
Conrad, Kirk H., Pr. Co. G 8th O.V.I.
Cunningham, Oliver M., Pr. Co. G 8th
O. V. I.
Dibble, Fred C., Corp. Co. G 8th O.
V. I.
Dibble, Harry H., Corp. Co. G 8th O.
V. I.
Dick, Frank P., Pr. Co. G 8th O. V. I.
Dick, James E., Pr. U. R. 8th O. V. I.
Dagenhard, Henry, Pr. Co. G 8th O.
V. I.
Fiscus, Stanton C., Pr. Co. G 8th O.
V. I.
Fretter, Albert H., Pr. Co. G 8th O.V.I.
Fouche, Ira, Pr Co. G 8th O. V. I.
Funk, Earl P., Pr. Co. G 8th O. V. I.
Gallagher, Nicholas, Pr. Co. G 8th O.
V. I.
Geisinger, Frank F., Pr. Co. G 8th O.
V. I.
Gerstenschlager, Valentine, Corp. Co.
G 8th O. V. I.
Good, Charles W., Pr. Co. G 8th O.
V. I.

Gunsaulis, William, Pr. Co. G 8th O.
V. I.
Hambleton, Thomas, Sergt. Co. G 8th
O. V. I.
Herrington, Bert B., Pr. Co. G 8th O.
V. I.
Huffman, Charles F., Pr. Co. G 8th O.
V. I.
Huffman, Edward E., Pr. Co. G 8th O.
V. I.
Hunsberger, Walter, 1st Sergt. Co. G
8th O. V. I.
Hunt, Earnest L., Pr. Co. G 8th O.V.I.
Keifer, Joseph W., Pr. Co. G 8th O.V.I.
Kraver, Frederick, Pr. Co. G 8th O.V.I.
Lee, Earnest R., Pr. Co. G 8th O. V. I.
Lee, John S., Pr. Co. G 8th O. V. I.
Long, John C., Pr. Co. G 8th O. V. I.
Loomis, Albert K., Artificer Co. G 8th
O. V. I.
Markley, Joseph C., Pr. Co. G 8th O.
V. I.
McIntyre, Charles G., Pr. Co. G 8th O.
V. I.
Merfield, Joseph, Pr. Co. G 8th O. V. I.
Mohn, John H., Pr. Co. G 8th O. V. I.
Nicely, Arthur H., Pr. U. R. 8th O.V.I.
Neiswander, Carl W., Pr. Co. G 8th
O. V. I.
Overholt, Charles H., Pr. Co. G 8th
O. V. I.
Overholt, George, Pr. Co. G 8th O.
V. I.
Richardson, Maurice, Pr. Co. G 8th O.
V. I.
Roleder, David T., Pr. Co. G 8th O.
V. I.

Roshon, Charles A., Pr. Co. G 8th O. V. I.
Santrock, Frederick W., Wagoner Co. G 8th O. V. I.
Sauer, Bert M., Pr. Co. G 8th O. V. I.
Sheets, Byron A., Pr. Co. G 8th O.V.I.
Siegfried, John J., Pr. U. R. 8th O.V.I.
Smith, Edgar. Pr. Co. G 8th O. V. I.
Stauffer, Abraham L., Pr. Co. G 8th O. V. I.
Tanner, Wilber J., Pr. Co. G 8th O. V. I.
Tuttle, Harry G., Pr. Co. G 8th O. V. I.
Van Epp, Arthur, Pr. Co. G 8th O.V.I.

Wait, Ralph H., Pr. Co. G 8th O. V. I.
Warner, Clare R., Pr. Co. G 8th O.V.I.
Weaver, Allen, Corp. Co. G 8th O.V.I.
Weisen, Mike, Pr. Co. G 8th O. V. I.
Wells, William J., Sergt. Co. G 8th O. V. I.
Wilson, Dudley D., Pr Co. G 8th O. V. I.
Yoder, Harvey O., Sergt. Co. G 8th O. V. I.
Yoder, Claud L., Corp. Co. G 8th O. V. I.
Yoder, Charles J., Pr. Co. G 8th O.V.I.
Yoder, Archie, Pr. U. R. 8th O. V. I.

WAKEFIELD

Hughes, Milton L., Pr. Co. D 3rd O. V. I.

WALLER

Hayden, John F., Corp. Co. H 7th O. V. I.
Hughes, Louis P., Corp. Co. H 7th O. V. I.

Jones, Forney C., Corp. Co. H 7th O. V. I.
Lauberschimer, Geo. W., Pr. Co. H 7th O. V. I.

WALNUT RUN

Ray, Homer C., Corp. Co. E 3rd O. V. I.

WAPAKONETA

Ahlers, Walter, Corp. Co. L 2nd O. V. I.
Anderson, Isaac, Pr. Co. L 2nd O.V.I.
Berry, George, Corp. Co. L 2nd O.V.I.
Bitler, George, Pr. Co. L 2nd O. V. I.
Blakeley, Samuel L., Sergt. Co. L 2nd O. V. I.
Botkin, Ellert, Pr. Co. L 2nd O. V. I.
Breese, Robert, Corp. Co. L 2nd O.V.I.
Carter, Calvin, Pr. Co. L 2nd O. V. I.
Clark, Frank M., Sergt. Co. L 2nd O. V. I.
Crider, Nathaniel, Pr. Co. L 2nd O.V.I.
Dearbaugh, Ferando C., Pr. Co. L 2nd O. V. I.
Dickas, William, Pr. Co. L 2nd O. V. I.
Dingler, Wilbur, Sergt. Co. L 2nd O. V. I.
English, Miller, Sergt. Co. L 2nd O. V. I.
Fisher, Clifford D., Pr. Co. L 2nd O. V. I.
Gessler, Otta A., Pr. Co. L 2nd O. V. I.
Hale, Harry, Corp. Co. L 2nd O. V. I.
Hassenier, George, Corp. Co. L 2nd O. V. I.
Herbst, Joe, Pr Co. L 2nd O. V.I.
Hunter, Roy C., Hos. Steward 2nd O. V. I.

Kinninger, Andrew, Pr. Co. L 2nd O. V. I.
Linder, William, 1st Sergt. Co. L 2nd O. V. I.
Mayer, Elmer E., Pr. Co. L 2nd O.V.I.
Means, Carl, Corp. Co. L 2nd O. V. I.
Miller, Albert J., Pr. Co. L 2nd O. V. I.
Morey, William B., Pr. Co. L 2nd O. V. I.
Musser, John H., Pr. Co. L 2nd O. V. I.
Reece, Lewis, Pr. Co. L 2nd O. V. I.
Ritchie, Franklin D., Pr. Co. L 2nd O. V. I.
Runyon, Clinton, Pr Co. L 2nd O. V. I.
Ryon, Edward W., Pr. Co. L 2nd O. V. I.
Schaffer, Anthony, Pr. Co. L 2nd O. V. I.
Schneider, William G., Pr. Co. L 2nd O. V. I.
Shockey, James W., Pr. Co. L 2nd O. V. I.
Snyder, Frank, Corp. Co. L 2nd O.V.I.
Stueve, William, Pr. Co. L 2nd O.V.I.
Tobias, Samuel L., Pr. Co. L 2nd O. V. I.
Wentz, Fred A., Pr. Co. L 2nd O. V. I.
Wentz, Elmer J., Pr. Co. L 2nd O.V.I
Wisener, Winfield B., Pr. Co. L 2nd O. V. I.

WARD

Ward, Adam, Pr. Co. E 7th O. V. I.

WARNER

Richey, Arthur, Pr. Co. D 7th O. V. I.
Richey, Lumley H., Pr. Co. D 7th O. V. I.

Wharff, Archie A., Pr. Co. D 7th O. V. I.
Wilson, Truman, Wagoner, Co. D 7th O. V. I.

WARREN

Camp, Phillip B., Pr. Co. K 10th O. V. I.
Forsyth, Lewis M., Pr. Co. I 10th O. V. I.
Hawkins, William H., Pr. Co. K 10th O. V. I.
Jones, Michael B., Pr. Co. K 10th O. V. I.
Kilpatrick, Dexter, Pr. Co. K 10th O. V. I.
Love, Frederick R., Pr. Co. K 10th O. V. I.
Love, John S., Pr. Co. K 10th O.V.I.
Loveless, Ward, Pr. Co. K 10th O.V.I.
Mace, John F., Pr. Co. K 10th O.V.I.
Musser, William D., Pr. Co. C 5th O. V. I.

Perry, Walter, Pr. Co. K 10th O. V. I.
Ray, Charles C., Pr. Co. K 10th O.V.I.
Smith, Edward S., Pr. Co. K 10th O. V. I.
Shafer, Fred C., Pr. Co. K 10th O.V.I.
Spade, George I., Pr. Co. K 10th O. V. I.
Thumm, Charles F., Pr. Co. K 10th O. V. I.
Truesdell, Earle B., Pr. Co. K 10th O. V. I.
Van Gorder, Monroe J., Pr. Co. K 10th O. V. I.
Vesy, Thomas A., Pr. Co. K 10th O. V. I.

WARSAW

Clark, James, Jr., Pr. Co. F 7th O. V. I.

WASHINGTON

McMaster, Jim F., Pr. Bat. H 1st O. V. A.

WASHINGTON C. H.

Allebaugh, Alvin A., Pr. Co. E 4th O. V. I.
Armstrong, William C., Pr. Co. E 4th O. V. I.
Baker, Morris O., Pr. Co. E 4th O. V. I.
Bales, John A., Pr. Co. E 4th O. V. I.
Bales, Howard, Pr. Co. E 4th O. V. I.
Barry, Joseph E., Pr. Tr. D 1st O.V.C.
Basye, William H., Pr. Co. E 4th O. V. I.
Bateman, Frank M., Pr. Co. E 4th O. V. I.
Beeler, John C., Pr. Co. E 4th O. V. I.
Bitzer, Charles W., Pr. Co. E 4th O. V. I.
Bonham, Robert A., Corp. Co. E 4th O. V. I.
Buzick, Arthur A., Pr. Co. E 4th O. V. I.
Coffman, Elivert, Pr. Co. E 4th O.V.I.
Coffman, Nathan J., Pr. Co. E 4th O. V. I.
Conway, Eugene J., Artificer Co. E 4th O. V. I.
Cook, James F., Jr., Pr. Co. E 4th O. V. I.
Cook, John W., Corp. Co. E 4th O. V. I.

Dailey, Michael, Pr. Co. E 4th O.V.I.
Dawson, Jacob H., Pr. Co. E 4th O. V. I.
Doddridge, John A., Pr. Co. E 4th O. V. I.
Douglass, Edward F., Pr. Co. E 4th O. V. I
Ely, Clyde B., Pr. Co. E 4th O. V. I.
Eyre, Will N., Musician Co. E 4th O. V. I.
Fandree, Henry D., Corp. Co. E 4th O. V. I.
Figgins, Charles E., Wagoner Co. E 4th O. V. I.
Ford, Franklin P., Pr. Co. E 4th O. V. I.
Gillum, John W., Sergt. Co. E 4th O. V. I.
Grass, John C., Pr. Co. E 4th O. V. I.
Gray, Will S., Pr. Co. E 4th O. V. I.
Hardway, Orestes E., Sergt. Co. E 4th O. V. I.
Hardy, Andrew J., Pr. Co. E 4th O. V. I.
Holcomb, Bartley C., Pr. Co. E 4th O. V. I.
Jacobs, Claud S., Pr. Co. E 4th O. V. I.

Jarnagin, Charles E., Sergt. Co. E 4th O. V. I.
Jenkins, Dio L., Pr. Tr. D 1st O.V.C.
Johnson, Morgan B., Corp. Co. E 4th O. V. I.
Keaton, James W., Pr. Co. E 4th O. V. I.
Kinesley, Carey C., Pr. Co. E 4th O. V. I.
Lydy, Sam., Pr. Co. F 4th O. V. I.
Marine, Arthur E., Pr. Co. E 4th O. V. I.
Marquet, Herbert C., Pr. Co. E 4th O. V. I.
McCormick, Harvey C., Pr. Co. E 4th O. V. I.
McDonald, Norman, Sergt. Co. E 4th O. V. I.
Mitchener, John H., Pr. Co. E 4th O. V. I.
Nixon, John T., Corp. Co. E 4th O. V. I.
Patton, John N., Pr. Co. E 4th O.V.I.
Palmer, Harry B., Pr. Co. E 4th O. V. I.
Pratt, Robert, Pr. Co. E 4th O. V. I.
Reeder, John S., Pr. Co. E 4th O.V.I.
Robb, John N., Pr. Co. E 4th O. V. I.

Sammons, Frank S., Pr. Co. E 4th O. V. I.
Sexten, Charles L., Sergt. Co. E 4th O. V. I.
Shimp, Burt O., Pr. Co. E 4th O.V.I.
Shingle, Arthur M., Pr. Co. E 4th O. V. I.
Simms, French, Pr. Co. E 4th O.V.I.
Smith, Harvey W., Pr. Co. E 4th O. V. I.
Smithers, Lynn F., Pr. Co. E 4th O. V. I.
Snapp, Joseph E., Pr. Co. E 4th O. V. I.
Stevenson, Lon E., Corp. Co. E 4th O. V. I.
Stogdon, Charles E., 1st Sergt. Co. E 4th O. V. I.
Stonaker, Galard J., Pr. Co. E 4th O. V. I.
Taylor, Jerome, Pr. Co. E 4th O. V. I.
Vincent, Elmer, Pr. Co. E 4th O.V.I.
Voss, Charles T., Pr. Co. E 4th O.V.I.
Walters, Elie N., Pr. Co. E 4th O.V.I.
Whited, Benjamin F., Pr. Co. E 4th O. V. I.
Wilt, Arthur W., Pr. Co. E 4th O.V.I.
Wyatt, James H., Pr. Co. E 4th O.V.I.

WASHINGTON, D. C.

Atwood, Henry O., Corp. Co. D 9th Batt. O. V. I.

WAVERLY

Burgess, Arthur, Pr. Co. M 1st O.V.I.
Burgess, Bert, Pr. Co. I 5th O. V. I.
Eisenhart, Joshua Scott, Pr. Co. H 7th O V I.

Emrich, Joseph M., Pr. Co. A 10th O. V. I.
Mercer, Jesse C., Pr. Co. H 7th O.V.I.
Silcott, Arthur, Pr. Co. I 5th O. V. I.

WAUSEON

Barhite, Harry G., Pr. Co. G 6th O. V. I.
Barnes, Harry A., Pr. Co. G 6th O. V. I.
Barnes, James W., Pr. Co. G 6th O. V. I.
Bayes, Christopher A., 1st Sergt. Co. G 6th O. V. I.
Bell, John J., Pr. Co. G 6th O. V. I.
Biddle, Charles E., Pr. Co. G 6th O. V. I.
Bollis, Marion E., Pr. Co. G 6th O. V. I.
Brailey, Orra L., Prin. Musician 6th O.V. I.
Calkins, Charles F., Pr. Co. G 6th O. V. I.
Casler, Maynard, Pr. Co. G 6th O.V.I.
Clark, Sylvanus S., Pr. Co. G 6th O. V. I.
Cornell, Fred V., Pr. Co. G 6th O.V.I.
Cunningham, John B., Pr. Co. G 6th O. V. I.
Dye, Dora, Pr. Co. G 6th O. V. I.

Funk, Albert L., Pr. Co. G 6th O.V.I.
Gardner, Kenneth E., Pr. Co. G 6th O. V. I.
Grandy, Frank, Pr. Co. G 6th O. V. I.
Graves, Marshall T., Pr. Co. G 6th O. V. I.
Hill, Charles R., Corp. Co. G 6th O. V. I.
Humphreys, Arthur G., Sergt. Co. G 6th O. V. I.
Klein, John, Corp. Co. G 6th O.V.I.
Lee, Harmon A., Sergt. Co. G 6th O. V. I.
Munal, Charles C., Musician Co. G 6th O. V. I.
Newman, Frank, Sergt. Co. G 6th O. V. I.
Overmeyer, Silas B., Pr. Co. G 6th O. V. I.
Pontious, Charles B., Pr. Co. G 6th O. V. I.
Quiggle, Thomas M., Corp. Co. G 6th O. V. I.

Reed, George D., Pr. Co. G 6th O.
V. I.
Reed, John J., Pr. Co. G 6th O. V. I.
Ritzenthaler, Fred, Pr. Co. G 6th O.
V. I.
Sales, Judson A., Pr. Co. G 6th O.V.I.
Saugston, William W., Musician Co. G
6th O. V. I.
Shaffer, James A., Pr. Co. G 6th O.
V. I.
Shaffer, Roll B., Pr. Co. G 6th O.V.I.
Smith, Will, Pr. Co. G 6th O. V. I.
Struble, Jasper, Pr. Co. G 6th O.V.I.
Stutzman, Samuel S., Artificer Co. G
6th O. V. I.
Swihart, Joe, Pr. Co. G 6th O. V. I.
Tremain, Ross, Pr. Co. G 6th O.V.I.

Traunppower, Homer, Pr. Co. G 6th
O. V. I.
Walker, Harvey S., Pr. Co. G 6th O.
V. I.
Wallace, Albert E., Pr. Co. G 6th O.
V. I.
Warner, Arthur E., Sergt. Co. G 6th
O. V. I.
Whitehome, Wellington B., Corp. Co.
G 6th O. V. I.
Williams, Harry E., Corp. Co. G 6th
O. V. I.
Williams, Leland S., Corp. Co. G 6th
O. V. I.
Williams, Sam., Pr. Co. G 6th O.V.I.
Zeigler, Bert, Pr. Co. G 6th O. V. I.
Zoll, Earl Clair, Pr. Co. G 6th O.V.I.

WAYNESFIELD

Cook, Hallie W., Pr. Co. I. 2nd O.V.I.
Dawson, Adolphus J., Pr. Co. L 2nd
O. V. I.

Earl, Mack S., Pr. Co. L 2nd O. V. I.

WELLSTON

O'Connor, James A., Wagoner Co. B 7th O. V. I.

WELLSVILLE

Holloway, Edwin C., Artificer Co. E 8th O. V. I.

WESTCHESTER, PA.

Fullerton, John, Pr. Co. D 9th Batt. O. V. I.

WESTERVILLE

Dempsey, Thomas A., Pr. Co. I 7th O. V. I.

WEST JEFFERSON

Bishop, William J., Pr. Co. E 3rd O.
V. I.
Burns, Charles, Pr. Co. E 3rd O. V. I.
Carr, Clarence A., Pr. Co. H 10th O.
V. I.
Cartwright, Wesley, Pr. Co. E 3rd O.
V. I.
Cartwright, William R., Pr. Co. E 3rd
O. V. I.
Dennison, Grant, Pr. Co. E 3rd O.V.I.
Frisbie, Charles A., Pr. Co. B 5th O.
V. I.
Furrow, William, Pr. Co. E 3rd O.V.I.

Garrick, Michael, Pr. Co. E 3rd O.V.I.
Giles, Frank M., Pr. Co. F 4th O.V.I.
Hann, John, Pr. Co. E 3rd O. V. I.
Hart, Charles, Pr. Co. E 3rd O. V. I.
Neighborgall, Harley, Pr. Co. E 3rd
O. V. I.
Pearce, Joseph W., Pr. Co. E 3rd O.
V. I.
Pryor, Harry, Pr. Co. E 3rd O. V. I.
Roberts, Homer W., Pr. Co. E 3rd O.
V. I.
Swetman, Manoah, Pr. Co. E 3rd O.
V. I.

WEST LAFAYETTE

Cochrane, Bert, Pr. Co. F 7th O. V. I.

Culbertson, Harry, Pr. Co. F 7th O.
V. I.

WEST MANSFIELD

Early, Joseph A., Pr. Co. I 2nd O.V.I.
Funk, Edward C., Pr. Co. G 2nd O.
V. I.
McCulley, Otto Frank, Pr. Co. G 2nd
O. V. I.

Ruehlin, Lewis J., Pr. Co. G 2nd O.
V. I.
Segner, William B., Pr. Co. G 2nd O.
V. I.
Stevens, Frank M., Pr. Co. G 2nd O.
V. I.

WEST MILTON

Beard, Calvin, Pr. Co. C 3rd O. V. I.

WESTVILLE

Sowers, Emory B., Corp. Co. D 3rd O. V. I.

WEST RUSHVILLE

Jenkins, Perry O., Pr. Co. K 7th O. V. I.

WEST SALEM

Berry, Joseph B., Pr. Co. C 8th O.V.I.
Hieler, Clarence A., Pr. Co. C 8th O. V. I.

Miller, Maurice E., Pr. Co. C 8th O. V. I.
Schott, Wilfred B., Pr. Co. C 8th O. V. I.

WEST UNITY

Brown, Frank W., Pr. Co. E 6th O. V. I.
Hickman, Bert C., Pr. Co. E 6th O. V. I.

Hollington, Arthur J., Pr. Co. E 6th O. V. I.
Niel, Norman E., Pr. Co. E 6th O.V.I.

WHEELING, W. VA.

Shefflin, John T., Pr. Co. G 7th O.V.I.

WHIPPLE

Abicht, James W., Pr. Co. D 7th O. V. I.
Hardy, Arthur G., Musician Co. D 7th O. V. I.

Wilson, Clyde E., Pr. Co. D 7th O. V. I.

WHITE COTTAGE

Booz, William P., Pr. Bat. C 1st O. V. A.
Smitley, George C., Pr. Bat. C 1st O. V. A.

Wiles, Florance J., Pr. Co. L 10th O. V. I.
Wilson, Harlan J., Pr. Co. L 10th O. V. I.

WIGNER

De Witt, Herschell M., Pr. Co. C 7th O. V. I.
Dyer, James S., Pr. Co. C 7th O. V. I.

Martin, Newton, Emory, Pr. Co. C 7th O. V. I.
Monk, John, Pr. Co. C 7th O. V. I.
Thompson, John, Pr. Co. C 7th O.V.I.

WILBERFORCE

Ballard, Wilson, Pr. Co. B 9th Batt. O. V. I.
Brown, Arthur, Pr. Co. B 9th Batt. O. V. I.
Howard, Charles, Pr. Co. B 9th Batt. O. V. I.
Howard, Frederick R., Pr. U. R. 9th Batt. O. V. I.

Lett, William C., Pr. U. R. 9th Batt. O. V. I.
Mitchell, Charles S., Pr. U. R. 9th Batt. O. V. I.
Shorter, Prattis, Pr. Co. C 9th Batt. O. V. I.

WILKESBARRE, PA.

Kleeman, Alfred E., Corp. Co. A 2nd U. S. V. E.

WILKESVILLE

Harrison, Rufus D., Pr. Co. C 7th O. V. I.

Phetteplace, Odell W., Corp. Co. C 7th O. V. I.

Rhodes, Jacob N., Musician Co. C 7th O. V. I.

WILLETSVILLE

Smith, Russel B., Pr. Co. F 3rd O.V. I.

WILLOUGHBY

Calkins, Fred M., Pr. Co. M 5th O. V. I.

Cowan, William J., Corp. Co. B 5th O. V. I.

Crobaugh, John E., Pr. Co. M 5th O. V. I.

Gibson, Charles E., 1st Sergt. Co. B 5th O. V. I.

McMahon, Michael L., Jr., Pr. Co. M 5th O. V. I.

Saxton, Harvey S., Pr. Co. M 5th O. V. I.

Zorbaugh, Frank M., Pr. Co. M 5th O. V. I.

WILLOW WILD

Foster, Alva C., Pr. Co. C 3rd O. V. I.

WILLSHIRE

Decker, Charles O., Pr. Co. D 2nd O V. I.

Streib, John F., Pr. Co. D 2nd O. V. I.

WITTENS

Mechling, Albert J., Pr. Co. K 7th O. V. I.

WOODFORD

Webster, Burt P., Musician Co. G 5th O. V. I.

WOODSTOCK

Clark, Guy W., Pr. Co. D 3rd O. V. I.

Connor, Thomas, Pr. Co. D 4th O.V.I.

Cushman, Charles W., Pr. Co. D 3rd O. V. I.

Gifford, Daniel H., Sergt. Co. D 3rd O. V. I.

Linville, Kemp Q., Pr. Co. D 3rd O. V. I.

Overfield, John A., Pr. Co. D 3rd O. V. I.

WOODVILLE

Clements, John T., Pr. Co. C 10th O. V. I.

Clink, Claude, Pr. Co. H 10th O. V. I.

WOOSTER

Barnes, John R., Pr. Co. D 8th O. V. I.

Barnhart, Charles W., Pr. Co. D 8th O. V. I.

Baughman, William H., Pr. Co. D 8th O. V. I.

Blake, George, Pr. Co. D 8th O. V. I.

Boyd, William H., Pr. Co. D 8th O. V. I.

Braustetter, Harry P., Pr. Co. D 8th O. V. I.

Brown, George W., Pr. Co. D 8th O. V. I.

Brown, Thomas P., Pr. Co. D 8th O. V. I.

Burg, George, Pr. Co. D 8th O. V. I.

Cameron, Nathaniel C., Pr. Co. D 8th O. V. I.

Cameron, Robert, Jr., Corp. Co. D 8th O. V. I.

Christine, Louis W., Pr. Co. D 8th O. V. I.

Clark, Jerome E., Pr. Co. D 8th O.V.I.

Clay, Alvin B., Pr. Co. D 8th O. V. I.

Conrad, Edward D., Pr. Co. D 8th O.
V. I.
Conrad. Willie A., Artificer Co. D 8th
O. V. I.
Critchfield, Lyman, Jr., Pr. Co. D 8th
O. V. I.
Cumberland, Charles E., Pr. Co. D 8th
O. V. I.
Cumberland, La Verne C., Pr. Co. D
8th O. V. I.
Curry, Will R., Pr. Co. D. 8th O. V. I.
Dice, Arch H., 1st Sergt. Co. D 8th O.
V. I.
Drushal, David H., Musician Co. D 8th
O. V. I.
Eaby, Harry P., Sergt. Co. D 8th O.
V. I.
Frazier, Charles W., Pr. Co. D 8th O.
V. I.
Funk, Sterling R., Pr. Co. D 8th O.
V. I.
Gasche, Louis E., Sergt. Co. D 8th O.
V. I.
Glenn, Joseph S., Pr. Co. D 8th O.V.I.
Glenn, Samuel M., Jr., Pr. Co. D 8th
O. V. I.
Gravath, Quintin W., Pr. Co. D 8th O.
V. I.
Griest, James E., Pr. Co. D 8th O.V.I.
Grossenbach, Cary W., Corp. Co. D 8th
O. V. I.
Heater, Charles A., Musician Co. D 8th
O. V. I.
Horn, Franklin B., Sergt. Co. D 8th
O. V. I.
Horn, Webster D., Corp. Co. D 8th O.
V. I.
Hughes, William H., Pr. Co. D 8th O.
V. I.
Johnson, Merton R., Pr. Co. D 8th O.
V. I.
Jolliff, Harvey F., Pr. Co. D 8th O.
V. I.
Kinkler, Harry, Pr. Co. D 8th O. V. I.
Langell, Clemet E., Pr. Co. D 8th O.
V. I.
Lautzenheiser, Irven, Pr. Co. D 8th O.
V. I.

Lautzenheiser, Perrine, Pr. Co. D 8th
O. V. I.
Leapold, Frederick J., Pr. Co. D 8th O.
V. I.
Lerch, William G., Pr. Co. D 8th O.
V. I.
Limb, George S., Sergt. Co. D 8th O.
V. I.
Mahaney, Edward, Pr. Co. D 8th O.
V. I.
Maize, Percy M., Pr. Co. D 8th O.V.I.
McKinney, Charles H., Pr. Co. D. 8th
O V. I.
McKinney, Frederick S., Hos. Steward
8th O. V. I.
Miller, Harry C., Pr. Co. D 8th O. V. I.
Miller, Horace W., Sergt. Co. D 8th
O. V. I.
Naftzger, Loyd A., Wagoner Co. D
8th O. V. I.
Oltmanns, Antoin, Pr. Co. D 8th O.
V. I.
Rieder, Edmond S., Pr. Co. D 8th O.
V. I.
Schuch, Fred. A., Pr. Co. D 8th O.V.I.
Schuck, William, Pr. Co. D 8th O.V.I.
Scott Charlie R., Corp. Co. D 8th O.
V. I.
Stevens, Thomas R., Pr. Co. D 8th O.
V. I.
Stotsbery, John F., Pr. Co. D 8th O.
V. I.
Stotsbery. William A., Pr. Co. D 8th
O. V. I.
Swartz, George M., Corp. Co. D 8th
O. V. I.
Unger, Charles E., Pr. Co. D 8th O.
V. I.
Webb, George B., Pr. Co. D 8th O.
V. I.
Winebrenner, Calvin A., Pr. Co. D 8th
O. V. I.
Woolman, Harry D., Corp. Co. D 8th
O. V. I.
Yoder, Ephriam S., Pr. Co. D 8th O.
V. I.

WORTHINGTON

Chapin, Albert, Pr. Co. F 4th O. V. I.
Chapin, Alfred. Pr. Co. F 4th O. V. I.

Putman, Charlie, Pr. Co. F 4th O.V.I.

WYNANT

Foust, Oliver M., Pr. Co. L 3rd O.V.I.
Luckey, James, Pr. Co. L 3rd O. V. I.
Luckey, Ruben H., Pr. Co. L 3rd O.
V. I.

Rhodefer, Harry W., Pr. Co. L 3rd O.
V. I.
Shannon, Stephen S., Pr. Co. L 3rd O.
V. I.

XENIA

Alexander, Peter, Pr. Co. C 9th Batt.
O. V. I.
Allen, Arthur, Corp. Co. C 9th Batt.
O. V. I.

Allen, Leon, Corp. Co. C 9th Batt. O.
V. I.
Anderson, Clarence Lee, Pr. Co. C 9th
Batt. O. V. I.

Anderson, Wesley, Pr. Co. C 9th Batt. O. V. I.

Archer, William, Pr. Co. C 9th Batt. O. V. I.

Battles, William, Pr. Co. C 9th Batt. O. V. I.

Bowens, Henry, Corp. Co. C 9th Batt. O. V. I.

Broadice, John L., Corp. Co. C 9th Batt. O. V. I.

Carter, Charles W., Pr. Co. C 9th Batt. O. V. I.

Cherry, Houston H., Pr. Co. D 3rd O. V. I.

Cherry, Houston H., Pr. U. R. 3rd O. V. I.

Cowles, George E., Pr. Co. C 9th Batt. O. V. I.

Coles, William, Pr. Co. C 9th Batt. O. V. I.

Curtis, Hampton E., Pr. Co. C 9th Batt. O. V. I.

Daunton, James, Pr. Co. C 9th Batt. O. V. I.

Davis, James F., Pr. Co. C 9th Batt. O. V. I.

Fennels, Tumes, Pr. Co. C 9th Batt. O. V. I.

Franklin, John W., Pr. Co. C 9th Batt. O. V. I.

Frazel, Jacob, Pr. Co. C 2nd U. S. V. E.

Goings, Tecumseh, Pr. Co. C 9th Batt. O. V. I.

Guy, Organ A., Sergt. Co. C 9th Batt. O. V. I.

Harris, Fred A., Sergt. Co. C 9th Batt. O. V. I.

Hatfield, Frank H., Sergt. Co. D 3rd O. V. I.

Hudson, John P., Pr. Co. C 9th Batt. O. V. I.

Hudson, Wilson, Sergt. Co. C 9th Batt. O. V. I.

Jackson, Edward, Pr. Co. C 9th Batt. O. V. I.

Jamison, Bert, Pr. Co. C 9th Batt. O. V. I.

Jenkins, Thomas, Pr. Co. C 9th Batt. O. V. I.

Ladd, Charles L., Pr. Co. C 9th Batt. O. V. I.

Lindsay, William, 1st Sergt. Co. C 9th Batt. O. V. I.

Logan, Walter S., Pr. Co. C 9th Batt. O. V. I.

Matthews, William, Pr. Co. C 9th Batt. O. V. I.

Maxwell, James E., Pr. Co. C 9th Batt. O. V. I.

McClure, George, Wagoner Co. C 9th Batt. O. V. I.

McElroy, William, Corp. Co. C 9th Batt. O. V. I.

Newsome, Joseph P., Pr. Co. C 9th Batt. O. V. I.

Oglesby, Edward C., Pr. Co. C 9th Batt. O. V. I.

Pearson, Calvin, Pr. Co. C 9th Batt. O. V. I.

Phelps, La Volta, Pr. Co. C 9th Batt. O. V. I.

Porter, Frank, Pr. Co. D 9th Batt. O. V. I.

Purnell, John H., Pr. Co. C 9th Batt. O. V. I.

Reed, George A., Pr. Co. C 9th Batt. O. V. I.

Riddell, Warren D., Corp. Co. C 2nd U. S. V. E.

Riddell, William S., Pr..Co. C 2nd U. S. V. E.

Robinson, James, Pr. Co. C 9th Batt. O. V. I.

Rodgers, Sidney, Pr. Co. C 9th Batt. O. V. I.

Smith, James, Corp. Co. C 9th Batt. O. V. I.

Smith, William, Pr. Co. C 9th Batt. O. V. I.

Steller, James H., Pr. Co. C 9th Batt. O. V. I.

Tolbert, Paschal, Pr Co. C 9th Batt. O. V. I.

Travis, Hugh, Artificer Co. C 9th Batt. O. V. I.

Washington, Frank, Sergt., Co. C 9th Batt. O. V. I.

Watson, James H., Pr. Co. C 9th Batt. O. V. I.

Wells, Horace O., Pr. Co. C 9th Batt. O. V. I.

Williams, Bennie, Pr. Co. C 9th Batt. O. V. I.

Winslow, Grant, Sergt. Co. C 9th Batt. O. V. I.

YARICO

Elliott, Henry, Pr. Co. C 7th O V. I.

YELVERTON

Hopkins, Ozra W., Pr. Co. G 2nd O. V. I.

YOUNGSTOWN

Barber. Joseph, Pr. Co. H 5th O.V.I.
Birmingham, James, Pr. Co. H 5th O. V. I.
Bliss, Bion, Pr. Co. H 5th O. V. I.
Brownlee, James O., Artificer Co. H 5th O. V. I.
Bufka, John W., Pr. Co. H 5th O.V.I.
Burkhart, Adolph, Pr. Co. H 5th O. V. I.
Burn, William M., Pr. Co. K 10th O. V. I.
Case, Frank V., Sergt. Co. H 5th O. V. I.
Christy, Wade, Musician Co. H 5th O. V. I.
Conroy, Stephen S., Pr. Co. H 5th O. V. I.
Cornell, John J., Sergt. Co. H 5th O. V. I.
Cowen, Isaac Allen, Pr. Co. H 5th O. V. I.
Crawford, William J., Pr. Co. H 5th O. V. I.
Cronin, William F., Pr. Co. K 10th O. V. I.
Cummins, Peter, Pr. Co. H 5th O.V.I.
Dalzell, C. H., Pr. Co. H 5th O. V. I.
Davis, Aaron, Pr. Co. H 5th O. V. I.
Dixon. John G., Pr. Co. H 5th O.V.I.
Edwards. Richard T., Pr. Co. H 5th O. V. I.
Flushgarden, Simon, Pr. Co. H 5th O. V. I
Freck, Clayton C., Pr. Cd. H 5th O. V.. I.
Frey, Paul J., Pr. Co. H 5th O. V. I.
Frost, Clarence E., Musician Co. H 5th O. V. I.
Greenwood, Fred H., Pr. Co. H 5th O. V. I.
Hamilton, Hale, Pr. Co. H 5th O.V.I.
Hamilton, Nicholas R., Pr. Co. H 5th O. V. I.
Haverstick, Elmer, Pr. Co. H 5th O. V. I.
Henry, George, Pr. Co. K 10th O.V.I.
Higgins, John, Pr. Co. I 5th O. V. I.
Howells, John R., Pr. Co. H 5th O. V. I.
Howells, Thomas, Pr. Co. H 5th O. V.. I.
Jackson, Andrew, Pr. Co. H 5th O. V. I.
Keeling, Harry, Wagoner Co. H 5th O. V. I.
Kennedy, John M., Pr. Co. K 10th O. V. I.
Keyser, William H., Sergt. Co. H 5th O. V. I.
Kingsbacker, Harry,. Pr. Co. H 5th O. V. I.
Mahan, John O., Pr. Co. H 5th O.V.I.
Matthews, Wade, Pr. Co. H 5th O.V.I.
McCartney, John W., Pr. Co. H 5th O. V. I.

McClure, John M., Pr. Co. H 5th O. V. I.
McCluskey, James R., Pr. Co. H 5th O. V. I.
McFarlane, David W., Pr. Co. H 5th O. V. I.
Merritt, George, Pr. Co. H 5th O.V.I.
Metz, Fred W., Sergt. Co. H 5th O. V. I.
O'Neill, Patrick J., Pr. Co. K 10th O. V. I.
Payne, Halsey D., Pr. Co. K 10th O. V. I.
Perry, John W., Pr. Co. H 5th O.V.I.
Pfund, Fred W., Pr. Co. H 5th O.V.I.
Phillips, William E., Pr. Co. H 5th O. V. I.
Porter, Wave W., Pr. Co. K 10th O. V. I.
Resch, Albert G., Corp. Co. H 5th O. V. I.
Robbins, George W., Pr. Co. H 5th O. V. I.
Rose, Archie A., Pr. Co. K 10th O. V. I.
Semple, Emery W., Corp. Co. H 5th O. V. I.
Shaffer, John C., Pr. Co. H 5th O.V.I.
Sharp, Charles C., Corp. Co. H 5th O. V. I.
Simmons, Fred A., Pr. Co. H 5th O. V. I.
Simpson, Perry A., Pr. Co. H 5th O. V. I.
Small, Indice L., Pr. Co. H 5th O.V.I.
Smith, Artemus W., Pr. Co. H 5th O. V. I.
Smoker, William, Pr. Co. H 5th O. V. I.
Spigler, George W., Sergt. Co. H 5th O. V. I.
Sprague, Allen W., Pr. Co. H 5th O. V. I.
Stambaugh, R. W., Pr. Co. H 5th O. V. I.
Steller, Henry, Jr., Pr. Co. H 5th O. V. I.
Stemple, Millard, Pr. Co. H 5th O. V. I.
Stowe, Milton, Pr. Co. H 5th O. V. I.
Thompson, Dallas L., Pr. Co. I 10th O. V. I.
Thompson, George V., Pr. Co. H 5th O. V. I.
Thullen, Albert W., Corp. Co. H 5th O. V. I.
Truman, Royal F., Jr., Q. M. Sergt. Co. H 5th O. V. I.
Uhlinger, August, Pr. Co. H 5th O. V. I.
Wagner, Joseph, Pr. Co. C 10th O. V. I.
Welch, Dolph, Pr. Co. H 5th O. V. I.
Wilson, Frank A., Pr. Co. H 5th O. V. I.

Wiseman, Burt L., Pr. Co. H 5th O.
V. I.
Wiseman, Frank G., Pr. Co. H 5th O.
V. I.
Wiseman, J. Clint, Pr. Co. H 5th O.
V. I.

Woolfe, Henry G., Corp. Co. H 5th
O. V. I.
Yergey, Thomas M., Pr. Co. I 10th O.
V. I.

ZANEFIELD

Richey, Charles M., Pr. Co. F 2nd O. V. I.

ZANESVILLE

Acheson, Charles Pr. Co. L 10th O.
V. I.
Adams, Julius F., Pr. Bat. C 1st O.
V. A.
Adrian, Edward, Corp. Co. L 10th O.
V. I.
Adrian, William, Pr. Co. L 10th O.V.I.
Aler, William A., Pr. Bat. C 1st O.
V. A.
Atkinson, Clarence F., Pr. Bat. C 1st
O. V. A.
Ayers, Charles C., Pr. Bat. C 1st O.
V. A.
Bailey, John T., Pr. Co. L 10th O.V.I.
Ball, Florence E., Pr. Bat. C 1st O.
V. A.
Barker, Louis, Pr. Bat. C 1st O. V. A.
Beaver, George R., Pr. Bat. C 1st O.
V. A.
Beckert, Frank H., Pr. Bat. C 1st O.
V. A.
Bell, Charles W., Pr. Bat. C 1st O.
V. A.
Bell, George F., Corp. Co. L 10th O.
V. I.
Beymer, Simon, Corp. Bat. C 1st O.
V. A.
Black, John S., Sergt. Bat. C 1st O.
V. A.
Blake, James H., Pr. Bat. C 1st O.
V. A.
Brenner, Albert A., Pr. Co. C 10th O.
V. I.
Bridwell, Albert, Pr. Bat. C 1st O.V.A.
Brown, William E., Pr. Co. L 10th O.
V. I.
Buell, Henry I., Pr. Tr. G 1st O.V.C.
Buerhaus, Henry A., Sergt. Co. L 10th
O. V. I.
Burns, Robert J., Pr. Co. L 10th O.
V. I.
Caldwell, John J., Pr. Co. L 10th O.
V. I.
Campbell, Frederick E., Pr. Co. L 10th
O. V. I.
Carpenter, Frank D., Pr. Bat. C 1st
O. V. A.
Carson, John L., Pr. Co. L 10th O.
V. I.
Carson, Robert M., Pr. Co. L 10th O.
V. I.
Cashbaugh, Ralph C., Pr. Bat. C 1st
O. V. A.

Chalfant, Ernest E., Pr. Co. L 10th O.
V. I.
Chapman, Hugh S., Pr. Bat. C 1st O.
V. A.
Clark, Earnest, Musician Co. L 10th
O. V. I.
Cobb, Sylvanus, Pr. Co. L 10th O.V.I.
Colman, Clinton L., Pr. Co. L 10th O.
V. I.
Coleman, Henry I., Pr. Bat. C 1st O.
V. A.
Crooks, Frank B., Pr. Bat. C 1st O.
V. A.
Crooks, George M., Pr. Co. L 10th O.
V. I.
Dawson, Charles A., 1st Sergt. Bat. C
1st O. V. A.
Dawson, Harry C., Pr. Bat. C 1st O.
V. A.
Deffenbaugh, James H., Pr. Bat. C 1st
O. V. A.
Deitrick, Alden M., Corp. Co. L 10th
O. V. I.
Dennis, Harry J., Sergt. Co. L 10th
O. V. I.
Dickman, William G., Sergt. Co. L
10th O. V. I.
Dickson, George W., Pr. Bat. C 1st
O. V. A.
Dosch, Lee C., Pr. Co. L 10th O.V.I.
Dover, Harry A., Pr. Co. L 10th O.
V. I.
Doyle, William J., Pr. Co. L 10th O.
V. I.
Dozer, Charles O., Pr. Co. L 10th O.
V. I.
Drake, Clarence E., Sergt. Maj. 1st
O. V. A.
Dunlavy, Anthony, Pr. Bat. C 1st O.
V. A.
Dunmeade, Samuel, Pr. Co. L 10th O.
V. I.
Evenas, Claude H., Sergt. Co. L 10th
O. V. I.
Farrell, Frank, Pr. Co. F 8th O. V. I.
Feasley, Henry E., Pr. Co. L 10th O.
V. I.
Felton, William H., Pr. Bat. C 1st O.
V. A.
Felumlee, Charles, Pr. Co. L 10th O.
V. I.
Fortune, Frank F., Pr. Bat. C 1st O.
V. A.

Fouts, Harry B., Pr. Co. L 10th O. V. I.

Fouts, Henry, Musician Co. L 10th O. V. I.

Fouts, Phineas, Corp. Co. L 10th O. V. I.

Freeman, Martin L., Pr. Co. L 10th O. V. I.

Fritz, Louis, Pr. Co. L 10th O. V. I.

George, Robert M., Corp. Co. L 10th O. V. I.

Giesey, Louis E., Pr. Co. L 10th O. V. I.

Gitter, Henry C., Corp. Co. G 7th O. V. I.

Grape, John A., Pr. Co. M 10th O.V.I.

Green, Harlan V. H., Pr. Bat. C 1st O. V. A.

Greene, Charles A., Pr. Bat. C 1st O. V. A.

Greiner, Harry C., Pr. Bat. C 1st O. V. A.

Grieves, Harry E., Pr. Bat. C 1st O. V. A.

Griffith, Harry B., Pr. Co. G 7th O. V. I.

Grubb, James G., Corp. Co. L 10th O. V. I.

Hammond, Lionel C., Pr. Bat. C 1st O. V. A.

Hauserman, Earnest, Pr. Co. L 10th O. V. I.

Hayes, John W., Pr. Co. L 10th O.V.I.

Hook, Beaumont, Pr. Bat. C 1st O. V. A.

Hooper, Fred D., Pr. Co. L 10th O. V. I.

Hornnuth, Sylvester, Pr. Co. L 10th O. V. I.

Hull, Curtis, Pr. Co. L 10th O. V. I.

Hull, William, Pr. Co. L 10th O. V. I.

Hutchison, Dewey, Corp. Co. L 10th O. V. I.

Jacobs, William W., Pr. Bat. C 1st O. V. A.

Jones, Edward J., Pr. Bat. C 1st O. V. A.

Jones, Fred H., Pr. Bat. C 1st O.V.A.

Kain, John, Pr. Co. L 10th O. V. I.

Keenan, Owen C., Pr. Bat. C 1st O. V. A.

Killian, Frank, Pr. Bat. C 1st O.V.A.

Klies, David A., Pr. Co. L 10th O.V.I.

Korn, William H., Pr. Co. L 10th O. V. I.

Larimer, James R., Pr. Co. L 10th O. V. I.

Lewman, Orthillo V., Sergt. Bat. C 1st O. V. A.

Loyd, Albert, Pr. Bat. C 1st O. V. A.

Loyd, John C., Pr. Co. L 10th O.V.I.

Lyda, Jacob E., Pr. Bat. C 1st O.V.A.

Mangold, Harry A., Pr. Bat. C 1st O. V. A.

Maroney, James, Pr. Co. L 10th O. V. I.

Matthews, Robert, Pr. Co. L 10th O. V. I.

McBride, Charles A., Musician Bat. C 1st O. V. A.

McCahill, Charles W., Corp. Co. L 10th O. V. I.

McCoy, Charles F., Corp. Co. L 10th O. V. I.

McCoy, William, Sergt. Bat. C 1st O. V. A.

McGee, Walter E., Pr. Co. L 10th O. V. I.

McLees, Thomas H., Pr. Bat. C 1st O. V. A.

Melvin, Charles J., Pr. Co. L 10th O. V. I.

Merrick, William A., Pr. Bat. C 1st O. V. A.

Mills, Chester S., Pr. Co. L 10th O. V. I.

Miner, William E., Pr. Co. L 10th O. V. I.

Mitchell, Alexander C., Pr. Co. L 10th O. V. I.

Mitchell, Harry F., Pr. Bat. C 1st O. V. A.

Mooney, Thomas H., Pr. Co. L 10th O. V. I.

Musselman, James, Pr. Bat. C 1st O. V. A.

Naylor, Fred, Pr. Bat. C 1st O. V. A.

Nicholas, Lewis E., Pr. Co. L 10th O. V. I.

Nichols, Amos, Pr. Co. L 10th O.V.I.

Norton, Vernie V., Pr. Co. L 10th O. V. I.

Nowell, Roy R., Pr. Co. L 10th O. V. I.

Oestermeyer, Carl, Pr. Bat. C 1st O. V. A.

Orwig, Archford, Pr. Co. L 10th O. V. I.

Osborne, George M., Pr. Co. L 10th O. V. I.

Osmond, Edward, Pr. Bat. C 1st O. V. A.

Parker, Harry F., Pr. Bat. C 1st O. V. A.

Parrish, Lewis H., Pr. Co. L 10th O. V. I.

Phillips, Carl B., Corp. Co. L 10th O. V. I.

Pletcher, Arthur G., Pr. Bat. C 1st O. V. A.

Purdy, Hugh, Artificer Co. L 10th O. V. I.

Reynolds, John J., Pr. Bat. C 1st O. V. I.

Richards, David E., Corp. Bat. C 1st O. V. A.

Richardson, John V., Pr. Bat. C 1st O. V. A.

Riley, Stephen, Pr. Co. L 10th O.V.I.

Roach, Richard, Pr. Co. L 10th O.V.I.

Robertson, Alexander, Sergt. Bat. C 1st O. V. A.

Ross, John F., Pr. Bat. C 1st O. V. A.

Ross, John F., Pr. Bat. C 1st O. V. A.

Rowe, John A., Pr. Bat. C 1st O.V.A.

Rowland, Henry, Pr. Co. L 10th O. V. I.

Rush, William I., Pr. Co. L 10th O. V. I.

Rusterholz, John J., Pr. Bat. C 1st O. V. A.

Sauer, Martin J., Q. M. Sergt. Co. L 10th O. V. I.

Scott, Frank O., Corp. Bat. C 1st O. V. A.

Search, Nimus E., Corp. Bat. C 1st O. V. A.

Search, Charles W., Sergt. Bat. C 1st O. V. A.

Sines, Thomas, Pr. Co. L 10th O.V.I.

Slack, Norris S., Pr. Bat. C 1st O. V. A.

Smith, Charles S., Pr. Bat. C 1st O. V. A.

Sprout, Frank E., 1st Sergt. Co. L 10th O. V. I.

Starkey, Edgar, Corp. Co. L 10th O. V. I.

Stockdale, Ralph W., Corp. Bat. C 1st O. V. A.

Stockdale, William A., Pr. Bat. C 1st O. V. A.

Stoneburner, Clarence, Pr. Bat. C 1st O. V. A.

Suttles, Walter W., Pr. Co. L 10th O. V. I.

Swan, John N., Pr. Bat. C 1st O.V.A.

Swope, Louie C., Corp. Co. L 10th O. V. I.

Tanner, William, Pr. Bat. C 1st O.V.A.

Taylor, Edward R., Musician Bat. C 1st O. V. A.

Taylor, Launce C., Pr. Bat. C 1st O. V. A.

Tilton, Dexter, Pr. Bat. C 1st O.V.A.

Turner, George H., Pr. Bat. C 1st O. V. A.

Tuttle, Frank, Corp. Bat. C 1st O.V.A.

Walters, Charles E., Pr. Co. L 10th O. V. I.

Walters, Scott A., Pr. Bat. C 1st O. V. A.

Wells, William, Pr. Co. L 10th O.V.I.

Welsh, James, Pr. Co. L 10th O. V. I.

Wendell, Otto W., Pr. Co. L 10th O. V. I.

White, William T., Wagoner Co. L 10th O. V. I.

Williamson, William, Pr. Bat. C 1st O. V. A.

Wilson, David F., Pr. Bat. C 1st O. V. A.

Wilson, Roy S., Pr. Bat. C 1st O.V.A.

Wood, George, Pr. Co. L 10th O.V.I.

ROSTER

OF

OHIO VOLUNTEERS

IN THE

SERVICE OF THE UNITED STATES,

WAR WITH SPAIN.

Prepared under direction of
HERBERT B. KINGSLEY,
Adjutant General of Ohio.

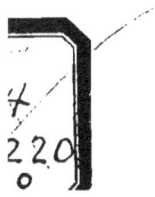

COLUMBUS, OHIO:
J. L. Trauger, State Printer.
1898.